Praise for *The Lives of Edie Pritchard*

"Characters so real they could walk off the page, virtuoso writing and up-all-night drama." —*People*

"Larry Watson is a riveting storyteller . . . This is a fast and compelling read, sparse and dusty as the open plain. Watson's journey is a sensory one, taking us down rippling highways and across weedy fields into basement rec rooms and out into shadowy sunsets. Though some scenes are gritty, the novel's dialogue and imagery awaken our senses and prove once again that when depicting small-town life in the West, Larry Watson is crushing it." —*Minneapolis Star Tribune*

"Watson has made [the implacable landscape of eastern Montana] his own as emphatically as Faulkner annexed Yoknapatawpha County . . . Watson remains incapable of creating characters who aren't fully formed individuals, as courageous as they are vulnerable, and here he again displays his rare ability to craft strong women and to describe their everyday lives with rare power." —*Booklist* (starred review)

"Watson's writing style is simple but powerfully effective. It's easy to sympathize with Edie and understand the difficult choices she makes. Everyone has a moment when they wish they could just chuck everything and start over. Watson leaves enough room for readers to ponder whether they should." —*BookPage*

"Watson's unfussy style makes room for nuggets of bitter humor, like a divorced and remarried woman telling a newcomer, 'Mister, everyone in this room is an expert on what a marriage *isn't*!'"

—*Milwaukee Journal Sentinel*

The Lives of Edie Pritchard

The Lives of Edie Pritchard

A Novel

LARRY WATSON

Algonquin Books of Chapel Hill

2021

Published by
Algonquin Books of Chapel Hill
Post Office Box 2225
Chapel Hill, North Carolina 27515-2225

a division of
Workman Publishing
225 Varick Street
New York, New York 10014

Printed in the United States of America.
Published simultaneously in Canada by Thomas Allen & Son Limited.
Design by Chris Crochetière, BW&A Books, Inc.

This is a work of fiction. While, as in all fiction, the literary perceptions and
insights are based on experience, all names, characters, places, and incidents
either are products of the author's imagination or are used fictitiously.

LIBRARY OF CONGRESS CATALOGING-IN-PUBLICATION DATA

Names: Watson, Larry, [date]– author.
Title: The lives of Edie Pritchard : a novel / Larry Watson.
Description: First edition. | Chapel Hill, North Carolina : Algonquin Books
    of Chapel Hill, 2020. | Summary: "A woman whose looks have always
    defined her, who has spent a lifetime trying to prove that she is allowed
    to exist in her own sphere, tries to be herself even as multiple men try to
    categorize and own her"—Provided by publisher.
Identifiers: LCCN 2019059066 | ISBN 9781616209025 (hardcover) |
    ISBN 9781643750576 (e-book)
Classification: LCC PS3573.A853 L58 2020 | DDC 813/.54—dc23
LC record available at https://lccn.loc.gov/2019059066

ISBN 978-1-64375-142-9 (PB)

10 9 8 7 6 5 4 3 2 1
First Paperback Edition

For Susan

CONTENTS

ONE

Edie Linderman

1967–68

Sunlight glints off the slope of the hood like a snowdrift, and Roy Linderman puts on his sunglasses. Like a man born to drive, he lets one arm hang out the window of his Chevy Impala while the other rests on top of the steering wheel to keep the big car in line.

The air flowing through the car is as hot as the August wind blowing across the prairie, and to make himself heard above the rush and the steady rumble of the Chevy, Roy raises his voice. "How do you know it isn't the flu?" he asks. "Maybe we'll all get it."

"My aunt in Bozeman is a nurse," Edie says, "and she says it's almost always something people ate."

"And what makes you so sure it was the hot dog?"

"Please. Sitting all day in that greasy water? It was the hot dog."

"And you didn't eat one? So you're safe."

"That's right," Edie says. "I'm safe."

"When we were kids, whatever was going around, he got. Measles. Mumps. Chicken pox. Like maybe with twins, only one of us had to get it. And Dean would be the one and it'd pass me by. Strep throat. Tonsillitis. He had his tonsils out and I still got mine."

"I remember when he had strep." She gives her head a rueful little shake. "I remember that very well."

"I wondered if maybe you did," Roy says.

On every side of them, nothing rises more than knee-high, and the wheatgrass, needlegrass, blue grama, and fescue—all the color of a sweat-stained straw hat—bend down lower in the direction they're always bent, west to east.

"What are we going after again?" Edie asks.

"It's a 1951 GMC half ton. Low miles."

"How did you find out about it?"

"It's Les Moore's uncle's. The uncle had to sell his ranch, so he doesn't need the truck."

"Doesn't anyone else want it?"

"Hell yes. But we'll get there first."

Ahead a dust cloud, high and thick enough to tint a corner of the sky a darker blue, swirls, and well before they draw close, they can taste its dirt. "The hell," Roy says. "Someone's plowing something. Close the windows."

They both crank up their windows, then Edie crawls over the seat to get to the rear windows. She has to swing one bare leg, then the other past Roy's head, and he takes his eyes off the road to watch her make this climb.

"Stay back there," he says. "You can roll them down again in a minute."

As the windows close, the air changes pitch from a steady whoosh to a fast-paced thump, as if a propeller powered their vehicle. Then the interior suddenly quiets, and their voices lower as though they've entered a church.

"My God," Edie says and draws a deep breath. "It's like the inside of an oven."

"I'm never getting a car again without air-conditioning," Roy says. "I swear it."

Edie keeps one hand on the window crank.

"Your place gets plenty warm, doesn't it?" says Roy. "I told Dean anytime you two need a good night's sleep, come on over and you can have my bedroom. Air-conditioned comfort. You can't beat it for sleeping."

"And turn you out of your bed? Where would you sleep?"

"I can always find someplace to bunk down."

"I bet you can."

"Or maybe you want your own unit? If the store has any left at the end of the season, they always put them on big sale. I could use my discount and get you an even better price."

"We'll let you know."

"Talk it over with Dean," Roy says, then twists his head as though he needs to know exactly where she is in the back seat.

"We'll let you know."

In another minute the sky clears back to its undifferentiated blue. Roy says, "You can roll them back down. And get back up here. I'm not your chauffeur."

The truth is, Edie would rather remain in the back seat, out of Roy's reach. These brothers . . . For some time now, Dean has acted as though he's been warned to keep his hands off her. Even in bed, he sleeps on a narrow space away from her. Meanwhile, Roy has been . . . well, Roy. Could it be that desire is something like mumps or measles, one brother coming down with it while it passes the other by?

Edie points a finger straight ahead. "Take me to the thee-a-tah, my good man."

"And I'm sure as hell not your good man."

As Edie climbs over the seat again, Roy reaches out a hand, but whatever he was going to do, he must think better of it because he puts his hand back on the steering wheel. Once she settles back into her seat however, he takes his hat from where it's been resting in the space between them and tosses it into the back.

Roy asks, "You ever been up to Bentrock?"

"When I was a little girl," Edie says, "my dad took us up to Canada. Just drove across the border and turned around and came back again. So we could say we'd been there. Would we have gone through Bentrock then?"

"You might have."

"Then I might have been there."

"Well, whatever you remember, it hasn't changed since."

Edie slips off her flimsy rubber sandals and hooks her toes up on the lip of the dashboard.

"You'll probably get your feet dirty today," Roy says. "I don't think Bentrock's got but the one paved street."

"I thought I'd wait in the car."

"Hell no. I need you to keep him distracted during the negotiations."

"Really? What was Dean's job going to be?"

"Drive. That's all. Just drive."

Roy takes a pack of Camels from the pocket of his white shirt and shakes a cigarette up to his lips. He offers the pack to Edie, then pulls it back. "I forgot. You don't smoke."

He pushes in the lighter. A moment later it pops out, and he presses its glowing coils to his cigarette. He inhales deeply and when he exhales, the wind whips the stream of smoke out the window. "Don't you have any vices, Edie?"

"You know better than to ask me that."

Roy turns his head toward her and with his finger slowly traces in the air the length of Edie's bare leg. "Tell me something," he says. "How do you get so tan working in the bank all day?"

Edie quickly lowers both feet to the floor. She says, "We've got a folding chair we set up behind the building. During breaks and lunch hour, I sit back there. And I'm out on weekends of course."

"I wouldn't think you'd get much sun in that alley." Roy pinches his cigarette between his lips and extends both arms. "Me? I'm like a steak cooked on just one side."

The car floats over the centerline, and Edie starts to reach for the steering wheel, but then Roy takes hold of it once again.

"About the only time I get out of the store," he says, "it's in the car, and then one arm hangs out the window and the other doesn't get any sun at all."

The only other car visible on this stretch of highway is at least a couple miles ahead, and then it vanishes, curving its way into the first of a series of low hills, each stitched to the next with a narrow dark strip of cottonwood or bur oak.

"Now you," Roy says, "you probably have to hike your skirt up plenty high to get so much sun." He leans forward to look at her. "And maybe undo a button or two."

She doesn't say anything.

"Of course with those miniskirts you've taken to wearing . . ."

"For God's sake, Roy. Can't we have a normal conversation?"

Roy smiles the smile of a man confident of its power to heal or beguile. "Why sure, Edie. What did you want to talk about?"

But she says nothing and turns her head away from her brother-in-law. She knows women whose husbands would never let their wives get into a car with Roy Linderman. But not Dean. No, not Dean.

THE BIG OVENS in Flieder's Family Bakery blaze all night long and into the day, turning out racks and trays of cakes, cookies, rolls, and loaves of bread, some of it trucked to stores around town. People might say they love the aroma of Flieder's baked goods, but they don't have it in their nostrils every day as Dean and Edie do in their apartment above the bakery.

Dean sits on the sofa in his underwear. A saucepan rests on the coffee table in front of him just in case he pukes. On his lap is the navy blue leatherette-bound *Prairie Harvest*, the 1961 yearbook of Gladstone High School, and it's open to the page picturing the homecoming queen and her court: five pretty girls in formal dresses standing in the middle of a football field on a windy day. The girls' carefully done-up hair-dos blow back from their faces, and the queen, Dorothy Bergstrom, holds up a white-gloved hand to keep her crown in place.

Dean stares at the page as if he's studying for an exam. Why does Edie look like a woman and the others like schoolgirls? Her body could furnish the explanation, of course, but there has to be something else. Is it in her eyes? Is there some measure of self-knowledge there that the other girls don't yet possess and perhaps never will? Or is Dean Linderman searching for something in the photograph that could provide the answer to the question that perpetually troubles him: Was Edie Pritchard a girl who could make a mistake among her suitors, believing she'd chosen one young man when she meant to choose another? Or is his uncertainty simply the kind that could trouble any twin: Do you mean me or my brother?

Someone knocks at the door, and Dean closes the annual and slides it under one of the pillows on the sofa. By this time his mother is already in the apartment, her blue-and-white floral-print housedress stretching as wide across her as it would billowing on a clothesline.

She's breathing hard from exertion and has to wait a moment before speaking. "You feeling any better?" she asks.

"You didn't walk here, did you?"

"Just from down the street. Your father and your uncle are at the Silver Dollar sampling the wares."

"I'm doing all right."

The apartment is not spacious, and its windows are high and narrow. The dim light makes the place feel even smaller, with every corner vanishing in shadow. Mrs. Linderman peers carefully at her son before bending down and pressing her palm against his forehead.

"Well, you don't have a fever. How long since you been on the pot?"

"Three hours at least."

"You're probably done then."

"I don't think I have anything left in there."

"You didn't have much to begin with." She points to his bare torso. "I believe I can count your ribs from here."

"I haven't had much appetite lately."

"I should have your problem," his mother says. "But you be careful. Just last year your father caught something, and he couldn't stop throwing up. He was down to blood and bile, but he kept heaving."

Dean says, "This was probably something I ate."

"You can be sure," she says and walks to the kitchen. She opens the refrigerator and surveys the interior. She closes the refrigerator and proceeds to open cupboard doors.

"Tonight you can have a couple soda crackers," she calls out, "and a little 7Up."

While his mother is conducting her kitchen inventory, Dean slips the annual out from under the pillow and carries it to the bedroom and puts it on the closet shelf. He takes a pair of Levi's out of a laundry basket and pulls them on.

Dean sits back down on the sofa, but his mother keeps circling and sniffing the air as if she's trying to separate the smell of white bread from wheat wafting up from the bakery below.

"Roy's paying her for making the trip?" Mrs. Linderman asks.

"That's what he said. Forty bucks."

"How about you? Was he going to pay you?"

"I would have done it," says Dean, "out of the goodness of my heart."

"Huh." Mrs. Linderman continues her circuit of the room. "I thought they'd be back by now," she says. "It generally don't take your brother long to close a deal."

"Maybe it took some time to track the owner down."

Mrs. Linderman walks over to the television set, a Motorola small enough to rest on a TV tray. Although the set is turned off, she adjusts its antenna anyway. "So I take it," she says, "you ain't concerned."

Dean closes his eyes and lets his head loll back on the sofa cushions. "What would I be concerned about, Mom?"

"It's not for me to say."

"No, go ahead. What should I be worried about?"

She bends over and looks at the blank television screen, though of course the set gives back no image but hers—cheeks as round and pronounced as plums, heavy jowls, close-set eyes, and all framed by improbably black hair enclosed in tight mesh.

She says, "You can get color in a little portable like this now, you know. I seen the ads. You probably have too."

Dean opens his eyes. "Stop changing the subject."

"Roy could get you a good price on one."

"Jesus, Mom."

Mrs. Linderman rises back up to her full height. She adjusts her hairnet. "What the hell. If you ain't worried, you ain't worried."

"That's my wife you're talking about," Dean says.

Mrs. Linderman shakes her head and says cheerfully, "It's not so much your wife as your brother. You know what your uncle says. Ice to Eskimos." She pauses then adds, "Panties off a nun."

Dean closes his eyes again. "Go ahead," he says. "You want to watch, watch."

His mother reaches eagerly for the knob and turns the television set on. "Lawrence Welk," she says, by way of explanation, and turns the channel selector to 12. She backs toward an easy chair and lowers herself onto its sagging cushion.

"Are Dad and Uncle John coming here?" Dean asks. "Or are you meeting them back at the Silver Dollar?"

"I'm meeting them. Soon as this is over."

From the television comes the wheezing, rollicking chords and notes of accordion music.

"That's about the sound," Dean says, "I made when I was heaving my guts out."

"It's only the one song," his mother says. "You want me to change the channel?"

Dean pushes himself to his feet. "Leave it. I'm going to lie down awhile."

As he walks barefoot toward the bedroom, Dean's mother calls after him, "I'll clear out soon as this is over."

"Watch as long as you like."

THE BEDROOM WALLS are painted a blue so pale that only in the faint light of late evening or early dawn do they look blue at all. At any other hour, the room passes for white. Edie received permission from the landlord to paint the apartment, and the color of the bedroom was her idea. Into a gallon of white paint she stirred in a little cerulean blue, a drizzle swallowed immediately by the white. But the blue was there. "Why bother?" Dean had asked her. "It's not even noticeable. Why not leave it white?" "It's private," Edie said. "Only we'll know. It's romantic." Dean didn't understand, but he didn't dare say so. The walls of every other room in the apartment remained white.

Dean lies down near the edge of the bed. He raises his knees up toward his waist. As his stomach and intestines flutter and pinch, his lips draw into a tight line, and he covers his eyes with his hand.

But nothing can keep those thoughts from seeping in. He's never been what you'd call confident or self-assured—just one more way he and Roy are so very different—but lately almost anything at all can set off another wave of uncertainty about his life. This morning he had a bout of vomiting right after Edie left, and he couldn't be sure what started it, the actual illness or the sound of a car door slamming as his wife climbed into a car with his brother.

From the living room comes the sound of his mother's laughter. High-pitched but steady. Then her laughter stops, replaced by the heavy tread of her footsteps. After a moment her laughter starts up again. The antenna must have needed adjustment.

When he wakes up, his mother is standing in the bedroom doorway. "I'm heading out," she says. "You want me to make you some soup before I go? Chicken noodle?"

Dean glances at the bedside clock. His mother has had time to watch more than a single episode of Lawrence Welk. "No," he says. "That's all right."

Mrs. Linderman braces herself in the doorframe. "Maybe you should give me a call when they get back."

"At home or the Silver Dollar?"

"I'm leaving for home soon. If your father and your uncle ain't ready to go, they can find their own way back."

"We'll see," Dean says. "I'll talk to you tomorrow for sure."

"Supper's around five. Heat or no, I'm roasting a chicken. If you get your appetite back, you're welcome to partake. The both of you."

As soon as the door to the apartment clicks shut, Dean gets the yearbook down from the shelf again. He switches on the lamp beside the bed and thumbs through the heavy glossy pages until he arrives at the portraits of the graduating seniors.

He doesn't linger on the photograph of Dennis Arneson, whose father died in Korea and who still wore a look of betrayal, nor on the practiced smile of Dorothy Bergstrom, nor on Doris Lantz, her pocked, pitted face smoothed over by darkroom magic. He skims quickly past Gail and Dale Peterson, the other set of twins in the class, and past the girl who was traded from boy to boy like a baseball card. Finally Dean's eyes come to rest again on Edith Pritchard. She isn't smiling, but many of the young men and women in these pages aren't. Eastern Montana doesn't fill its young with a lot of false promises. Like the faces in many other portraits, Edie's is angled to the side. But just like her picture as part of the homecoming court, something is different . . . No one else seems as lovely and alive on the page as she does, staring out at the eyes that stare at her. Dean once asked her how the photographer caught that look. She laughed and said, "He told me to act like I knew something no one else knew." And that was years before cerulean blue.

ROY PARKS IN a driveway of sorts, two dirt tracks worn through sparse grass, and under a lone cottonwood, the only shade on this dusty edge of town.

"You still want to wait in the car?" he asks Edie.

"If it's all the same to you."

"Can't say I blame you."

The front porch of the tumbledown little house is missing boards, and a window screen has torn loose and curled upward. Masking tape covers a crack in a front window. A corner of the house is splintered, as if an animal has gnawed on it.

Roy climbs out of the car and shuts the door quietly. The keys still dangle from the ignition. "Turn the radio on if you like," he says. "The battery's got plenty of juice."

"You're sure this is the place?"

Roy waves a hand in the direction of the gravel road running past the house. "You see any other possibilities?"

Yet Roy seems reluctant to walk away from the car. Finally he says, "I'll check around back first. Maybe I can get a look at the truck before the haggling starts."

He takes a few steps, then looks back. "Wish me luck."

"You don't need it," says Edie.

That brings his smile back. "We all need it."

You'd think Roy Linderman had been the track star. Shoulders back, a bounce in his long stride—nothing like Dean's loose-limbed slow, slouching walk.

Edie turns on the radio and adjusts the dial until the static clears and a station comes in. CHAK—Moose Jaw! But in another moment, the song that seems to play once or twice every hour comes on, and Edie switches off the radio. My God, she thinks, even in Canada they can't get enough of that boy jumping off a bridge. Overhead the cottonwood leaves applaud the silence.

She opens the glove compartment and begins a desultory inspection of its contents. A flashlight. An unopened pack of Camels. Match books. A comb. Maps of Montana and North Dakota. When she lifts the maps, she jerks her hand back as if she'd been stung.

Under the maps is a gun, a revolver with a wood handle and a blue-black barrel that gleams even in the dark glove box.

Edie has seen guns before. She's lived in Montana all her life. Not a highway sign or a rural mailbox is without its bullet holes. The gun racks in living rooms and rec rooms. The rifles and shotguns boys brought to school for hunting after the bell rang. The dead deer strapped to car roofs and hanging out the back of truck beds. In high school Edie dated a boy who said he had a pistol under the front seat of his car, though he never showed it to her. Her own father's rifle and shotgun leaned in a corner of the front closet where everyone hung their coats, and when her father died, her uncle went directly to that closet to claim those guns as his own.

And yet Edie has never touched a gun. She reaches into the glove compartment and takes hold of the revolver's grip. So many curves in the wood and warm steel . . . the round barrel, the cylinder, the hoop of the trigger guard. The gun fits her hand as if it wants to be held . . . but after only a few seconds, Edie puts the revolver back and covers it again with the maps.

She continues to go through the glove box. An opened roll of Life Savers. An owner's manual for the Impala. The car's registration. A parking ticket for the Gladstone street where Warren's Furniture and Appliance is located. A folded manila envelope containing a few cartridges. A tin Band-Aid box, but when Edie opens it, she finds prophylactics. Roy, Roy . . .

As gently as Roy closed the car door, Edie shuts the glove box. She flexes the fingers that gripped the handle of the revolver as if she needs to rid herself of the sensation of holding it. From her purse she takes out a stick of gum, unwraps it, and chews it vigorously, bringing a little saliva back to her mouth, which has gone suddenly dry.

She hears a yowl and looks up to see two girls coming around that gnawed-on corner of the house. The girls are perhaps seven or eight, both wearing brightly colored bathing suits, pink and lime green, and one of the girls carries a tortoiseshell cat in the crook of her arm. The cat is not only meowing loudly but also pawing and kicking at the air in its struggle to escape. The girl simply tightens her hold around the animal's neck. The other girl has a towel and a galvanized metal bucket, heavy with water.

It's plain they intend to wash the cat, and when the one girl puts the bucket down, they manage to sponge the cat's fur with a little soapy water. But once they lower the cat toward the pail, it manages to get its paws on the ground and in an instant leaps free and bounds off.

The girl who'd been holding the cat examines the scratches on her arm. A thread of blood trails down toward her wrist. "That little bastard," she says.

"He got you good," her friend says.

"That bastard."

Then they notice Edie and the long white car and, as if of one mind, they approach together.

The little girl with the scratched arm says, "We'll wash your car for you."

Edie has to laugh. "Cats *and* cars?"

"For just a dollar," her companion adds. Roy had mentioned the town's unpaved streets, and the feet and ankles of these children are darkly powdered with dirt.

"Sorry," says Edie, shaking her head.

"For fifty cents?"

"It's not my car."

The girl who carries the pail has a face so smeared with freckles it looks dirty. "Is it your husband's?"

"It's not my husband's."

"Is it your boyfriend's?"

Edie says no.

The girls step back and examine the Chevy from front bumper to back, as if Edie's relationship to the owner could best be determined by careful scrutiny of the car itself. The freckled girl smiles slyly and whispers something to her companion. The remark brings giggles from both of them.

"Go ahead," the scratched girl says. "Ask her."

"No. *You*."

The girl who carried the cat steps close to Edie's open window. She balances on one leg to scrape at that leg with her bare foot. She looks past Edie and into the car's interior. "Are you a whore?" she asks.

Edie draws back. "What do you know about whores?"

The girl nods toward her freckled friend. "Her brother said . . ."

"Really? What did he say?"

The freckled girl steps forward eagerly. "Are you? Are you?"

Edie points toward the house. "Do either of you live here?"

"Her grandpa does," the girl with the scratched arm says.

"What if I go tell your grandpa what you just said?"

"He don't care," the freckled girl says.

Edie makes a shooing motion with her hand. "You better go catch your cat before it gets run over."

"He ain't our cat," the girl with the scratches says, but both girls back away from the car. Just before they arrive at the corner of the house, the freckled girl turns back to Edie and gives her the finger. Then the children run off out of sight.

Edie opens her purse again. The familiar, comforting smells of spearmint and cosmetic powder rise from the interior. She clicks open her compact and surveys her features. Whore? She isn't even wearing any lipstick or mascara today. This summer she'd cut her dark hair so short it can't be brushed or combed, just ruffled—and now when she runs her hand over her hair, it rises and falls as if she's standing out in a breeze. Edie brings the mirror close to her face, and then she too raises a middle finger at that woman.

ROY STARTLES HER when he leans in the open window on the driver's side.

"Scoot over here," he says. "You're the driver now."

"Did you—?"

"I sure as hell did," Roy says, wearing a conqueror's smile. "Signed the papers, handed over the money, and put the keys in my pocket. The whole shebang. Now I'm going to buy you supper."

"Let's just head back," Edie says.

"Not a chance. We're celebrating with a steak dinner. Afterward you can go back to your sick husband. I'll bring the truck around and you follow me."

As Roy walks away, he knocks twice on the hood of the Chevy.

THE HIGHWAY LEADING in and out of Bentrock runs right through the business district, past the pillars of the First National Bank, the wide plate-glass windows of Shipley's Auto Supply, and the brass-handled doors of the Mon-Dak Hotel. And past both the Bison Café and Wolf's Diner. But Roy Linderman doesn't stop at either of those eateries. Instead he leads Edie to the Spur Supper Club and Lounge, better known to as the Spur, situated on a low bluff just outside town.

The evening has a little sunset light left to offer, but none of it finds its way inside the Spur. The dark paneled walls, the carpet the color of dried blood, the candles in their red-glass jars—there's barely enough light to glint in the glass eyes of the deer, antelope, and elk heads mounted on the walls.

Roy's sense of triumph hasn't left him. He leans closer to Edie over their dinner table and says softly, "The hell of it is, the old man didn't even want to haggle. I started him off with a number even lower than Les Moore said he might go for and, boom—he says yes, right off the bat. Hell, by this time I'm feeling a little sorry for him.

I'm about ready to tell him I could go a little higher. But there's no sense in me carrying on both sides of the negotiations. Then after we shake hands on the deal I say, 'You mind if I ask why you're selling the truck?' No farm, the old fellow says, no need for a farm truck. Well, hell. You can't argue with that logic."

From their table in a dark corner of the Spur, Edie has a view of the front door and the patrons trickling in. Saturday night. All the men and a few of the women head into the bar before returning to the restaurant space to sit down for supper. The women are in bright full-skirted dresses and high heels, the men in string ties, good boots, and Stetsons. There isn't another woman dressed like Edie, in sandals, shorts, and a sleeveless blouse. But Roy's short-sleeved white shirt? Good enough just about anywhere in this part of the world.

"To tell you the truth," Roy says, "he reminded me a little of Dad. For about a month after he sold the ranch, he looked like death itself. Drinking more than ever. Staring off at nothing. Then Mom sort of gave him a kick in the ass. Stop feeling sorry for yourself, she told him. Get with it. This is your life now."

"Easy advice," Edie says. "If you can follow it."

"Usually isn't much choice in the matter, is there?"

"I suppose not."

The waitress, a shy young woman with stooped shoulders, appears and takes their orders. A T-bone and hash browns for Roy, chopped sirloin and a baked potato for Edie. Roy holds his highball glass aloft and rattles the ice. "And could I get another one of these?" He points to Edie's half-full glass of beer. "How about you, Edie? Another Budweiser?"

"I'm okay."

As the waitress walks away, Roy says, "That's something you wouldn't have seen not too many years ago."

"What's that?"

"A place like this hiring an Indian gal."

"I hadn't noticed."

Roy leans closer and when he speaks, even in his lowered voice, his breath causes the flame of the candle on their table to flicker. "They had a big scandal up here a while back," he says. "A doctor or politician or somebody was raping Indian women. He'd been at it for years."

"My God. They finally caught him?"

"Killed himself before it could come to a trial."

"My God." An air-conditioning vent is nearby, and Edie is sitting right in the path of its cool breeze. She rubs her hands on her bare shoulders.

"I have a jacket out in the trunk," says Roy.

"I'm all right."

"And then a few years ago, the local sheriff was shot and killed. I'm telling you, Edie, it's the Wild West up here."

The waitress returns with Roy's Jim Beam highball and places it on the starched white tablecloth. "Your salads will be right out," she says.

"No hurry," Roy replies.

Roy sits back in his chair, and for a long wordless moment, he gazes at Edie. From another corner of the restaurant comes a man's booming laugh. Knives and forks scrape and clink against dinner plates. The smell of whiskey, of cigar smoke, of charred meat drifting through the shadows. Saturday night in Bentrock.

"Anybody sees us here together," Roy says, "they'd assume we're a couple."

"But we're not."

"We could have been, Edie. If you'd have let things go on a little further. We both wanted something more to happen, didn't we? And after, then it would have been you and me for sure. I'm right about that, aren't I?"

"Stop, Roy. Please. Just *stop*."

The waitress brings their salads, and it looks as though a single head of lettuce has been sliced in half for each bowl. She places a carousel of salad dressings on the table.

Neither Edie nor Roy lifts a fork. Edie again rubs her shoulders for warmth, and Roy lights a cigarette.

"I can go get that jacket for you," he offers again.

"I'll be all right." Edie looks around the Spur. The dining room is filling up. Maybe they could have been a couple. After all, it hadn't been Dean—her boyfriend—who showed up on the doorstep on that winter morning when she was home from high school—home *alone*, and in her pajamas. And she'd been angry with Dean, giving her strep. Roy didn't care that she was sick and looked it. And she was curious about Roy. She'd heard what other girls had said about him . . . and he was Dean's *twin*. What must that be like? But they'd stopped. *She'd* stopped. She was curious about Roy, but she loved Dean.

There isn't a table in the Spur now that doesn't have at least one man and one woman seated at it. At one a man covers a woman's hand with his own. At another a man strikes a match to light a woman's cigarette. Yes, perhaps she and Roy could have been a couple, but that's not the same as *should* have been.

"You want to trade seats?" Roy asks.

She shakes her head no.

Roy takes another long drink from his Jim Beam and water. "Look, Edie. I'm sorry if what I said in the car earlier offended you. But, damn, since when can't you tell a good-looking woman she looks good?"

"My grandmother said if you say 'I'm sorry, *but* . . . ,' you aren't really sorry."

"Was that your grandmother Fitzgerald or Pritchard?"

"Grandma Fitz."

"Wise woman."

"Was she? In the last year of her life, she told me if she'd been smart, she'd have moved to Sacramento when her son and his wife invited her to come live with them. Instead she said, 'I have to stay in Montana, but for the life of me I can't think what for.'"

"I remember she used to roll her own smokes."

Edie laughs. "Even when her hands got bad, she could still roll her own."

"Would you like to live in Sacramento?"

"Dean and I used to talk about moving. But we're okay where we are. For now."

Roy leans forward again. This time he pushes the candle to the side as if he might need to climb across the table. "Here's what I'd like to do. Take off with nothing but the clothes on my back, a few dollars in my pocket, and the car I'm driving. I'd leave Gladstone and go to, say, Great Falls. There I'd swap the car for another. Then I'd go to maybe Pocatello. Or Denver, even. Make another deal. See if I could add to my bankroll. Make enough to stay in the Brown Palace. You ever been there? Incredible hotel. Just beautiful. But that would be part of the plan—stay in a fancy hotel in every town. And then finally end up in California, driving a convertible alongside the ocean and with more money than I left with. I was reading this article the other day, about San Francisco and all the kids going there— hippies I guess they are—just to hang out. What do you think? You'd fit right in with your sandals. Maybe I'd grow a beard. Wear some of those love beads. Can you feature that?"

Edie's large green eyes gleam with something other than candle-light. "I've always wanted to go to New York," she says. "Just to be there . . ."

"We could do that," Roy says eagerly. "We wouldn't have to go west. East would work too. No reason why not—"

"We?"

"What do you say? We have two vehicles to get started. I've got a little money. We could buy you some clothes in . . . I don't know. Fargo, maybe? Minneapolis?"

Her face darkens as she sits back out of the reach of the candle-light. "*We?*"

"We'll leave here and head out on Highway Two. Straight across North Dakota. I know that road. We can make good time—"

"Stop it." Edie covers her ears with her hands. "Stop it-stop it-*stop it!*"

"All right. All right," Roy says. "Just having a little fun. You know me." He takes a swallow of his whiskey. "I never know when to quit. Always taking a joke too far."

"Jesus *Christ*, Roy."

"And then for a minute there I thought . . ." Roy stubs out his cig-arette. "Well. It doesn't matter what I thought."

The waitress arrives with two platters of sizzling meat. The pota-toes are on separate plates, and she isn't sure who had the hash browns and who the baked potato.

"We'll straighten it out," Roy says, waving the waitress away.

He unfolds his napkin and tucks it inside his shirt collar. He does this with such a flourish it isn't clear whether this action is also supposed to be a joke.

"I hope I don't embarrass you," he says. "I'm so damn hungry, I might pick up this steak with my hands and start gnawing away."

He doesn't of course. He cuts his meat into small pieces before he takes a single bite. Just like his brother.

Edie pries open her beef patty and examines its interior.

"Something wrong?" asks Roy. "You didn't eat any salad either."

"Not much of an appetite."

"You feel sick? Maybe you have what Dean has."

"I don't."

"You want to order something else?"

Edie shakes her head no.

"Suit yourself." He spears another piece of steak and swipes it through the bloody juices on the platter before lifting the meat to his mouth.

And then there it is. The look that's in the high school yearbook. The same look that's in Edie and Dean's wedding album as well. In the snapshot taken at their wedding reception, she and Dean were sitting on the couch in front of a stone fireplace, and Edie—Mrs. Linderman for less than an hour—had just turned around to look at something or someone who had commanded her attention. Eyes open wide, the sensual mouth unsmiling—it might as well be called the Edie Linderman Look. And she has it trained now on the entrance to the Spur, where two burly young men stand just inside the door and survey the restaurant.

They look as if they could be twins, with their identical crew-cut blond hair; their moon faces; their thick, short necks; their powerful chests and shoulders. They're both wearing short-sleeved white shirts, though one is a T-shirt and the other a dress shirt like Roy's.

Their inspection of the room passes over the two older couples who are laughing because one of the women has decided to begin her meal with dessert; over the gentleman who carries on a more animated conversation with the young man who came to clear away their dishes than with the woman sitting across from him; and over the young couple that had to bring their baby to the Spur. Then the man in the T-shirt points to the corner of the restaurant where Roy and Edie sit.

Even their walks are identical, with their muscular arms curled slightly at their sides and held away from their torsos.

"I think we have company," Edie says, but by then the two men have arrived at the table and loom over Roy and Edie.

The man in the dress shirt asks, "Are you Linderman?"

The young man in the T-shirt stares at Edie, who of course could answer yes to the question but keeps silent.

Roy puts on that smile that's supposed to bring everyone over to his side. "I'm Roy Linderman," he says. He extends a hand, but when no other hand comes out to meet his, Roy pulls his back and removes his napkin from his shirt collar as if that's what he intended to do all along.

"What can I do for you gentlemen?"

Up close it's apparent that these men are brothers all right but not twins. The man in the white dress shirt is obviously older, though both men appear to be in their thirties. He's taller too, by at least a couple inches, and the better looking of the pair, but both brothers have the small eyes that, in their ruddy round faces, give them a porcine look.

"You buy a truck today?" the older one asks.

"More like, did he *cheat* someone out of a truck today?"

"Whoa!" Roy tilts his chair back as though he needs a longer perspective on his interrogators. "I don't know where you're getting your information, but that deal was on the up-and-up. Nobody cheated anyone."

"Bull. *Shit*," says the younger man. He has a mouthful of bad teeth, and they lean and slant every which way like old stone markers in a graveyard.

"You two must be related to Mr. Bauer," says Roy.

"He's our grandpa," the younger man says, but his older brother thrusts out a hand to silence him as if he doesn't want that information revealed.

"I don't know what your grandfather told you," Roy says, "but he agreed to the price I offered. We shook hands on the deal and we signed the papers. And he accepted the money. If that's not your idea of a fair deal, I don't know—"

"You know that truck's worth more," says the older brother. "You goddamn well know that."

"And it ain't his to sell anyway!" the younger brother says. When he speaks he has to manipulate his lower lip to keep it from snagging on a tilting lower front tooth. "That truck was meant to be *ours*."

"Look," Roy says, gesturing toward Edie's plate and then his own, "we're trying to have supper here."

"Eat up," says the younger brother. "We ain't stopping you."

"Excuse us then," Roy says, and he picks up his knife and fork and turns back to his meal. But before taking another bite, he lays his silverware aside and then pushes his platter away. "Maybe you fellows want to find a table of your own?"

"We want," the younger man says, "the keys to the fucking truck."

Roy shakes his head, a little sadly. "I wish I could help you out there, but the deal's done."

"Well, now we'll undo it," says the younger brother.

Once again the older brother holds out a calming hand. "Here's the thing," he says, lowering his voice and trying to find a reasonable tone. "Our granddad more or less promised that truck to us. And we went ahead and made plans, and the truck was part of them. I don't have any idea where he got that wild hair to sell, but he sure as hell never consulted us. What do you say we give you your money back and we call it square?"

"Can't do it," Roy says. "I might be willing to go for that, but it's not up to me. I've already got a buyer for the truck. I'm here more or less as his representative."

This little speech might be nothing more than a negotiating tactic on Roy's part, but he wears such a pained expression it's difficult to believe he's anything but sorry.

"And did this fellow send you up here to screw an old man out of his truck?" the younger brother asks.

Throughout the entire push-pull of this conversation, Edie has sat quietly, demurely, not touching her food, not looking at the men hovering over her. She's kept her hands in her lap and said nothing. But now she looks at the three men in quick succession.

"This is ri*dic*ulous!" she says.

The color rises to her cheeks, two dark pink blotches as distinct as if someone had pressed thumbs to her flesh. "You've got no right— *no right*." She throws her napkin on the table. "I'm going to call the police or the sheriff or someone. This *isn't right*."

Edie starts to rise from her chair, but Roy reaches across to touch her forearm. "Easy, Edie," he says. "There's no need—"

"So that's who this is," says the younger brother. "Easy Edie. Yeah, Easy Edie, there's no need—"

"Shut up, Bob," says his brother. To Edie he says, "I apologize, Miss . . ."

"*Mrs.*," Edie says. "Mrs. Linderman."

Mrs. Linderman. It's the truth of course. But the pronouncement seems to change everything, as if the earth beneath the Spur buckled and the room tilted, and no one could be quite certain now where they sat or stood. Who did the Bauer brothers believe was sitting across from Roy Linderman? Had they spoken to that little girl? Had she told them it was a whore who rode in that white car?

Roy glances gratefully at Edie, and the brothers look at Roy as if they need to reassess the man. But the younger brother quickly switches his gaze back to Edie.

"Maybe," she says, "I should talk to the owner. I'm sure they don't want their customers disturbed."

"So I'm disturbing you?" Bob says with a gap-toothed leer.

"Mrs. Linderman," Bob's brother says softly, "we just came in here to see if we couldn't talk reasonably about this situation."

Edie glares at him. "You've said what you have to say then?"

"I believe I have." The older brother takes a step back, but Bob remains in place until his older brother reaches out and tugs at his T-shirt. They almost back into a table where two older couples nurse their beers while waiting for their steaks. Before the brothers reach the front door, Bob Bauer turns around and points a threatening finger at Roy and Edie.

THE CHEVY AND the truck are parked behind the Spur, but there's enough light back there for Edie to see what's happened.

"Uh-oh," she says. "Roy?"

"Yeah?"

Edie points to the long scar along the driver's side of the Chevy, stretching from the side-view mirror to the back door.

Roy licks his finger and rubs at the scratch. "Uh-huh," he says. "Maybe a key. Or a church key. Or a knife, I suppose."

"I'm sorry, Roy."

"Well, hell. I guess the boys had to have the last word."

Roy steps back and looks over the other cars parked nearby. Then he lifts his gaze into the darkness beyond the Spur, over the ravine where trees rustle in the dying wind and on to the bluff across from theirs, a palpable darkness silhouetted against the night sky.

"I'm the one who ought to apologize," he says. "I'm sorry you had to be a part of that. But that business about the sheriff? That wasn't good. You just set them off with that remark. And I was handling it."

"Did I violate some kind of manly code or something?"

"Like I said. I was handling it."

"Fine," Edie says, crossing her arms against her chest. The day's warmth has vanished so completely it's as if the season changed while they were inside. "Are you calling the police about *this*?"

"And say what? I don't have any proof, but I'm sure I know who did this? No, hell no. The Bauers had to have their revenge. Fine. But I've got their truck."

"If I can ever persuade Dean to leave Montana, it'll be to get away from their kind."

"They're everywhere. Don't blame Montana." Roy steps closer to Edie. "But if you're serious about a change of scenery, you know I'm your man."

Edie sighs and opens the car door carefully, as if the entire automobile has been compromised by that scratch in the finish. "I just want to go home."

The car's dome light comes on, and Roy steps in front of Edie and looks around the interior. After she climbs in, he closes the door then motions for her to open her window.

"I don't know what kind of speed I can coax out of the truck, so you go on ahead. Don't wait on me. Drive the Chevy as fast as you're comfortable. It'll keep up with you."

ROY CAN'T SEE exactly who's in the car following him—a Ford Galaxie by the look of the grille—but he can make out the silhouettes of the driver and a passenger. The Bauer brothers. He'd bet money on it.

The Ford had suddenly appeared a few miles outside Bentrock. By then Edie was well out of sight. She drove the Impala fast, even on this unfamiliar highway. And as it turns out, Roy is having trouble getting much speed out of the truck. He can cajole it up to sixty-five but that's it. And at that speed, the truck begins to shimmy.

So he's not about to outrace anyone. He tries a different tactic. He slows down to forty-five. The Ford slows as well.

"All right, stay there," Roy says out loud. "I don't give a damn. As long as we're poking along like this, Edie can put more miles between us."

Underneath the expected smells of grease, oil, and cow shit, the truck smells faintly of tobacco, maybe the smoky-sweet fragrance of Mr. Bauer's pipe. One of his children or grandchildren could no doubt climb inside the truck and identify the smell in an instant as belonging to that bandy-legged, sad-eyed little old man.

Even on high beam, the truck's headlights are feeble, but the slower speed has the virtue of allowing Roy to see every curve and drop in the road in plenty of time to adjust. He doesn't know this highway well; he isn't one of those people who can travel a route only once and then remember it.

Not like Dean: as boys they could wander off into the hills with their .22s or follow the bends and backwaters of the Elk River with their fishing poles, and no matter what trail they followed—or didn't—Dean could always find the way back. The truth is, Roy can still get lost in Gladstone if he crosses the bridge and ends up on the other side of town.

The car following him finally pulls out to pass, and Roy lets out a sigh of relief.

But it doesn't pass. It keeps pace with him, its front end even with the truck bed. They continue down the highway like that for almost a mile, and then the headlights of an oncoming car appear up ahead. The Ford will either have to pass or pull back. Its engine whines as the driver shifts down and slips behind Roy once again.

"Fine," Roy says to the rearview mirror. "Follow me all the way to Gladstone, fucker. I'll lead you right to the police station."

Once the approaching car passes, Roy permits himself a look up at the night sky. Clouds have blown in since they left the Spur. He can't see a star or any light from the almost-full moon. The highway climbs. Lightning flashes far off on the western horizon. The Linderman family ranch sat on a rise, just high enough to give their father the long view. On summer nights he'd stand out on the porch and watch the storms approach, silently at first, then grumbling as if thunderheads had a mind to be made up. Then the cannon fire. But when the country is hard up for rain like this, the clouds seem likely to do nothing more than flash their lights and then retreat.

From this height Roy can also see the road ahead. A car's taillights glow less than a half mile away. Has Edie slowed to let him catch up?

"No, Edie," Roy says in the barely audible voice of a man accustomed to talking to himself, a man who has spent too many hours alone in a car. "Go," he says. "Go. *Go.*"

EDIE PRITCHARD LEARNED to drive in her uncle's 1939 Packard Super Eight, though it wasn't Uncle Earl who gave Edie her first lesson but his wife, Nora. They drove out to a dirt road along the Elk River, and Nora put Edie behind the wheel and instructed her in the H pattern of the gears, the synchronization of the clutch and the gas, and the correct foot to use on the brake pedal. "Now go," Aunt Nora said.

Edie stalled the car the first few times she tried to get it going, but she caught on quickly—and before long she had that big black automobile flying down the road, a dust cloud rising behind her and the treetops rushing by overhead.

Once Edie had demonstrated her proficiency behind the wheel, Aunt Nora said, "All right. I've got one more lesson for you. Don't ever get into this car or any other with your uncle Earl. Not alone. You hear me? Not ever."

Edie didn't say, "Uncle Earl? Your husband? Mom's brother?" And she didn't tell her aunt that she, Edie, had already had to slap the hands and wrestle out of the grasp of boys her own age and older, boys bigger and stronger than Uncle Earl.

She has found few pleasures as pure as driving fast, even in the car she and Dean own, an underpowered Volkswagen with a slipping clutch.

But in this Impala? My God! She has the windows open, the volume on the radio turned up high, and the speedometer holding steady at eighty. After dark the signal from Moosejaw's CHAK comes in stronger than ever, and Edie sings along with nearly every song: "Come on baby, light my fire." "My baby, just-a wrote me a letter." "I know that my baby loves me." . . . The wind flows through her short hair with no more resistance than over a grassy field.

ROY IS LOOKING for that collapsed, abandoned barn not far off the highway. "Like a shipwreck," Edie had said when they drove by it earlier.

A dirt road turns off the highway near the barn, a road Roy could turn onto, and in the process lead that Ford off Edie's trail.

There it is, the barn's hulking shape looming not far ahead.

And is that the road? It might be. He shifts down, the gears grinding, and turns the wheel hard, aiming for what might be a road and might be nothing more than a dirt trail that runs into a ditch. For an instant it feels as though the truck is tilted on two wheels and in danger of rolling over. But it rights itself, and Roy is able to keep the truck moving ahead, bumping and scraping across the prairie, the headlights illuminating nothing in their bouncing, wavering beams but brush, weeds, dirt, and stones. Within fifty yards he's able to shift back into third and pick up a little speed across the flat land.

He hazards a glance in the rearview mirror. The Ford seems to be following him off the road but with far more caution than Roy exercises. "Go, Edie, go," he says under his breath.

A creature—a jackrabbit most likely—bounds across the truck's path, leaping from darkness to light and back to darkness.

He realizes, too late, that this was no road, though maybe it was a trail the cows used to come home. Roy is climbing now, steering the truck up a hill steep enough that he has to shift down again. Once he reaches the top, he can look back and determine whether the Bauers gave up the chase or are still coming on.

But the crest of the hill does not lead to a gentle slope down the other side. Instead the hill falls off sharply, as if a giant knife has sliced off its other half, the earth dropping away and exposing its rocky underside. The truck's headlights suddenly illuminate nothing but night air, the beams traveling out over space like starlight.

Roy brakes and turns, and in so doing he avoids going over the steepest edge. But he's still headed downhill and sideways, the truck sliding, skidding, and banging against the boulders that jut out of this ravine. Hang on, he tells himself, *hang on*, because the truck suddenly seems to have become a living creature with the intent to go its own way and to get rid of him in the process. The truck leans hard into its descent, tilts, then tips, and when its great weight begins to tumble and roll, Roy spreads out his feet and hands as if it's *his* balance that can be regained. But he's a passenger now, riding inside these tons of steel along the earth's slope with no more power or control than an infant caught in a strong man's arms. One headlight blinks into darkness while the other flashes, like miniature lightning bolts, first across the horizon, then into the earth, then across the horizon again, and then into the earth once more.

Time itself becomes a casualty of this accident, and events seem to happen out of sequence, as if everything is ordained only in the instant before it occurs. The sound of shattering glass seems to precede the windshield breaking under the weight of the roof caving in. The truck's frame groans before it bends in its roll down the ravine. Roy already seems to be tumbling out of the truck before the door pops open. The taste of brass is in his mouth before he bites through his lip. The warm gush of blood precedes the pain of the gash across his forehead. The soggy *crack* of his femur arrives at his ears before the pain rises up to and registers in his brain.

The truck finally comes to rest. Laws, properties, and sequences are restored to their natural order. Roy Linderman's first utterance, "Shit," comes out of his mouth as it must—as close to *ship* as *shit*—spoken through the space where his front teeth were only seconds ago. He rolls onto his back and takes a cautious breath, deep, deeper, right up to the pain and then past it. He exhales slowly, and the air whistles and seems to scrape bone on the way out. He struggles to sit up. He raises both arms over his head as if he's signaling the gravedigger: "Hold your shovel, I'm alive, *I'm alive!*"

He must have skidded face-first out of the truck because when he spits, he tastes not only blood but also dirt. He clears his vision by delicately wiping away the veil of blood that has slipped down his forehead. He won't touch his broken leg; the bone might be poking through the skin. The leg's rapid swelling feels as if it's tightening its own tourniquet.

Roy can't rise from that sitting position. He can't walk, and he can't crawl, but if he stays where he is, he'll surely die—and so he pulls his way up the hill, his hands and elbows digging into the earth below, and his leg dragging uselessly behind. He moves along the route lit by the one headlight, though its beam, never strong, will soon leave him.

What is time out here, far from all the clocks and measures of human purpose? If only that storm would come closer, its flash and thunder a means to calculate both minutes and miles, but it won't move from the distance it has settled into. Nevertheless Roy begins to count, "One, two, three, four, five." And rest. "One, two, three, four, five." And rest. Each five count moves him perhaps three feet. "One, two, three, four, five." And rest.

He's not the first man or the last to be confronted with the futility of trying to move forward and the futility of staying put.

THE HI-TOP TRUCK Stop and Diner has only two customers sitting at its counter: Edie Linderman and an old cowboy who bends down so low to his slice of huckleberry pie, it looks as though he might slurp it right off the plate. Nothing but coffee for Edie. She'd stopped just to use the restroom, a smelly, begrimed, cinder-block closet for both gas station and café customers. But once she headed back to the car, fatigue caught up to her.

Now she swivels around on her stool to face the plate-glass window and its view of the highway. When Roy comes along, she figures, he'll doubtless see his white Impala parked under the gas station's bright lights and stop. Maybe he'll want a piece of pie too. At the Spur he said he was going to end his meal with coffee and dessert, but they'd left before he even finished his steak.

The waitress refills Edie's cup without being asked. She's as big and wide as Edie's mother-in-law though closer to Edie's age and with similarly short hair.

"You sure he's coming?" she asks Edie and chuckles. "It's awful late."

"I'm sorry," Edie says. "Are you closing?"

"Didn't you see the sign? Twenty-four hours gas and food. I get paid if I don't do nothing but sit on my ass all night long for the two or three customers who walk through the door."

"You have some long nights, I bet."

"I got my trucker regulars," the waitress says. "And lonely cowboys." She laughs in the direction of the old cowboy. "And just a week or so ago, a carload of young folks—not much younger than you and me— come in about three o'clock in the morning. Headed to Missoula, they said. Five girls and a guy. Can you imagine? And he had hair down to his shoulders. I kind of wanted to ask him what kind of shampoo he used. This was about the prettiest, shiniest head of hair I ever seen.

I'm guessing you're like me," she says, pointing to Edie's close-cut hair. "Sick of trying to deal with it, so you chopped it all off."

"Something like that," says Edie.

"What does he think of it?"

"What does . . . *who*?"

"The fellow you keep looking out the window for. What does he think of your crew cut?" When the waitress laughs her shoulders bounce up and down. "Hell of a time to be meeting someone out here in the middle of nowhere. Can't say it don't happen though. This here's a Greyhound stop. But if no one's getting off or on—*whoosh!* The bus keeps right on a-rolling."

"My brother," Edie says. "We were up in Bentrock on family business. He was supposed to be following me."

The waitress's face puckers with disappointment. She glances over her shoulder at the clock. "Maybe he had car trouble."

"Maybe."

"Or you had a hell of a head start."

"We left at the same time."

The waitress looks out the window with concern that matches Edie's. "How far you have to go tonight?"

"Gladstone."

"You still got a few miles ahead of you. You wide-awake now?"

"I believe I am."

"You know what this trucker I know does? When he's feeling sleepy? He pulls out nose hairs." The waitress bends down to peer into Edie's face. "You could maybe do eyebrows."

Edie opens her purse. "How much?"

"Free with a meal. Ten cents without. Refill's free."

Edie puts down a fifty-cent piece. "I don't need any change."

The waitress picks up the coin, flips it in the air, catches it in her palm, and slaps it onto the back of her other hand. "Heads or tails?" she asks Edie.

"What? Oh, heads. Heads."

The waitress peeks under her hand but keeps the coin out of Edie's sight. "Heads it is. You're a winner."

Edie smiles. "What have I won?"

"Hell if I know." The waitress's shoulders bounce up and down again.

EDIE DOESN'T GET back in the Impala. She paces the Hi-Top's parking lot, pausing occasionally to look down the highway. The air has grown cool. She hears the faint, rhythmic *thud-thud-thud* of thunder.

No, it's not thunder. Parked not far from the Impala is a truck and horse trailer, probably the rig belonging to that old cowboy. And there's a horse in that trailer, stamping a hoof against the boards with a rhythm so regular it could be a message in Morse code. *Finish your pie. It's time to go.*

Edie drives out of the parking lot, heading north, back toward Bentrock.

ROY STARES AT the dirt, weeds, and stones only inches from his face and continues to haul himself across a landscape that seems to vary only in offering different patches of dirt, weeds, and stones. All around him are faint noises, the scratching, scurrying, crawling, creeping sounds of creatures hunting and being hunted, yet Roy has not seen another living thing.

Edie drives the length of highway that she drove earlier, waiting and watching for an indication or a sign she can't even be certain she'll recognize. How, in this world—with its immense empty spaces—can people find each other?

That white shirt.

The creature least suited for negotiating this terrain, Roy moves at perhaps one mile an hour. Past his swollen lips and gums, each breath heaves out and in. The taste of blood is like a mouthful of copper pennies. The blood drying on his forehead and down the side of his face cracks like parched earth. Either during the truck rollover or in the repetition of pulling himself forward, something has happened to Roy's right wrist—and each time he curls his fingers, the muscles in his forearm cramp and rebel with pain. Both the physical sensation of his broken leg and the thought of it sicken him, and just as he starts down the other side of the hill, he has to stop, raise himself farther off the ground, and vomit. The retching causes so much pain he cries out and has to lie down in the tall grass. After a few moments of rest, he begins again to creep forward.

In the days and weeks to come, when she tells her story of this night, Edie will say again and again that she has no idea how she managed to see Roy. *No idea*. She was driving slowly, yes, but she had no reason to believe he was out of the truck, much less lying out on the prairie, almost a hundred yards from the highway.

But that shirt, that white shirt.

The highway, of course, is Roy's goal, his reason for crawling forward for one agonizing hour after another. Occasionally cars speed past—the sudden welcome pour and sweep of headlights, then the red blink of taillights.

Now Roy sees a different light, a bouncing searching beam, almost as though it's in flight.

Then the light has a voice and its voice is Edie's, fainter than a whisper across the dinner table. "Roy? Roy? Oh God, Roy, *Roy!*"

She's running toward him, running through the coarse, sharp silver sagebrush with her bare legs and those flimsy sandals.

When she bends down toward him, he can see that she has brought not only his flashlight but also his revolver.

"My leg's broken."

Edie puts both flashlight and gun down in the dirt and reaches for him. "Oh God, what happened? What are you doing out here?"

"What the hell are *you* doing out here?"

At this she laughs and sobs in relief as if the humor of his remark is the best indicator not only that he will live but will live as himself.

She shines the light on him, and Roy flinches away from its brightness. "Don't look at me," he says.

She sends the flashlight beam searching across the prairie. "Where's the truck?"

"Totaled." He spits out a small clot of blood, and a fragment of tooth flies out with it.

"I'm sorry, I'm sorry. You don't have to talk. But we have to get you back to the car. We have to get you to the hospital."

She kneels down next to him and runs a hand gently down his back. "Can you get up? I can help you."

"My leg's broken."

"I know, I know. But first things first—we have to get back to the car."

Their world has shrunk down to these few square feet of Montana prairie, this small plot of land barely larger than a grave site, this land and the two people on it, their concerns a single concern: *we have to get you back to the car.*

Roy has to roll onto his back to sit up, and once he's sitting up, Edie tries to lift him—and then he pushes himself up until he's standing on one leg, and he has an arm across Edie's narrow shoulders. Then, as a broken, bleeding, three-legged creature, they hobble toward the highway. Roy holds the flashlight and keeps its small circle of light fixed on the ground a few feet ahead of them.

Somehow Edie is able to open the back door of the Chevy and maneuver him inside.

He lies down across the seat. He says again, "Don't look at me." He drops the flashlight, and it bounces and rolls under the front seat but continues to send out its weakening beam.

"I think I'm going to pass out." *Pass* comes out as *path.*

"Don't, Roy. Stay awake. Stay with me. We're going to the hospital."

"Not in Bentrock," he says. "*Not in Bentrock.* Go back to Gladstone."

"It's so far . . ."

"Just go. Go."

Edie goes. She puts the Impala into gear and speeds onto the highway with a tire-spinning lurch and a spray of dirt and gravel.

In the back seat Roy groans, and Edie says, "I'm sorry I'm sorry."

"It's all right." Roy will still not touch or even look at his broken leg.

"Tell me if you need to stop."

"Just keep going."

A car approaches, and Edie's tears spangle and blur its headlights. With her thumb she wipes the tears from her cheeks.

From the back seat comes Roy's voice: "Hey, Edie." It's weak and the words come out slowly, but its tone is calmer, as though Roy has reconciled himself to something. "What were you doing with the gun? You didn't bring it out there to put me out of my misery, did you?"

"The gun! Oh God. Oh, I'm sorry, I'm sorry. I forgot your gun out there!"

After a long pause, Roy says, "That's all right. What the hell do I need a gun for?"

The miles pass. The lightning comes no closer. The car radio remains silent. Nothing distinguishes one mile from another but the broken or unbroken highway line. And time passes with the miles, enough time for a man to black out, to lapse into a coma. Enough time for a man to die.

But then from the back seat comes a voice. Her name again, its syllables sweeter to her now than if whispered during lovemaking.

"Hey, Edie?"

"Yes?"

"We don't have to tell anyone about the Bauer brothers, do we?"

"I suppose we don't."

ONLY THE BEDS on the sunlit side of the ward are occupied, and Dean's brother's is at the far end next to a window. Their mother is at Roy's bedside, and when she sees Dean she waves him over.

On his slow walk down the aisle of beds, Dean must pass the two other patients on the ward: one an older man whose eyes are closed and whose skeletal body seems sunk into the mattress and the other a boy who is sitting up while a heat lamp dries the cast covering his right arm from wrist to shoulder.

Like the boy's arm, Roy's leg is encased in plaster. And it is held above the bed by an elaborate system of weights and pulleys. But the sight of the leg in traction is not what's most startling. Nor is it the contrast of that elaborate mechanism and the heavy white cast with Roy's torso, bare above a girdle of gauze. It is Roy's face that's most shocking. Above his left eye his forehead is purple and swollen, as if an egg has been sown under the skin. The sutures closing the gash alongside that bump look like miniature train tracks. His mouth hangs open, his lips are puffed out as though he's trying to form a word, and between his swollen lips is the dark space where his upper front teeth once were. His face looks made of mismatched parts.

Their mother puts her hand on Roy's shoulder. "I told you he'd come," she says.

"Hey, little brother," Roy says to Dean. His words come out slowly. "I finally got something and you didn't."

"And you can have it," Dean replies. He grips the bed's footrail as if he's worried about losing his balance.

"Go ahead," their mother says to Dean, "get a little closer. He ain't catchy."

Dean remains where he is. "What the hell happened?" he asks his brother.

"Compound fracture," says Roy. "Of the femur?" He looks at his mother and she nods. Roy adds, "They pounded nails right into the bone."

"And they're pumping him full of antibiotics," their mother says. "On account of infection. Because the skin was broke. And he was crawling around in the dirt."

"I meant with the truck," says Dean.

Their mother says, "I didn't know bones could get infected, did you?"

"Edie didn't tell you?" Roy says to his brother.

Dean shakes his head no. "She's still not sure."

"His ribs," Mrs. Linderman says, "ain't broken. They're cracked. There's a difference, I guess."

"I rolled the truck," Roy says. "Going too fast on a hill."

"Yeah, but—"

"He might need another operation," their mother says.

"I just want," says Roy, "to get the goddamn dentist in here."

His mother lays her hand gently on her son's shoulder. "They won't do nothing until the swelling goes down. You know that."

"So," Dean says, running his index finger along the bed rail as if he were tracing a route, "Edie had gone ahead, and then you had the accident—"

"Did you feel anything?" Roy asks abruptly. "You know, like when we were kids. You said you could feel it when Kenny Wertz nailed me with a fastball. Did you feel anything last night?"

"I—no. No, I didn't feel anything."

"Good," says Roy. "I wouldn't want you to. Not this." His eyelids flutter and close.

Their mother whispers to Dean, "He kind of comes and goes." She adds, "While you're here I'll go grab a cup of coffee."

Mrs. Linderman lumbers across the room. When she gets to the door, she turns and looks back at her sons. Not even in the hours after their birth, when they lay swaddled in the nursery on the floor below, could one boy be confused for the other. "Dean's the sad-eyed one," the doctor and nurses had said, to which the boys' father replied, "What the hell does a baby have to be sad about?"

In another moment Roy's eyes open, and he looks up at his brother with an expression that is, for an instant, clouded with incomprehension. "She's gone?" he asks Dean.

"She went for coffee."

"She's wearing me out, man. Every minute it's 'How are you doing?' 'Feeling better?' I think she's worried I'll die if she doesn't keep checking. But I'll probably be getting into a private room, thanks to her. And no extra charge."

"She probably walked up and down the hall looking for empty rooms."

"That's *exactly* what she did."

"Look," says Dean, "do you want me to drive up there and do something about the truck? Have it towed somewhere? You said it's totaled, but maybe something can be salvaged? Scrap maybe?"

"Fuck it," Roy says. "Leave it. Let it rot."

"Wrecks don't rot."

"Rust then. I don't give a shit." His eyes droop closed, and within an instant he's asleep again, his breaths chuffing in and out past those swollen lips still traced with thin dark lines of blood.

Somewhere on the floor a bell rings, a chime that is doubtless a call of distress or complaint. Dean steps closer to the bed. Just beneath the sharp, pungent smells of bleach and antiseptic is a faint fetid odor like rotting vegetables. Dean touches his brother's hand, its tendons relaxed, its veins like mapped routes leading . . . where? Roy wears a ring commemorating their high school and graduating class, a thick, heavy circle of engraved metal and polished stone. A sentimental adornment on the finger of a man who professes to be free of sentiment. To the heart of course. That's where the map leads. To the heart.

SUNDAYS ARE USUALLY busy times at the Seventh Avenue Laundromat, but today Edie has the business and its machines all to herself. Though the front and back doors and all the windows are open, no cooling air moves through the screens. The laundromat is stifling, and though its heat is fragrant, scented with soaps and fabric softeners, it is heat nonetheless, like a heavy blanket that can't be thrown off.

The last load is drying now, and while those sheets and towels twine and separate in their slow-motion swirl, Edie folds and stacks Dean's and her clothes on the long white table. Dean's underwear is frayed and yellowing. Her own slips and brassieres look gray. The stitching on the patch on one of the short-sleeved shirts Dean wears on the job has come undone and is in danger of falling off. Edie presses down on the embroidery—Cheyenne Sporting Goods—as if the pressure of her finger is enough to secure the patch. She'll have to sew it on. Again. And a cuff on one of the two pairs of Dean's cotton work pants has come unstitched, and Edie will have to tack that down too. Two socks are without their mates. Edie closes her eyes and lowers her head as if nothing could be more dispiriting than one black sock and one brown sock. Then she comes to the only garments left to be folded, the powder blue shorts and the white sleeveless blouse she wore to Bentrock.

The stains did not wash out. Dirt, where she sat down on the prairie next to Roy. Blood. Did she cradle his bleeding head to her chest? She must have. And she must have allowed his head to rest on her lap. These stains—great, faded wine-colored blotches shaped like unmapped continents—will never come out.

She carries the shorts and the blouse to the back of the laundromat and drops them into a trash can.

"Must be nice."

Edie turns around. Janice Twilly carries a wicker laundry basket, and her two daughters follow her—the older one, no more than five or six, toting a baby in diapers.

"Hi, Janice," says Edie.

Janice nods in the direction of the trash. "Was that something that'd fit me?" she asks. The women are close to the same size, though Janice Twilly's body looks as though it's been put to harder use than Edie's.

"That's not something you'd want. I couldn't get the stains out."

Janice barks out a laugh. "You think some little stains would bother me?" She puts down her basket and heads for the bin. She takes out the blouse and holds it aloft.

"Jesus," says Janice. "Is this—?"

Edie nods.

Janice examines Edie carefully, looking perhaps for the wounds that might have produced this quantity of blood.

Janice takes Edie's shorts out of the trash as well. "Jesus," she says again. "Did you put anything on these before you washed them?"

"I didn't."

Janice shakes her head. "That'll just set the stains, you know."

"I suppose."

"My mom uses baking soda and vinegar. That'll take out damn near anything." She drapes the blouse and the shorts over the edge of the trash bin, where she can continue to appraise them.

The baby begins to whimper, and Janice says to her older daughter, "Put her over on the table. And check her diaper."

The child obeys without question. "She's dry," she says to her mother.

"But is she stinky?"

The older girl shakes her head no.

Janice reaches into her laundry basket and extracts a pack of Old Golds. She lights one and says, "I hear Roy Linderman was in a bad accident."

"Where did you hear that?"

Janice exhales a stream of smoke. "My brother-in-law takes the X-ray pictures at the hospital."

"Then you know all about it."

Janice glances in the direction of her daughters and lowers her voice. "I heard you was with him."

"You heard wrong."

Janice's forehead wrinkles with disappointment. "Roy isn't yours?"

"I'm married to Dean if that's what you're asking."

"Shit. I know they ain't identical, but I could never keep them two straight."

Edie stacks her folded laundry into a basket, and Janice begins to unload hers, the top layer of bright pinks, blues, and yellows of children's clothing giving way to the mud and steel colors of the garments of working adults.

"Go get the diaper pail," Janice commands her older daughter.

Janice finds an empty Coke can to use as an ashtray. "I knew you was married to one of them. And the other one wasn't married. My cousin went out with him a few times. You know her? Kids used to call her Bug because of her eyes. But get this—Bug's mom went out with him too. Yeah. Mother and daughter. I mean, come *on*."

"*Roy*," says Edie. "That's Roy you're talking about. Not my Dean."

"I guess it's just the names I couldn't get straight." Janice has her cigarette pinched between her lips while she sorts the laundry and blinks from the smoke rising into her eyes. "Steve's brother says he's busted up pretty bad."

"He'll be laid up awhile, but he'll be okay."

The baby starts to crawl toward the edge of the table, and Janice deftly turns the child around. "Why don't you ask Roy about that sometime? Why don't you ask him what it's like to get with a gal and her mother both?"

The dryer buzzes, and Edie looks toward the machine where the sheets and towels are fluttering and falling to a rest.

"If Bug ever knew about her mom and him," says Janice, "she'd flip *out*. I mean it."

Edie opens the dryer and pulls out the still-warm towels and sheets. She stuffs them into the basket without folding them.

"And you wasn't with him when he had the accident? I thought sure Steve's brother said—"

"I have to go."

Janice's daughter comes in just as Edie's going out. The child is carrying the diaper pail with two hands, and she gazes up at Edie as if she's looking at a photograph in a magazine. Behind them Janice calls out, "I'm going to try to get them stains out. Then what if somebody sees me in your clothes? They might think I'm you!"

FROM THE BOTTOM of the stairs, Edie looks up. Dean is right outside the door to their apartment, sitting on a milk crate and drinking a beer. When he sees her he puts down the bottle and descends the steps.

"Did you lock yourself out?" asks Edie, allowing her husband to take the laundry basket from her.

"I wanted to talk to you about something."

"And what—you were afraid I'd drop off the laundry and drive away?"

He leads the way into their apartment and sets the laundry basket on the sofa. Edie has brought his beer and she hands it to him. "We have any more of these?" she asks.

The curtains in the living room are drawn against the heat. This dusky hour could be the one before dawn or after sunset, the shadowy indeterminate minutes of beginnings or endings. Dean brings out two long-necked brown bottles of Schlitz beaded with condensation and hands one to his wife. Edie doesn't drink but holds the bottle against her forehead.

"I went to the hospital. He looks like shit. But he cares more about getting his teeth fixed than anything else."

Edie takes a long swallow from her beer. "Your brother's vain. If he can't turn on that smile, he'll be helpless. So what if he has trouble walking for the rest of his life?"

"Jesus, Edie."

Edie shrugs. Then she performs the maneuver that never fails to astound Dean, no matter how many times he's seen it. She reaches behind and under her shirt, unclasps her brassiere, slips off its straps by reaching inside her sleeves and shrugging her shoulders, and then pulls the bra off under the front of her T-shirt, all without exposing any skin. She flips the undergarment on top of the clothes in the laundry basket. "What did you want to talk about?" she asks.

For a moment Dean stares at the brassiere. Then he backs into the doorway separating the living room from the kitchen.

"What happened up in Bentrock?"

"I told you. Roy bought the truck and on the way home he rolled it. The truck's totaled. And your brother damn near was too."

"But you found him . . ."

Edie looks up at the ceiling and then at her husband. She sets her jaw. After a long pause she begins to speak. "I was driving on ahead. I stopped at a little diner. I'd tell you the name of the town, but I have no idea what it was. Maybe it wasn't even a town. A gas station and a diner. I had to pee. I was tired. I had a cup of coffee. I watched for Roy. And when he didn't drive past, I drove back looking for him. If he hadn't been wearing a white shirt, I don't know that I would have seen him."

"Out on the prairie."

"Out on the prairie. That's right."

Dean's shaking his head slowly.

"What?" Edie says. "*What?*"

"Something you're not telling me."

Edie starts to walk away, but the apartment is small. Almost every direction will eventually move her closer to her husband. She stops and faces Dean once again. "Like what?"

"I just know there's something you're not talking about. And neither is Roy."

"You *know*. How do you *know*?"

"Because I know my brother," says Dean. "And I know you."

"Do you?" asks Edie. "Do you know me? I wonder. There's a me who exists in your mind and you know her. But that's not me. You've made her up and you seem to have a whole life for her."

"The thing is, Edie, I know how Roy feels about you."

"Do we have to go over this again? Your brother doesn't like to admit defeat, and I'm a conquest he didn't conquer. That's all it is."

"He came close . . ."

"Close only counts in horseshoes and grenades."

"And love. Close counts in love."

"How many times have I told you? Jesus, why did I ever say anything about that. We kissed. *In high school*. And you're still fucking obsessed with that."

"Still. It counts. It definitely counts."

"Don't you get it?" Edie sets her beer down and walks close to Dean. "It's not what *he* feels that matters. It's what *I* feel."

"Roy usually finds a way to get what he wants."

"You don't think I have anything to say about it?" She reaches out and grabs the waistband of Dean's Levi's, loose enough that she has no difficulty getting all her fingers inside. "Now come here," she says.

"I'm here." He still has his beer in one hand, but he puts the other hand at the back of Edie's neck.

"Closer."

"If I was any closer, I'd be on the other side of you," says Dean. It's an old joke and not theirs alone, but in a moment like this every utterance becomes private and original.

With her hand still inside the waistband of his jeans, Edie pulls him into the bedroom.

The light in this room is even dimmer than in the living room. Edie pulls her T-shirt up and over her head. She tosses it toward the chair where their clothes usually end up when they undress. She wriggles out of her cutoffs, removing her underpants in the process.

"Is this," says Dean, " just to shut me up?"

Edie steps into his embrace and presses herself against him. "Shut up," she says.

THE SHEETS THAT were supposed to go back on the bed are still in the laundry basket, so Dean and Edie lie asleep on the bare mattress. The fan on the dresser blows across their naked bodies, their sweat long since cooled. Nightfall is complete now. The only light that enters their bedroom is from the bare bulb burning over the back door of the bakery. In only a few dark hours, the truck will pull into the alley for the day's deliveries, releasing its exhaust along with the smell of baked goods through the apartment's open windows.

Even in sleep the muscles in Dean's arms still quiver from the earlier effort of supporting his weight above his wife, naked and open beneath him. And even in the darkened room, Edie's body, from breasts to hips, is as pale as the interior of a loaf of bread, torn open in one of Dean's rare moments of terrible hunger.

ROY WAKES UP from an afternoon nap to see his boss, Delbert Thayne, sitting at the bedside, puffing on a Pall Mall.

"How are you doing?" Delbert says with an easy, unforced smile. His business card announces: Thayne Home and Appliance Center. But it's the line below that says it all: *Sales and Service with a Smile*.

A few days earlier Roy was moved to a private room, and a nurse he's come to know looks in his open door as if to ask: "Are you up to this company?" Roy nods to her and she walks away.

"I've been better," Roy says.

"My cousin Lee busted his leg worse than you. He was hunting and he stepped over a fence right into a hole. He said the crack sounded like a goddamn tree branch breaking. You hear yours?"

"I didn't."

"My point is, Lee's doing fine. He was laid up for a while, but now there isn't a thing he can't do as good as before." Delbert crushes out his cigarette in the ashtray on the table next to Roy's bed. "I hear the dentist is coming this afternoon."

"Dr. Nord," says Roy. "About time."

"That's on me, you know. Whatever you need done, I'll foot the bill."

"I appreciate that. Blue Cross doesn't cover dental. But I guess I don't need to tell you that."

Delbert waves away the gratitude. He says, "I got a few changes in mind for when you come back to the store too. First of all, we'll have you working out of Bill Strobel's office. That way you don't have to try to clump around the floor on crutches or whatever the hell you'll need to get around."

"Bill won't like it."

Delbert waves this notion away as well. "Bill needs to get out with the merchandise and meet the customers. But he'll steer them your way. We all will. And you can seal the deal like you always do."

While his boss talks, Roy Linderman closes his eyes, and the energy seems to drain from him as though hearing about these activities is more exhausting than the actual work.

"Another change we'll have to try," Delbert continues. "We'll cut back on your salary." Roy registers no more protest than opening his eyes, but Delbert holds up a hand anyway. "Hold on," he says. "Your commission won't change. But we'll need a little trial period to see if the sales hold up like always. And if they do, why, your salary will pop right back to where it was."

The room, like every room in every hospital, has a distinctive odor: floor wax and isopropyl alcohol mingling with the sweet scent of ether and the smell of vomit from patients waking from its effects. As if Delbert Thayne is the source of an odor Roy cannot tolerate, Roy turns his head away and toward the window.

"And as long as I'm going on about changes," Delbert says, "I'll tell you what we'll have no more of. No more of your romancing the ladies you sell a stove or refrigerator to. And right now you're proba-bly thinking who you fuck is none of my business, and usually you'd be right about that. But when you let the prospect of a piece of ass affect the price tag on my merchandise, it's a different story."

Roped in place with traction and bound tight with plaster and sutures and bandages, Roy keeps staring out the window. Finally he says, in a voice as flat as window glass, "I quit."

"I heard what you said," Delbert Thayne says. "But for a minute or so I'll pretend I didn't."

Roy's head turns listlessly back toward Delbert Thayne. "I quit," he says again.

THE DOOR IS open no more than a foot, and through this space Edie peers in. "Roy?"

The only light in the room is from the sunset seeping through the slats of the blinds. All the room's whites—bedding, bandages, charts, and plaster cast—have darkened to tones of gray, and the actual grays—chair, lamp, bed stand, locker—look as though they're about to vanish in the shadows.

"Edie?"

She slips through the opening and takes a few cautious steps into the room. "Did I wake you?"

"No, no. I was just—is Dean with you?"

"He's at work."

"Oh, sure. Sure. The store's open tonight. Sorry. I'm losing track of the days in here."

Edie steps farther into the room but stops at the foot of the bed. "How are you this evening?"

"You're a sight for sore eyes. Did you come from work?"

"I had to stop at my mom's," she says. "She's not feeling well."

"Sorry to hear that."

Edie shrugs. "Just a cold."

Roy tries to sit up but raises himself only a few inches. "What's happening at the bank?"

"Irene Easter, this woman I work with? She has a son who just got his notice to show up for his physical, and Irene's sure he'll get sent to Vietnam."

Roy laughs. "Hey, that's one worry I won't have. The doctor says I'll probably end up with one leg a couple inches shorter than the other. I'll be walking like Chester from *Gunsmoke*."

"Oh, don't, Roy," Edie says, shaking her head.

"Don't what? Talk about being a goddamn cripple?"

"You're not going to be crippled."

"Whatever you say. Hey, could you get my cigarettes out of the drawer here? The nurse's idea of keeping this place clean is to put everything out of my reach."

As Edie walks to the bed stand, she's subject to Roy's scrutiny. "How do they feel about your short skirts at the bank?"

"I stand behind the counter all day. You know that."

"And do you notice the bank officers looking for any excuse to walk around behind the counter?"

She gets out his pack of Camels, shakes out a cigarette, and raises it to his lips. If he has to be disabled in some way, she thinks, why couldn't it be his vision that's affected? If he were blind or nearly so, his remarks, his unrelenting remarks, about her appearance would finally cease. And how different their relationship would be then.

"I can tell you're feeling better." She strikes a match and holds the flame to his cigarette, then points to the telephone on the bed stand. "You have your own phone?"

"I've got Doc McCarthy to thank for that. I told him I needed a phone to keep up with customers while I'm in here. And since I gave him a great deal on a freezer a couple months ago, he went for it. Told the nurse to attend to it right away. When she plugged it in, she said, 'A private room, a private phone . . . You have to be the most privileged patient in this hospital.' And it's a direct line. So if you want to call me, you don't have to go through the switchboard. The number's right there on the phone."

Edie steps back toward the window.

"Why'd you cut off your hair, Edie? Your hair looked great long."

"My God, Roy. My skirt. My hair. Maybe I should consult you before I make any decisions about my appearance."

"Maybe you should." Roy has figured out how to speak without exposing the space where his front teeth were. "I know what looks good on a woman," he says. "Now, you, you don't need much help. Short skirts? Hell yes. Short hair? Huh-uh. At least not fixed like that."

"*Fixed?*" She laughs and runs her hand back and forth through her hair.

"What does Dean think about your hair?"

"He hasn't said."

"And you didn't consult him. What about how you dress?"

"What about it?"

"What does Dean think?"

"What else," she says, "has the doctor said?"

Roy smiles as if he understands her strategy. "Not much," he says. "Wait and see how the bones heal. Or don't."

"I bet you'll be fine."

"Is that your expert medical opinion?"

"Isn't it better to look on the bright side?"

Roy smiles again. "Is that what you do, Edie? Do you look on the bright side?"

"I try."

He reaches toward the ashtray, stubs out his half-smoked cigarette, and attempts again to sit up a little straighter. "Here's the thing. My life is divided in two now. Before and after. I can feel already how my memory will work. From now on, every time I try to remember something I'll think, When was that? Was that before the accident or after? But you're right there, on both sides. You're like the hinge holding my life together."

"What the hell are you talking about? Dean was your brother before and he's your brother now. Your mother's your mother. Your apartment's your apartment. You're not making sense."

"But you were there. You were out there on the prairie. You found me. If not for you . . . Hell, you know the answer to that as well as I do."

"A 'hinge.' You sure know how to flatter a woman."

"Do you need to be flattered? I didn't think you were that kind of woman. But if that's what you need, I can sure as hell oblige you."

"I just stopped by to see how you were doing. Physically."

"Physically? You want to know how I'm doing *physically*? Well, let's see." He raises his head from the pillows and looks down the length of his body as if he'd forgotten a body was there. "How *am* I doing?"

He lets his head fall back on the pillows. "But since you're here, and since you're concerned about how I'm doing—how I'm doing physically—there is something you can do." He crooks his finger for her to come closer.

Reluctantly Edie steps forward.

"Come around to the other side," Roy says, and she does as he commands.

He lifts the sheet. "Reach under here, will you, Edie?"

She flinches.

"Come on," says Roy. "You know what I need. I'm a prisoner here, Edie. There's a box of tissues right over there on the shelf. Just put your hand under here and give me a little relief." He laughs. "Shouldn't take more than a minute."

Yes, she understands what he needs. She understands very well. He's flat on his back, swaddled in gauze and plaster, and helpless as an infant. He has to find some source of power, some way to impose his will. And if he can humiliate her in the process, so much the better.

"I'm asking you for a favor, Edie."

And how does he know that Edie won't tell Dean about this incident? Or perhaps he simply doesn't care one way or the other.

For a moment it looks as though she will do as Roy asks. She steps close to the bed. But rather than reach under the sheet, she bends down and kisses her brother-in-law chastely on the forehead.

"You have to learn to do things for yourself, Roy," she says as she backs out of the room.

FATHER AND SON look nothing alike. Elmer Linderman is a short, compact bald man, perpetually smiling, and bowlegged from the years he spent on horseback. Dean is tall, slope-shouldered, and usually overdue for a haircut. On this warm evening Mr. Linderman is wearing a sweat-stained work shirt while his son is shirtless. Yet when they step back to assess the carport they've built, they fall into the same posture—hands in the back pockets of their jeans and heads cocked to look at their handiwork.

"What do you think?" Mr. Linderman says.

"It'll work," says Dean.

"I don't know what the hell good it'll do. The car won't start any easier on a cold morning. I'll still have to plug it in."

Dean shrugs. "You won't have to sweep snow off the car."

"Not if the snow comes straight down. But how often does that happen?"

"Well, it's better than nothing."

Mr. Linderman grips one of the posts that the corrugated fiberglass sheets are attached to. "The hell of it is," he says, "all those years on the ranch, we always left our vehicles out in the open."

"You're in town now."

"You sound like your mother."

Dean turns away from the carport and looks off in the direction of the unbounded prairie beyond the trailer park. "I remember one blizzard when the snow piled up so high you weren't sure which drift the truck was under."

"You might be remembering more than one."

"I'm thinking of a time when Roy and I did the shoveling."

Mr. Linderman walks away from the trailer, and his son seems to know that he is to follow.

"Is that thunder?" Dean asks.

"More likely trucks out on the highway. An eighteen-wheeler with an empty trailer makes a hell of racket." He turns toward his son. "Your brother quit his job. He say anything to you about that?"

"Nope."

"Us neither. Your mother come across that bit of news when she went in to talk to Delbert Thayne."

"About?"

"You know your mother. Wanting to make sure Delbert understood about Roy's condition and to go easy on him when he returned to work. And Delbert says, 'He won't be returning.' Seems Delbert visited Roy in the hospital, and your brother up and announced he's quitting."

"Huh. So did Mom ask Roy about it?"

Mr. Linderman walks a little farther from the rows of trailers. From the roofs of a few trailers, the stalks, wires, and wings of television antennas protrude like the skeletons of great birds, and from a few windows come the gray-blue ghostly glow of television signals.

"You know your mother," says Mr. Linderman. "She don't like to push her boys in any direction they might not want to go. Roy will tell us when he's good and ready, she says."

The sweat Dean worked up earlier has dried, and he crosses his arms against a breeze that blows across the open land. He says, "Sam Wylie would hire Roy at the drop of a hat."

"Just what I told your mother. A wheeler-dealer like your brother will never be out of a job for long. Still," Mr. Linderman says hesitantly, "maybe you could ask Monte if he needs another hand at the store."

"I think," says Dean, "one Linderman is enough for Monte."

"Sure, sure. I just thought I'd put it out there."

"You mean Mom put you up to it."

Mr. Linderman starts walking back toward the rows of trailers. "You know your mother."

IT'S THE THIRD call from Roy in as many days, and this one begins like the others—with an apology.

But this time Edie doesn't hang up. She's home alone. Dean went over to his parents' trailer after work and he's still there, helping his father with another project that Mrs. Linderman dreamed up.

". . . It's just that . . . well, hell, you know you make me a little crazy. And then cooped up here . . ."

"Is this another 'I'm sorry, *but* . . .' ?"

"All right, all right. I apologize. I apologize for my behavior. Period. There, how's that?"

The phone cord is long enough to allow Edie to sit down at the kitchen table.

"Okay."

"I'm forgiven then?"

"Until the next time."

Laughter comes across the line. "Ah, you know me too well. But that isn't the only reason I called. Laying here like this I've had a lot of time to think. And you know I'm not big on that. I'd just as soon be up and doing."

"Roy Linderman, man of action."

"Hey, it's no joke. Dean was always the one who could sit for hours and do nothing but think about which way the world spins. But why the hell am I telling you what he's like? You married the guy."

"You've known him longer than I have."

"That's true. But I sure as hell haven't figured him out."

"Let me know when you think you have."

"Anyway. Just laying here with nothing to do but wonder which nurse is going to hold the bedpan has been getting to me. Then I realize I don't have to think. I can remember. And I've been remembering like a son of a bitch. So can I tell you what I was remembering tonight? You were a big part of it."

"I'm not sure."

But Roy proceeds. "This was, I don't know, maybe the summer we graduated. Anyway. Hot, sunny day, and we're all down at the Elk River. Sandbar was packed with kids. You were sitting on a log, and right next to you was Carla Hall—and you were both wearing swimming suits. I walked up behind you two and you didn't know I was there, so I'm staring at your backs. And remember, I was going with Carla then. And Carla—well, hell, Carla was a knockout. Everybody thought so, right? But what I see when I look at the two of you is how different you look. And this is your backs, just your *backs*. But your back, Edie, yours was like, like—I don't know what to say. It was smooth, not a goddamn blotch or a mole or a blemish. And you're tan, both of you, but you looked like caramel. Suddenly I realize there's skin and there's skin. You know what I'm trying to tell you?"

"I don't know, Roy. You liked my back?"

He groans. "Jesus. You don't get it. I *saw* you, Edie. I appreciated you. I saw how you were different. How many other guys could have done that? Every guy at the river that day would have thought, Two good-looking girls. A back's a back. Isn't that what Dean would have thought? Isn't it?"

"Some girls," Edie says, "used to mix iodine and baby oil and spread that on before lying out in the sun."

"Come on. Has Dean ever said anything about your back? Has he?"

Edie rises from the table and walks to the sink. A dishrag is draped across the faucet, and she takes the cloth and wipes it desul-torily across the counter. She says, "He's said a lot of things . . ."

"Okay, okay. Let me give you another one. And I know this is a time you remember too. You weren't in school, so I skipped chemis-try and went to your house. To check on you."

She drops the washcloth in the sink and walks back to her chair. "I had strep throat," she says. She closes her eyes, holds the tele-phone a few inches from her ear, and presses her forehead onto the heel of her free hand.

"Yeah, yeah. Strep throat. You answered the door in your paja-mas. God damn, I still remember exactly what you looked like in those pajamas. Baby blue, right? Am I right? Baby blue pajamas?"

"Blue," she says and sighs. "Yes, blue flannel." It wouldn't make a difference if he were blind, she thinks. He doesn't even need her there to look at her in that way.

"And they buttoned up the front," he says.

Roy and Dean Linderman aren't identical twins, but they share identical obsessions. "High school, Roy. Do you hear yourself? You're talking about something that happened years ago. I wore a bathing suit, and I had a good tan. We made out once. In *high school*, Roy."

"It was more than that, Edie. You know it was. You in those blue pajamas. That was more than making out. Tell me it wasn't . . ."

Edie says nothing but crosses the room and terminates the call. But she doesn't set the receiver back in its cradle. She keeps it pressed to her ear.

FROM HIS HOSPITAL bed Roy looks up at his brother and says, "I want you to sell the Impala. Take out an ad in the *Gazette* and the *Shopper* both." He points to a folded sheet of paper on the bed stand. "I wrote down what the ad should say."

"The hell," Dean says. "What for?"

Roy nods in the direction of his leg in its cast. "I'll probably need something with an automatic transmission."

"Are you sure? Why don't you wait?"

The swelling in Roy's face has gone down, but the bruising, though it has faded, remains. A yellow-lavender smear covers one side of his head from his hairline to his jaw.

"I could use the money," says Roy.

Dean raises his eyebrows.

"Don't give me that look. That's Mom's look."

"She's going to talk to Delbert, you know."

Roy turns his head from side to side. "*Shit*. I don't suppose you can call her off. Or tell her I've got something else lined up."

"Sooner or later she'll want to see your pay stubs."

"I just need to buy a little time. Once I get on my feet, I can work something out."

Dean picks up the glass of water on the bed stand, raises it to his lips, and drinks. Then before he puts it back down, he looks at the glass curiously, as if he has just realized what he's done. They grew up drinking from the same glass, eating off the same plate. So close for so many years it seemed as though one of them could taste what the other one bit into. Wearing each other's coats and shoes. Sharing the warmth of their blankets and bodies on cold winter nights. And then, around the age of thirteen or fourteen, they were suddenly different—and no difference seemed as profound as the fact that Roy was now sure of almost everything and Dean was not.

"That price you're asking," says Dean. "That already seems low. And then 'or best offer'? You really want that?"

Roy nods. "And put a For Sale sign in the window. Wash the car and park it on the street."

"Edie and I have a little saved," says Dean. "We could help you out—"

Roy waves away the offer. "How the hell did you two manage to save any money?"

Dean shrugs. "We keep it pretty simple."

"And is that your idea? Or Edie's?"

"Just let me know if you need anything."

"Sell the fucking Impala," says Roy. "That'll hold me for a while. In the meantime, spend a little of your savings on your wife. Buy her something nice."

"She makes more than me." Dean refolds the paper with its instructions and puts it in his shirt pocket.

"That's not what I'm talking about."

"Thanks for the advice," Dean says and turns toward the door. "Even if I didn't ask for it."

"Hey, *hey*. Wait up. I've got something else I want to ask you."

Dean stops.

"Did you ever think I was going to die? From the accident?"

Dean stands up a little straighter, as if his brother's question comes as a challenge. He says, "When Edie called from the hospital, she said right away you were okay. 'Roy's been in an accident but he'll be okay,' she said. So, no. I didn't think you'd die."

"Yeah, but what if . . . What if I died?"

"What if you moved to Denver? What if, what if . . . How the hell do I know?"

Roy laughs. "I die or move to Denver? It's all the same to you?"

"You know what I mean."

"I'm not sure I do, brother. I'm not sure I do."

"Well. You work on it."

This time Dean makes it almost to the door, and it's not anything his brother says that stops him and draws him back to the bedside, but once he's there he bows his head as if he expects Roy to place his hand and a benediction upon him.

"She couldn't say it fast enough," says Dean. "That you were okay. It took a fraction of a second before she got those words out, and it wasn't fast enough."

ROY, IN HIS pajamas and robe and supporting himself on his crutches, surveys the trailer's living room. The sofa and an over-stuffed chair have been covered with sheets.

"What the hell, Ma," Roy says. "Did you think I'd bleed on your furniture?"

"Your mother thought the chair and sofa would be too itchy for you," Mr. Linderman says.

"They both got that kind of tweedy fabric," Mrs. Linderman says.

"They're a set," says Mr. Linderman. "Remember?"

Mrs. Linderman puts a hand on her son's shoulder. "You were saying in the hospital how the itching was driving you crazy."

"Inside my cast, Ma. *Inside.*"

"I'll show you how we got the bedroom rigged up," she says.

Roy's crutches, his mother's girth, his father's rolling side-to-side gait—they have to proceed single-file down the hallway, at the end of which Mrs. Linderman opens a door and gestures for all of them to enter.

"Here you be," she says. "Welcome home."

Roy looks around the small room. The single bed with no frame or headboard, its head pushed up against the wall. The worn white chenille bedspread. The straight-backed chair at the bedside. The chest of drawers painted a shade of blue more common to exteriors. If there's anything here that pleases or surprises Roy, his face doesn't register it.

Mrs. Linderman points to the room's window, where a box fan sits on the ledge of the frame. "Your dad," she says, "put that there. Should keep the room cool at night."

Mr. Linderman says, "Not that we'll have that many more warm nights."

"Well, just in case," she says.

Not a picture, not a sampler, not a mirror, not a crucifix hangs anywhere in the room, yet the three Lindermans look from one wall to another, and while they do a dog wriggles out from under the bed.

"Hey, Rusty," says Roy.

The dog, a beagle-Lab mix not much bigger than a coyote, slinks tentatively toward Roy and begins to sniff his cast. Roy removes the crutches below his armpits, balances on one leg, and reaches down to scratch the dog's head. Rusty flinches away from his touch.

"Don't tell me," Roy says, "you've forgotten me?"

After a moment of cowering, Rusty pushes his graying muzzle into Roy's open hand.

"He's been hiding out in here lately," says Mr. Linderman.

"Am I putting you out of your room, Rusty? I don't mind if you bunk down in here."

"Remember that big old tom," Mrs. Linderman says, "that used to crawl in bed with you and Dean?"

"With Dean," says Roy. "He always slept on Dean's side of the bed we shared for years at the ranch."

"Well, that ain't how I recall it." Mrs. Linderman reaches down and smooths the bedspread, which doesn't need smoothing.

Roy hops over to the bed on one leg and pulls back the spread to expose a pillow that's almost as flat as a creature run over on the highway. "You got an extra pillow?" he asks his mother. "I like to put my leg up when I can."

"I reckon I can scrounge one up," she says. "You feel like laying down now, or you want to sit up awhile?"

Roy turns to his father. "You have any cold beer?"

DEAN LINDERMAN EXITS Cheyenne Sporting Goods by way of the back door, stepping into the alley that runs from Winchester Avenue on the north end to Merchants' Avenue on the south. And when he steps out of that brick canyon, deep in shadow and barely wide enough for a car to drive through, he runs right into sunlight . . . and his mother.

"They keep you late?" she asks. "Seems like every other store's cleared out already."

Dean shakes his head. "My turn to help total out the registers."

"Can I buy you a piece of pie?" she asks, nodding in the direction of the Mint, the café across the street.

"No thanks. Too close to supper for me."

"Come watch me eat then."

Dean looks apprehensively up and down the street.

"What the hell," his mother says. "It's not like Edie's got supper on the table."

At this hour the Mint's only customers are the men and women who have no one at home to prepare their meals or to prepare meals for. They hunch over the hot roast beef sandwich or the Swiss steak, and they turn the pages of the *Gladstone Gazette* as they lift forkfuls to their mouths. Two of these solitary diners are present when Dean Linderman and his mother enter. Mrs. Linderman says hello to Doris Carroll, who has finished her day of work at Shaw's Rexall, and Dean nods at old Earl Dunbar, who no longer sells shoes at Harmon's Bootery but still walks downtown and takes his meals at the Mint.

Dean and his mother sit at a booth by the window. "Busy day?" Mrs. Linderman asks.

"Not particularly," Dean says. "A few high school boys coming in to get fitted for their football cleats."

The waitress, a lean woman with her gray hair caught up in a net, walks over with her pencil and pad poised. "You see the specials?" she asks, pointing toward a small chalkboard leaning against the cash register.

Mrs. Linderman squints at the handwritten sign. "I couldn't read that little writing if I had my nose right up against it. What kind of pie you got back there?"

"Apple, rhubarb, and banana cream."

"I'll have a slice of the apple. With ice cream. And coffee."

"How about you?" the waitress asks Dean.

"A glass of water, please."

"Oh come on," his mother says.

"A glass of water," he repeats.

The waitress walks away, and Mrs. Linderman says, "Well, we got your brother settled in."

Dean turns his gaze to something outside on the street, but unless you count the way late afternoon sunlight glints off store windows and windshields, there's nothing out there to lay particular claim to his attention. "How's that going?" he asks.

"He ain't interested in doing much of anything but drinking beer and watching television."

"Not much else he can do, is there?"

"He could call around. See if he could get something lined up for when he's back on his feet."

Dean shrugs.

"He's let his apartment go," she says. "Did you know that?"

"Not much sense in paying rent on that place if he's staying with you. Who moved him out—you and Dad?"

"Your father mostly," she says. "We put all his belongings in a few boxes, and now they're stacked up in that little bedroom."

"You should have said something. I'd have done that for you."

"Not much to do," she says, shaking her head. "I don't know how a man accumulates so few goods."

"He trades them away, that's how."

"You get any takers on the car?"

"Lookers but no buyers. One fellow took it for a test-drive. Maybe it's me. Roy would probably have sealed the deal by now."

"I can't get used to seeing him with them new teeth. They're just too damn big and bright or something."

The waitress brings the apple pie and coffee, and sets them on the table. Mrs. Linderman lifts the plate and touches its bottom. "I thought maybe they might heat the pie."

"It's hot when it comes out of the oven," the waitress says. "That's the last time."

Mrs. Linderman picks up her fork, and that's all the answer the waitress needs. She walks back over to her stool by the cash register.

Neither mother nor son says a word until Mrs. Linderman finishes her pie. "Nobody can make a decent piecrust nowadays," she says. She pushes her plate aside. "You could come over. Talk to him."

"About what?"

"Maybe he could show a little interest in something other than a six-pack of Schlitz and a rerun of *Gunsmoke*."

"Nothing I could say you haven't said already."

"But it'd be coming from his brother."

"Roy and I have never been much for telling the other how to live. You never noticed that before?"

Mrs. Linderman scrapes her fork through the crumbs on her plate. "It's because no one uses lard anymore. You can't make a good piecrust without lard."

OCTOBER IS A little late in the year for a party down by the river, but a gathering to celebrate Roy coming home from the hospital had to wait until he actually came home. And the party has been a good one. A warm day. Plenty of food and beer, and a great turnout of friends and relatives.

But it's winding down now. Most of the older folks have gone home, and a few of them took grandchildren with them. Mrs. Linderman, Mrs. Pritchard, and Mrs. Anderson remain, and they're cleaning and packing up, rounding up paper plates and cups, empty beer cans and soda bottles, and putting the leftover potato salad, baked beans, chips, and chocolate cake back in the coolers until the picnic area is as tidy as their kitchens.

The football and the Frisbee both sit on a picnic table. The men who had been out in the parking lot looking under the hood of Butch Field's new GTO have returned to their wives and girlfriends. The jackets and sweatshirts have come out. A fire has been lit, and the remaining partygoers bring their chairs and blankets close to the flames and the heat. The guest of honor basks in the fire's glow, his leg in its cast stretched out straight on the webbing of a lawn chair. His crutches lie in the grass next to him. Dean sits at Roy's right side, Edie on his left. Someone—Jerry Krueger? Big Bill Den Dooven?—has uncapped a bottle of Southern Comfort, and it's going around the circle.

"Hey," Big Bill says, "whose idea was this shindig?"

"Edie," says Dean. "This was Edie's idea. It was all Edie."

The gibbous moon hangs in the evening sky like a bent pie tin. The fire's sparks rise as if they want to take their place among the first stars.

And between these flickering luminosities, a flock of ducks flies—no doubt looking for some quiet backwater of the river to settle on for the night. One of the men in the group raises an imaginary shotgun and leads one of the ducks as if he intends to blast it from the sky.

"How'd you decide who to invite?" Bunny Hildebrand asks Edie.

"It looks," says Larry Kraft, "like she just opened the phone book and started dialing."

"The hard part," Edie says, "was making sure everyone understood it was a surprise."

"And was it, Roy?" asks Bunny. "Was it a surprise?"

"Didn't you see me? I damn near dropped my crutches."

Mary Jo Shewmake asks Edie, "Is it true you invited his doctor?"

"I invited every one of his nurses too!" Edie says, and only now is it plain she's had too much to drink. "Hell, I damn near called Bentrock and invited the Bauer brothers."

"Who? Bauer?" The question comes out of more than one mouth.

"Oh, those two assholes who ran us out of Bentrock—" Edie says.

"*Hey*," says Roy.

"Who said Roy cheated them on the truck. But it was fair and square, wasn't it?" Edie asks.

"They ran you out of town?" says Big Bill. "The hell."

Bunny asks, "Is that how the accident happened?"

Roy slumps back in his chair.

The alcohol, the crackle of burning wood, the wind, the noise of too many questions going in too many directions. And then Jerry Krueger's voice rises above the confusion to make what almost immediately becomes an official announcement: "Those fuckers caused Roy's accident!"

And that's that. Like a fire that jumps its boundaries or a river that breaks its channel, this news will now find its own way: *the Bauer brothers ran Roy off the road.*

They think they can get away with that?" says Big Bill. "That's *bullshit*."

Bunny says, "I can't believe anybody would actually do something like that. Like in the movies."

"We should go up there." This is a new voice—Roger Reichert, who graduated with Roy and Dean and Edie and Jerry and Bunny and Big Bill. But Roger went straight from Gladstone High to the state prison in Deer Lodge, where he spent three years for breaking into an auto parts store. "Show those sons of bitches," Roger says, "what's what."

From somewhere in the circle comes the metallic crunch of a beer can being crushed.

"Put together what's left of the old football team and drive up there," Jerry Kreuger suggests.

It's a woman's voice that says, "Oh please."

"What's the name again?" asks Butch Field. "Bauer?"

"Shouldn't be too hard to find them," Larry Kraft says. "I got cousins up there. Bentrock's your original one-horse town—"

"And the horse died!" shouts Jerry.

Roy and Dean are twins. Of course they are. What other explanation could there be for the identical look they both turn on Edie, a look that flares with shock, anger, disappointment, and perhaps even sadness as both think: Edie, Edie. What have you done?

"I GET THAT you're pissed off at me," Edie says to Dean. "Are you trying to kill us both to make your point?"

They're in the Volkswagen, speeding along River Road, away from Frontier Park and the site of Roy's party.

"And why the hell are *you* mad?" Edie asks. "It was Roy who asked me not to say anything about the Bauer brothers. Is this another one of those goddamn twin things that nobody knows anything about it until it's too late? I swear to God, you two ought to come with an instruction manual or something."

The road is unpaved; its rises, dips, and curves are unannounced, and Dean leans out over the steering wheel as if he's trying to see beyond the reach of the headlights.

"Just slow down," Edie says. "Please."

Dean ignores his wife's plea, and when it becomes apparent that he's not going to slow down, Edie turns her head from the road ahead and stares instead at the darkness of the trees streaming past. "Fine. Kill us both. I don't give a damn."

And then the narrow road widens enough for Dean to pull over without the Volkswagen slipping into the ditch. The car has barely come to a stop when Edie has her door open, and she gets out and starts walking back the way they came.

"Hey!" Dean calls after her, his shout echoing down the long corridor of towering ash and cottonwood trees. "*Hey!*"

Edie doesn't slow. She's wearing the same flimsy footwear she was wearing that night she rescued Roy, and the sandals are no better suited for walking the gravel of River Road than for running through the sagebrush.

For a long time Dean watches his wife's figure recede. Does she intend to walk all the way back to Gladstone? It's at least five miles. When she has all but vanished into the night, Dean says, "Oh hell," and he gets out of the car and starts after her.

In the years since high school, Dean hasn't run any farther than across a street, but he still has the miler's easy distance-eating stride—and it doesn't take long for him to draw alongside his wife. But Edie doesn't stop walking. Dean grabs her arm, but she shrugs out of his grip and keeps going.

"God damn it, Edie. Stop."

She obeys, halting abruptly but staring straight ahead.

"I want to talk to you."

"Really? You didn't say a goddamn word in the car."

A car is approaching, its hum and whine becoming louder. Dean has no choice but to step away from the middle of the road and stand at his wife's side on the shoulder. Then the car's headlights blind them, and they turn away as the car speeds past.

For a moment neither of them speaks, both keeping their mouths closed until the dust cloud settles. "All right," says Edie. She has pulled her hands inside the sleeves of her sweatshirt, and her arms are folded against the cold. "What did you want to talk about?"

"Here?"

"We're here."

"When did you run into those brothers—the Bauers?"

"We were having supper and they came into the restaurant."

"And? Big guys? Tough guys? What?"

"Shit, I don't know. Yeah, I suppose. One of them anyway. He looked creepy. But I never saw them again after we left the restaurant. So if something happened with them and Roy on the road, I wasn't around."

Dean backs out into the middle of the road again. "And why, Edie—why didn't you tell me about any of this?"

"Roy asked me not to say anything."

For a long moment neither Dean nor Edie Linderman speaks. Is that the sound of another car approaching or simply the wind moving in the tops of the trees?

"And supper in the restaurant?" Dean finally asks. "Did he ask you not to say anything about that too?"

"Can we get back in the car? I'm freezing."

"Did he tell you not to say anything about the Bauers? Or the restaurant? What?"

"Please, Dean."

"And when he asked you not to say anything, you decided that meant me too? You decided that extended to your fucking *husband*?"

The chill has found its way into Edie's voice. "I'm not sure," she says, "I can always tell you two apart."

In an instant Dean grabs his wife's narrow shoulders. "Don't say that." He shakes her hard. *"Don't ever fucking say that."*

She doesn't resist him in any way, and her passivity must be like a reproach to him. He releases her suddenly.

"I'm sorry," he says, backing away from her. "The keys are in the car. I'll walk back."

But he doesn't walk. He begins to run, and the pace that moments ago carried him to Edie's side now carries him away.

THREE DAYS BEFORE Halloween a snowstorm drops half a foot on Gladstone. And trailing right behind the snow is air cold enough to keep that snow on the ground until spring. Up and down the streets

there's a chorus of grumbling: "Winter in Montana—*Chee-rist!*"
And the remembering: "Back in '47 we got snow in September and it
lasted to May, eight goddamn months of winter!"

Dean has been moving Roy's Impala around to various locations
in the city. High-visibility residential streets. In front of the post
office. In parking lots—at the Red Owl, at the Conoco station on
Main Street, at the Northern Pacific Depot.

Today the car's on a street behind the high school, and Dean no
sooner has it swept free of snow than the fellow who has looked at it
on two other occasions drives up and, without getting out of his own
car, rolls down the window and makes an offer.

"Mister," says Dean, "that's a hundred fifty dollars lower than
what we're asking. And we're not asking much."

Louis Florent is a short, stocky fellow with black hair so oily it
looks as though he just stepped out of the shower. "Or best offer,"
Florent says. "That's what your own sign says. Or best offer."

"I have to talk to my brother about this," says Dean.

"You do that," Florent says. "You get his permission. Then call
me and tell me when I can come pick up my fucking car. I'll bring a
check. And you know what the amount will be."

ROY RAPS ON his cast and makes a sound like knocking on a hollow
log. "I don't recommend a broken leg to anyone," he says, "but it gets
a man out of shoveling snow. You want a beer?"

"Little early in the day for me," says Dean.

"Yeah? What's your start-up hour?"

"Not before noon."

"Well, clocks and calendars don't mean what they used to for me."

From outside the trailer comes the sound of a shovel scraping
across concrete. "What the hell is he doing?" asks Dean.

"Dad? After he cleared off the walk and the driveway, he started
in on the neighbor's. He won't be happy until the whole goddamn
trailer court is cleared of snow."

"Where's Mom?"

"There's a gal who lives a few trailers down," says Roy, "and Mom watches her kids some days while this gal works an early shift at the Roundup."

"Maybe Mom thinks that's as close as she'll get to having grandkids," Dean says. "Edie's mom has it even worse. She comes right out and asks. Begs, practically."

"Did I ever tell you how close I once came?" Roy says. "This was a few years after high school. Carla Hall was home from college at Christmas, and she was between boyfriends. Or just bored. Anyway, the two of us got together and we pretty much started up right where we left off. Which meant hot and heavy. Then she went back to school, and a couple months later I get a call from her: 'Roy, I'm late.' Well, I'd heard that a few times before, and I knew the best thing was to wait a little. Sure enough, a week goes by, I get another call. Carla. 'You're off the hook,' she said. I had the feeling she was as relieved as I was."

"But you were ready to do the right thing?"

"The right thing for who?"

"Come on," says Dean.

"I mean it," Roy answers. "If you would have asked Mom, she'd say, 'Whatever gives me a grandbaby.' But Carla? Not right for her. Sure as hell not right for me."

"I guess you had it worked out then."

"You better believe it." Roy lights a cigarette. "Now what's this Florent fellow offering?"

Dean holds out a small piece of paper. "I wrote it down."

Roy examines it. "Well, it's not like he's trying to steal it," he says and hands the paper back to his brother. "But pretty fucking close."

"His argument is we said 'or best offer.'"

"That doesn't mean if someone comes along and offers a buck, we have to sell it for that. Jesus."

"What do you want me to tell him?"

Roy exhales a cloud of smoke. "Shit. Try to get him closer to what we're asking."

"And if I can't?"

"Don't let him have his price. I don't give a damn if you can't get him higher than another ten bucks. Just don't let him think he's winning."

"Whatever you say," Dean says and leaves the trailer.

He gets into his car, and for a moment he simply sits behind the wheel with the engine off.

Dean ran the mile and the 880 in high school, and he and Tony Brower, a pole-vaulter, were the stars of their track-and-field team. It's possible that Dean still holds the school record in the mile. But almost as soon as he started competing, he knew he'd never be a great runner. It wasn't for lack of ability. He just didn't care enough. Or, more accurately, he didn't care about the right things. Running a good race was more important to him than winning. If he won, yet the other runners were slow or the track was in poor condition, he was disappointed. But if he ran a good race—if he hit his splits, if he had a decent kick at the end, if he *felt* good but lost . . . Well, that was all right. There'd even been times when Dean wished he hadn't won. Like the race in Miles City when he finished a second ahead of Bob Eagle Staff. Now that Indian kid *was* a great runner; he'd tripped, but he got up and still damn near won.

What Dean cared about was the activity itself. Practice was more enjoyable to him than the track meets, and he'd put in extra time on the weekends, logging mile after mile for the pure pleasure of it.

Roy had been a decent athlete when they were kids, but he gave up virtually all sports when he was a teenager. Smoking, drinking, chasing girls, and driving fast, he'd often said, were sport enough for him. Yet he was the one who measured almost everything in wins and losses. Even now—his leg in a cast and the rest of his body still under repair, unemployed, and back in his parents' house—he has to find ways to win.

On the day of Dean and Edie's wedding, just before the ceremony, Roy handed Dean a flask and offered him a drink of whiskey. Then he clapped Dean on the shoulder and said, "Congratulations, brother. You won the prize."

Is that what marrying Edie had been—winning? Yes, Dean supposes that's true. But he ran enough races to know that any competition that can be won can be lost, especially if the competition is stiff.

AS SOON AS Roy hears the Volkswagen's engine whine, cough, and ratchet to life, he picks up the telephone.

"Edie? Now don't hang up. Don't. Just listen to me. Dean just left here. He might have a buyer for my Impala, but the guy's coming in really low. Would you go with Dean? Maybe talk to this guy?"

Roy's call catches Edie in her bathrobe, and while he talks she reties the belt, tightening its knot.

"If Dean can't get him to go up a few bucks," Roy says, "maybe you can goose him a little."

"I can't do that, Roy."

"Yeah, Edie. You can. You damn well can."

IT WAS EDIE'S idea to start the car and warm it up, and now she and Dean sit on the Impala's red upholstery and wait for Mr. Louis Florent to arrive.

"He's going to regret selling this," Dean says, running his hands around the steering wheel.

"Maybe."

Edie takes off her wool coat and tosses it into the back seat. Then, while she's still turned away from her husband, she unbuttons another button on her blouse. It is, she's sure, what Roy meant when he told her that she could help make this sale. Then, disgusted with herself, she immediately buttons up again. If she can do what he asked, she'll do it her way, not his.

"You don't think so?" Dean is staring straight ahead as if the car is in motion and he has to keep a careful eye on the road.

"I think," says Edie, "it reminds him of something he doesn't want to be reminded of."

"And that would be—?"

"That trip to Bentrock really damaged your brother. And I'm not just talking about broken bones and missing teeth."

"Well, you were there. You'd know."

There is silence and there is silence, and Dean and Edie wait in the special marital brand.

Dean watches in the rearview mirror, and when he sees Florent climb out of his Chevy Bel Air, Dean gets out too.

"I thought you might have changed your mind," says Dean.

"I'm still thinking on it," Florent says.

"Anything I can do to help you decide?"

Florent doesn't answer. He walks slowly around the Impala, stopping when he comes to the scratch in the finish inflicted by the Bauer brothers.

"You didn't see that before?" Dean asks. "A little paint will take care of it."

Florent bends down close to Edie's window. He stares in at her as though she's behind a one-way mirror. "I want to drive it again," he says to Dean.

Dean shrugs. "Suit yourself."

Florent slides in behind the steering wheel and slams the door, and Dean barely has time to open the back door and jump in.

"Test-drive," Dean says to Edie.

"You can stay," Florent says to Edie. The mingled smells of Vitalis and fried onions have entered the car with Louis Florent.

"I wouldn't think of leaving."

Louis Florent asks permission to take the Impala out on the highway, and Dean says, "You can drive it all the way to Denver if you like."

Florent says, "I just want to see what it'll do on an open stretch."

Florent recently transferred from Nebraska to work for a petroleum company in Gladstone. He's twenty years older than Dean and Edie, a businessman wearing wingtips, a white shirt, and a wedding ring. But once he has the Impala out on the open highway, it doesn't take him long to assume the familiar position. He has his left hand resting lightly on the steering wheel and his right arm stretched across the back of the front seat, the open invitation for Edie to give him the gift that every man behind the wheel wants: Come closer.

Florent points casually to the speedometer. "Is this too fast for you?" he asks Edie.

"I'll scream when it is."

Florent speeds up to ninety, but this speed frightens him and he slows down to seventy.

They're heading west, and Dean looks out his window to the south and the buttes where snow clings to a few sheltered ledges making those rock walls look as though they're striped black and white. What he'd give for it to be just him and Edie in the car, heading not *away* but *to*. But where that would be is a place that lies outside the reach of even his imagination.

Finally Edie turns to Florent and says, "I know what you offered for this car. Real proud of that, are you?"

Louis Florent has an awkward smile that jerks up first one corner of his mouth and then the other. "What do you mean?"

"A man like you . . . you know what this car's worth. And that offer was an insult."

"Lady, do you know how this works? Buying a car?"

"Edie. My name is Edie." She doesn't move any closer to Louis Florent, but she twists around in her seat until she's facing him. "I know what it means to be fair. And you're not being fair."

Florent glances over his shoulder, but of course Dean Linderman is sitting directly behind him and can't or won't be enlisted in the discussion.

"Lady—"

"Edie. Linderman. *Edie Linderman.*"

"Edie. I made my offer—"

"And you look like a fair man to me."

"I brought a check with me," he says and pats the black-leather checkbook in his shirt pocket. "For the amount I said I'd pay."

"Oh come on," Edie says. "You expect me to believe you're carrying around a check made out for that much money? That's a line, Mr. Florent. A pretty good one. But it's a line."

Dean moves over in his seat and leans forward as if here is a performance he can't miss.

Edie reaches up and puts her hand on Louis Florent's arm. Certainly it's an innocent touch, but Florent risks a glance down at her hand, trying hard to read meaning in her gesture.

"Besides," says Edie, "you could always make out another check."

This time Louis Florent's smile seems to arrive at both sides of his mouth simultaneously. "Checks cost money."

"Mr. Florent," Edie says, with a laugh, "I work at a bank. I know what checks cost. I'll reimburse your ten cents out of my own pocket."

Negotiations cease. The land has flattened out to the south and the north while ahead a series of hills, half covered with snow, hump up from the prairie. But before the road begins to rise, Louis Florent slows and, with no traffic coming from either direction, turns the car around.

As he heads back toward Gladstone, he asks Edie, "So what's your idea of a fair price?"

Edie says, "That amount you said you made the check out for? Add a hundred dollars to it. And you'll still be getting a damn good deal."

Florent says nothing for a mile or two. Then, with both hands still on the wheel, he says, "I got this cousin in Omaha. Quite a bit younger than me. Good-looking guy. Kind of a goof if you want to know the truth, but the ladies seem to go for that. Anyway. He's got a car just like this. So when I saw this Impala for sale, I suppose I thought, you know, fresh start. But hell, I'm no Stan. I know that."

Edie says softly, "But that doesn't stop you from wanting his car."

Florent barks out a laugh. "No, I guess it doesn't."

Before they reach the Gladstone city limits, they've agreed on a price—they call it Florent's but with Edie's hundred added on so everyone can feel as though they've won—and settled on the final arrangements: Once the check clears, Florent can take possession of the Impala. In the meantime the car will remain parked by the high school.

After they watch Louis Florent drive away, Dean hands the keys to the Impala to Edie.

"I'll walk back," he says.

"Oh come on, Dean."

He shakes his head and backs away. "It's all yours," he says. "And be sure to tell Roy what a good job you did."

Edie climbs inside the Impala. The interior still smells faintly of Vitalis. Edie puts the key in the ignition, but she doesn't turn it. She watches Dean walk away, his shoulders hunched against the cold. At this moment Mr. Louis Florent seems less a mystery to her than her own husband.

The ignition has not sparked to life. The gears are not engaged nor are the wheels revolving. This automobile is as motionless as every house up and down the block. Yet, Edie thinks, it's possible to feel as though something is carrying you away from your own life at a speed faster than any speedometer can measure.

DEAN ENTERS THE trailer on this Sunday afternoon and finds his brother in his usual place and posture, sitting in front of the television with his injured leg up on an ottoman. The cast looks dirty, and at Roy's foot and upper thigh the plaster is chipped, and a few strings from the inner lining dangle loose.

Weeks have passed since the sale of the Impala. Roy had his father cash the check for him, but he hasn't spent the money on anything but cigarettes and beer, plucking a few bills from the stack on top of his dresser whenever his supply of either begins to run low.

"Who's winning?" Dean asks.

"The Browns. I think. But this picture is so shitty I can't be sure. Once the ball is in the air, I can't see it worth a damn."

"So much for the new antenna." Dean looks around the trailer. "I didn't see Mom and Dad's car."

"They drove out to Harville. Another church supper."

Dean smiles. "Mom and her church suppers. 'Better food than you get in any restaurant.' Jesus, how I hated going to those."

"And she'll probably come home bitching about how lousy the food was." Roy motions for his brother to sit down.

Dean perches on the edge of a sofa cushion as someone might sit in a doctor's waiting room, ready to be called in for judgment.

"You never told me," Roy says to his brother. "What did Edie say to get Mr. Florent to come up on the price?"

"Damned if I know," says Dean. "I was right there watching the whole thing, and I still didn't see it happen."

"You have to make them feel like they're getting a good deal. No matter how bad you're screwing them, they can't know it. And you sure as hell can't let them know how good it feels to screw them."

"If it gave her any particular pleasure, it didn't show."

"It didn't show? Or you didn't see it?"

Dean stands abruptly. "Can I bring you a beer?"

"You ever heard me say no to that question?"

Dean returns with two cans of Budweiser and hands one to his brother. For a moment he stares at the little mound of foam that has bubbled out of his can. Then he takes a deep breath and says, "I think we should go up to Bentrock."

"Why the hell would we want to do that?"

Before he answers, Dean crosses the room to turn down the volume on the television. He sits back down. "We should look up the Bauer brothers."

"Oh we should, should we?"

Dean nods. "You know it."

"I've already met the Bauers. I'm not sure I care to renew the acquaintance."

"I don't mean now," says Dean. "Once you're up and around."

Roy shakes a Camel out of the pack. He lights it, inhales, and exhales before he asks, "Anything more to this plan of yours?"

"I'm working on it."

"You didn't think much of this idea when someone brought it up at the park that night."

"This time it would be coming from us."

Roy blows a stream of smoke in his brother's direction. "Us? Sounds like this is all yours, brother. What do you propose we do when we get up to Bentrock? Assuming we can track down the Bauers."

Dean shrugs. "Maybe tell them they owe you the money you put out for the truck."

Roy laughs and shakes his head. "I can't imagine that'll go over too well!"

"Well, if they won't listen to reason . . ."

Roy leans toward his brother. "What the hell's got into you? I don't know where any of this is coming from."

"We can't let them think they put the run on the Lindermans."

"You know what that is? That's cowboy talk. Or even worse—cowboy *movie* talk. Either way it's bullshit. You think we just roll into town, kick some ass, and then ride out again? Jesus."

"Hey, if you don't want to—"

"What? You'll go up there alone? I'd laugh if that wasn't so fucking stupid. Let me tell you what's just as likely to happen. The Bauers will cut off your nuts and feed them to you one at a time."

Dean realizes that he's wound himself so tight in working up to present this plan that he must find a way to loosen the tension. He rises and walks to the trailer's front door, then looks out the small window where a curtain of dripping water falls before his sight.

Roy stares at the television set, watching the blurry figures collide with each other. "Maybe," he says to his brother's back, "we should see how many former football players we can recruit. Who was it suggested that at the park?"

"Jerry Krueger," Dean replies.

"Jerry. Yeah. And what was he—the fucking student manager?"

"I don't remember."

"You'd for sure want some help. I mean, that's the Bauers' territory up there. And who the hell knows how many of them there are? We could be going up against a goddamn army of Bauers, not just the two of them."

"So we ask around," Dean says, returning to his seat on the couch. "I'm sure there are guys who'd want to get in on something like this."

The dog waddles into the room and flops down on the floor between the brothers. "Hey, Rusty," Dean says softly, his voice entering that register usually reserved for animals and babies.

"He sleeps under my bed," says Roy. "Snoring and wheezing and farting under there like a goddamn steam engine."

Dean slides off the couch to bring his face close to the dog's. When he scratches Rusty's head, the dog's eyes all but close and his tail weakly slaps against the floor. "Hey, boy," Dean says. "Do you miss the ranch? All that room to roam?"

Roy finishes his beer and says, "Dad said when the time comes, he'll bury Rusty back there with the other critters. He's already made arrangements with the new owners."

"At the foot of that hill behind the barn? Jesus, how many do you think we buried back there?"

"I don't know and I don't feel like counting. But it's a fucking boneyard back there." Then Roy stabs out his cigarette. "All right. The Bauers. We need to have some kind of plan."

But no plan is forthcoming. The dog wheezes. The snowmelt drips. The football announcer drones on. The electric wall clock hums. But the Linderman twins sit silently in the company of a dog that has known them both since they were boys playing make-believe.

AT THE END of her workday, Edie walks out of the bank into a November evening so mild she gives a little gasp. She'd walked to work that morning in fog thick enough to eliminate all distances, but by noon the fog had lifted and now the day's vanishing light lingers just long enough to give Gladstone's business district a smoky amber glow and the sky a darkening rose and deepening blue.

A car that Edie doesn't recognize, a humpbacked rusting gray-black Plymouth right out of the 1940s, pulls to the curb alongside her.

The car's horn bleats, and then Roy climbs out, grinning and shouting, "Edie! Edie!"

He limps around the front of the car, making his way toward her. "The cast! It's off!"

His joy invades her, and she steps into his open arms.

He takes a few steps back from her and says, "Come on. Let's go get a drink. I'm buying. And don't try to say no, Edie. This is a celebration."

"Dean—"

"We'll call him when he gets home from work and he can join us."

Her hand on the door handle, Edie hesitates. Once again she's about to do what husbands forbid their wives to do. Dean has never issued her that kind of warning—he can't, not about his own brother. Yet she knows he's jealous of Roy. If he'd just say so, she could tell him he has no reason to be.

Oh, the hell with it. She's tired of trying to figure out what goes on in Dean's head. She opens the door and climbs in.

Roy revs the engine and puts the car into gear, but it lurches and stalls.

"Sorry," Roy says. "Sorry, sorry. I'm not used to . . . Hell, I'm not used to much of anything. And that includes being out of the house."

He restarts the car, and this time he's able to pull away from the curb smoothly.

"Whose car?" Edie asks.

Roy pats the dashboard. "This good-looking set of wheels belongs to our uncle LeRoy Linderman."

Edie sniffs the air. "It smells like . . . hay?"

"And that would be Uncle LeRoy."

It doesn't take them long to exit Gladstone's business district.

"Where are we going?" Edie asks.

"I thought I'd drive out to Vincent's. Then if we decide we want to have something to eat, we'll be right there."

"What about Dean?"

"I told you. We'll call him. He can join us."

"If we stay downtown," says Edie, "he could just walk over."

"You think if he has to drive a few miles, he won't bother?"

"He might not."

"That boy. Jesus."

"He's pissed that I didn't tell him we had dinner in Bentrock."

"And why didn't you?"

"It just didn't seem important." There's no point in telling Roy about Dean's jealousy, something Dean would almost certainly deny. And she knows that it would only embolden Roy.

Vincent's Supper Club is on a mesa on the outskirts of town. As Roy pulls into the parking lot he says, "I'm surprised this car doesn't hold any memories for you. This was the first car Dean and I drove. I mean, we learned to drive on Dad's truck, but the folks didn't have a car for most of the ranch years. Dean never pulled up to your curb in this fine automobile?"

"Never anything but the truck. And hardly ever that. I drove more than he did."

"Huh! I wonder why that was. Uncle LeRoy would let us borrow it just about anytime we wanted. All we had to do was bring it back with more gas in the tank than we left with." Roy opens the driver's door, and when the dome light comes on it illuminates his smile. "Matter of fact," he says, "I lost my cherry in this car."

"You remember the car. Do you remember the girl?"

"Edie. Please. Give me some credit. Rebecca O'Connell."

"The Becky O'Connell who went to St. Joe's? You're kidding!"

"One and the same."

"She lived just down the street from me. Until her folks got too good for the neighborhood. And sent her to Catholic schools. *Becky?* Are you sure?"

Roy walks around to the passenger side and holds the front door open for Edie. He says, "I'd never make a mistake about that."

To prevent her skirt from riding up too high, Edie swings her legs carefully out of the car and steps onto the running board first and then down to the asphalt. "Becky O'Connell?" she says again. "Really? She didn't have that kind of reputation."

He extends his arm and Edie slips her arm through his, and together they enter Vincent's Supper Club.

They go into the dimly lit space, empty of customers at this hour, and opt to perch on stools at the bar. The bartender is smoking and reading the *Gladstone Gazette*. Once they're seated he crushes out his cigarette, closes the newspaper, and puts two felt coasters in front of Roy and Edie. She orders a Seven and Seven, and Roy asks for a bourbon and water.

Edie takes off her coat and lays it across the stool next to her. "I'm sorry," she says, lowering her voice, "but I have to ask. You and Becky . . . how did . . . why did she say yes?"

Roy claps both hands over his heart. "Now I *am* insulted!"

Edie playfully slaps his arm. "You know what I mean."

"I made a deal with her."

"And? What was your end?"

Roy lights a cigarette, and with his first exhalation he blows a smoke ring that holds together remarkably well before dissipating in its drift over their heads. "Simple," he says. "I told her I'd never forget her."

"And that did it . . ."

"Nobody wants to be forgotten."

The bartender sets their drinks down. Edie says softly, "I'm not so sure."

Roy raises his glass. "Here's to walking on two legs!"

Edie touches her glass to his and they both drink.

"So," says Roy, "has Dean shared his plan with you?"

Edie's eyes widen.

"I take it that he has not. He thinks he and I ought to go up to Bentrock."

"*Bent*rock? What the hell for?"

Roy shrugs and directs a stream of smoke out the side of his mouth and away from Edie. "He's none too specific on that account. Something about trying to get the Bauers to return the money for the truck. But mostly to show them the Lindermans can't be buffaloed."

"And what did you say?"

"He's my brother, what am I supposed to say? And if I don't go with him, he's all set to go on his own."

"You have to talk him out of this. You *have* to."

"He's thinking maybe we can recruit some others to make the trip with us."

"Oh Jesus. Like who? Who's going to sign on to something like this?"

"You'd be surprised." Roy finishes his bourbon and water with one long swallow. "He's talked to Jerry Krueger, and Jerry thinks it sounds like a damn good idea."

"Men. I swear to God . . ."

"I told him we'll have to wait until I get my legs under me. Maybe with a little time he'll come around."

Edie looks at her watch. "He should be home by now. You said you'd call him."

"Maybe you should," Roy suggests.

"You said you'd do it. Now *go*."

"Okay, okay." Roy hobbles off to use the pay telephone located just inside the front door of Vincent's.

Right after Roy leaves, the bartender walks over and puts a fresh drink down in front of Edie. "Seven and Seven, right?"

The bartender wears a white shirt with the sleeves rolled to his elbows, exposing forearms thatched with black hair, and he leans those arms on the bar to move closer to Edie when he speaks. "When did the cast come off?"

"Today."

"He *might* lose the limp," the bartender says, glancing in the direction Roy walked off in.

"You know Roy?"

"Just by reputation. You hear stories."

"And what do you hear about Roy Linderman?" Edie asks.

The bartender just smiles and points to her glass. "How is that?" he asks. "Too strong? Too weak? Say the word and I'll pour it out and start over."

"It's fine," she says, though she has not yet drunk from the glass.

"You work at First National," he says. "I seen you there."

"Have you heard stories about me too?"

"I can see for myself," he says. The bartender stands up and raps on the bar. "You walked in here with the wrong brother," he says and walks back to his earlier post.

Roy reenters the bar. For a few seconds Edie watches his stiff-legged progress, and then she turns away.

"He's not coming."

"Did he say why?"

"He said he's tired."

Edie picks up her fresh drink. Before bringing it to her lips, she says, as if she's speaking to the ice cubes, "Anything else?"

"Not much."

"What did he say?"

"He wants us to enjoy ourselves. And then he hung up on me."

She sweeps her coat off the stool. "Let's go. The son of a bitch. He doesn't want to come here, we'll go there."

WHEN EDIE OPENS the door of the apartment, Dean is on the floor by the stereo, flipping through the stack of record albums leaning against the wall.

"What the hell, Dean," she says, turning on a lamp just inside the door. "What *the hell.*"

At her approach he stands up.

"Are you *trying* to get rid of me?" she says. "Is that it? Do you *want* your brother to take me off your hands?"

Roy enters the apartment, and Dean stares at his brother for a long moment and then says, "I thought it wasn't supposed to come off for another week."

"I got out early for good behavior."

Edie takes off her coat and slings it on the couch. She points an accusing finger at her husband. "We're not finished talking."

Roy asks, "You have something to drink?"

Dean nods toward the kitchen. "There's a bottle of Ten High under the sink." He says to Edie, "I didn't feel like going out, okay? It's been a long day. Besides, I have a TV dinner in the oven."

From the kitchen Roy holds up the bottle and calls out, "Who's ready?"

Edie stares steadily at Dean. "It was supposed to be a celebration. Your brother wanted to take us out."

Roy opens the freezer. "No ice?"

"Us?" says Dean. "But he found *you*. He came looking for you and he found you."

Now Roy is searching the refrigerator's interior. "There's a Coke in here," he says. "How about it, Edie—a whiskey and Coke?"

"Pour it," she says.

From the stereo's speakers come the sounds of the singer's sorrowful whine, his ringing guitar, and his rhymes that seem to accumulate for no sake other than their own: "And your face like glass . . ."

Edie can't help but wonder if Dean would rather sit alone in their darkened apartment and feel what this music makes him feel than to be with her . . . or his brother. She could ask, but she's not sure she's ready for the answer.

Roy comes out from the kitchen and hands a tall glass to Edie. "How about you, brother?" he asks.

Dean shakes his head no.

Roy looks from Edie to Dean and then back to Edie. "Should I clear out? I can find a drink somewhere else."

"No. Stay," Edie says.

"Hey," Roy says to Dean, "Edie said she's never been in Uncle LeRoy's Plymouth. How the hell is that possible?"

"You're driving LeRoy's car?" Dean asks. "How come?"

"He's having stomach problems again, so he's staying with Mom and Dad while he gets checked out. It's just an excuse to stay in town a couple days."

Edie sips from her drink and shudders. "Is there *any* Coke in here?"

Roy reaches for the glass. "Here. I'll pour some out and put in more Coke."

"I'll get used to it."

"You've been in that car before," Dean says to Edie. "We were out together with Dick Dryden and Patsy Steele. Junior year."

"Huh-uh," Edie says.

"We went to a movie. And if you give me a minute, maybe I'll remember the name."

"Are you sure?" she asks.

"You think I'm confusing you with your twin?"

"Is that supposed to be funny, Dean?"

"Nobody's laughing, so I guess not. My TV dinner is getting cold," he says and walks into the kitchen. He reappears to announce, "*Last Train from Gun Hill.* Kirk Douglas and Anthony Quinn."

"How about you?" she asks Roy. "Do you want something to eat?"

Roy holds his glass aloft. "I'm fine. But I have to sit down. This leg isn't used to doing all I'm asking of it."

Edie moves her coat from the couch. "Here," she says. "Do you need to put your leg up?"

"That'd help." Roy sits down gingerly and extends his leg.

She looks around the living room and then goes into the kitchen.

Dean is seated at the table, hunched over his tin tray of Salisbury steak, mashed potatoes, and peas and corn. Edie picks up one of the kitchen chairs. "Your brother," she says, "needs to put his leg up."

"Help yourself," Dean says without looking up from his meal.

Before she's out of the kitchen, Edie stops and comes back to the table. "Would it have killed you," she says softly, "to get in the car and drive to Vincent's? I mean, for God's sake. He wanted to celebrate. He asked you to come."

"I was tired. And he had *you* there," says Dean. "Which is what he wanted. Why didn't you stay there? Whose idea was it to come here?"

"Does it matter?"

"Yeah. It does."

"It was his."

"And there you have it," Dean says and turns back to his food. Without looking up, he says, "Roy needs his chair, doesn't he?"

Edie picks up the chair with one hand. She needs to keep the other hand free to give her husband the finger. If Dean registers the insult, he gives no sign. From the couch Roy Linderman is able to observe this brief marital exchange, but when Edie enters the living room with the chair, he opens the *TV Guide*.

After situating the chair for Roy's leg, Edie turns off the stereo and turns on the television. *The Girl from U.N.C.L.E.* is playing, and when Stefanie Powers appears, Roy points to the screen and says to

Edie, "See—now that's what I was trying to tell you. That's how you ought to wear your hair."

Edie sits across from him on the couch, with her legs folded under her and her drink in her hand. "I'm working on it," she says, "at this very moment."

From the television come the sounds of explosions, gunshots, screeching tires, cries for help, exhortations to violence, and whispers of seduction. Dean rises from the kitchen table, his chair scraping across the linoleum. His silverware clatters in the sink. His foil tray gives off a metallic creak as he bends it into the garbage can. Roy's lighter opens and closes with a clink, and his exhalations of smoke sound like sighs of futility.

Dean stands in the doorway. The television gives each of them something to look at so they don't have to look at each other.

Edie says to her husband, "I've never been in that fucking car before."

Dean does not smoke and never has, but he seems to be paying very close attention to everything that is being shown and said about the virtues of Viceroy cigarettes. Twenty thousand tiny filter traps.

"Do you hear me?" Edie says. "Never."

"Before today you mean," says Roy.

"We know what she meant," Dean says. He turns away from the television to his wife. "Yes," he says, "you have."

"I think I'd remember."

"Yeah," says Dean. "I think you would too. But you don't."

"You remember my life better than I do?" Edie asks. How tiresome and familiar this is. Dean always has to be the more conscientious one, the one with the memory that can be relied upon.

Dean shrugs. "Maybe I've paid closer attention to it than you have."

"Maybe," Edie says, "it was somebody else in the car with you."

"No," Dean says calmly. "No, it wasn't."

"I was telling Edie," Roy says, "I got my first piece of ass in that car."

"And did you give her a blow-by-blow description?"

"Jesus *Christ*," Roy says. "What the hell's with you tonight?"

Edie reaches over and pats Roy on his leg. "Don't worry. This isn't about you." She finishes her drink with one long swallow and hands the empty glass to Roy. "Fix me another, will you? And easy on the Coke."

"Don't you think you've had enough?" Dean asks her. "When you drink too much, you have a tendency to give away secrets. Like at the park? So if there's something you don't want to say, maybe you should call it quits."

Roy has taken her glass, swung his leg off the chair, and he stands, stalled, between the living room and the kitchen.

"Keeping track of men's secrets," Edie says, letting her head fall back against the sofa cushion, "is just too fucking much work."

Roy holds Edie's empty glass as if it is the talisman that will allow him to pass, but Dean doesn't step aside. Roy tries to slide past his brother, but now Dean stiffens and squares his shoulders. In the next instant Roy is no longer attempting to go around Dean but to push through him. And Dean pushes back. Edie's empty glass falls from Roy's hand to the carpet and then rolls onto the kitchen's linoleum floor.

Both brothers try to brace themselves against the other, but Dean's not wearing shoes and his socks slide on the linoleum, and Roy's injured leg can't help him hold Dean back. Yet those handicaps only serve to keep them evenly matched, a surprise to Dean considering that only today has Roy gotten off his crutches.

"Stop it," Edie says. "*Stop!*"

But the brothers have locked arms now, and they're straining hard to shove their way past each other.

Then Dean glances over Roy's shoulder and notices that Edie has left the room. Immediately he gives up, yet he still holds on to Roy in an attempt to keep them both from crashing to the floor. But Roy's bad leg gives way completely, and he collapses. This in turn causes Dean to topple against the doorframe, banging the side of his head in the process.

Roy looks at the space on the couch where Edie sat. "She might not need a drink anymore," he says. "But I do. Give me a hand here."

Dean reaches down to his brother and helps him stand.

"Your ear's bleeding," Roy says.

Dean wipes his ear with his hand. He looks closely at the smear of blood and then says, "That was fucking stupid."

"Tell me about it," Roy says and limps his way toward the whiskey bottle.

EVEN THOUGH EDIE has locked the bathroom door, she still leans her weight against it as though she fears someone might try to push his way in.

After a few minutes she steps away from the door. She undresses and turns on the shower. Under spray as hot as she can bear, she stands, trying to understand. They were fighting to impress her; she knows this. And she wasn't impressed; she was disgusted. Yet that didn't matter at all. *She* didn't matter either, not really, not her disapproval or her anger. The fight was over her, yet they didn't even need her there. Edie turns off the water and climbs out of the tub. She towels herself dry and puts on the flannel pajamas that hang from the hook on the door. She exits the bathroom, and when she does, fog swirls in her wake, just as it did that morning when she walked to work.

EDIE WAKES UP when Dean enters the bedroom and undresses, but she keeps her eyes closed.

"Roy's out on the sofa," Dean says. "He's too drunk to drive, so I told him to bunk down here."

The pale green glowing hands of the alarm clock indicate that it's almost one o'clock. "What," Edie asks, "have the two of you been doing?"

"Nothing much. Watching Johnny Carson. Talking."

"About what, if you don't mind my asking?"

"The past mostly. And Roy worked his way through what was left of the whiskey."

"You think he has a problem?"

Dean snorts softly. "We've all got problems."

"I meant the drinking."

"I know what you meant."

"Did he take his plate out?"

"*What?*"

"His partial plate. His new *teeth*. Did he take them out? I heard about a man who was drunk, and he choked on his false teeth."

"Christ, who thinks of such a thing? No. He didn't take his teeth out. At least as far as I know."

"Please, Dean. I don't want to fight anymore."

They lie quietly then, Dean on his back and Edie curled next to him.

Finally, after a long silence during which neither of them moves any closer to sleep, Dean says, "Do you want to know how I remember us being in Uncle LeRoy's car? We'd been to the movie—"

"*Last Train from Gun Hill*," Edie says. "Is that what you said?"

"Not that it's important but yeah. And when we came out of the theater, Dick Dryden asked if he and Patsy could catch a ride with us. Dick usually had his own car, but I think he'd had his license revoked or something. Or maybe his old man had just taken the keys away. If they couldn't ride with us, Patsy'd have to go home with her brother. Sure, we said, it was okay with us. I mean, what could we say? Remember how Patsy lived out in the country? Dick told me about a road to turn off on before we came to Patsy's folks' place. A perfect spot to park, he said. And there we were. You and me in the front seat and Dick and Patsy in the back. Dick had a pint of lime vodka, and we took turns pulling on that. But then we settled into doing what we were there to do. You and I hadn't progressed beyond the making out stage yet and besides, there was Dick and Patsy in the back seat. If there was a way around that, I didn't know what it was. But Dick had it figured out. We hadn't been there very long when you whispered, 'We have to go.' You said Patsy was in trouble back there. I don't know what the hell you heard or saw, but I didn't ask questions. I started up the car and when Dick said, 'What the hell?' I told him, 'Edie's got to get home.' God *damn* was Dick pissed off at me. After we dropped the two of you off, he called me every kind of chickenshit bastard in the book. Now, Dick Dryden and I were never what you'd really call friends, but whatever we were we sure as hell weren't after that night. So . . . Uncle LeRoy's car. Front seat and back seat. Dick and Patsy. You and me. If you don't remember, you don't remember. But don't say it didn't happen."

"And we never talked about it after?"

"I guess I was embarrassed to bring it up," Dean says. "I used to think girls had a set of secret distress signals they used in situations like that."

"That was sweet of you. Rescuing Patsy."

"Patsy? The hell. That was you."

Edie reaches over and rests her hand on his sternum, almost as if she were feeling for his heartbeat. They have fallen silent now, and she trails her hand down his torso and then slips it inside the elastic of his briefs. She wraps her hand around his cock and almost instantly it stirs under her touch.

Dean says, "Roy's right out in the other room."

"So? You don't want him to know we fuck?"

"He might still be awake."

Edie keeps her hand right where it is.

Then Dean rolls onto his side and not toward his yearning wife but in the other direction. Her hand slips from its hold and soon, in the space between them, the sheets lose the heat they momentarily held.

THREE O'CLOCK. EDIE no longer pretends to sleep. And there's no sense listening for the bakery trucks lining up in the alley or for the clink of milk bottles or the thud of the *Gladstone Gazette* against the door. It's too early for any of that.

She climbs out of bed and walks out of the room.

In the living room she confronts the sight of her sleeping brother-in-law on the couch. He has twisted free of the blanket that covered him, and he's sprawled out in nothing but his underwear. There's enough light from the street for Edie to make out Roy's injured leg, and she sees its thinness and its pallor—that whittled stick couldn't possibly belong on Roy Linderman's thickly muscled body. She steps closer. The leg looks as if it's molting, shedding its flaking, dried skin, yet with no sign of new growth underneath.

Edie rearranges the blanket and covers Roy's leg. The rhythm of his breathing does not alter. On the end table next to the sofa is the glass from which he drank his whiskey. His new teeth smile out of the glass.

Roy Linderman would never turn away from her in bed. Edie's sure of that. But she's also sure he'd never lift a finger to rescue Patsy Steele.

ON THIS QUIET Tuesday morning, Dean checks the used skates that Cheyenne Sporting Goods sells and, after satisfying himself that all have sufficiently sharp edges, he strolls over to the Guns and Ammo section.

Gus Vogel is smoking one of the cigars that, along with gun oil and the leather of gloves, shoes, and various balls, gives the store its distinctive odor. He leans on a display case, rows of handguns arrayed under the glass.

As Dean approaches, Gus taps the newspaper spread open in front of him and says, "Give me your expert opinion, Mr. Linderman. Who do you like this Friday?"

"I'm embarrassed to say I don't even know who's playing," Dean says.

"Glendive. They got a kid who's fuckin' near seven foot."

"No shit? Is he any good?"

"He can't hardly walk and chew gum at the same time, but hell, seven foot. That makes up for a lot. He can just park his ass under the basket."

"Huh. And the game's here?"

"Yessir."

"Maybe I'll try to take it in."

"Show up early," says Gus. "Hell of a lot of folks want to see a seven-foot high school kid."

Dean bends down and rests his hands on his knees. "Say I wanted a handgun," he says. "What would you recommend?"

"First I'd ask you what you want to shoot. Bottles and cans? Gophers? Maybe that Colt Woodsman .22. Somebody coming at you with a pitchfork? Maybe that .38. Just like what's hanging on the hips of our local constabulary. Grizzlies? That's your .44 Magnum."

Dean laughs nervously. "I don't know that I want to fire the thing at all. But the other night Edie said she heard someone jiggling the door."

"And where were you? Out on the town?"

Dean laughs again. "Probably sleeping."

"So home protection, huh? Truth is, we don't hardly have burglars or prowlers in our town. Leastways not half so many as womenfolk seem to think are lurking around here."

"Edie's not the kind to hear or see things that aren't there."

Gus Vogel shrugs. "Most folks who come in looking for something to protect hearth and home, I tell 'em, 'Go over there and buy yourself a Louisville Slugger. That'll give you all the protection you need—and you don't have to worry about shooting the milkman. Or a husband creeping home after hours.'"

"I think Edie'd feel better if she had some protection."

"All right," Gus Vogel says. "I said my piece." He places his cigar in an ashtray and slides open the display case. He brings out a blue-steel revolver with a wood grip. "This here is a Smith and Wesson .32 and inaccurate as hell as any snub nose will be. Add to that, it's got a fairly long trigger pull. Gives a shooter a chance to change his mind. Or *her* mind, as the case may be. And the ladies are likely to think, Oh, I can handle this. It'll fit nice in my purse."

"Or on the nightstand," says Dean.

"Or on the nightstand," Gus agrees. "What have you. It doesn't have a hell of a lot of recoil. So if you take the little lady out shooting for the day, she won't come home feeling like she slammed her hand in the car door."

"A .32 though . . . not much stopping power."

Gus Vogel laughs. "Stopping power! What the fuck do you care about *stopping power*? You want the sight of the gun to scare the living shit out of any intruder. And if that don't do the job, the bang should send him running."

Dean does not take the gun from Gus Vogel's hand, though Gus extends the butt toward him. "You have something like this in a .38?" Dean asks.

"Maybe you want to jump all the way to a .45. Then you got that scary big barrel working for you."

Dean presses a finger against the glass. "Is that a .38?"

"That it is." Gus Vogel pulls out the revolver and, again, holds its handle out to Dean. "Colt Detective Special," he says. "Just like on TV."

Dean takes the gun in hand but does nothing more than heft its weight.

"It's used," says Gus. "But what the hell do you care?"

"How much?"

Gus Vogel reaches over and lifts the small tag hanging from the trigger guard by a short length of string. "I'd give you ten bucks off that," Gus says. "Call it the family discount."

"And a box of bullets."

"You sure you need a whole fucking box? I'd be willing to throw in six."

"Practice," Dean says.

"You can practice all you like, you still won't be able to hit a fucking thing. But what the hell. You're the customer and like the boss says—"

Dean and Gus say in unison: "The customer don't know shit!"

DEAN TAKES ONE of the heavy wool socks that customers put on when they try on a pair of skates, and he puts the gun and the box of cartridges inside the sock. Then he wraps an old rag around the gun, the ammunition, and the sock, and he wedges that package under the front seat of the Volkswagen.

FOR ANOTHER OF their planning sessions, Jerry Krueger and the
Linderman twins have settled into a booth at the Elk's Tooth, one of
four bars at the intersection of Third Street and Mead Avenue. The
Elk's Tooth is the oldest and quietest of the four. Many of the town's
young men, and its young women too, had their first legal drink in
the Elk's Tooth, where the lights are always dim.

"Maybe," Jerry Krueger suggests, "we should make a scouting trip
first just to get the lay of the land."

Dean says, "One trip to Bentrock is plenty for me."

"I get that," Jerry says, "but we should find out where we want to
take those fuckers on."

Roy picks up the pitcher of beer and refills his glass and Jerry
Krueger's. "And how will that be up to us?"

"Hell, we come right out and tell 'em. Meet us at . . . I don't know . . .
a parking lot somewheres."

"And here's what they'll do," Dean says. "They'll round up their
whole clan and as many friends as they can, and when we show up at
that parking lot we'll be surrounded and outnumbered."

"Jesus Christ!" Roy says, flinging a book of matches across the
table. "This is getting old, you know that? Every fucking time someone comes up with a plan of action, you find a way to shoot a hole in
it. Do you want to do this or not?"

"I want to do it right."

Roy laughs. "Right? There's no fucking *right*. It's a half-assed
scheme that'll probably end up with us getting a shit-kicking or
worse. But we're doing it anyway, so let's see if we can come up with
some kind of plan."

"Even a half-assed one?" asks Dean.

"Yeah," Roy says. "Even a half-assed one."

"You really think we'll get our asses handed to us?"

"You tell me how it can be otherwise. Take your time," Roy says.
"I'll wait."

"We just need to recruit a few more guys."

"And what kind of luck you been having with that?"

"At least I'm willing to ask around," says Jerry.

Dean has a glass of whiskey in front of him, and he pokes at the ice cubes with his index finger. "We drive up there," he says, "get an address for a Bauer out of the phone book, and knock on his door."

"Knock on the goddamn door." Roy pats his brother on the head. "Elegant in its simplicity. I like it."

Jerry says, "A Bauer answers the door. Then what?"

Dean shrugs as if the matter is of no consequence to him. "We sue him. We present him with a bill for the fucking truck. We carve our initials on his front door. We shoot him. We hit him in the head with a baseball bat. I don't give a shit."

Roy shrinks back from his brother and then says, "We *shoot* him?"

Dean shrugs again and sucks whiskey from his finger.

"We shoot him," Roy says, nodding thoughtfully. "Interesting."

Jerry turns to Roy. "Do *you* understand him?"

"On some days," Roy replies.

Jerry shakes his head. "I could use a bump," he says. "Who else? I'm buying."

Dean holds up his glass and rattles the ice. "I'm ready."

"But none of that Southern Comfort or Yukon Jack shit," Roy says. "Nothing sweet."

As soon as Jerry Krueger is out of earshot, Roy addresses his brother. "We *shoot him*? Where the hell did that come from?"

"I work in a sporting goods store," Dean says. "I'm around guns all day."

"And baseball bats."

"And baseball bats. That's right."

Tonight the wind is rolling right down Main Street, bringing with it all the grit of winter—sand, grains of snow, scraps of paper—and flinging it against the window with a sound like radio static.

Roy lights a cigarette. "You know, this going to Bentrock business was your idea in the first place, little brother, and now you seem to be losing your enthusiasm for the enterprise."

"I'm just fucking sick of talking about it."

"You'll scare Jerry off with that gun talk."

"And that would be a great loss? I'd rather this be just you and me anyway. Or maybe you don't care about doing what's right. If you don't, I'll go without you."

Roy merely smiles and shakes his head.

Jerry returns to the booth, somehow balancing three brimming shot glasses in a little nest he's made of his cupped hands and fingers. "Hey," he says, "have a looksee over at the bar. Couple of honeys up there."

Both Dean and Roy stand to get a better look at the bar and the young women sitting there. One of them wears a snug pink mohair sweater and white stretch pants. The other is in a tight red jersey dress. That they're heavily made up is apparent even from across the room. The crimson bloom of their lips. The deep shadows of their eyes in a room full of shadows. And both of them blondes with teased and ratted bouffant hair. Dean sits back down, but Jerry and Roy continue to stare at the women.

Then Roy practically shouts, "Shit, that's Edie! Hey, Edie!"

Dean jumps back to his feet. Yes—the woman in the red dress is his wife. And sitting on the stool next to her is Russell Hildebrand's wife, Bunny.

"Hey, Edie!" Roy says again. "Bunny—over here!"

The women do not look over. They lean their heads close and whisper to each other. The bartender on duty tonight is Loretta Sooner, the owner's wife, and she stands apart from the women, drying glasses and placing them carefully on a shelf behind the bar.

Roy tries again. "Edie, Bunny!" He signals for them to come over to the booth, but they continue to ignore him. But his shouts have gotten the attention of other customers. Ike and Farley Rose, co-owners of Rose's Ace Hardware, sit at the opposite end of the bar from Edie and Bunny, and the Rose brothers can't seem to decide whether to keep their eyes on the women or the Linderman twin who's waving his arms like a drowning man. At another booth are a nicely dressed couple, he in a dark suit and she in a skirt and blouse. They're strangers in Gladstone, in town perhaps to take a deposition in a lawsuit or to buy up mineral leases, and they wear expressions of annoyance and disapproval, as if a contract has been broken—the Elk's Tooth is where you go for a *quiet* drink.

Of course the women have heard Roy. Of course they understand what he wants them to do even though he doesn't say it—"Pick up your drinks and walk over here!"

Edie slides off her stool and readjusts her too-tight dress. But then she heads in the opposite direction, toward the jukebox. She leans on its big bright belly and stares at the selections. She turns to Bunny to ask, "How about—?"

"I told you," Bunny says. "You decide."

Edie drops her coin in. She punches the buttons. E-7. C-17. D-4. The machine hums and clicks, and rows of lights blink in sequence. The mechanical arm finds the first record and places it on a turntable. And when its first jangling chords begin to play, the women just stare at each other. Then—"Don't you want somebody to love"—the women begin to laugh.

Edie returns to the bar, where her Seven and Seven waits. She finishes it with one long swallow, and Bunny does the same with hers. Then Edie reaches out to her friend. In the next moment the women are dancing in front of the bar. They swivel and slide and shimmy a few feet apart, their eyes only half open, alone with the music.

Roy hurries over to the women, clapping his hands not quite in rhythm to the music. Jerry Krueger follows close behind, but Dean remains at the booth, hunched over his whiskey.

When Bunny spins close to Roy, he taps her on the shoulder and says, "Do you mind if I cut in?"

Edie shakes her head no at him and scolds him with a waggle of her finger.

The record stops, but the women don't return to their bar stools. They continue to sway in time to an echo only they can hear. Then Edie's next selection begins. "Gimme a ticket for an aeroplane . . ."

Loretta says to Jerry Krueger, who's standing by the bar waiting for the show to resume, "Don't blame me. They come in like this."

And they're off, gyrating harder and faster than before, as if obeying an impulse apart from the song's rhythm.

"Jesus Christ, Bunny," Jerry says. "Where'd you learn to dance like that?"

The song ends and before the third song starts—the jukebox clicks and hums once again—Dean rises quickly from the booth and walks determinedly to the bar.

"Come on," he says, taking Edie roughly by the hand. "We're going home."

She shakes free of his grip. "I *was* home," she answers. "And you weren't."

Dean grabs Edie's coat and holds it for her but says nothing.

"It's all right for you to go out to a bar every night?" Edie says. Then she looks at Bunny and adds, "You and Russell?"

"Fine," Dean says. He drops her coat back on the bar stool.

Edie watches him walk away, but before he reaches the door, she says, "Oh hell."

She grabs her coat and catches up to him just in time for them to walk out together into the winter wind.

IN THEIR WALK toward the bakery, Dean and Edie pass Montgomery Ward, and though his wife is beside him, Dean slows and looks intently through the glass as if he were trying to see the teenage Edie working there. "Am I correct," he says, "the Elk's Tooth wasn't your first stop tonight?"

"We tried the Silver Dollar first. Bunny thought Russell and his buddies might be there."

"You put on a show there too?"

"Not really. We just had a drink."

"Hell, that dress is a show all by itself," says Dean.

"We were looking for you, you know. You and Russell. Bunny and I have both had some trouble lately getting our husbands' attention, so we thought we'd try a different approach."

"And do you think Bunny's still trying?"

"I feel bad about that," says Edie. "Leaving her there. We were doing this together. It was supposed to be fun. And funny."

"She won't be lonely," Dean says. "Not with Roy there. Where'd the wig come from, by the way?"

"Bunny's sister," Edie replies. "Both of them. She and her husband are visiting from California, and she left most of her stuff at Russ and Bunny's. Said she didn't want her mother to see the wigs. She's got two more. Black ones."

"But you decided to go with the blond . . . And how about the dress?"

"Bunny's. It's old. But she said it would still work."

"I forget—has Bunny always been a whore?"

"Dean! My God! Why would you *say* that? Because she . . . ? Jesus. What if someone said that about me tonight?"

"Wouldn't surprise me," he says.

Edie stops on the sidewalk and turns on Dean, her eyes flaring with anger. "I told you," she says, "we were trying to get your attention. Men are always looking at women who look like that . . . Well, we decided to look like that. But now you need to tell me: What made you so mad—the way I looked? Or the way men looked at me?"

Dean doesn't say anything. Edie shakes her head in frustration and then starts to walk again.

After a few steps she stops again. She turns back to Dean, who has lagged behind.

"And if Bunny and I want to go to a bar," Edie says, "we have a perfect right. And if we want to dance, we can dance to our fucking hearts' content."

Dean's jaw has stiffened with the cold, and he has to work hard to get the words out. "I've never blamed you," he says, "for men noticing you."

"Well. Thank you for that at least." She leans into the wind and keeps walking.

They enter the alley behind the bakery, and when they come to the stairs that lead up to their apartment, Dean says, "Careful, there's still a little ice there. I have to chip that away one of these days."

Edie is first to step inside, and she switches on a light. Almost immediately Dean slaps the switch and the light goes off.

Dean shrugs out of his jacket before helping Edie remove her coat. He lets her coat drop to the floor, and while she still has her back to him, he unzips the red dress and tries to push it off her shoulders but it's too tight to slip off easily. Then he unclasps her brassiere. In defiance of the frigid night, Edie's bare back gives off heat and the faint scent of perfume. Soon Dean is pushing her across the room and bending her over the back of the couch. He seems uncertain—should he keep trying to slide the dress off her shoulders or reach down and lift up the hem? But even in his uncertainty he keeps pushing, pushing, as if his desire has its own momentum that can't be resisted. Edie tries to reach back, tries to find a way to be involved in what's happening, groping helplessly for her husband, but her arms are still caught in the dress. Dean runs his fingers up the dark groove of Edie's spine, and when he reaches her neck he grabs the wig and throws it across the room. For an instant the blond filaments seem to lift like the feathers of a bird's wing, but then the wig falls behind the television.

The act finished, Edie stands up and turns around to face her husband. She seldom wears mascara, but tonight she layered it on thickly, and when she wipes at her tears now, she smears her cheeks with black. Her lips tremble with the effort to speak.

"I guess that approach worked then, didn't it?"

She walks away, tugging her borrowed dress back onto her shoulders.

TWO NIGHTS LATER Bunny calls. The wig. Bunny's sister needs her wig back.

Although Edie searches everywhere, she can't find it. Dean ripped it from her head in the living room, but it doesn't seem to be there, so she tries the bedroom, the bathroom, even the kitchen.

Finally she asks Dean if he knows where it is.

He's eating another one of his TV dinners. Fried chicken.

"How would I know?" he says.

"You seemed to like it," Edie replies. She knows this remark is likely to anger him, but she doesn't care. She's tired of having to step quietly around his feelings; an angry Dean would be preferable to the sullen, silent version that she's had entirely too much of lately.

"Maybe you tucked it away somewhere," she says. "So you could pull it out when you need the help."

Dean slams his fork down. The aluminum tray of food jumps and skitters on the tabletop. When he stands he pushes his chair back with such force it topples to the floor. With his fists clenched he lunges toward her. Edie flinches, but she doesn't cower. She stares defiantly at him.

Dean pushes past her, and once he's in the living room he yanks the cushions off the couch and pushes magazines off the coffee table. It looks as though he's about to kick over the TV tray that the television rests on when he stops. There, on the plastic-coated wire that leads from the rabbit ears antenna to the connection at the back of the television set, is the wig, hanging so precariously it's surprising that any vibration in the room didn't send it sliding to the floor.

He throws the wig at Edie, but it has so little weight it flutters uselessly to the carpet between them. Edie scoops up the wig. She grabs her coat from the hook and walks out of the apartment.

"I'm taking this to Bunny," she says. "Don't wait up."

As she descends the stairs, she wonders what ignited in Dean's mind when he charged at her. Did he intend to strike her? He never has, and she doesn't believe he ever would. But does he know that?

How exhausting and bewildering it can be, Edie thinks, to live with someone you understand better than he understands himself.

EDIE DOESN'T COME home until after ten o'clock, her breath smelling of whiskey. She doesn't offer any explanation, and Dean doesn't ask for any. The cushions are back on the couch, and the magazines are stacked on the coffee table.

If Dean wanted to know where his wife has been, he might have returned to the Elk's Tooth to make his inquiry. Loretta Sooner could tell him, yes, she was here. She sat right where she sat two nights ago, this time as a brunette however. She drank three Seven and Sevens, and she played the jukebox over and over. E-7, C-17, D-4. E-7, C-17, D-4. E-7, C-17, D-4. The only time she spoke was when a young cowboy approached her. He didn't know her as anyone's wife; to him she was just a pretty girl sitting alone at the bar. Loretta didn't hear what Edie said to him, but as the cowboy walked away, he said, "Jesus Christ, lady. Why the hell would you go and say a thing like that?"

A WEEK LATER when Dean enters their apartment after his work-day, he finds Edie sitting at the kitchen table, her coat on, an opened bottle of Budweiser in front of her.

"What's going on?" he asks. "Is the heat off?"

Edie says, "I need to talk to you." She quickly adds, "This is nothing for you to get mad about. I'm not mad. I'm . . . I don't want us to fight, Dean. But we've hardly spoken ten words to each other for days."

He pulls out a chair and sits down.

She pushes the beer toward him. "This is for you," Edie says. "I opened it when I heard you on the stairs." Then she smiles and leans across the table to reach toward him. "Let's leave here," she says. "Let's move."

Dean lifts up the beer bottle. "And go where?"

"I don't care. It doesn't matter. Just away. Away from here."

"You don't mean now."

"We can give the landlord and the bank and the store a month's notice. The car's paid for. We've got a little money in the bank." Edie sweeps her hand through the air to take in the entire apartment and its contents. "It won't take much to pack up. And we can sell what doesn't fit."

"And go where," he asks again. "It's the middle of winter."

"San Francisco? I read an article about how so many people are going there and—"

"Kids. *Kids* are going there. And living on the streets. Is that what you want?"

"It was just an idea. It doesn't have to be California. Denver? Or we could go the other way. Minneapolis maybe. Or someplace smaller if you like. I don't care. I just want to leave here. If we stay here, we're not going to make it."

He doesn't say anything in response, but he draws a sharp intake of breath and sits up straighter.

"As long as we're here," she says, "you'll always be one of the Linderman twins. I'll always be Edie Pritchard. And we'll always be—"

"I *am* one of the Linderman twins. No matter where I am."

"I'm not saying this right. It's just that as long as we're here, we'll keep living our lives in the same way. Please don't look at me like that. Please say you understand."

Dean finally drinks and puts the bottle back down on the table. "I can't."

"You can't what? Leave? Of course you can—"

He's shaking his head before Edie finishes speaking. "Not yet. I can't leave yet. Not until I'm finished here."

"Oh God. Don't tell me. Is this about going to Bentrock? Is that what you mean?"

"It's something I need to do."

"You don't. You *don't*."

"All right then," says Dean. "It's something I *want* to do. I want to be able to hold my head up in this town."

"Have you heard anything I said? We can leave. This town doesn't give a damn about you."

If this remark wounds him, he gives no sign.

Edie slips her coat from her shoulders. She smiles and says, "I'll dye my hair blond. What do you say? We can go someplace new and I can be a blonde." She gives a nervous laugh before adding, "Or I can get a wig."

"You don't have to do that."

"You seemed to like me as a blonde."

"I told you. Leave that be. Please." There's no anger in his words. He puts his head down as if he's ashamed.

She tugs tentatively at the hair right behind her ear. "I'm trying to grow it long again."

"You don't have to do that for me."

"I just thought . . . I don't know. Long would be easier."

"I liked it that way." His voice has grown softer. "But I like it the way it is too."

Edie reaches across the table again. She takes his hand in hers and squeezes it affectionately. But something in the pressure of her hand causes his mind—or his heart—to lurch in the wrong direction.

He stands abruptly and steps back from the table. "Is this about you and Roy?" he asks. "Is that what you're trying to tell me? If I don't get you away from here, you'll end up with him?"

Edie's head sinks to the tabletop. After a long moment she looks up at him. "Is that all you can think of? No. What I'm afraid of is that *you'll* end up with him."

A DIRT ROAD runs along the margin of one of the old Linderman pastures before winding its way up into the foothills, and in most winters it would be drifted over, accessible only by a tractor or a truck. But Dean has been able to drive the Volkswagen—the *Volkswagen*—out here with no more difficulty than if he were cruising down a highway on a summer day.

He gets out of the car and locks it. The morning is calm, but the leaden sky looks as though it's about to close the lid on the day. Hoar frost clings to every stalk and stubble, giving the prairie the appearance of having grown white fur overnight.

Dean's dressed for the cold in a knit cap, two sweatshirts, and sweatpants. In his mittened hand he holds the revolver.

No coach ever told Dean that the best way to train for distance running was to find a steep hill and run up it as hard as he could, but that's exactly what he did back in high school. This very hill. Over and over again.

Now he paws the bare, frozen ground as if he were waiting for the report of a starter's pistol. Finally he takes off, not sprinting exactly, but pumping his feet, knees, and arms at a speed he can't possibly sustain. At fifty yards his lungs feel as though they're burning. Or freezing. Not that it matters. Whether his lungs are filled with ice or fire, they can no longer provide him with the oxygen he needs to keep moving up the hill.

After a moment of rest, Dean starts up again, this time at a slower pace that carries him farther but still leaves him short of the top of the hill. He rests again. Then he walks to the crest.

There the land levels out. Off to the right is a rocky outcropping that he and Roy used to call the Crooked Teeth. In the lee of those rocks is a little dip where cedar and chokecherry grow. A Linderman cow and her calf once got tangled up in that gully, and it took the better part of a day for their father and his sons to get the animals out.

There's less frost at this elevation, but in that patch of dark vegetation a few branches and leaves still bristle with white outlines. Dean stands perhaps twenty yards from the tree with the thickest trunk. He takes off his mitten, assumes a shooter's stance, and raises the pistol to eye level. Squeeze. That's what shooters are advised to do, whether novice or experienced marksmen. Squ-ee-ee-ze. The gun jumps in Dean's hand as if the weapon were a muscle that could suddenly contract. The *bang*—like the slamming of a heavy, hollow door—rolls out across the empty land.

He looks at the pistol as if it has betrayed him. Then, without seeming to aim or even care where a bullet will strike, he pulls the trigger five more times. He seems to be firing the gun for no other purpose than to empty it.

But he hits something. From that thicket of trees and bushes, a few knots of frost flutter down.

THE WIND IS howling tonight, ripping loose anything that isn't latched, tied down, or too heavy for a gust to lift.

Even before Edie knocks, the trailer's flimsy storm door is rattling in its frame. Her fist is raised to knock again when Mrs. Linderman pulls open the inner door. Edie steps inside, and Mrs. Linderman closes the door behind her but keeps her hand on the knob.

"Roy ain't here," she says to Edie.

"I know where Roy is. He and Dean are sitting in a bar somewhere."

"Them two," Mrs. Linderman says, chuckling and shaking her head.

"They're planning the trip they're going to take. That's what I wanted to talk to you about."

Mrs. Linderman leads her daughter-in-law into the small kitchen. "Sit yourself down," Mrs. Linderman says.

Edie sits but does not remove her coat. "Is Elmer here?" The trailer smells of Sir Walter Raleigh, the tobacco Mr. Linderman uses in his hand-rolled cigarettes.

"He's gotten in the habit of laying down after supper. Don't do it, I tell him. You nap now, you'll be up till all hours. He and Roy stay up and watch the late show most nights. You want me to call him out here?"

Edie shakes her head no. "Let him sleep."

"So . . ." Mrs. Linderman rests her ample arms upon the table. "What's this about a trip?"

"You haven't heard? They're planning on driving up to Bentrock."

Mrs. Linderman gives a little start, but she recovers quickly and says, "Do tell."

"They have some idea of confronting the Bauer family. Who Roy bought the truck from? The ones who followed Roy out of town when he had his accident?"

"I know who the Bauers are. *Confronting*, you say?"

"Oh, I don't know. I don't know if they expect to be reimbursed for the truck or if they want revenge or what."

"Not a bad idea," Mrs. Linderman says. "Especially with the both of them going."

"It's a *terrible* idea," Edie says. "Roy almost got himself killed up there."

Mrs. Linderman raises her eyebrows. "Alone. But now with Dean—"

"No. *No*. Please. You can tell them not to go."

Mrs. Linderman nods thoughtfully. "I could. But I won't. Besides, it'll be good for 'em. Dean especially. He's always had a tendency to mope, but it's got worse. And Roy needs to learn that a little limp don't mean he's any less than he ever was."

"*A little limp!*"

Mrs. Linderman leans forward as if she has a secret to convey. "I don't think you know what it means to be a Linderman. Maybe nobody ever said nothing like this to you, but when you got the Linderman name you got yourself a good deal, honey."

"And it's time," Mrs. Linderman continues, "those boys remembered what it means to be a Linderman."

"But you're not," Edie says. "A Linderman, I mean. You're a Hindemith."

"I used to be. Until them boys were born."

ROY CARRIES HIS whiskey and water to the booth by the window, where his brother waits with his own glass.

When Roy sits down, Dean asks, "Are you going with the folks to Denora this Sunday?"

"Another one of their damn church suppers? Why would I?"

"I told Mom I'd drive them. I don't think she trusts Dad driving on the highway anymore."

"Be careful," Roy says. "You don't want to get stuck being their chauffeur."

"Just on the highway," Dean answers.

"Well, that should get you the good-son-of-the-month award," Roy says. "By the way, I got a call from Jerry Krueger today. He's out, thanks to your comment about shooting the Bauers. He wants no part of 'any gunplay,' his words."

Dean shakes his head dismissively. "He was never going anyway."

"No?"

"It was never going to be anyone but us. You know that."

"Do I?" says Roy.

"Come on. Would you be willing to sign on for something like this if you didn't have to?"

Roy smiles and cracks an ice cube between his molars. "Brother, I don't *have to*. Neither of us does."

The Elk's Tooth's side door rattles, and the brothers fall silent and look in that direction. It's only Dr. Thayer, a Bentrock dentist. He sits on a stool at the bar.

"Are you ready for the Bauers?" Roy asks his brother.

"What the hell does that even mean?"

"I have no idea," says Roy. "When were you last in a fistfight?"

"Junior year," Dean says without hesitation. "Lasted maybe ten seconds. I took a swing at Vince Wiens and sort of banged my fist on his elbow. He hit me on the top of the head and put me on my ass."

"Vince Wiens? Jesus. Did you have some kind of fucking death wish?"

Dean ignores the question. "'Now don't get up, Linderman,' Vince said, 'and I won't have to kill you.' But I tried. My legs just wouldn't work."

"And you threw the first punch, huh? At Vince-fucking-Wiens. What the hell got into your head?"

Dean stares into his whiskey for a long moment. "I had the crazy idea I was defending someone's honor."

A sheaf of newspaper suddenly blows against the window, flattened as though giant hands have opened it and held it there for the brothers to read. In the next instant it's gone.

EDIE SITS IN the Volkswagen while two tumbleweeds, tightly tangled balls of Russian thistle, scrape slowly along the aluminum outer wall of her in-laws' home. Inside the trailer it must sound as though a creature is scratching to be let in.

The wind gusts and the tumbleweeds pick up their pace, rolling away from the Linderman home and out to the open land beyond the trailer court. Tattered masses of high white clouds move rapidly past the sun. Then the sun blinks brightly into view, and still Edie waits. She has turned off the Volkswagen's engine, but the key remains in the ignition, and she flicks at the key ring, making a discordant little chime inside the car. Her fingers are right there; it would take hardly any effort at all to turn the key again, start the Volkswagen, and drive away. All the effort would be in making the decision. "Fuck it," she says and gets out of the car.

Edie knocks on the door of the trailer. From inside a voice calls out, "Yeah, come in!"

She walks in. From out of the little kitchen Roy Linderman appears, the dog waddling along behind.

"Hey, Edie! I wasn't expecting company," Roy says. He's wearing a plaid flannel bathrobe and moccasins, and he has an open Budweiser in his hand. "How about that wind, huh? What's it been now—the fourth day of it?" He raises his beer can. "Can I get you one?"

"No thanks."

"Something stronger? A whiskey and Coke maybe? Or something weaker? I can put on a pot of coffee."

"No, I'm fine. Thank you."

"Sit yourself down," he says. "But I have to tell you, if you sit in that chair, you'll come away covered in dog hair. Rusty's sort of made that his."

She smiles at the dog, and then she finds a place for both herself and her coat on the sofa. Roy sits at the other end.

"Everybody else has gone up to Denora," he says. "One of Mom and Dad's beloved church suppers. Beats the hell out of me why anyone would drive seventy miles just to eat a stranger's fried chicken." He reaches into the pocket of his robe for his cigarettes and lighter. "Hell, you look like you just came from church yourself."

Along with the white blouse she wore when she was trying to sell Roy's car, Edie's wearing the navy blue wool skirt that she bought with the Penney's gift certificate that Dean gave her for Christmas. She's also wearing more makeup than what's usual for her, though not nearly as much as she wore that night she and Bunny danced at the Elk's Tooth. She sits up straight, perched on the edge of the sofa cushion with her hands folded in her lap. She looks as though she's been called into the bank manager's office for her annual job review.

Roy lights a cigarette. "But you knew they wouldn't be here." He blows a stream of smoke toward the ceiling. "That means you're here to see me. I'm flattered. To what do I owe the honor of this visit?"

Another of those cloud-frigates drifts in front of the sun, and the room suddenly dims and the shadows thicken, then just as quickly, the brighter light returns.

Edie tugs at the hem of her skirt. "I want to ask you for a favor."

Roy leans back. "Let's hear it." Something in his voice and manner has turned hard.

She clears her throat. "Don't let Dean go to Bentrock."

"Don't *let* him? Dean's a big boy. He does what he wants."

"You can stop him."

"And you can't?"

She shakes her head no. "I thought I could. I can't." Her eyes glisten with tears, but she blinks them back.

"Maybe you're giving me too much credit."

"You could tell him you won't go. He won't go without you."

"Yeah," Roy says. "Yeah, you're probably right about that."

For a long time neither of them says anything. He drinks his beer, and he smokes his cigarette. He looks appraisingly at Edie. She says nothing, wondering how much will need to be said.

"All right, say I do this for you," Roy says. "Are you prepared to do something for me in return?"

Well, there you have it, Edie thinks. Not much at all.

"I asked you for a favor," she says and smiles. "I didn't propose making a deal."

"But you asked *me*, Edie. And you know me. Hell, we started dealing the minute you walked through the door."

"I didn't think it would be quite so quick," she says. "And I wasn't sure if it would be with words."

"You thought I'd just throw you down and have my way with you? That's a joke, by the way. In case you can't tell." Roy finishes his beer, crushes the can in his hand, and drops it on the coffee table. "But we can close this deal right now. They won't be back for hours."

Edie knows the trailer's arrangement of rooms, and she looks down the hall in the direction of the bedrooms. The hell of it is, she still finds him appealing. She always has. Easy to be with. Handsome. And yes, sexy. Even now, reeking of beer and cigarettes, looking like a slob in that ratty old bathrobe, if he'd only smile his Roy Linderman smile instead of staring at her as if he were calculating her worth on the open market.

"I sat out in the car for a long time," she says, "until I was sure. Until I was *ready*." She picks up her coat, and though she doesn't put it on, she lays it across her lap and smooths the fabric. "But it turns out, I'm not. I can't do something to save my marriage when that something would actually cost me my marriage. I'm sorry."

"What are you apologizing for, Edie? For being you? Come on."

She stands up and puts on her coat. "I guess I'm not as good a negotiator as you once thought I was."

Roy shrugs. "It's a gift. Not many people have it."

Edie leaves the trailer. When she opens the car door, she has to fight the wind to close it. It was that last gust, she tells herself, that finally caused her tears to spring free.

DEAN KNOCKS ON the bedroom door. When there's no answer, he opens it a few inches and peers inside. "Hey, you in there?"

Roy sits up a little higher in the bed. "I'm here."

Dean steps inside. The room smells of whiskey and cigarette smoke. "Jesus. Sitting in the dark feeling sorry for yourself?"

Roy raises a pint of Jim Beam. "I got a little project here I'm working on."

Dean switches on the overhead light.

"Fuck!" Roy cringes and tries to tuck his head inside his bathrobe. "Turn it off. God *damn*."

Dean turns the light off. He crosses the room and sits on the foot of the bed. "Well, Dad got shit-faced. You remember Bud Rodenbaugh?

The old foreman on the Howell ranch? He and Dad got to reminiscing. And drinking someone's home brew out in the church parking
lot. Damn near had to carry him to the car. Then he slept all the way
home."

"Uh-huh."

"So Mom's on the warpath. You're better off staying in here.
Especially if you're stinking too."

"Exactly my intention. Exactly."

"I'm thinking next Saturday," Dean says.

"Saturday?"

Dean's voice drops to a whisper. "Bentrock. We can head out early.
Be back maybe by nightfall."

"Whatever you say."

"Christ, what's with you? If you don't want to do this . . ."

Roy raises the bottle to his lips and pulls hard. A shudder runs
through him. "You talk to your wife about this?"

"This is ours," Dean says and stands up from the bed. "She's been
to Bentrock. Remember?"

"Oh, I remember. I surely do." He screws the cap back on the
bottle of whiskey and sets the bottle on the chair next to the bed.
"Saturday. Gotcha. The brothers Linderman ride again."

Dean has his hand on the doorknob. "You better write it down,"
he says. "You're too fucking drunk to remember."

DEAN SITS IN the Volkswagen outside the Linderman trailer, with
the engine running. After a few minutes, the trailer door opens and
Roy steps out. The vapor of his breath in the morning cold mingles
with the smoke from his cigarette.

He climbs into the Volkswagen. "Fuck," he says, "I thought it was
supposed to get up to fifty today."

Dean puts the car into gear and eases away from the trailer. "Is
Dad up?"

"You know it."

"What'd you tell him?"

"That we're driving up to Jordan. That I have a lead on a Chrysler with low miles up that way."

"And he bought it?"

"'Back to wheeling and dealing,' he said. 'Your mother will be pleased.'"

Dean drives slowly through the narrow, curving streets of the trailer park.

"And what'd you tell Edie?" Roy asks.

"I left her a note."

"Saying . . . ?"

"The truth."

"Must have been a hell of a long note."

"Not really," Dean replies. He exits the park and accelerates onto the street that will take them to Highway 16, the road that runs all the way to Bentrock.

EDIE LINDERMAN WAKES up from an alarm that goes off only in her own mind. The sheets cooling at her side. The mattress no longer tilting from her husband's weight. His touch is now nothing but a memory—as if he were training her not to feel his presence at all . . .

Edie throws back the blanket and sheet and leaps from the bed.

Frantically she searches the apartment, though she's not surprised that Dean isn't there. Then she sees on the kitchen table the pencil and the notepad on which Dean records his and Roy's gin rummy scores. But there are no numbers written there. Just words: *Roy and I are driving up to Bentrock. Back tonight. Dean*

Edie pulls on a pair of jeans and a sweatshirt, and steps into her loafers. She grabs her coat and purse, but at the door she stops and looks back at the rooms she has called home. Then she hurries out of the apartment and down the stairs.

Their Volkswagen is gone. But in the alley is a white panel truck with FLIEDER'S BAKERY—TASTY AND GOOD emblazoned on its side. One man sits behind the wheel while another stacks metal racks of bread loaves in the back of the truck. When he slams the back doors of the truck, the clang echoes up and down the alley.

Edie knocks on the driver's window. He's an older man, swarthy, balding, unshaven, and he looks at Edie with rheumy eyes that register neither annoyance nor pleasure, as if a pretty woman banging on the window of his truck is simply one more thing he must face before his morning duties are done. He rolls the window down.

"Where are you going?" Edie asks him. "Can you give me a ride? Please?"

"I got deliveries, lady. And we ain't supposed to take on riders."

"Do you go out to the highway? To Sixteen?"

"I got a drop-off at the Oasis."

"Close enough," Edie says. "*Please*. I'll pay you."

"Keep your dang money," he says. But he reaches across the front seat to open the passenger door.

AS THEY TRAVEL Roy and Dean keep the silence of men who have a long road and a hard day ahead. The neon red of the rising sun has finally made an appearance, while at the same time the bone-white sliver of the setting moon hangs low in the west. One of these is visible out Dean's side of the car and the other out Roy's.

Roy turns on the radio. But at this hour he can't find anything but livestock reports and *Swap Shop*, and he soon switches the radio off.

After a few more miles of silence he says, "Look, when we get back home? I'm thinking of packing up and heading out."

"Yeah? Where you headed?"

"Not sure," says Roy. "Maybe I'll flip a coin. Heads, I go east. Tails, west."

"North and south are out, huh?"

Roy swats at his brother. "Smart-ass."

"And this is a permanent move you're talking about?"

"That's what I'm thinking."

"How're you going to make the move?" Dean asks. "Without a car, I mean."

"I'll pick up something cheap. Something I can sell somewhere and make a buck."

Dean says, "I told you before. Edie and I could give you a little cash to tide you over."

Roy laughs. "No, brother. I don't want your money."

Dean looks off into the distance as though he's trying to determine which direction would be best for his brother to take. "Funny," he says, "Edie wants to move too. I came home from work the other day, and she jumped me with it. 'Let's move,' she says. And just like you, she doesn't give a damn where. Just somewhere else."

Roy shakes a cigarette from the pack and raises it to his lips, strikes a match, and lights the cigarette, "Why does she want to leave?"

"She says she wants to get me away from you."

Roy inhales deeply and allows the smoke to drift from his nostrils. "But here we are," he says.

THE BAKERY TRUCK pulls into the parking lot of the Oasis, a restaurant on Gladstone's northern edge.

"Far as I can take you, missy," the driver says to Edie. "Where'd you say you're going?"

"Bentrock."

He shakes his head sadly. "I hope you get a ride quick," he says and points down to her ankle, bare above her shoe. "Or you're going to freeze your tootsies."

Edie opens the passenger door. "I appreciate what you've done. Thank you."

He's still shaking his head when she shuts the door and walks away.

She takes a moment to scan the vehicles in the parking lot. Then she walks in the direction of Route 16, though at this hour traffic is so sparse it seems as if she might be heading toward a deserted highway. She stations herself on the gravel shoulder of the road, ready to raise her thumb at any approaching car or truck.

Two cars go by before a black Corvair pulls over. The driver reaches across the seat to open the door for her. "Where you headed, ma'am?"

"Bentrock?"

"I can get you there," he says. In an instant all the cautions of a woman's lifetime coalesce into a single voice in Edie's mind—Don't get in a stranger's car. But she climbs in anyway, believing that today it would be a greater mistake not to.

But surely those warnings can't have meant him. He looks as though he's not much older than high school age. His hair is close-cropped and he's spent a lot of time in the sun, yet his tan can't hold back the pink of his smooth cheeks. He must have been traveling for a time because the car's interior is warm and he's wearing a T-shirt. He tells her he's Bobby March, home on leave after completing his basic training at Fort Benning, Georgia. His voice is deep, and his Adam's apple, which protrudes like the knob on a cupboard door, bobs up and down in his long neck when he speaks or swallows.

"I figured army," Edie says. "The haircut."

Bobby laughs and rubs his skull. "Ain't so different from how it's always been. Me and the sheep. Dad sheared the both of us."

"You grew up on a sheep ranch?"

"Yes, ma'am. South of Hardin. And if my folks have their way, that's where I'll return."

"What if you have your way?"

Bobby laughs ruefully. "I reckon not."

The rising sun is hitting Edie's side of the Corvair, adding to the warmth of the interior. She slips her arms out of her coat but leaves it wrapped around her shoulders.

"You must have got off to an early start," Edie says. "You know I'm going to Bentrock. But you didn't say where you're headed."

"I went through basic with this fellow from Williston. Over across the border in North Dakota. Me and a couple other buddies, we're all going to meet up at his place. Just hang out for a few days. Drink a few beers. Shoot the shit. Excuse my French."

"You don't have to watch your language around me." Edie says with a smile. "Do I remind me of your mother or something?"

That question brings a laugh from Bobby March. "Ma'am, you sure as *hell* do not."

"Then maybe you could save the 'ma'am' for your mother as well."

"I know *where* you're going," he says to Edie. "But I don't know *why*. Hitchhiking. No luggage or nothing. Out at the crack of dawn. Seems a little strange. A gal like you, if you don't mind my saying."

"My husband's working up in Bentrock. With his brother. I thought I'd surprise him."

"And your husband will be okay with you thumbing a ride? Ain't really the safest thing."

"Like I say," Edie replies. "it's supposed to be a surprise."

THE SOUND OF the Volkswagen's tires droning along the highway is almost in a musical key, and at some point Dean begins to hum along with a tune of his own.

"Oh Jesus," Roy says. "Don't tell me."

"What?"

"The humming? You're turning into Pop."

They both laugh. "It helps me think," says Dean.

"And what do you need help thinking about today?"

"When you move. Wherever you go, you think you'll tell people you're a twin?"

"What the fuck kind of question is that? Why wouldn't I?"

"I don't know," Dean replies. "Why would you?"

"Jesus, sometimes I wonder how that mind of yours works."

"You and me both."

AS SHE'S TWISTING in her seat, trying to get comfortable, Edie glances in the back seat. A sleeping bag is rolled up there. Next to it is a cardboard box with a few of its contents visible—boxes of Quaker Oats, a jar of peanut butter, a loaf of bread, and cans of Campbell's soup. Also on the seat is a sheepskin coat. On the floor is a rifle or a shotgun in its cloth scabbard.

"Looks like you've brought plenty of supplies," she says. "Everybody appreciates a visitor who brings his own groceries."

Bobby March says, "We're planning on going camping."

"At this time of year? You be careful you don't get buried under a foot of snow. It could still happen."

"I got a tent in the trunk."

"You don't get enough of sleeping in a tent in the army?"

He laughs. "I reckon not."

Edie likes this young man, this earnest young man with his good manners and his ruddy cheeks and his boxes of oatmeal. She wants to ask him if he has a girlfriend. But she's afraid he might say, "Yes ma'am." Then Edie would have to know that he'd rather spend his precious leave playing house with his friends than being with her.

Instead Edie looks out at the monochrome landscape of early spring. She isn't sure she'll recognize in daylight that field where she saw the flash of Roy's white shirt. But Roy will certainly know it. And will he point it out to Dean? Will he say: "That's where Edie found me, broken and bleeding"?

"What did you say he's doing up there?" Bobby Marsh asks. "Your husband?"

"He's buying a truck. And then his brother will drive it back home."

"And you'll ride home with him," says Bobby.

"That's right," Edie says. "I'll ride home with him."

ROY SITS UP a little straighter. Is that the barn in the distance? Its boards are splintered and weathered to the color of the feathers, weeds, dirt, and stones of the surrounding world. It lies collapsed at the foot of a hill. Even in ruin it continues to lean northwest to southeast, the direction that the prevailing wind pushed, pushed, and pushed on the structure over the years.

"Pull over, will you," he says. "I have to take a leak."

"What are you? Four years old?" But Dean drives onto the narrow shoulder. Stones bounce into the wheel wells, and the car rolls to a stop. When Roy opens the door, the smell of sage enters the car. From nearby comes the burble and whistle of a meadowlark's song.

He climbs stiffly from the car and takes a few steps into the ditch, stopping finally amid the dry stalks of last summer's knapweed and toadflax. His urine stream hisses and steams in the dirt.

When he returns to the car, he doesn't get in, not right away. He stands by the open door and lights a cigarette. He leans on the roof of the Volkswagen and surveys the miles of prairie that surround them in every direction.

"You want to know what I think?" Roy says. "I think this whole fucking expedition is so you can prove something. To Edie, probably. Or maybe to me. And here's the thing that just doesn't figure." Roy lowers himself to look into the car. "Edie doesn't want you to do this. You know that, don't you? She came and talked to me about it."

Dean says nothing. He grips the steering wheel and stares straight ahead as if he were not stopped on an empty stretch of road but speeding along a highway with one hairpin turn after another.

"But you never talked any of this over with her, did you?" Roy asks. "You never asked her what she wants, did you? " He slumps into the car, but he sits with his back to his brother and with his legs sticking straight out toward the ditch.

"I can't do this," says Roy. With the heel of his shoe, he gouges a line in the dirt of the road's shoulder. "I can't. I'm sorry, brother. Those Bauers did a number on me. I'm not going up against them again. Fuck, I still haven't got used to these false teeth."

"Call me a fucking coward," he continues. "I don't care. You want to do this, you'll have to do it alone." The Volkswagen's heater keeps gasping out heat, but it can't compete with the cool air coming in through Roy's open door. "If you like," he says, "I'll get out here. You can go on ahead. I'll hitch a ride back."

"What the hell was your plan for today, anyway?" asks Roy, turning now to look over his shoulder at his brother.

"We'd scare them, I guess," Dean says and points toward the dashboard. "Glove box."

Roy opens the glove box. Inside is the .38 revolver. "Oh fuck." He lifts the gun out. "No. Don't tell me."

Then as swiftly as he can with that bad leg, Roy clambers out of the car. He jogs into the ditch again and beyond, stumbling up the other side. He stops when he comes to a barbed wire fence. Then he winds up and throws the pistol as far as he can. "There," he says, in a voice only he can hear. "Now we've both got one out there."

He walks slowly back to the Volkswagen and climbs in again. This time he closes the door.

"I paid good money for that pistol," Dean says.

"I'll reimburse you."

"I thought you were hard up for cash."

"We can work out a trade."

The Volkswagen's transmission is balky, and it takes a couple tries for Dean to shift into gear. He checks the side and rearview mirrors. Nothing is approaching from either direction, yet Dean rolls down his window to look at the highway behind them. "I don't believe," he says to his brother, "you have anything I want."

Then he makes a U-turn in the middle of Route 16 and heads them back toward home.

"THERE AREN'T BUT a few Volkswagens in this part of Montana," Roy says, breaking the silence between them, as he's done since they were boys just learning to speak, "and I bet you dollars to doughnuts yours is the only one with a gun in the glove box. Or *was*."

"Is that how you can tell who's armed?" Dean asks. "The make of car?"

"Go ahead. Try me."

Another mile passes before a car comes up fast and passes them. A dark green Cadillac. "That one?" asks Dean.

"Oh for sure. Hell yeah."

A Ford station wagon goes by in the other lane. "Well?" Dean asks. Roy shakes his head. "Doubtful. Possible but doubtful."

Soon they're laughing and pointing at every car that passes or approaches—an old Chevy pickup, yes; a new Dodge Charger, maybe . . . The Linderman brothers, who have often had to find their own fun in this world, are making up a private game to pass the time before they return home together.

"That black Corvair?"

"Nope," Roy says confidently. "Unarmed."

So focused are they on the automobiles that they don't notice the woman in that car. And if they did, they'd talk themselves out of it. Edie? How could it be? She's back in Gladstone.

BUT EDIE SEES them.

Who else could it be in a red Volkswagen at that hour on Highway 16? Dean and Roy, and laughing over something only the two of them can share.

Edie couldn't feel more betrayed if she walked in on Dean with another woman. Laughing, they're *laughing*, and in her mind she's the object of their mirth.

"Mr. March," she says, "here's what I want you to do—"

"Bobby."

"Bobby. All right. There's a truck stop and diner not far up the road. I want you to drop me off there—"

"No, ma'am, I can—"

"No, Bobby. That's as far as I want to go. My plans have changed."

"If you say so, ma'am." Bobby March hunches over the steering wheel and, like a horse with blinders, stares at nothing but the highway.

"This place will be on your right," Edie says.

The Hi-Top Truck Stop and Diner comes into view. Bobby slows down as he turns into its parking lot. He drives up as close to the door as he can and stops the car.

"Are you sure?" he asks.

"As sure as I can be of anything. Thank you, Bobby. You came along at just the right time."

Edie opens the door, and Bobby says, "Wait—"

But it's too late, and as astonished as Bobby March seemed when Edie Linderman climbed into his car he seems equally astonished now that she's gone, running toward the diner and out of his life forever.

He steps down on the gas pedal so hard it takes an instant before the tires can gain traction on the gravel and send him on his way.

THE STOUT WAITRESS is not working today. In her place behind the counter is a young woman who looks not much older than twelve.

Edie stands by the cash register and waits. The girl comes over, wiping her hands on a dirty apron. "Yep?"

Pointing to the Greyhound bus sticker on the back of the register, Edie says, "I want to buy a ticket."

The girl's face is pocked with acne and her hands reddened from dishwater. She shakes her head no. "I'm not allowed to sell bus tickets. You got to talk to the agent." Then she steps behind a curtain into a back room and calls out, "Mom!"

A moment later a woman steps through the curtain. They have the same slope-shouldered build and chins that look sharp enough to poke holes in a newspaper.

"Where you headed?" the woman asks Edie.

"When's the next bus leaving?"

The woman glances over her shoulder at the clock next to a shelf of pies. "About three hours. Going west."

Edie opens her purse. She takes out a wallet, unclasps it, and pulls out every bill inside. "How far will this take me?" she asks.

The woman takes the money and counts it. "On the westbound bus you say?"

"If that's the next one."

"Yep. West." The woman looks down at the money again. "One way?"

"One way."

"This'll get you to Shelby for sure. Maybe Wolf Point."

"Fine," Edie says. "Whichever."

"Shelby it is," she says. She picks up the money but hands a ten-dollar bill back to Edie. "You'll need something for when you get there."

Edie stuffs the bill back in her wallet. "Thank you."

"You traveling alone?"

"You know it," says Edie.

"Be ready to jump out there when the bus pulls in," the woman says. "That driver hardly slows down if he isn't dropping off."

DEAN PARKS IN front of the Linderman trailer. Their mother is outside, slashing with a hoe at the barely thawed ground next to the front step.

"Shit," Roy says. "She'll want to know why I'm not driving up in that Chrysler."

"You want to come over to our place? Play some cards?"

"No, brother. You'll be enough of a surprise for your wife. She doesn't need to see both of us."

EDIE HAS BEEN on the bus less than an hour, and its easy bounce and sway are already transporting her toward sleep. Looping the strap around her wrist, she tucks her purse close to her side and away from the aisle, then closes her eyes.

But in another moment she's jarred back to consciousness. A large woman in a man's wool overcoat is lurching up the aisle toward the front of the bus. She's waving her arms and yelling, "Wait! Stop! We have to stop!"

When she reaches the driver she bends down to tell him something. Edie can't hear what the woman says, but the driver extends an arm in an attempt to calm her and move her back toward her seat. His effort is in vain however. She continues to hover near him and to plead her case.

In another moment the bus slows, and the driver steers the vehicle to the side of the road. The vehicle leans, totters, and finally stops, half on the blacktop and half on the crumbling shoulder. The driver shuts off the engine and pulls on the emergency brake.

He stands and turns to face the bus passengers. "Folks, we have a little situation. This lady has forgotten her medication in her luggage and it's medication she says she needs. So we'll dig out her suitcase, get her pills, and we'll be on our way again. Feel free to step out and stretch your legs."

Edie follows everyone else off the bus, but while they gather near the driver as he opens the luggage compartment, she walks behind the bus and stands by herself on the cracked, frost-heaved blacktop.

It might not seem like much, this country. A few bare hills, each seeming to rise out of the shadow of the one behind it. Miles of empty prairie, and all of it, hill and plain, the color of paper left out in the sun. You might be out here alone someday with what you thought would be your life. And a gust of wind might blow your heart open like a screen door. And slam it just as fast.

TWO

Edie Dunn

1987

Edie picks up the telephone and hears the breathy hiss peculiar to long-distance calls. For a moment she simply stares at the trapezoid of sunlight shining on the kitchen floor.

A long-distance call. Daylight. Nothing good can come of those in combination.

But it's too late. Even if she hangs up the phone, bad news will only find another way to enter her house.

She exhales and says hello.

"Edie? Is that you?"

The voice is familiar, but she still has to ask: "Who is this?"

"It's Roy. Roy Linderman."

"Roy . . ."

"Jesus, you're a tough gal to track down."

"How did you find me?"

"You remember Jeannie Johnson? Jeannie Walbert now. She was secretary of our class, and she's the one in charge of our reunions. She does a hell of a job keeping track of everyone. Damned if she didn't have your address and phone number."

"I haven't been hiding."

He laughs. "Okay, if you say so. You haven't gone out of your way to keep in touch either."

"My life is here, Roy." She closes her eyes and rests her forehead against the wall. "If it was so much trouble," she says, "why did you bother tracking me down?"

Roy Linderman pauses and clears his throat. "Dean asked me to call you. He's got cancer. Prostate. Mom and I took him to Billings to see a specialist. They operated but it had already spread. His chances don't look good. What the hell am I saying. *Chances*. He doesn't have any. It's just a question of when. Six months maybe at the outside."

"Oh no, I'm sorry. How's he doing?"

"You know. Good days and bad days. And now the bad days are pushing out the good."

"How about your mom? How's she taking it?"

"You know Mom. This can't happen to her boy. She thinks maybe the doctors made a mistake. Or they'll find a drug or something."

"I'm so sorry. Please tell Dean how sorry I am."

"Like I say. He wanted you to know. And Edie? Something more—"

She pushes away from the wall and opens her eyes. The lunch dishes in the sink. The radio on the counter. The empty coffee cup. The mail on the kitchen table. Sunlight's bright geometry on the floor. The sound of water from the lawn sprinkler pattering against the side of the house. Nothing says that her life is changed from what it was before she picked up the telephone. Nothing but the voice in her ear.

"He wants to see you. One more time."

"But *he* didn't call me."

"You know how hard it would have been for him. I told him I'd do it."

"Still wheeling and dealing, Roy?"

"That's not fair, Edie. He's dying."

"And I said I'm sorry. But there's nothing I can do. He's there and I'm here. Good-bye, Roy. You can tell Dean I said good-bye too. Or not. That's up to you."

As she hangs up the phone, she hears his voice, still pleading, still trying—"Wait, Edie, *wait*—"

She walks quickly away from the telephone, but why flee its silence? She turns on the radio: "Ain't got time to take a fast train . . ." The oldies station.

Her husband says that in this heat, they should leave the curtains drawn, but Edie usually opens them once he leaves for work. She closes them now.

She goes to the sink and turns on the hot water, lifts a plate, rinses it, and places it in the dishwasher.

A letter. Yes, she could have received this news in a letter: *Dear Edie, I'm writing to let you know I have cancer.* Just the way he might have phrased it in high school when they passed notes in study hall. And his brother would have written it the same way: *Dear Edie, I'm writing to let you know Dean has cancer.* As different as they are, as easy as it is—and was—to forget they're twins, the fact could still assert itself in surprising ways. Or the news might have come after the fact: *Dear Edie, I'm sorry to say Dean passed away.* She could have seen the name and return address on the envelope—or recognized the loopy handwriting—and decided whether to allow this news to come any closer. She could have thrown a letter away unopened. Why would she think it held news she needed or wanted to know?

Even if she began to read she could decide at any time to stop— after the greeting perhaps, before the crucial information. But once someone speaks into your ear, you can't decide not to hear it.

The back door faces west, and opening it today is like opening an oven door. This part of Montana, in the lee of mountains always cold at their heights, never has heat like this, never until this summer, and now it has gone on for eight days, creating its own suspense. Edie walks across the grass, as dry and prickly under her bare feet as wheat stubble. At the far end of the yard, out of the reach of the shade of the cottonwoods that mark their property line, her daughter is lying in an aluminum-and-plastic lawn chair, her taut, trim teenage body glistening with sweat. Jennifer is wearing a two-piece red bathing suit, and she's adjusted it to allow the sun access to parts of her body usually covered, the straps off her shoulders and the bra top pushed down an extra inch.

Her eyes are closed, but she must hear her mother's approach. "Who called?" she asks.

"You'll have to move," Edie says. "I need to pull the sprinkler over here."

"Was it for me?"

"I would have let you know. I'm not intercepting your calls."

Edie maneuvers around so she's standing between her daughter and the sun's rays. "I don't know how you can do it," she says.

Suddenly shadowed, Jennifer opens her eyes. "Do what?"

"Just lay out here."

"You should try it. It feels good."

"Does it? I thought maybe you were just willing to suffer for your beauty."

"Wow." Jennifer sits up and pulls the straps back up onto her shoulders. "Where did *that* come from, Mom?"

"Sorry," she says. "Sorry. Maybe I'm just jealous."

Jennifer is folding up the lawn chair. "I'll move the sprinkler," she says.

As she walks toward the house, Edie looks back over her shoulder. She hasn't been in hiding, and she's made no attempt to keep her life secret. So why does she feel as though she's been found out?

THAT NIGHT THE telephone rings, and though Jennifer scrambles up from the living room floor where she's been lying and watching *St. Elsewhere*, she can't beat her father to the phone. Gary Dunn has been sitting at the kitchen table, his broad shoulders bent over his forms and his calculator. He rises to his full, considerable height and with an exasperated sigh picks up the receiver.

"Dunn residence," he says.

A man's voice asks to speak to Edie.

"Who's calling?"

The man gives his name and without saying a word in reply, Gary Dunn simply lets go of the phone. It dangles from its cord and bumps against the wall.

Jennifer strides into the kitchen, and her father shakes his head no and says, "It's for your mother."

Into the living room Gary marches, his daughter close behind. His wife is paging through a copy of *Good Housekeeping.*

"It's for you," he says.

"Who is it?"

"Answer it," he says.

He follows Edie into the kitchen, and when she picks up the telephone, he stations himself on the other side of the room, his arms crossed, his back against the stove. He's wearing a white shirt and dark slacks, but he's built as if stiff-arming a tackler and perhaps bucking hay might be in his past. And you wouldn't want him looking at you the way he's looking at Edie, his dark eyes glowering.

Edie turns toward the phone and focuses her gaze on the numbers printed on its buttons. "Hello," she says.

"Hey, Edie. It's me again. I thought of something I should have said earlier."

"What's that?" she says, her voice an uninflected whisper.

"I could pick you up. Or Carla and I could."

"Carla?"

"Oh shit. You don't know. Hell, why would you. You remember Carla Hall? Sure you do. She's Carla Linderman now. Going on twelve years since we got hitched."

"You and Carla . . . Well, congratulations."

"Yeah, thanks. Anyway. We could drive up to Granite Valley and bring you back to Gladstone. You could look in on Dean, and then we'd take you back home. Same day, if you like. Though that's a hell of a lot of miles in a day."

"I told you, Roy," she says, and now she looks back at her husband, who has not moved from his station. "I can't do that."

"You can't or you won't?"

"Whichever."

"Nothing I can say then?"

"No. There's nothing you can say."

"Okay," he says. "I can't pretend I'm not disappointed. But setting everything else aside, I have to tell you, Jesus *Christ* it's good to hear your voice again."

"I'm saying good-bye now, Roy." She places the telephone receiver gently on the hook.

From across the room Gary Dunn addresses his wife. "What the hell was that all about?"

"My ex-husband has cancer," she says. "He's dying."

"He sounded pretty damn chipper to me."

"That was Roy."

"I know who it was."

"Dean's *brother*. I was married to Dean. They're twins. Maybe you have trouble telling them apart."

"Is that supposed to be a joke?"

"I thought it was funny," Edie says but she's not smiling either.

There aren't many crew cuts left in America, but Gary Dunn still has his. His close-cropped hair bristles from his scalp like iron filings on a magnet. He brushes his palm across his skull and says, "But the one with cancer couldn't make the call himself?"

Edie remains by the telephone, leaning against the wall, her hands behind her back. "He wants to see me . . ."

"The hell."

"You asked why he called."

"This Dean—do you still have feelings for him? Is that what his brother thinks?"

"My God, Gary. It's been twenty years since I last saw him."

"That's not exactly an answer to my question, is it?"

Usually the central air hums almost constantly, so when it shuts off momentarily it seems as though someone has suddenly left the room. In the silence following Gary Dunn's question there's time for the air-conditioning to cycle off and then on once again.

"He's going to die," Edie says. "I feel sorry for him."

"And that's not an answer either."

Jennifer comes back into the kitchen, and for an instant the distance between her parents seems to disconcert her. But she has her own curiosity to satisfy. "Who called?" she asks.

"One of your mother's old boyfriends," says Gary.

Edie shakes her head sadly. "Don't listen to your father," she says. "Someone I used to know is sick."

"Go watch your show," Gary says to his daughter.

Jennifer looks to her mother.

Edie tells her, "No one you know, honey."

Jennifer has long legs and when she backs slowly out of the room, it seems a maneuver as awkward as a filly's. Once she's gone, Edie says to her husband, "Shame on you."

"Me! Look who's talking!"

If there was any sadness in Edie's eyes earlier, it's gone now, and she looks at her husband with pure defiance.

"So if he wants to see you," says Gary, "I guess that means he's up to traveling."

"He wants me to come there."

Gary emits a chuffing little laugh. "Like hell you are!"

She says, "I haven't decided yet." She walks out of the kitchen.

JUST AS IN her first marriage, Edie usually stays up later than her husband. She'll watch *The Tonight Show* or a movie. Or read one of her mysteries. But finally she'll shut down the house for the night. She makes certain the front and back doors are locked.

In the bathroom she washes her face and brushes her teeth. On her way down the hall, she checks for a strip of light under her daughter's closed door. There's no light tonight.

She opens the door to the bedroom she and her husband share. The lamp beside the bed is burning, and the bed is still made and her husband is nowhere to be seen. Edie steps into the room, and when she does the door closes behind her. Before she can turn around, a hand clamps down hard on the back of her neck and shoves her forward.

"You 'haven't decided'?" Gary Dunn says. "You haven't *decided*?"

Edie can't free herself from his grasp, and she can't do anything to keep him from rushing her toward their bed.

"Here's your decision," Gary says, his words a harsh whisper in her ear. "You aren't going *any*where."

He pushes Edie facedown on the bed, but he keeps his grip on her neck. The bedsprings squeal under their weight. Edie tries to crawl away from him, and she makes a little progress toward the other side of the bed, but then Gary grabs her legs in those big hands of his and pulls her back. She slides easily across the satin bedspread, and as she's hauled backward her nightie rides up, exposing her backside.

Edie begins to thrash. But Gary has planted his knee on her back, right above her tailbone, and he leans forward and places his hand on her spine and runs this hand right up to the back of her neck again.

"You hear me?" he says. "You aren't going *anywhere*." His knee pushes down harder.

"You hear me?" he asks again.

Gary briefly relaxes his grip on her neck, and when he does, Edie is somehow able, with his knee as a pivot point, to rotate herself out from under him. She twists over onto her back and kicks herself free of his weight. When she slides onto the floor, most of the bedspread slides off with her. She is quick to her feet and she starts to run toward the door.

"Wait, Edie!" Gary says, and his tone has changed utterly, from that of a man filled with rage to a husband who wants only to finish his side of an argument. He reaches out to grab her, and his hand clamps onto her right wrist.

When Edie tries to yank her arm away, he tightens his grip, and in her desperation to be free she slips to the floor.

Both of them hear the *pop* of ligaments breaking loose from bone, and at the sound Gary Dunn lets go and Edie yelps in pain—the first time she has cried out since she entered the room.

FOR NEARLY AN hour, Gary sits fully clothed on the bed with its spread and sheets askew. He is slumped over, a man made weak by waiting and contemplation. Finally something in him resolves and he leaves the room.

He finds his wife sitting in the darkened living room in her favorite easy chair, her legs folded under her, a plastic sandwich bag filled with ice pressed to her swollen right wrist.

She watches him. Her look is wary, but she doesn't flinch as he approaches.

He falls to his knees beside her chair. He presses his forehead to the armrest. "Hey, Edie. I'm sorry. I . . . I'm sorry."

Edie says nothing.

He lifts his gaze to meet his wife's shining, impassive eyes. "It was the thought of you going away," says Gary. "No, not just going away. Going there. You know I have trouble thinking of you and . . . of you having that life before. And that you'd go back to it. Back to him."

She lifts her injured arm and the ice bag off the armrest.

Gary reaches tentatively toward her right wrist. Even in the dark he can see how swollen it is. "God, did I do that? Jesus, I'm sorry."

She pulls her legs in tighter to her body. "It's fine," she says.

"It's not fine. I can see it's not fine. Do you want to go to the ER?"

"It'll be fine," she says, and she looks away from her husband to their daughter standing in the hallway.

"Mom?" Jennifer says. She's wearing the Van Halen T-shirt that belonged to a boyfriend from the previous school year.

"What is it, sweetheart?"

Jennifer hesitates. The sight of her parents in the dark living room and in this arrangement obviously confuses her. Has she intruded on a quarrel? Or something sexual? Her mother's in her nightie, yet her father is fully clothed and on his knees. Is this some kind of family crisis? But in the next moment, her adolescence reasserts itself and she says, "I don't feel good."

Edie pushes the ice bag between the chair's cushion and one arm. Then Edie rises, careful not to touch her husband in the process.

"How don't you feel good, honey?" Edie asks.

"I think maybe I have a fever."

Edie turns back to her husband, who is still crouched beside the chair. "Go back to bed," she tells him. "I'll be in soon."

"Are you sick to your stomach?" Edie asks Jennifer.

"Not really."

Although Jennifer is at least two inches taller than Edie and has a woman's body, she allows her mother to lead her like a child.

Gary Dunn follows them down the hall, but when they come to Jennifer's room, he keeps walking. Edie and Jennifer enter, and Edie closes the door behind them.

Clothes, cassettes, and magazines are scattered about. Posters of musicians leer from the walls, and a tennis racket leans in a corner. On the bed a black-and-white cat wakes up and looks suspiciously, with its eyes narrowed, at Edie and Jennifer.

"Scoot over, Mickey," Edie says and pushes the cat aside. The cat meows in protest but moves toward the foot of the bed. Jennifer lies down in the vacated space.

"I think," Edie says to her daughter, "you just got too much sun today." She pulls the sheet over Jennifer, then bends down and presses her lips to her forehead. "No fever," says Edie. "Cool as a cucumber."

"Is something wrong?" Jennifer asks. "You and Dad . . . Was it about that phone call?"

"You try to get to sleep," says Edie. "You have an early day tomorrow."

"I told you. I might not go. Alison said you can try out even if you don't go to cheerleading camp. It doesn't really help you that much."

"You might feel differently in the morning."

Jennifer regards her mother with eyes as narrowed as the cat's. "And nothing's wrong?"

"Nothing's wrong."

"You wouldn't tell me even if there was."

"Go to sleep," Edie says.

She walks back to the living room, to her easy chair and the bag of ice melting between the cushions. From that station she can watch the hallway and with eyes adjusted to the dark see her husband, should he come searching for her—or see her daughter, should her temperature rise.

Eventually Edie dozes off but she sleeps fitfully, waking up at the sound of the Ellisons' dog barking at who knows what and later at the song of birds that detect light in the eastern sky before any human eye is able to. She keeps her eyes closed when her husband comes into the living room to check on her. He makes no effort to wake her before he leaves the house.

But once the door clicks shut behind him, she quickly gets up from her chair.

AN HOUR LATER Edie, showered and dressed, walks into her daughter's room, pulling a large suitcase behind her. "Up," she says to Jennifer. "Up-up-up!"

Jennifer rolls over sleepily. "Mom! I told you. I'm not going."

"This is not about cheerleading camp," Edie says and gestures to the suitcase. "We're taking a trip. Get up and pack as much of your stuff in here as you can. Pack for cold weather too. If there's something you want to take and it doesn't fit in the suitcase, stuff it in your backpack."

Jennifer asks, "What are you talking about? I'm not going—"

"And bring your pillow. I already have your sleeping bag in the car."

"Mom!"

"If there's something you absolutely have to take and you don't have room, let me know. Maybe I can fit it in my suitcase."

"Mom, Mom—wait. Just *wait*."

Edie sits down on the edge of Jennifer's bed. "No, *wait* is just what we can't do. We have to go. You pack and get dressed as quick as you can."

Jennifer edges away from her mother. "I'm not going anywhere. What's the matter with you?"

Edie stands and throws back the sheet covering her daughter. "Did you hear me? Get up, God damn it—right *now*!"

"Okay, okay," Jennifer says. "What about Dad?"

"We have to be gone before he comes home for lunch."

Jennifer is standing beside her bed now. "I don't get it—Dad doesn't know?"

Edie pulls the sheet back over the mattress and tries, using her injured arm as little as possible, to make her daughter's bed.

"What happened to your arm?"

"Go take your shower," Edie says.

"Did *Dad* do that?"

"And I'll pack for you."

"I can do it." Jennifer jerks the bedspread from her mother's hand. "And I can make the bed."

"You can. But you won't. Now *go*."

JENNIFER HAS A full-length mirror in her room, the only one in the house, and Edie positions herself with her back to it. She takes off her skirt and hikes up her T-shirt. She twists her neck, trying to see her reflection in the mirror. Yes, there it is. The empurpled imprint of a knee at the base of her spine. There it is.

JENNIFER'S SUITCASE IS already packed in the Rabbit under a sleeping bag, pillows, and a cardboard box filled with photo albums and family documents. But Jennifer pulls out the suitcase and opens it.

"My God, Mom! My down jacket? And sweaters? What's going on? How long do you think we'll be gone?"

"I don't know."

"And a dress? What do I need a dress for? And *these* jeans? I don't even wear these." She begins to pull garments out of the suitcase, but her mother stops her and stuffs the clothing back inside.

"That's enough," Edie says. "This will have to do."

Jennifer backs away from the car and out of the garage. She's halfway down the driveway before her mother stops her.

"Get in the car, Jennifer. Right now."

"Not until you tell me where we're going."

"Gladstone. All right? Now get in."

Her hair is still wet from her shower, and Jennifer shakes her head no so strenuously that it swings around her. "I'm not going," she says. "You're trying . . . you're trying to take me away . . . from *everything*."

Her tears begin to fall now, and her cheeks blotch through the tan that she has worked so hard for.

Edie approaches her daughter slowly, as if she is a half-wild creature that might bolt at any moment.

"I need you with me, honey. Please? Can't you understand? I have to go but I have to have you with me too." She puts her arms around her daughter, and together they move toward the car.

Jennifer stiffens and pulls back. "Mickey! I can't leave Mickey!"

"Honey, we don't have room," Edie says. The car's rear seat has been folded down, and the space is filled with suitcases, pillows, jackets, boxes—all arranged in an unbalanced fashion as befits packing done by someone with only one good arm.

"Please, Mom."

"Mickey'll be okay."

"He won't. He *won't*. Dad doesn't know how to take care of him. He'll leave a door open and Mickey will run away."

Edie sighs. "All right. Go get him. And his litter box."

"And his bowls?"

"And his bowls. And the cat food. And his leash."

"He hates that."

"I don't care. Bring it."

Jennifer runs back into the house.

Edie lowers her injured arm onto the car roof and then rests her head against it. She doesn't look like a woman about to begin a trip. She looks like someone who has already spent a long day staring at the highway.

THEY LEAVE GRANITE Valley, a small city nestled between two mountain ranges, on Highway 91. In the first mile or two out of town, the road is as straight as a chalk line and as flat as a griddle top. Just past the turnoff for the Prairie Meadow Mobile Home Park, the road begins to rise, and then it's a gradual two-thousand-foot climb before reaching Dutchman's Bend. There the highway will begin to wind its way through the Spindle Mountains. Just before reaching the bend, Jennifer turns around in her seat. She lifts Mickey—he's been squatting on the floor at her feet—and tells the cat to look back on the city they've left behind.

The heat wave has broken, and in place of the endless blue that has hung over the valley for the past week is a sky mottled with high clouds sailing in on the strength of a northwest wind. As the clouds briefly block the sun, everything spread out across the valley floor— the houses and businesses, the streets, cars, parks, and treetops, the wide course of the Song River—blinks in and out of shadow, which means that for a moment any bright surface, glass and chrome, polished steel and rippling water, glitters as if it's sending signals up to the heights. Dark pines climb the mountainside until they run out of warmth and moisture and oxygen—and then they give way to rock. Towering above the town across the valley stand the snow-streaked peaks of the Isabelle Mountains, nine thousand feet at their highest.

This view of Granite Valley is enough to elicit a gasp from any traveler, all the more so from someone who's looking back on a town that's been the only home she's ever known. Jennifer swipes away her tears. "Say good-bye, Mickey," she says.

FOR THE FIRST two hours of the trip, Edie has to keep two hands on the wheel as they negotiate the blind sharp curves, the engine-laboring steep grades, and the brakes-burning descents that finally, finally lead to easier traveling.

Just east of Missoula, Edie pulls into a gas station, as much to rest her throbbing right wrist as to refill the tank. She climbs out of the car and heads for the pump.

When Jennifer sees her mother cradling her injured arm, she climbs out of the Rabbit too. "Mom, are you sure it's not broken?" she asks. "It looks really bad."

"It'll be all right."

"Maybe we should find a hospital or a clinic, and you can have it
x-rayed."

"It already feels better than it did this morning. You don't have
to worry."

"At least let me drive for a while," says Jennifer.

"We'll see. Maybe once we get past Bozeman."

"Here," Jennifer says, taking the nozzle from her mother's left
hand. "I'll do that."

Later, when Edie is in the restroom, and Jennifer is cleaning the
Rabbit's windshield, a young man comes out of the station to watch
Jennifer squeegee the windows. He's grease-stained up to his elbows
and he's not wearing a shirt, revealing his hard, stringy muscles.
When Jennifer sees him she drops the squeegee in the bucket with
its dirty gray water. She glares at him and then gives him the finger.

Edie exits the station in time to see her daughter and her gesture.
"Get in the car, Jennifer. Right now."

Jennifer obeys, and as they are speeding down the highway once
again, Edie says, "Do you know how angry that makes men? Do you?"

"I don't care."

"You'll care if—just don't do it."

"You know what we call that, Mom? Excuse me, but that's eye
fucking."

"I don't care what you call it. Don't do that."

"We're supposed to just let them stare?"

The highway is mostly empty ahead of and behind them, but Edie
looks frequently in her side and rearview mirrors. Jennifer scoops
up Mickey into her lap from his perch at her feet.

Jennifer notices her mother's vigilance. "Oh for God's sake, Mom.
Do you think he'd come after us just because I flipped him off?"

The landscape has changed. The distant mountains look less like
eruptions of cold stone and more like great gray beasts lounging
under the sun, their patches of black pine the coats they're shedding
from a previous season. The road is tamer too, and Edie is able to rest
her swollen discolored wrist on her lap and drive with one hand on
the wheel.

After miles of this silent, almost leisurely traveling, Jennifer suddenly laughs and says, "God, how stupid can I get! It's not some gas station guy you're worrying about—it's Dad! It's Dad you think will be coming after us!"

Edie says nothing.

"Did you even tell him where we're going?"

"He'll know," replies Edie.

"So you didn't tell him?"

"He'll figure it out."

Jennifer shakes her head in bewilderment. Then she says, "Well, you can stop looking for him. He's got a game tonight. He's not going to miss that."

"Who are they playing?"

"Pioneer Bank. But it doesn't matter. He wouldn't miss a game no matter what." Jennifer closes her eyes and lets her head fall back against the front passenger seat. "You told me where we're going. But you still haven't told me why."

"Gladstone is my hometown."

"Yeah, Mom. I know. But *why* are we going there? You have to tell me."

Edie sighs. "Someone I used to know is sick."

Jennifer yawns. "You can just say, you know. You got me in the car. It's not like I'm going to jump out or anything. Who is it, Mom? Come on."

"My ex-husband."

Jennifer's eyes open and she jerks upright. "Holy shit! No wonder Dad's pissed!"

"Okay, that's enough. Watch your language."

The cat slides from Jennifer's lap to the floor, scratching the girl's bare leg in the process. "Ouch! God damn it, Mickey!"

"I said that's enough," Edie admonishes her daughter.

"I'm going to meet him? The man from my mom's other life? Wow!"

"It's all one life, Jen. You need to know that."

"Has Dad ever met him?"

"No."

Jennifer reaches an open hand down toward Mickey to make amends. The cat sniffs the hand warily. Jennifer says, "But you love Dad . . . right?"

Edie points toward the cat. "Keep him over on your side. I can't have him getting under my feet while I'm driving."

"Mom?"

After a long moment Edie says, "Your father and I have been together longer than . . . longer than Dean and I were. And your father and I have you."

"*Dean?* That's his name? God, I didn't even know his name. Dean what?"

"Linderman."

"Maybe I knew that," Jennifer says. "Edie Linderman. Yeah, I think I knew that. Mrs. Linderman."

"Okay, Jen."

The cat leaps back up onto Jennifer's lap. "Is that who called last night?" Jennifer asks. "Dean Linderman?" As she says the name she taps out its rhythm on the dashboard. And because she must like not only the drum beat of the syllables but also the feel of the vowels and consonants in her mouth, she says it once again: "*Dean Linderman.*"

"His brother," Edie says. "Dean would never ask me to come. Roy called. His twin brother."

"Yeah? Are they identical?"

"They're fraternal twins."

"So you could tell them apart?" Jennifer asks.

"That's what *fraternal* means."

"You know the Sager twins, don't you?"

"They're in your class, aren't they?"

"A year younger," Jennifer says. "This guy I know has been going with Vicky Sager and one night—he was kind of drunk—he said, 'I think it's Vicky I'm in love with. But I'm not always sure. Because sometimes I can't tell Vicky and Sandy apart.' That's not exactly how he said it. But that's what he meant."

"It sounds like he has a real dilemma."

"But you could tell them apart, huh?"

"Always."

Edie has the Rabbit doing eighty, fast enough that they come up quickly on an old pickup pulling a horse trailer, the horse's blond tail hanging over the back gate and swaying with the wind and the motion of the truck and trailer. Edie pulls out to pass, and as they go by they can see that the driver is an old man clinging to the steering wheel as if it's the only thing keeping him from collapse.

"This Dean," Jennifer says. "He's pretty sick?"

"Very sick, his brother says."

"I don't do that great around sick people."

Edie says, "You were good with Grandma."

"That was Grandma."

They're on a stretch of highway now that makes few demands of drivers other than that they stay awake. They've left the high country far behind and entered the treeless, scrubby prairie. Any low hill they climb affords a view so far into the distance it seems as though reaching any destination is now possible. Yet after an hour of unvarying miles, nothing seems closer. To drive this road is to feel that humans are meant to travel yet never arrive.

Jennifer turns and folds her body into the narrow passenger seat. Edie too is beginning to tire. She opens her window a couple inches. The fresh air isn't particularly invigorating, but the whistle of wind immediately rouses the cat from his station at Jennifer's feet. He leaps onto Edie's lap, determined to get his nose into that two-inch gap in the open window where the scent of sage is blowing into the car.

"Get down, Mickey." Edie tries to push him away, but he keeps stretching toward the window. "God damn it—"

Her curse startles Jennifer and she sits up. "What?"

Edie cranks her window back up, and it closes with a gasp and then silence. "Get your cat, Jen."

"Can I drive now?"

"Can you stay awake?"

Edie slows and then pulls the Rabbit off the highway, two of its wheels sinking into the soft dirt off the pavement. "Don't try to pass," she tells her daughter, "unless you're sure."

The two of them climb out, careful to make sure that Mickey doesn't escape, and walk around the car to exchange seats. The wind buffets them as if it's trying to push intruders out of its territory.

"Jesus," Edie says, once she's back in the car and the door is closed behind her. "Hang onto the wheel."

Jennifer pulls her fingers through her hair. She adjusts the seat to accommodate her longer legs. She turns the radio dial.

"You won't find much out here," says Edie, referring to the music options.

"Just so it isn't more of that country shit."

"I don't really like to hear that, Jen. Not from you."

Her daughter laughs. "Okay. We'll look for *more* of that country shit."

Edie gives up and closes her eyes.

The station Jennifer settles on is more static than music, and she turns the volume down until the announcer's voice is barely audible.

"Why did you and Dean Linderman get divorced?"

"Oh, you know," Edie says, her eyes still closed. "The usual reason. We just went in different directions."

"Did he cheat on you?"

"Dean? No. No, he didn't."

"Are you sure?"

"I'm sure."

"If Patrick was sick," Jennifer says, "I wouldn't go visit him. If he was dying on our front lawn, I wouldn't set foot outside."

"Wouldn't you?"

"Or like Helen said, 'I wouldn't piss on him if he was on fire.'"

"Helen certainly has a way with words," says Edie. "You never did tell me what happened with you and Patrick."

The car speeds up, and Edie leans across to check the speedometer.

"Keep it under seventy, Jen."

"We kind of have the highway to ourselves."

"Just hold it down."

"Remember when you made me go to that thing of Dad's in Missoula?"

"*Made you?*" says Edie. "I thought you might like to be there when your father received his award."

"There was a big party that night at Dave Holland's. Patrick went, and he and Monica Lynch were making out in Dave's parents' bedroom. And that's just what he'd admit to. Who knows what else they did."

"I'm sorry, Jen. I wish you would have said something before."

"Monica *Lynch*, Mom. She's a total slut."

"Are you sure you know all the facts?"

"He didn't deny anything."

"I just mean . . . Things aren't always what they seem."

"Jesus, Mom! Are you *defending* him?"

"No, no. Not at all. But Patrick always seemed—"

"'So if that's what you like,' I said to him, 'I hope the two of you are very happy together.'"

"And are they?" Edie asks tentatively. "Together?"

"He just wanted to see how much he could get, and when I wouldn't put out he went somewhere else."

A road sign, blinking with bullet and buckshot holes, tells them that Locklin, Montana, is twelve miles away. "Can we stop there," Jennifer says, "and get something to eat? I'm starving."

"I brought a few snacks," Edie says and turns to the back seat and a grocery bag on the floor behind the driver's seat. "I have crackers. Carrots. Apples. What would you like?"

"Did you bring any pop?"

"No."

"So we don't have anything to drink?"

"Fine," Edie says. "But let's try to find a drive-up so we're not stopped long."

Locklin is a mile from the highway. Its few streets are unpaved, and dust has not only settled over every building and vehicle but also swirls in the air, a scrim to view the town through. Not that there's much to look at. A Conoco station. Two bars—Jerry's and the Red Hat. A general store selling groceries and renting videos. A laundromat. A few trailers up on cement blocks and a few houses crouched under a stand of cottonwoods. No stop signs and no traffic lights. And no eatery, drive-up or otherwise.

As Jennifer drives slowly down the street that the county highway has turned into, her mother says, "Just turn around. We can find someplace else to stop."

"I'm really thirsty," Jennifer says. "And I *really* have to pee."

Edie says, "Go back to the gas station then. We'll get something there."

Jennifer pulls into the side lot of the gas station. Edie hands her daughter a ten-dollar bill.

"And don't dawdle."

"*Dawdle?* God, Mom, you're turning into Grandma Dunn."

"Do you think Mickey needs to get out?"

"Probably."

"I'll walk him around while you go in. And please—don't give anyone the finger."

On her way into the gas station Jennifer pivots and, walking backward and holding her hand close to her chest, smiles and raises her middle finger to her mother.

Edie snaps the leash on Mickey's collar. "Let's go, big guy." She lifts the cat out of the car and carries him toward the weedy edge of the lot. She sets him down in the dust and gravel. "Okay," she says. "Do your thing."

Nothing in the surrounding landscape suggests that rain has fallen here in days, possibly weeks, yet the lot is dotted with small pools of water. Immediately Mickey strains at the leash, trying to get to one of those puddles.

A man walks up behind Edie and says, "Careful, Miss. You don't want her drinking out of them puddles. That there is poison to cats."

Edie turns around. A long-haired middle-aged man is approaching. He's tall and his Allman Brothers T-shirt has the sleeves cut off to reveal his weightlifter's musculature. He stops advancing when

Edie faces him, but he's the kind of man who can't conceal the intent of his gaze. *Eye fucker.*

"But it won't do humans no harm," he says. His smile is wide and his dimples deep.

She scoops Mickey up and starts back toward the car.

"Hey," the man says, "she didn't do her business."

His boots crunching on the gravel tell Edie that he's following her. "I got cats myself," he says. "They generally don't like to do their business out in the open."

Edie keeps moving toward the Volkswagen.

He hurries alongside her. "Let me carry her for you."

"It's a he," Edie says and winces at her own remark.

He steps ahead of Edie to open the car door for her.

Edie sets Mickey inside on the floor and climbs in after him. She keeps her hold on the leash, but the cat shows no inclination to leave the car. Edie shuts the door, but her window is still open.

"Holy shit," he says. "That's some bad-looking wrist you got there."

"It's nothing."

"The hell. That ain't nothing. I seen a lot of nothing in my time, and that there ain't nothing like nothing."

Jennifer is walking out of the gas station, her arms laden with bags of potato chips, cans of Coke, and candy bars, and when she sees the man standing at the car, she starts to run toward it.

The man steps away from the car door in a move that seems almost courtly. "Who do we have here?" He bends down and looks at Edie and then back at Jennifer. "You two sisters?"

"Come on, Jen," Edie says.

Jennifer walks around to the driver's side and opens the door. "Here, Mom," she says and hands her purchases in to her mother.

"Couple glamour girls is what we got here," he says. "You two in the movies? Or TV maybe?"

Jennifer climbs in behind the wheel and puts the key in the ignition.

"Are you maybe in that show about the cops?" he asks. "The lady cops?"

"We have to go," Edie says and rolls up the window. "Start the car, Jen."

Jennifer turns the key and the engine grumbles like a man trying to gather his thoughts, but the car doesn't start. She tries again but the engine won't turn over.

The man signals for one of them to roll down a window.

Edie says, "Press the gas pedal all the way to the floor and hold it there for a few seconds. Don't pump it."

Now he has walked to the front of the car. "Pop the hood!" he shouts. "Let me take a look."

"That'll flood it," Jennifer says.

"Do it," says Edie. "Right to the floor."

Jennifer obeys her mother.

"Try it now."

The engine coughs again, but then it catches and roars to life. The man takes a step back but he's still standing in front of the car.

"Go," Edie commands her daughter.

"Mom, he's right *there*—" Jennifer puts the Volkswagen in gear but keeps her foot on the brake.

"*Go*. He'll move."

Move he does, stepping to the side and making a passable imitation of a matador waving his cape as the car accelerates within two feet of him on its way out.

Not until all of Locklin will fit in the rearview mirror does either Jennifer or her mother speak.

"God, Mom. What was that all about? Who was he?"

"I'm sorry," says Edie. "I should have been the one driving."

"So *you* could run him over?"

"That's right," Edie says, still turned in her seat and watching the highway behind them. "So I could do it."

THE ODORS OF gasoline, combustion, and sun-heated plastic now become as familiar as the smells of home. Edie and Jennifer have their food and drink—open bags of potato chips and sweating cans of icy soda in their hands. The landscape repeats itself like the songs on the radio.

And then here it comes. Stevie Wonder. "I just called to say . . ."

A mile passes before Edie notices Jennifer wiping at the tears that have already streaked a trail down her cheeks.

"Jen? What is it? What's wrong?"

She sniffs hard and replies, "Nothing."

"Come on, honey. Tell me."

Now it's an actual sob Jennifer must swallow. "That song. It was kind of Patrick's and my song. I know it's stupid but when I hear it . . ."

"It's not stupid. It's not stupid at all. But I thought . . . Do you want to pull over?"

Jennifer waves her hand in front of her face. "It's okay. I'm okay."

"Are you sure? Maybe I should drive awhile."

"Why? Did you see someone you want to run over?"

Edie laughs. But she reaches toward the radio.

"That's okay," Jennifer says. "You can leave it on. It's a good song. And I have to be able to listen to it without blubbering."

"So maybe," Edie says, "it's not over between you and Patrick?"

Jennifer laughs derisively. "Oh, it's over! It's just that . . ."

"Jen. Please pull over."

"Of all the guys he was the one who did it for me, you know? It was like the two of us—oh, *crap*. I don't know. He did it for me, that's all."

"I know, honey. I know. But you have to let me drive now."

Jennifer shakes her head but pulls over and stops the car. Without saying a word, mother and daughter get out and change places.

Jennifer has stopped crying. She's watching her mother closely now, her gaze settling finally on her mother's hands gripping the steering wheel.

"Did Dad do that?" she says abruptly. "To your wrist?" She asks those questions with a cool detachment.

"He reached out for me and I twisted away. He didn't mean to."

"But you're leaving him, right? Over *that*?" Now the detachment in Jennifer's voice has given way to judgment.

"We're going to Gladstone," says Edie. "To see someone who's very sick."

"The way we're packed? You don't plan to go back! *Ever!* Whatever's between you and Dad, it isn't fair to take it out on me! I didn't want to leave at all! You didn't even *ask* me. And now you're trying to take me away for *good*, away from my friends and school . . . and from . . . from . . ."

"Is this about Patrick?"

"He wants us to get back together. That's what he told Helen."

"He cheated on you, Jen."

"Yeah, but—"

"You know I try not to interfere in your life. And I don't give you advice unless you ask for it. Which you never do. But that's a separate issue. If Patrick cheated on you once, he'll do it again. Cheaters cheat."

Jennifer slumps in her seat. She turns away from her mother and leans her head against the window.

Edie keeps her eyes focused on the highway, though she can't help but see her daughter.

After all these hours in the car, the bruise on Edie's backside has begun to throb, its cadence nearly matching that of the car's engine. Or her own heart. Their rhythms are very close.

SOMEWHERE UP THERE is a moon almost full, and Roy Linderman blows a lungful of smoke in its direction and damns the clouds that won't get out of the way. The view won't be any better on the other side of his mother's trailer, but he walks around back anyway. Gladstone has grown, yet open prairie still surrounds it on two sides. From the alkali flats that run all the way to the foothills a mile away comes a smell like someone pissed on a hot rock. Roy flicks his cigarette toward the sky and sparks pinwheel off it.

He walks through the front door and into the living room. Every light is on as well as the television. *Cagney & Lacey* is playing, though no one is in the room. He walks down the narrow hallway that leads toward the trailer's two bedrooms. He tilts from side to side as if the trailer were in motion, but this is simply the limp he's had for two decades.

A light is on in one of the bedrooms, its door open a few inches. Through that gap Roy asks softly, "How we doing in there?"

"Sleeping," his mother says and steps out of the bedroom.

Roy remains in the doorway. His brother is propped up on pillows, his eyes closed and his arms at his sides. But his hands are open, and the palms are turned up, as though he had to let go of something to let sleep come. The room is the only one in the trailer with air-conditioning, a clattering unit balanced precariously in the window. Despite the room's chill, Dean is wearing nothing but a pair of gray gym shorts. He's always been thin, but now his arms and legs look like knotted rope. Roy pulls the door closed and backs away.

Before he leaves the trailer he says to his mother, "Call me if anything—"

Without looking away from the television, she waves him on his way with the back of her hand.

ON A QUIET tree-lined street, Carla sits in the dark on a creaking porch swing. She's drinking a glass of wine, and in her white shorts and white polo shirt she looks as if she just stepped off the tennis court. While she's staring off into the night, a car comes fast down the street, and then it slows and the engine growls amiably. The car pulls into the driveway, and the engine shuts down but for another moment the driver leaves the headlights on, and their beams shining on the garage door look like underwater light. Then the lights go dark, the car door opens, and Roy Linderman climbs out. He stands still for a moment and looks up again into the summer sky. Still no moon or stars.

Carla watches Roy as impassively as she might a stranger driving by. When he steps onto the porch, he points at her wineglass and says, "Wine? In this heat?"

"A fine cabernet," she replies and raises the glass to him. "There's half a bottle left in there if you care to join me."

"Maybe a beer," he says, but neither of them makes a move to fetch it. "Are you drunk?" he asks her.

"Quite possibly," she says. "How's your brother this fine evening?"

"About the same." Roy takes a pack of Marlboros from his shirt pocket, shakes loose a cigarette, raises it to his lips, and lights it.

"You didn't smoke in the trailer, did you?"

"Jesus, Carla. Give me a little credit."

"A simple question," she says. "And a simple yes or no would do."

"You are drunk."

"I'll take that as a no," she says. She takes a long swallow from her wineglass. "Jay called. He's bringing the boys back early. So if you have any plans you need to implement before their return, you have until Saturday."

"Plans? Like what plans?"

"How should I know? Fucking on the dining room table maybe. You always seem to have plans and occasionally you share them with me. And maybe this would be one of those occasions."

Roy asks, "Why early?"

"Something about Julie's parents coming for a visit."

Roy turns away and looks toward the street. A mountain ash has been planted out on the berm, a tree that's never been healthy, and on this warm, breathless summer night, the tree drops a few leaves that flutter in the light of the streetlight.

"And," Carla says, "a woman called. She wanted to speak to you."

"About?"

"She didn't deign to share with me the reason for her call. But she quite specifically asked for Mr. Roy Linderman."

"Did she say who it was?"

"No, but then she wouldn't, would she?"

"Hey, Carla. Do we have to do this? I'm really tired tonight."

"Perhaps," Carla says, "the caller was someone interested in buying a car."

"Yeah. I don't know. Could be."

"And to get the best deal, the very *best* fucking deal, she thought she'd call you at home."

"You know what? I'm going to call it a night."

Once again she raises her glass to him. "Sleep well."

MICKEY HAS LEAPED from the bed onto the dresser and from the dresser to the top of the television set. From there he surveys the motel room: the cheap wood paneling, the black-and-white television, the two sagging beds, the mismatched chairs, the wind-up alarm clock, the framed print of ocean waves breaking on the shore—and this in a town about as far from an ocean as it is from anywhere else in the country. But room 106 in the Rimrock Inn is clean, as the smell of Pine-Sol testifies; the proprietor accepts pets; and the rate is probably as cheap as any they're likely to find. Despite its name, the Rimrock Inn is nowhere near any of the sandstone and scoria bluffs that look down on Gladstone. It's in the older center of town and on a street that has as many residences as retail businesses. But Edie had no trouble finding the inn because it's just where it was when she lived in Gladstone. Which is more astonishing—what's still there or what's not?

Light takes its time leaving the summer prairie sky and still lingers on the western horizon in a strip of dark lavender. Moths cluster under the streetlights. The weather forecaster—if she can be heard accurately above the rattle and buzz of the air conditioner—promises that tomorrow will be cooler and the winds calm.

Jennifer is already in bed but shows no interest in sleeping. Mickey curls his paws under his chin and closes his eyes.

Edie is rearranging clothes in one of the suitcases.

"Did you call Dad?" Jennifer asks.

"What do you want to wear tomorrow?" Edie says. "I'll hang something up for you."

"A T-shirt. And I don't care if it's wrinkled." She sits up in bed. "I said, 'Did you call Dad?'"

"I heard you. No, I didn't."

"You said you were going to the office to use the phone. So who'd you call?"

"Do you want me to take out a sweatshirt for you?"

"Who did you call?"

"I think I'll wear jeans," says Edie. "Since it's supposed to be cooler . . . You're sure you won't need a sweatshirt?"

Jennifer kicks her way free of the sheet and bedspread. She grabs hold of her mother's shoulders and shakes her the way a parent might shake a child.

"Mom, *Mom*! Why won't you talk to me? I ask you questions and it's like you don't even *hear* me."

For the second time in as many days, Edie Dunn is trapped in the desperate grasp of one of her own family members. She waits until Jennifer seems to be done. Then Edie takes a step back.

"I'm sorry, Jen. I should have said something. I tried to call Mr. Linderman."

"Now it's *Mister* Linderman? You already told me—"

"His brother," Edie says. "Roy. I wanted to let him know we're in town. He wasn't home. I suppose I could have talked to his wife. She and I used to be friends. But I doubt she'd remember me."

"She does I bet," says Jennifer. "So now what?"

Edie shrugs. "I'll call again in the morning."

"Why don't you just go see him? Dean, I mean. That's what you came for."

"Well, for one thing, I don't know where he is."

"Maybe he's in the hospital," Jennifer suggests. "After you see him can we go home?"

"I can't say right now."

"You're doing it again."

Edie sighs and sits down on the edge of the bed. "I need some time away from your father."

"I knew it!" Jennifer says. "I knew it! You and Dad are getting a divorce, and *I'm* the one who has to leave home! That's not fair!"

Jennifer walks around to the side of the bed opposite her mother and sits down. "I could go home," Jennifer suggests, "and you could stay here."

"We'll talk about it, Jen. But not tonight. Let's wait and see how Dean's doing."

"I could take the bus or something."

Edie's shoulders slump a little.

"Are you even thinking about Dad? He's probably so worried. He doesn't know where we are."

"He'll figure it out," says Edie.

"Dad needs someone there. And I don't want to live in this shitty motel."

"Your father will be fine."

AS THEY LIE in their beds in the dark, Edie says, "Jen? I'm sorry if what I said about Patrick hurt you."

Jennifer doesn't say anything.

"I don't want to see you hurt. Again. And you said yourself that he . . . Well. You make your own choices, Jen. But I want you to be loved properly."

Jennifer barks out a laugh and sits up. "Oh God, Mom. 'Loved properly?'" This she says in a poor imitation of a British accent. "What the hell does that even mean? Properly!"

"It means—"

"Didn't Dad love you properly?"

"All right, Jen."

"That's what you want. What about what I want? Me and Patrick . . . that's about what we want."

A sound enters the room, faint but distinct, and Edie and Jennifer instantly fall silent and listen. The sound could be a key scraping at the wrong lock. Or a window screen being cut. But an instant later, its source becomes obvious. Mickey is in the bathroom, scratching in his litter box.

Neither mother nor daughter says another word.

ROY LINDERMAN IS in his bathrobe, roaming the edges of his back lawn, his bare feet wet with morning dew, a coffee cup in one hand, a cigarette in the other.

Then, from the back door, his wife calls out to him: "Hey! You have a phone call!"

Roy tosses the remainder of his coffee on the peonies and walks toward the house.

When he enters the kitchen his wife hands over the phone and leaves the room.

"Hello," he says.

"Roy? It's me. Edie."

"Edie? Jesus. Edie . . ."

At the sound of that name Carla comes back into the room.

"I'm in town. We're at the Rimrock Inn. My daughter is here with me."

Carla is mouthing something to her husband—"What does she want?" perhaps—but Roy just shakes his head at her.

"Well, my God, Edie. My God."

"I was hoping I could see Dean."

"Dean. Hell yes, you should see him. He won't believe this."

"I don't know where to find him."

"He's at Mom's. God, he's going to be so happy to see you."

"Can I just—I mean, is he okay with visitors? Is there a time—"

"Hey, I'll pick you up. I'll take you over there. And I'll check with Mom first to see how he's doing today."

"All right."

"God *damn*. It is you. How about I pick you up in an hour?"

"We're in 106," she says. "I'll wait for you outside."

"Hold on a second. Will I recognize you? Have you changed?"

"Don't worry. I'll know you."

Roy hangs up the phone. "Is that who called last night?" he asks his wife.

"Could be," she replies. "As I said, the caller did not identify herself. And she didn't this time either. To me."

"She's here with her daughter."

"Just passing through?"

"She's here to see Dean."

"She knows about his condition?"

"Yeah," Roy says. "She knows."

"How? How does she know?"

"Dean wants to see her before . . . He wants to see her one more time."

Carla Linderman is dressed for a day at the office. White silk blouse tucked into perfectly creased navy blue slacks that show off her long legs and the ass that she's worked so hard to keep high and tight. Her streaked blond hair cut to shoulder length and perfectly coiffed. A simple gold chain around her throat and a gold cuff around her wrist.

"Well," she says, snatching up her briefcase and the red blazer that all the agents in the real estate company wear, "Dean will get his wish. I hope the reunion is a happy one." She heads toward the door leading to the garage. "Or as happy as it can be under the circumstances."

Then Carla stops. "Wait. Did Dean call her?"

"I called her."

"Oh my goodness," Carla says, smiling her practiced but unconvincing smile. "Oh my fucking goodness. This does change things." She walks back into the kitchen and sets her briefcase and blazer down.

"All right," she says, gripping the top rail of a chair. "Let me see if I've got this straight. You called Edie. How you came to have her number is a fucking mystery we'll leave for another time—"

"I asked—"

Carla raises a halting hand. "You call your brother's ex-wife and tell her—what? That Dean's dying? But that he'll die a happy man if he can see her just one more time? And did Dean *ever* bring up her name? Or was this totally your idea? Did you figure, well, as long as Dean has to die anyway why not see if you can't get something good out of the deal? And what could be better . . . what could be fucking *better* than to have Edie Pritchard back in town?"

"That's not fair, Carla."

"Fair? Do you really want to talk about what's *fair*?"

"Carla . . ." Roy walks toward her and puts out his arms. "Come on."

"*Don't.*"

Roy's arms hover in the air between them. "You have to believe me, Carla."

At this she smiles and says, "That's the one thing I *don't* have to do."

"That's right, Carla. You don't have to do anything you don't want to do. Now, I have to get going."

"Where are you picking her up?"

"She's staying at the Rimrock Inn. With her daughter."

"The Rimrock Inn," she says and shakes her head. She lifts her blazer from the chair and puts it on. The garment's incongruously wide shoulders make her look as though she's impersonating a much stronger woman. "How long are they staying?"

"I have no idea."

"Well, I can't imagine they're comfortable in the Rimrock." Carla snatches up her briefcase again. "Tell Edie that she and her daughter are welcome to stay here."

"That's very generous—"

"Fuck you," she says on her way out the door.

EDIE IS STANDING in front of Room 106, and at the sound of Roy's tires on the parking lot gravel she turns in his direction.

Roy stops the car and reaches across to open the passenger door. He smiles widely and says, "Hop in, Edie. Damn, it's good to see you!"

"How have you been, Roy?"

"You know me. Same old, same old."

"I hear that expression all the time," Edie says, "and I never know what it means."

"Where's your daughter? She's not joining us?"

"I told her she could sleep in. She's a teenager, Roy. You remember what that was like."

"I sure do."

"So I don't want to be gone too long this morning."

Roy has been looking everywhere but at Edie's face. He looks at her feet in their leather sandals. At the purse she's put between them on the seat beside her. At her knees and thighs, bare below the hem of her denim skirt. But finally, like a man looking up at a break in the clouds, he lifts his gaze. That face. Yes. The large green eyes. The cheekbones. The dimpled smile. The lips, perfect in their curve but chapped in this morning's dry Montana air.

"God damn, Edie. Here you are. Here you are and it's starting all over again. Except I don't believe it ever stopped."

"Don't, Roy. Please."

"I'm happy to see you. That's all. Man, twenty years just fell away like they were nothing."

Edie points vaguely toward the street. "Just go."

But Roy's searching examination is not over. "What happened to your wrist?"

"Oh, I slipped on a throw rug. And I landed wrong."

"There's a right way to land?" He puts the car in gear and drives slowly away.

Edie is looking back at the motel when she says, "Sometimes I have to remind myself it wasn't you I was married to."

"Whoa! I'll take that as a compliment."

"Don't. It just turned out I couldn't tell the two of you apart as easily as I thought I could."

"You'll see a hell of a difference now. And back then I never would have let you get away."

She continues to stare out the window. "You couldn't have stopped me," she says.

"Well, I would have made a hell of a sales pitch," Roy says. "Wait—I should have said this right away. Carla says you can stay with us. We've got plenty of room. Maybe a little less when her boys come back. But you and your daughter can have the whole basement. We've got a bedroom down there and a full bath. Wet bar. Cable TV. And I'd have what I've always wanted—you sleeping under my roof. I'm kidding, I'm kidding. You'd have all the privacy you could ask for. You and your daughter."

"Thank you, Roy. That's very kind of you. But I already paid for another night."

"So? You want to spend another night in that dump just because you paid for it?"

"It's not a dump, not at all, it's—"

"Don't bother, Edie. Circumstances have forced me to spend a few nights in the Rimrock. I know what it is."

"We have our cat with us. Mickey. Our big old Tom."

"Hell, that's not a problem."

"Thank you. But you have to let me pay you something."

He waves away her offer. "No need. Carla and I are doing pretty well. She's the best-selling real estate agent in eastern Montana. If you have any ideas about coming back to Gladstone, she's the person you'd want to see."

"Carla . . . selling houses."

"Commercial buildings too. And I'm selling Toyotas." Roy pats the steering wheel of the Celica as if it's a creature whose goodwill must be maintained. "Who'd have thought Montanans would go nuts over a Japanese car? You keep your money in your purse. You'd be our guest. You and your daughter. And Mickey."

"LOOK WHO'S HERE," says Mrs. Linderman. "I never thought I'd see you darken my door again."

"Hello, Mildred," Edie says as she steps inside the trailer. "It's good to see you."

The two women spend a few seconds assessing what the years have done to the other. Edie has gained a few pounds, but they've distributed themselves evenly and she still has that figure that can induce gasps when it's displayed just so. Mildred Linderman is exhausted and whittled down by the decades, but she still has her height—close to six feet—and those big bones.

She nods in the direction of the hallway and the bedroom beyond. "He's sleeping."

Roy says, "I'll leave you two to catch up. I have a customer coming in, and I can't afford to take a chance he'll spit the hook."

Edie casts a pleading look in his direction, but he's as good as gone.

Neither woman speaks until the sound of Roy's car dies away. Then Mrs. Linderman points to the couch. "You might as well sit."

Edie sits. She looks around the living room. The console television. The picture on the wall—mustangs in full stampede. The La-Z-Boy recliner, its mauve velour worn smooth in spots. "Not much has changed," she says.

"Unless you count one dead and one dying."

After a moment's hesitation Edie says, "I was sorry to hear about Elmer."

Mildred Linderman flicks a hand in the air. "He was never the same after we sold the ranch. He couldn't get used to town life. Not enough to keep him occupied. So he drank too much. I kept telling him what he was headed for but he wouldn't listen."

"He always seemed so cheerful."

Mildred pokes a loose swirl of hair back into the bun at the nape or her neck. "I might as well get this said," she says. "When you left it took something out of Dean he never got back."

"That was a long time ago," Edie says.

"You get to my age," says Mildred, "the years don't mean like they used to."

"How's Dean doing?"

"Good days and bad. Though if anyone wanted to keep count, they'd probably say more bad than good now."

From somewhere outside comes the sound of children at play, gunplay if the mouth noises—the *kra-chows* and *kra-jings*—are any indication. And just when that battle seems at its height, one gunshot in rapid succession after another, Dean appears in the living room, shirtless and barefoot and clad only in gray gym shorts.

"Jesus Christ! *Edie?* Is that you?"

At the sight of him Edie gives out a little gasp that slides into a moan, as if all his sharp edges of bone—hips, ribs, shoulders—were slicing into her flesh as well as his.

She stands up but doesn't move toward him. "Hi, Dean."

"Jesus. I woke up and I thought I heard your voice, but I knew that couldn't be. I thought maybe I was going nuts."

Dean falls into the recliner. "Christ almighty. *Edie.*" He's short of breath now but manages a question. "What the hell are you doing here?"

"I came to see you."

"Roy . . . did he? Because I'm dying?"

"I wanted to see you again. Can't we leave it at that?"

His head is thrown back. His arms hang over the sides of the chair. "Edie," he says yet again. His eyes cloud over with tears. "I'm not about to kick just yet, you know."

Edie smiles and sits back down. And when she does, Mildred Linderman rises and heads for the trailer's kitchen.

"You see how skinny I am?" says Dean. "It's not the cancer. I took up running a few years back. Like everybody else in the damn country."

"Are you in pain, Dean? How bad is it?"

Before he can answer his mother sticks her head in from the kitchen. "He don't complain," she says. "Not one word."

Dean and Edie both smile, remembering a time when Mildred Linderman was a joke between them.

"I just can't seem to get comfortable," he says. "Can't sleep. Can't stay awake."

"But you have medication? When it gets bad?"

He nods. Then, eagerly changing the subject, he asks, "When did you get in?"

"We got in late last night."

"We?"

"My daughter Jennifer's with me."

"You got a daughter?"

"She's seventeen."

He tries to brighten at this news, but he can't manage it. He has to turn away, and when his head is turned toward the window he says, "Gladstone always looks better when the sun's shining. That's my notion anyway."

Mildred Linderman steps into the kitchen doorway. "We got changes aplenty around here," she says. "There's a Indian family a couple trailers over. And I mean Indian like in India. The country. Nice folks too."

"So you see," Dean says to Edie with a wry smile, "you'd hardly recognize the place."

Edie slides her sandaled foot back and forth on the floor. "And," she says, also smiling, "I believe this carpet is new since I've been here."

"Paid for that," says Mildred, "with Elmer's insurance. His idea. When he was just barely hanging on he told me, 'Mildred, get yourself some new rugs. Something soft underfoot and warm on those winter mornings.'"

Mildred ducks back into the kitchen, but only a second or two later she returns, wiping her hand on a dish towel. "So you got yourself a teenager," she says to Edie. "Good Lord. I first met you when you was about that age." She shakes her head in disbelief. "What the years fashion for us."

In a whisper Dean says, "I'm embarrassed to say I don't know your married name."

"Dunn. *D-u-n-n.*"

"Edie Dunn," Dean says, and his eyes close slowly. "That's easy to remember. Edie Dunn."

JENNIFER WALKS OUT of Unit 106 into the calm August morning. She closes her eyes and lifts her face to the sky. The sunlight dapples her features as it shines through the leaves of a towering cottonwood. She pushes the room key into the back pocket of her shorts and looks up and down the block. After a moment of indecision, Jennifer begins to walk in the direction of the morning sun.

Within a few blocks the neighborhood shows signs of age. The sidewalk crumbles in places and tilts along its cracks. The houses are smaller, closer together, and built of mismatched parts—one side of a house clad in aluminum and another side in unpainted planks, a roof with a sheet of tin nailed to the shingles, plywood in place of window glass. The air smells of motor oil and dead grass. The yards are mostly dirt, and occasionally littered with the things of children's play—trikes and bikes, inflatable swimming pools and beach balls. On the block ahead is a windowless, abandoned building that was once the home, as its sign says, of Lueck's Creamery. Jennifer turns around and walks back.

GRANITE VALLEY TORE down its Carnegie library in 1977 and built in its place a glass-walled building that in the afternoon allows in so much light and heat it's impossible to sit near any of the west windows. On one of the low shelves in the middle of the main floor is a collection of telephone directories from Montana cities and towns. Gary Dunn sifts through the piles until he finds the one he's looking for. He takes it to a desk and opens the white pages of the Gladstone telephone book.

There are three Lindermans—a *D*, an *R*, and an *M*. He takes an index card from his shirt pocket and copies down all three numbers. Then he puts it back in his pocket and drives home.

In the kitchen he picks up the telephone and begins to dial one of the numbers. A recorded voice announces that this number is no longer in service. Gary Dunn hangs up but only for a moment. Then he dials the second number on the card.

A woman's voice says hello.

"I'd like to speak to Edie Dunn, please."

"Jesus! You're calling here for Edie? Is this long distance?"

"Is she there?" asks Gary.

"No, she's not here. God." And Carla Linderman hangs up the phone.

Gary Dunn hangs up on his end as well.

In the voice of a man comfortable listening to his own speech, Gary Dunn says, "You mean she's not there *now*."

JENNIFER HAS JUST entered the parking lot of the Rimrock Inn when she sees the door to their unit standing open and, outside the door, a cart stacked with sheets, towels, and cleaning supplies.

"No!" Jennifer cries and breaks into a run.

She bursts into the room just as a squat older woman is walking into the bathroom with a few white towels draped across her arm.

"Mickey!" Jennifer calls out. "*Mickey!*"

The older woman stops in the bathroom doorway and looks at the girl.

"My cat!" Jennifer says as she frantically scans the room. "You left the door open! Where's my cat?"

The woman stares at Jennifer without comprehension.

"There was a cat," Jennifer says, her words tumbling over each other like pebbles loosed on a mountainside. "A cat, a cat, a black-and-white cat. And he was in this room and the door, if the door was open, he'd go out. Did you see him go out?"

The woman shakes her head no, but it's by no means clear that she has understood.

Jennifer falls to her knees and looks under the bed. She gets up and looks behind the dresser, the chair, the curtains. She pushes past the woman and looks in the bathroom, in the tub, behind the toilet. "My God," she says. "My God, my God. Mickey!"

She runs out the door and half sobs half shouts, "Here Mickey, here Mickey! Please, please, Mickey!"

Once again she drops to her hands and knees, this time to look under their Volkswagen. There's no cat there, but Jennifer crawls over to the only other car in the lot, a rusting Ford Galaxie. Mickey is not under that vehicle either.

Behind the Rimrock is a vacant lot overgrown with weeds, and Jennifer walks around its perimeter, heedless of the way her bare legs are being scratched. As she walks she says again and again in a voice barely above a whisper, "Mickey, Mickey—please, Mickey."

When Jennifer returns to the room, the door is closed, the maid having moved on to another unit. Jennifer steps inside and asks loudly, "Mickey? Are you here?"

The beds are made, the coverlets pulled so tight and smooth that if a cat had jumped on either bed, its paw prints would show. The wastebasket has been emptied. Clean towels hang in the bathroom. The bowls of cat food and fresh water are full.

Jennifer backs out of the room, pulling the door closed as she goes. But she has not even gotten out of the parking lot when she returns. She unlocks the door and leaves it open a few inches, just wide enough for a cat to push its way inside.

ROY PULLS INTO the covered carport, but he makes no move to get out of his car. Inside the trailer are the three people he's loved deeper and longer than any others, yet he remains here, thirty feet away. The Celica's engine throbs insistently. It would be so easy to put the car in reverse and drive away from his town, his job, his marriage, from every duty and obligation in his life. But some hooks can't be shaken.

JENNIFER MAKES HER way slowly down the block where she recently walked. It's a route an animal might follow if it were following its owner's scent. Every few steps she stops and looks carefully into the yards. She calls softly, "Here kitty-kitty-kitty. Here Mickey. Good kitty."

She stops in the middle of a block and turns a slow circle, looking in every direction of the compass. The tears smearing her cheeks are tears of hopelessness.

MRS. LINDERMAN STIFFLY pushes herself up from the sofa. "Excuse me," she says. Dean has fallen asleep in his chair, and Edie has not spoken a word since he closed his eyes. "I hear a car out there."

She steps outside and marches over to the passenger side of the car with its idling engine. She bends down and leans her head through the open window.

She says in a whisper, "You think I don't know what's what? You think I don't know what you been plotting ever since your brother brought her through the door all them years ago? And now you got her here for you, not for him. And you're sitting out here because you got what you wanted and it scares the hell out of you."

Roy Linderman doesn't say anything, but the face he turns to his mother is that of a haunted man.

"Now," his mother says, "instead of sitting out here like a coward, you'll take me for a little ride and we'll let the two of them have their moments alone. And when we come back you'll do what you can to help your brother live out his days in peace. And not one word, not one goddamn word, to him or that woman about what's in that scheming black heart of yours."

Mrs. Linderman opens the car door and climbs awkwardly into the low seat. She slams the door behind her. "Once your brother is dead and buried," she says, "you can do what you want to get your way. But not before. You hear me? Now drive. And I don't give a good goddamn where."

DEAN LINDERMAN HAS slept through his mother's departure, but when Edie rises to investigate the sound of a car driving away his eyes open.

"Edie?"

She turns toward his voice. "I think your mother went somewhere with Roy."

A shudder starts at his head, shakes his shoulders and torso, and runs right down to his feet. "I get so damn cold," he says. "My thermostat must be screwed up or something."

"Can I get you a blanket?"

"I better get back in bed." He tries to sit upright in the recliner, but his weight doesn't seem sufficient to move the lower part of the chair back to the floor. Then he tries to climb out over one side of the chair.

Edie rushes over to him. "Dean, wait. Let me—"

His strength gives out, and he collapses back into the chair.

"Here," Edie says, extending her hands, "I'll help you."

Dean reaches out but then stops and withdraws his hands. "What happened, Edie?"

The question seems to confuse her, and she steps back uncertainly, as if she's suddenly been called upon to explain everything the years can do—death, divorce, cancer, love, the death of love, departures, returns . . .

"Your wrist," Dean says.

"It's nothing," Edie says.

"What happened?" he asks.

"I slipped. I fell. You remember how clumsy I was."

"No," says Dean. "No, I don't remember that."

She smiles and lifts her shoulders helplessly.

Is it that they were once in love and lovers are forever attuned to the other's lies or that Dean is dying and he guesses at truths that others must let pass? He asks her, "Did your husband do that to you?"

Because he's dying does she decide it's all right to nod?

"Oh, Edie, Edie."

Now he's able to sit up in the recliner and get his feet on the floor. He reaches out for her again, and Edie steps inside his outstretched arm.

GARY DUNN CARRIES in his wallet two photographs, one of his wife and one of his daughter. The picture of Edie is from five years ago at the Granite Valley Merchants' Association Christmas Ball. The association hired a professional photographer for the evening to take pictures of couples upon their arrival. Gary asked for a second photograph, this one of Edie alone. In that holiday photograph Edie is unsmiling, and she looks uncomfortable in the clinging, low-cut green-velvet dress that Gary purchased for her.

The photograph of Jennifer was taken two years ago for her school yearbook, before her prettiness overcame her adolescent awkwardness—the too-large nose, the overly made-up unfocused eyes, the hairstyle she hadn't yet learned to make her own, the expression that's closer to grimace than grin.

But at every stop Gary makes on his drive from Granite Valley to Gladstone, he makes it a point to take out the photos and ask gas station attendants and waitresses if they've seen these pretty women.

"They went on ahead of me," Gary explains at the Mobil station in Butler, Montana. "We're on the family vacation. I'm wondering how far out in front they are."

"Uh-huh," says the young man who takes Gary's money.

"Have you seen them?" Gary asks. "They'd have come through yesterday or earlier today."

"Nope."

At the Steel Wheel Truck Stop and Diner just outside Duncan, Gary shows the photos to the waitress, a gray-faced woman as skinny as the pencil tucked behind her ear. She barely glances at the photos before saying, "Haven't seen 'em."

But a pair of highway construction workers sitting only one stool away perk up at the sight of the photos. The one closest to Gary, an older man tanned as dark as saddle leather, says, "Let me see those."

Gary doesn't hand over the pictures, but he holds them both out for inspection.

The younger worker, who wears a dirt- and oil-stained Seattle Mariners cap, reaches out and puts his index finger right on the image of Edie as if he were probing ripe fruit. "This the wife?" he asks.

"God damn," the older man says. He looks up at Gary. "She's out on the road ahead of you?"

Gary says, "That's right."

"If I was you," the older man says, "I'd keep her on a shorter rope."

Gary puts both photographs back in his shirt pocket and signals for the waitress to bring the check.

"SHALL I PULL back the covers?" Edie asks. It's apparent Dean's been lying on top of the bedspread.

"Please," he answers. He climbs under the sheet gingerly. "Sorry," he says, "to be such a party pooper."

"Shh."

He shivers once more but then relaxes with the sheet and blanket pulled up to his chin. He closes his eyes and says, "But that's the way it always was, wasn't it? We'd go to a party or something, and you wanted to stay and I wanted to go home."

"Just rest now."

"Now I'm going and you're staying . . ."

Edie starts to back away from the bed, but he reaches out with surprising speed and grabs her uninjured arm. "Wait, please. I need to say something to you."

She shakes her head. "No. There's nothing you have to say to me."

"Edie. I never thought I'd see you again, much less have a chance to say any of this."

Edie shakes her head. "We don't have to say a thing to each other. Not anymore."

But she doesn't walk away.

"You know what I lay here thinking about when I can't sleep?" Dean says. "Which is a hell of a lot of the time. I fall asleep easy enough but I just can't stay asleep. Something hurts or . . . or I just wake up. Maybe it's the medicine. Or maybe it's because I'm scared. And it's my mind telling me, 'Come back, come back—it's not time, not yet.' Anyway. I lay here and what I end up thinking about is all the times we didn't fuck. Is that all right to say? Is that too crude?"

Edie gives a little shake of her head.

"No? Okay then. And I know it was me. It was all me. What the hell was the matter with me? I had a sexy wife—why wouldn't I fuck her every chance I got? Why wouldn't I, Edie? Why? I ask myself that over and over and over, and goddamned if I can figure out an answer. Other than that you were married to a fool. And the hell of it is then I could and I didn't, and now I can't and I'd give anything, *anything*, even what I got left of my life, if I could fuck you again."

He releases her arm now and with both hands makes a sweeping gesture that takes in the lower half of his body. "Hell, I can't even get a hard-on anymore. Not since the operation."

She hasn't seen this man in decades. The bond between them was dissolved by a court decree. And when they were husband and wife, Dean would never have spoken so intimately. If he had . . . But that's a thought as hopeless as Dean's condition. Edie understands that the nearness of death has a power to induce forgiveness that not even love can match. And she and Dean did love each other. She never doubted that, and she hopes he didn't either.

She says, "I'm another man's wife, Dean."

He looks at her for a long moment with eyes that glisten darkly as only the eyes of the dying do. Then he points to her swollen right wrist. "Wife to a man who did that? Are there marks I'm not seeing?"

Edie shakes her head no.

"I'll kill him for you. What the hell do I have to lose? He can't be doing that to you."

Edie's smile is the smile that indulges a child. But now it is her eyes that glisten. "Oh, you'll kill him, will you?"

"Say the word. Gun or knife. Or poison."

"Or bomb?" she says with a laugh.

"Or bomb. What the hell." Now Dean is laughing too.

Then Edie steps back but only a foot or two. While Dean watches her, she reaches behind herself, her hands sliding up inside her red T-shirt. She unhooks her brassiere and then moves closer to the bed again.

"Give me your hand," she says.

He raises his arm, and Edie takes his hand and guides it up inside her shirt and presses it to her breast.

Dean closes his eyes. "Jesus. Jesus H. Christ. The back seat of Tom Dove's old DeSoto. After a basketball game. Must have been twenty below that night. Jesus, Edie."

She leans harder into his hand. "What year?"

"Nineteen fifty-six?"

She smiles and slides slowly, gently away from his touch. "Fifty-seven," she says. She fastens her brassiere.

His eyes open. "A good year. A very good year."

"We had a few. More than a few."

He just nods but that motion alone seems to exhaust him.

"You rest now." She smooths the bedcover.

"Are you coming back?"

"I'll be back," she says.

WHEN MRS. LINDERMAN returns she finds Edie sitting on the end of the couch with her arms crossed for warmth as if her thermostat is broken too.

"Roy's waiting for you," Mrs. Linderman says and nods toward the door.

He's leaning against his car and wearing a little groove in the gravel with the toe of his shoe.

"How long does he have?" Edie asks.

"On TV," Roy says, "the doctors are always telling their patients, three months, six months. A year. In real life they don't like to say. I tried to get it out of the doctor in Billings, but the best I got was, 'It's hard to say.' I kind of lost my temper. 'Hard to *say*?' I said to him, 'You son of a bitch, try watching it happen.' He looked me right in the eye and said, 'I have, Mr. Linderman. More times than you can imagine.' Put me in my place." Roy reaches for his cigarettes but then leaves the pack in his pocket. "Mom told me she expects to find him dead every time she opens the bedroom door. But then the next day she says she thinks he'll beat this thing. So . . . You're welcome to take a guess. I'm a little too close to assess the situation."

"It hurt my heart to see him."

"Of course there's the whole will-to-live thing," says Roy. "I hear that talked about a lot. The will to live."

"As far as I can tell," Edie says, "we don't seem to have much choice in the matter. One way or the other."

IT'S NOT AS high or as long as the hill leading in and out of Granite Valley, but this bluff, where Gary Dunn has pulled off the highway and gotten out of his car, affords a view of the whole of Gladstone, from its newer houses on the northwest bench to its shacks south of the railroad tracks. Gary walks to the edge where the sandstone has eroded over the years, leaving deep grooves carved in the rock face. He crouches, picks up a stone the size of a lemon, and tosses it underhanded over the rim.

Then Gary steps back, and with a finger in the air he traces a pattern in the city's streets. "Got you," he says, and then he gets back into his car.

ROY STOPS AT a red light at the corner of Cheyenne and Third Street. "I suppose," he says, "Dean wanted to know all about how being Mrs. Dunn has worked out for you."

"Not really. He didn't ask me much about my life at all." She looks at Roy. "Come to think of it, you haven't either."

"Hey, just seeing you is enough for us."

Edie says nothing.

When they pull into the motel parking lot, Jennifer is sitting on a curbstone in front of the Volkswagen. Behind her the door to room 106 is still open a few inches.

At the sight of her mother, Jennifer's tears begin again. "Mickey. He got out . . ."

"Oh, honey." Edie puts her arms around her daughter, but Jennifer looks over her mother's shoulder at the man getting out of the Toyota.

Edie releases Jennifer and asks, "Did you look—"

"Everywhere, Mom. I've been up and down the block, and I've called him and called him. What if he tries to go back home?"

Roy Linderman ambles over, and Edie says, "Jennifer, this is Mr. Linderman. Mr. *Roy* Linderman."

Roy holds out his hand. "I thought for a minute I'd traveled back in time," he says. "You look like your mom back when we were in school together."

Jennifer shakes his hand and says, "Pleased to meet you." But then she turns to look at her mother as if she needs to check any such resemblance for herself.

"I bet," says Roy, "you'll be the homecoming queen just like your mom."

"Except I wasn't," Edie says and steers Jennifer toward the motel room. "Let's look in the room again."

Once inside, Jennifer leans against the dresser while her mother gets down on her hands and knees and lifts the spread on one of the beds.

"You can get your things together," Edie says while looking into the dark space under the bed. "We're staying at the Lindermans' tonight."

"No, Mom, *no*! If Mickey comes back, he'll come back *here*."

Edie gets up from the floor. She lifts her suitcase onto the bed, opens it, and rearranges the clothes inside. Then she goes into the bathroom and packs her toiletries in a small pink plastic bag.

Jennifer hasn't moved from her position by the dresser.

When the suitcase is closed and latched, Edie says, "You need to pack up too, Jen."

She lifts the suitcase from the bed and carries it outside where Roy is waiting. He takes the suitcase from her and puts it in the trunk of the Toyota.

Edie looks back at the open door of the motel room. Her daughter is standing there, her face streaked with tears. Meanwhile Roy waits with his hand on the trunk's open lid.

Moral fatigue suddenly settles on Edie like a weight. She's been back in Gladstone for less than a day, and she's already caught between competing demands—and one involves a Linderman.

And there's her car . . . She wishes she could climb in, start the engine, and head off in a new direction, one that would lead to neither of the towns that have a claim on her. Yet she doubts that such a place—call it the City of No Obligations—exists, or that she could find her way there.

"I'm sorry," she says to Roy. "We have to stay." She shrugs helplessly. "The cat . . ."

Edie walks to the trunk and lifts her suitcase out.

"Are you sure?" he says. "Carla's going to be disappointed. She was taking off work early today to help you and your daughter get settled in."

She shakes her head no.

"How about you just stop over and say hello," Roy suggests. Jennifer is still in the doorway, and he says to her, "Would that be okay? If I took your mom away for an hour or two?"

"Sure, sure!" Jennifer assents eagerly. She hurries forward to take Edie's suitcase and carry it back into room 106.

"All right," Edie says. Then she asks Roy, "What's your phone number?"

He tells her, and Edie goes back into their room. On the notepad on the nightstand she writes down the number. She adds the names Roy and Carla Linderman.

"If Mickey comes back," she tells her daughter, "call me. And you wait here for him. Do you hear me? Don't go looking for him. He knows where you are."

As Edie is climbing into Roy's car, she says, "You said you and Carla have kids? Boys?"

"Brad and Troy. Carla's from her first marriage. Except for a couple weekends a month, they live with us."

"How old are they?"

"Thirteen and fourteen," says Roy. "But when it comes to the child-rearing duties I mostly keep my distance."

Edie's eyebrows rise. "Nice trick," she says.

GARY DUNN FINDS the Meadowlark Mobile Home Community without difficulty, but he can't seem to figure out the system of addresses inside the trailer park. Some of the streets turn into other lanes, and some simply end when the pavement gives way to sagebrush and prairie.

He finally stops at a washed-out yellow double-wide with a carport. The trailer's aluminum siding is covered with small dents, the result no doubt of a hailstorm.

Gary steps up to the door and peers through the screen. He can feel the heat coming from the dark interior. His knock rattles the flimsy door.

In another moment an old woman in a floral-print housedress lumbers toward the door. "Hold your horses!" she calls. "I'm on my way."

When she sees Gary she says, through the screen, "You better not be selling something. This here's a Green River ordinance town."

"I'm looking," Gary says, "for an Edie Dunn." He looks at the slip of paper in his hand, though written there is not a name but the directions given him by a gas station attendant.

Mrs. Linderman leans forward until her forehead is almost touching the screen. "Did you call here before?"

Still staring at the paper, Gary says, "Her daughter is likely accompanying her."

"Christ on a crutch," Mrs. Linderman says. "Are you the law or something? She ain't here. And I got my hands full without trying to keep track of her."

She turns her back on Gary Dunn and despite the day's heat shuts the interior door.

ROY AND EDIE enter the house through the back door. He flips a switch lighting the stairs that lead to the basement.

"Carla will be here shortly," he says, "and she'll give you the grand tour. But I want to show you something down here first."

Edie follows him down to a rec room with paneled walls, a dark wood bar complete with stools, a large Naugahyde recliner, and a sofa upholstered in a fabric printed with charging horses. The air smells faintly of mildew.

"Back there is a bedroom that was supposed to be for the boys," Roy says. "Now it's where their toys go to die. Probably more Star Wars shit in there than they used in the movies." He points to a console television set. "With cable we get maybe fifty channels. Most of it crap if you ask me. But I watch a lot of sports down here."

He turns a slow circle as if he's only now realized where he is. "Hey, Edie. Doesn't this make you think of high school and the time—"

"No, Roy. No reminiscing. I didn't come back to Gladstone to remember."

"All right. Whatever you say." He places his hands on her shoulders to turn her attention toward a far wall and its built-in shelving.

She twists away from his touch. "You said you wanted to show me something."

"Yeah, yeah. Over this way."

The shelves are heaped with books, paperback mysteries and romances mostly but with a few children's picture books as well, along with piles of comic books. Next to the stacks of games—Sorry, Clue, Monopoly, Chutes and Ladders, and Parcheesi—and boxes that look as though they haven't been opened in a long time, there are photo albums, grade school projects, and sports trophies and awards. A plastic milk crate full of record albums is on a shelf by itself.

"Here we go," Roy says, lifting the crate. "Maybe you want to sit down and take a gander at these."

Edie sits on the sofa, and Roy places the crate at her feet. She looks at the records and then up at him, waiting for an explanation, but he simply smiles and nods as though they share an understanding of this moment.

The telephone rings upstairs in the kitchen. "Shit," Roy says. "I better get that."

He hurries up the stairs, at least as much as a man with a bad leg like his can hurry. He picks up the phone in the middle of a ring.

He has no sooner said hello than the voice on the other end says, "Something ain't right here."

"What isn't, Ma? What are you talking about?"

"Your brother. His temperature is up again. A hundred three maybe. I can't read that thermometer worth a damn."

"Okay. And what is it you want me to do?"

"I believe he should go to the hospital."

"Have you called Dr. Hall? Is that what he said?"

"You know what it's like getting him to return a phone call."

"I'm kind of in the middle of something here."

Mrs. Linderman says, "This is your brother we're talking about."

Roy slumps against the wall and sighs. "Go ahead and call an ambulance, Ma. I'll meet you at the hospital."

He hangs up the phone, but he continues to hold on to it as if it were a handle he needed to keep himself upright. Then he lets go and pushes away from the wall. He walks to the head of the stairs and calls down, "Edie? I've got something I need to attend to. Carla should be home any time now. You okay waiting here by yourself?"

"I should be getting back to the Rimrock soon."

"Sure, sure. One of us will take you back there."

The back door closes, and Edie reaches into the crate and lifts out five or six albums. The colors of the covers have faded and warped, and their cardboard shows the circular imprint of the record inside.

Simon and Garfunkel. The Rolling Stones. To whom could these belong? Credence Clearwater Revival. They're too old for Carla's sons—they're younger than Jennifer, and she would never have these albums in her possession. Otis Redding. Aretha Franklin. The Doors. She picks up a few more. The Beatles—*Revolver, Rubber Soul, Sgt. Pepper's Lonely Hearts Club Band.* She turns an album over and from the songs listed there, she begins to hum a tune.

And then she knows.

Footsteps sound overhead, and from the top of the stairs a woman's voice calls down, "Hello? Brad? Is that you? Troy?"

"It's me—Edie!"

The woman's high heels tap rapidly down the stairs. She stops, puts her hands on her hips, and says, "As I live and breathe. Edie Pritchard."

"Hello, Carla."

"I must have misunderstood," she says. "I didn't know you were already here."

"Roy had to go somewhere," Edie says when she notices Carla glancing toward the bedroom.

"I see you found Dean's records."

"Yes," Edie says.

Carla nods and says, "When Dean had to move out of his apartment, he got rid of damn near everything but those old records. He wanted Roy to hold on to them. Roy asked him why. 'You love music. Don't you want to listen while you're . . . you know . . . bedridden?' That was Roy trying to be delicate. Considering how good a talker he is on the sales floor, he sure has trouble getting some things out. You know what Dean told him? 'As long as I'm dying I don't want to have anything around to remind me of all I'm going to miss.' 'But *music*?' Roy asked. 'Nothing beautiful,' Dean said. Well . . . If that's how he wants it, he's in the right place over at Mildred's."

"He wanted Roy to keep them though?" asks Edie.

"I guess. And then when Roy heard you were here, he said he thought you'd like to have them."

Edie stares at the album cover in her hands. A young man and a young woman walk arm in arm down a snowy city street. She drops the album back in the crate and says, "We don't even have a record player anymore. Just cassettes."

Carla shrugs. "It didn't sound like all that great an idea to me, but I wasn't about to say anything. I gave up trying to figure out those two long ago. It's funny," she says, "my first husband, Jay Stepke, was a record collector too. For him it was all jazz and big bands. Stuff I couldn't stand. But one day I was looking at an album, and Jay says, 'Go ahead. Give it a listen.' I told him I was just looking at the cover. 'Because I used to know a girl,' I said, 'who looked a hell of a lot like this woman.' 'I buy them for the music,' Jay says, all superior like. But that woman? I was talking about *you*."

"I guess I missed my calling," Edie says.

"Damn right. Give 'em that sexy look, and you could have sold a million copies. So—you're settled in? I hope the room's okay. The boys have sort of used it for a locker room, so there might be a stray jock strap under the bed."

"I appreciate your hospitality," Edie says. "Thank you. But we won't be staying here. Our cat went missing at the motel, and my daughter doesn't want to leave until he turns up."

"You brought your *cat*? Well, I guess not being a pet owner I can't relate."

"We've had him for almost fifteen years. Jennifer can't remember a time when he wasn't around."

"Like I say—never been a pet person." Carla points to the stairs. "I was about to have something to drink. Can I tempt you? You haven't turned into a teetotaler, have you, Edie?"

"No."

As they ascend the stairs, Carla turns and says over her shoulder, "White wine? Will that be all right?"

THE ENTRANCE TO the trailer park is right off Hoffman Road, and that's where Gary Dunn has parked, so he can see every car that drives in or out.

When he is not scrutinizing each passing car, he watches four boys across the street playing something that resembles baseball, though they're playing with a tennis ball and an aluminum bat—and their only object seems to be to hit the ball over the roof of a steel storage building. Each time the tennis ball is struck with the metal bat, making a distinctive *pung*, Gary shakes his head as though he's offended to see something even remotely similar to baseball played so frivolously.

But Gary turns his attention away from the boys when an ambulance enters the trailer park. Ten minutes later the ambulance exits onto Hoffman Road and turns on its siren. Gary makes a U-turn and follows.

CARLA PUTS A glass of wine down in front of Edie and says, "So you brought your daughter *and* your cat to see Dean?"

"I didn't want to leave them."

"But your husband? There *is* a husband?"

Edie nods.

"And he's okay with you making this mercy trip to see your former husband?" She points to Edie's swollen wrist. "Or is that him trying to make you stay?"

Edie pulls her arm off the table and rests the injured wrist on her lap. "He didn't really approve of the journey."

"That's a hell of an argument he made." Carla takes a long swallow of wine. "Which motel did you say you were in?"

"The Rimrock Inn."

"The Rimrock? Why that place?"

"I could find it," Edie says.

"And your daughter is there now? Honey, Gladstone's not the folksy, friendly little community you might remember. A year ago someone was arrested for dealing coke out of the Rimrock. I wouldn't even try to sell a property in that neighborhood."

"Shit," Edie says. "Shit, *shit*."

Carla picks up their wineglasses and carries them to the refrigerator. "Come on," she says. "Let's go get—what's her name again?"

"Jennifer."

"Jennifer. We'll go get Jennifer and bring her back here."

"She won't want to come," Edie says. "Not without—"

"Then maybe we'll stay there and keep her company."

Edie rises and heads toward the door with Carla. When they're outside and about to climb into Carla's white Toyota Corona, Carla looks at Edie across the top of the car. "God damn it," Carla says. "Why couldn't you be fat?"

BOTH ROY AND his mother rest their heads against a cinder block wall in the waiting room. From where they sit they have a perfect view of the clock across the room, and they can observe how hospital time passes like no other.

"What did the doctor say again?" Mrs. Linderman asks her son.

"He was a nurse. We won't know a damn thing until the doctor comes."

Minutes of silence pass, and then Mrs. Linderman says, "Say, who else knows Edie's visiting? A fellow come to the door earlier asking after her. Edie Dunn? Ain't that right? *Dunn?*"

Roy opens his eyes. "Who was asking for Edie? Are you sure?"

"Fellow about your age I'd say. Big square shoulders. Big square head too, come to think of it."

"Why didn't you say something? What did he want—"

"I told you. Edie. He asked for Edie."

"How would anyone know she was in Gladstone?"

"Maybe he saw the damn parade they were holding for her. Hell if I know. And I wasn't about to ask him. I had Dean in there with his temperature going through the roof. I couldn't stand out there gabbing with a stranger."

She looks down the hallway again. "Didn't they say that infernal doctor'd be here soon?"

Another half an hour passes before Dr. Hall appears in the waiting room. His hand-tooled western boots give him an extra inch or two, but he still barely tops five feet tall. The doctor repositions a chair so he's facing the Lindermans.

"Is his fever come down any?" Mrs. Linderman asks.

"I'll come around to that fever in just a minute. I'm more concerned right now with his breathing. Dean has himself a touch of pneumonia. More than a touch. *Pneumonia.* He has pneumonia."

Mrs. Linderman turns to her son. "Pneumonia is what finally did your father in."

"I know, Ma."

Dr. Hall makes a calming motion with his hands. "Antibiotics are the usual treatment for pneumonia, and we'll get him started on that right away. And we can bring the fever down. But this might be the time to talk about what's down the road. What measures we might want to take when—"

"If there's things that can be done," Mrs. Linderman says. "We'll do them."

The doctor turns to Roy. "Has Dean expressed any—"

Mrs. Linderman interrupts. "So he don't need to stay here? You can give him the antibiotics and we can take him home?"

"Maybe there's someone else you want to talk to," suggests Dr. Hall. "I could have Reverend Rowe come around. He's a good man to consult at times like this."

"And what the hell kind of time is this?" she asks.

Dr. Hall looks helplessly at Roy.

"Ma—"

"We're not a regular churchgoing family," she tells the doctor.

"I'm sure that won't matter to the reverend."

"I can't imagine that man's got a damn thing to say that I need to hear."

Dr. Hall says, "I was only—"

"You was only, all right," Mrs. Linderman says. "You go write that prescription and let us take him out of here."

The doctor rises and walks away without saying another word to the Lindermans.

Roy says to his mother, "What the doctor was trying to say—"

"You think I don't know? Christ, give me some credit!" She's silent for a long moment. Then she turns to her son and says, "You ask him. He's your brother. You be the one to ask him what he wants."

"I think I know what he'll say, Ma."

JENNIFER SITS CROSS-LEGGED on one of the beds. Balanced on one leg is the notepad with the Rimrock Inn's name on the top of each page, and with the Rimrock's pen, she's trying to compose a letter.

> *Dear Patrick,*
> *I know you will think this is crazy but can*
> *you come get me. My mom brought me here*
> *because her first husband is dying, did you*
> *even know she was married before? and she*
> *wanted to see him to say goodby. I kind of*
> *feel the same way. I didn't even say goodby to*
> *you before I left or when we broke up and last*
> *night when I couldn't sleep I thought what if*

you died and I didn't say goodby. I couldn't
stop crying just thinking that. I'm afraid now
mom's not going back to Granite Valley ever
and that scares me so much—

She tears this sheet off, then she tears it into tiny pieces and drops them in the wastebasket. She leaves room 106—but with the door still left open a few inches—and walks across the parking lot and down the sidewalk. "Here, Mickey, here, Mickey, here Mickey," she whispers over and over in a voice so faint a cat's ears would be necessary to hear her call.

CARLA DRIVES LIKE Roy, with one wrist draped over the steering wheel. She asks Edie, "Anyone else you planning to look up in Gladstone? Relatives? Old friends?"

"No. No one."

"Let me ask you this," says Carla. "Are you going back to him?"

"Him?"

"The Husband?" She points at Edie's right wrist. "Who tried to make you stay?"

"Oh. I don't know. I can't see myself back there. But I can't see myself anywhere else either."

"So," Carla says, "definitely not lovelier? As in, the second time around?"

Edie lets this question pass. "Your first husband," she says, "was he from Gladstone? A name I'd know?"

"Billings," says Carla. "I was living there, working in my uncle's carpet store. One day this big-shot developer came in wanting a deal for a new apartment complex. He made some kind of filthy joke about laying carpet, and when I didn't blush I guess he thought I was the girl for him. We were okay until his business went bust. Then we did too. I came back to Gladstone with the boys because my mother had ovarian cancer. I thought I'd take care of her, but the way we fought I probably cut her life shorter. Roy and I just . . . He was here.

I was here. No introductions needed." Carla shrugs. "How about you and your mister?"

"Not so different from your story," Edie says. "After I left Gladstone I landed in a kind of roundabout way in Granite Valley. I'd made friends with an older woman, Gladys Frost. Or it was more like she adopted me. She gave me a place to live and a job working the counter at her bakery, which I thought was funny because the apartment Dean and I had, you might remember, was over Flieder's Bakery. This cheerful nice-looking guy started coming in every morning for a glazed doughnut. That was Gary. We started going out, Dean's and my divorce came through, and pretty soon I was Mrs. Gary Dunn. It seems like the story should be more complicated, but that's pretty much it. One bakery to another, one marriage to another."

"Well, how's this for symmetry: After Roy and I got together, my ex-husband moved to Gladstone. To be closer to the boys, he said. Now he and I are real estate competitors."

"I think you and Roy make a great couple."

"Well, I could tell you some stories. But you go ahead and think that."

Carla abruptly pulls the car to the curb in front of a two-story white Colonial with an American flag flying from its wide front porch. "God damn it," says Carla.

Carla climbs out of the car, walks across the front lawn, picks up the For Sale sign lying flat on the grass, and jams it back into the turf, leaning hard on it to use her weight to drive the prongs deep. Once she seems satisfied the sign is exactly where it ought to be, she returns to the car.

"Do you know whose house that is?" she asks Edie.

"I haven't any idea."

"Come on. The family lived there forever."

"I don't know. Really."

"Judge Flowers."

"As in *Miss Flowers*?"

"Yep. His sister. And get this, after the judge died, Miss Flowers called me about putting the house up for sale. And you know why she called me? Because she remembered me. I about shit. How long ago was that? Fourth grade? Fifth? But get this—once I agreed to handle the sale, she said, 'You were a bright girl, Carla Stepke. You could have done something with that brain of yours. But you were boy crazy.' Can you imagine? She's saying that about a *fourth* grader." Then Carla laughs. "She was probably right. Once I discovered boys, I was done for."

"You, Carla?" Edie says. "It was the boys who were done for."

"Look who's talking," Carla says. "They were lining up to drink your bathwater. But I forgot to ask—do you work anymore? Outside the home, I mean."

"I was a receptionist at a chiropractor's office for a while. But Gary didn't want me to work. He said, 'We need to keep you out of the public eye.' 'Gary,' I said, 'what does that even *mean*?' 'You're a divorced woman,' he said. I was flabbergasted. Does anyone say that anymore? *Flabbergasted*?"

"They should," Carla says. "If it's about husbands. Because they are fucking *flabbergasting*. And, Edie, didn't any teachers ever tell you that you should go to college? You were always the smartest one in the class."

"I think you're confusing me with Ralph Varner. But Mrs. Allen, the guidance counselor, suggested I think about secretarial school or beauty school. Hell, when I got the job at the bank I thought I was lucky."

"Mrs. Allen," Carla says and puts the car into gear. "That bitch."

As they pull away, Edie continues to gaze at the house, its hipped roof, its dormers, and its columns. "How can you stand it?" she asks Carla. "To be remembered for who you were in the fourth grade."

ROY REACHES DOWN and jostles his brother's shoulder, but Dean remains asleep. Roy tries once more, and this time his brother stirs.

"There you are," Roy says.

Dean blinks a few times. "Wow. I was *out*. Did they give me something?"

"Must have been the ride in the ambulance. Too much excitement."

Dean looks around the room. "Mom—?"

"She's getting you signed out. Early release for good behavior, I guess. Speaking of Mom. How'd you like to come over to our place for a while? Give Mom a break. She's getting a little frayed. She and Dr. Hall sort of had a set-to."

"That sounds fine," Dean says.

"And if you miss your own bed, we'll take you right back."

"Sure. I mean, if I wouldn't be putting you out or anything."

"No trouble at all, brother. No trouble at all. Hey, Mom said someone came to the door asking for Edie. Do you know anything about that?"

"For Edie? No. Who?"

"That's what I'm trying to figure out," Roy says. "A man. That's about all she said."

"Who else knows she's here?"

"Damned if I know. Maybe she called ahead and told somebody she'd be in town."

"Her boss at the bank?" Dean suggests. "What was his name? If he knew she was here, he'd for sure come sniffing around."

"Cuthbertson? He'd be about the last person she'd call."

"Where's Edie now?"

"She and her daughter are staying at the Rimrock. But she's over at our place right now. She and Carla are getting caught up."

Dean points to the wheeled tray that's just out of his reach. "Could I have some water?"

Roy lifts the cup close to his brother's lips and steadies the straw so Dean can drink. After only a few sips he falls back again. Roy puts down the cup. He lifts the edge of the thin cotton blanket covering his brother and tucks it in tighter around his shoulders. "Did you and Dr. Hall talk?"

"About as much as we ever do. Why? Did he talk to you?"

Roy nods.

"What about?"

"You have pneumonia. Did he tell you that?"

"I guess."

"They can give you something for it."

"I believe they already have. Penicillin probably. That's usual."

Roy nods in agreement. "You're getting to be quite the expert."

"And I'm about done with all of it."

"I'm not sure you—"

"Pills. Shots. Tubes. Treatments. Machines. All of it. I'm done. Isn't that what you wanted to talk to me about?"

"How did—?"

"How did I know? Don't twins know what the other one's thinking?"

"You're sure?"

"I'm no hero," Dean says. "So no heroic measures." His weak laugh ends in a cough.

"Okay." Roy sighs deeply. "Okay. Do you want to talk to Dr. Hall or should I?"

"If you talk to him, I'll take Mom. Deal?"

"I'd sure be getting the easy part," says Roy. "But maybe we should both be in on those conversations."

"Strength in numbers."

"Exactly," Roy says. "Now I'll go see about getting you out of here. Didn't Dad always say a hospital is no place to be sick?"

But before Roy can step away, Dean reaches out and grabs his brother's hand. Roy doesn't move. He remains by the bed, his hand inside his brother's. Up and down the hospital corridors the sick and scarred are being attended to. A doctor orders a drug, and the nurse shakes her head in hopelessness. A teenage hospital volunteer carries a tray of Jell-O and consommé to a patient who wants only to be able to chew. A priest peers into a room to determine if this is the hour. A mother tries to nurse her new child. And the Linderman twins hold tight to each other's hands.

EDIE POINTS TOWARD room 106 and Carla pulls right up to the door. She parks next to the only other car in the lot, Edie's Volkswagen Rabbit.

"This is yours?" Carla asks. "You packed that little car with all you need to start a new life? Plus a teenager? And a cat? Jesus!"

"When I left Gladstone twenty years ago," Edie says, "it was with nothing but my purse and the clothes I was wearing. That turned out to be a good lesson for me. I learned how much I could leave behind. You've heard of traveling light? I learned to settle light too."

Edie has a motel key in her hand, but then she notices the door has been left open a few inches. "That's strange," she says as she pushes the door open and enters the room, Carla following close behind.

"Jen?" Edie calls out.

Her daughter isn't there, but sitting regally in the center of one of the beds is a black-and-white cat.

"The missing cat?" Carla asks.

"One and the same." Edie scoops Mickey up into her arms and earnestly asks him, "Where's Jennifer?"

She carries him into the bathroom. "Where's Jen?" she asks again. "And where did you run off to?"

The bathroom, of course, is empty, so Edie and the cat go out to the parking lot. Carla joins them and says, "I'm sure she hasn't gone far. Maybe down to the office?"

"Would you check there for me? Please?"

Just at that moment Jennifer comes into view, walking slowly, her gaze fixed on the buckling sidewalk at her feet. When she finally looks up, she shouts, "*Mickey!*" and breaks into a run. Mickey squirms out of Edie's grasp and leaps to the gravel. He doesn't run off into the street or the weedy lot but back to the motel room.

"Mom! Where'd you find him?" But Jennifer doesn't wait for an answer. She runs after the cat.

"The daughter?" Carla asks.

Edie nods. "The daughter."

When Edie and Carla enter the room, they find Jennifer on the floor, looking under the bed. "He's not here!" Jennifer says. "He ran under here but he's not there!"

"Say hello to Mrs. Linderman," says Edie.

"Where is he?" Jennifer says to the darkness under the bed.

Now Edie is down on the floor too. "Mickey," she says softly, "come out."

And at the sound of Edie speaking his name, the cat appears, poking his head out from a rip in the fabric covering the bottom of the box spring.

"You little shit!" Jennifer says and grabs Mickey around the neck and hauls him out from under the bed, meowing in protest.

"Now pack up your things, Jen." Edie says. "We're staying with the Lindermans tonight."

GARY DUNN HAS parked at the base of the long drive leading up to St. Michael's Hospital and the emergency room bay where the ambulance deposited Dean Linderman hours earlier. There's no shade here, and Gary has the windows rolled down. He waits with his left arm, mostly bare in a short-sleeved shirt, exposed to the sunlight. Every so often he moves that arm inside and compares its reddish-brown color to that of his right arm. But only for a few seconds. Then he puts his sunglasses back on and resumes his watch.

JENNIFER AND MICKEY now situated in the basement bedroom, Carla and Edie return to the kitchen and the wine they began drinking earlier.

"Your Jennifer is a looker," Carla says. "And those long legs! I expect the boys are already barking at her door?"

"One in particular. Patrick. They broke up over his cheating, but Jen says they're thinking about getting back together."

"And you don't care for the idea."

"He broke her heart once and now she wants to get back together with him? He'll just do it again. And I don't want to see her hurt. Again."

Carla points again to Edie's injured wrist. "You're something of an expert on the subject?"

"Dean never hurt me," she says. "He annoyed me. He puzzled me. He frustrated me."

"But," Carla asks, holding up a finger, "did he *flabbergast* you?"

"He *definitely* flabbergasted me!"

Carla says, "But I wasn't asking about Dean, was I?"

"Oh, Gary is like one of those little boys on the playground who just plays too rough. More clumsy than mean."

"But possessive. Obviously."

Edie nods. "And you know how men can be about their possessions."

"They hang on tight."

"Thank you again for putting up with all of us. You have a good heart, Carla," Edie says.

Carla ignores the compliment and jumps to her feet. "Are you hungry? I have some cheese and crackers. I think."

"I'll wait for the others," Edie says. "When did Roy say they'll get here?"

"They shouldn't be long. They were going to stop at Mildred's and pick up a few of Dean's things."

Edie holds up her glass. "I should probably slow down on the wine."

"Oh, drink up! You don't have any place you have to be. Besides . . ."—Carla raises her own glass—"this is a celebration. Edie Pritchard returns to Gladstone!" Carla tips the glass to her lips and drinks. "And you know, don't you, Dean probably won't eat anything when he gets here? You see how skinny he is."

"It won't be easy for Roy. When, you know."

"He's always thought Dean's the one who depended on him. I think he'll find out different."

"Have they been close since . . . since I last knew them?"

"For maybe six or seven years after you left—and by the way, for a long time they'd talk about how you ran out on Dean, and don't tell me they didn't learn that from their mother's lips—they hardly ever saw each other. Holidays. An occasional Sunday dinner at the trailer. Mostly they were both going their own way. Roy doing what he always did, screwing women and customers. Dean kind of turned into a hermit. Went to work and that was about his only human contact. Oh, he dated a couple women but never anyone long term. Then at some point the two of them got closer again. Even before Dean got sick. They don't do much of anything when they're in each other's company, but that seems to suit both of them. I asked Roy once, 'What do the two of you talk about when you're sitting down there in the basement all evening?' 'Nothing,' he said. 'You have to talk about *something*,' I said. 'No, Dean doesn't need to talk and I've learned to do without too.'" Carla laughs. "Any of this sound familiar?"

"I remember nights when he wouldn't say a word," Edie says. "We'd sit in front of the TV for hours in total silence. 'Are you mad?' I'd say. He'd shake his head. 'Is everything okay?' He'd nod. 'Will you please just tell me what's bothering you?' 'Nothing, nothing's bothering me.' I'd get so angry, which didn't do either one of us any good."

The telephone rings, and Carla gets up to answer it. To Edie she mouths the name "Roy."

"All right," Carla says. "So how much longer will you be?"

After another pause, she asks, "How's he doing?"

While Carla listens to the answer, she holds her glass out to Edie and nods. Edie empties the bottle into Carla's glass.

Carla says good-bye, hangs up the phone, and comes back to the table.

"What did Roy say?"

Carla shrugs. "He won't die tonight."

WHEN THE TWINS arrive, Carla, Edie, and Jennifer all go onto the porch to greet them, though Jennifer soon ducks back into the house.

"Your daughter?" Dean asks Edie.

"Did you think you saw a young Edie there?" Roy says.

"*There's* Edie," Dean says and smiles in her direction.

Edie steps forward to help Dean into the house but then steps back. It's plain that the Linderman brothers have perfected this dance.

Roy guides Dean into the living room and the big leather chair. Then Roy sits on the sofa with Carla and Edie.

"I'll be right back," Edie says and leaves the room.

Jennifer is in the kitchen, staring out the window. Edie touches her on the shoulder. "Come and meet Dean," she says.

Jennifer shakes her head no.

"Come on, Jen. This is what we came here for."

"This is what *you're* here for."

"Oh, Jen. Don't."

Jennifer moves away from her mother. "I told you before. I don't like being around sick people."

"He's not sick, not exactly."

"Are you kidding? Look at him."

Edie steps close to her daughter again and puts her arm around her shoulders, holding her tighter than mere affection would require. "Just come and say hello. Then you can go downstairs and watch TV or something."

Jennifer allows herself to be led.

"Here she is," Edie says when she enters the living room with her daughter. "Everyone? This is Jennifer!"

"What'd I tell you?" Roy says to his brother.

Dean shakes his head. "She looks like herself," he says. "I'm pleased to meet you," he says to Jennifer. "All this must be pretty strange for you."

Jennifer's shoulders rise and fall. "I guess."

Dean tries to push himself up to a standing position. After only a second however he gives up and slides back down into the leather cushions. "Well, it's pretty damn strange for me."

Edie nods to her daughter and mouths the words, "You can go."

And then the four of them, with their long, broken history, fall silent. The light from the setting sun travels its last journey of the day across the neighbors' rooftops and enters through the sheer curtains.

"I thought the boys would be here by now," Roy says.

"Jay called earlier," Carla says. "He said they'd be a little late."

At this dusky hour the mourning doves have begun to perch on the branches, telephone wires, and rain gutters. If their call weren't so familiar, the people in this room might believe a low tremulous question were being asked of them: "Who? Who? Who? Who?"

FROM WHERE HE has parked down the street, Gary has a perfect view of Roy and Carla's front porch. He's watched the red Celica pull into the driveway and winced when one of the men had such difficulty getting out of the car that he had to be helped.

"The dying son of a bitch," Gary says softly.

Then the two women come out onto the porch to see what assistance they might offer, and Gary says, his voice even softer, "My wife."

ROY STANDS UP. "Anyone else thirsty? I'm getting myself a beer."

Carla points to Edie and back to herself. "We'd drink a glass of white wine, wouldn't we?"

Edie nods.

"I'll have a beer," Dean says to his brother.

"You sure? You haven't even had any supper."

"I didn't want supper. I want a beer."

"You're the boss." Roy leaves the room.

"Your brother," Carla says to Dean, "is just trying to look out for your health."

"A little late for that. So I might as well drink a beer."

Edie says to Carla, "I'm looking forward to meeting your sons."

"They'll probably terrorize your daughter. That's their specialty." Carla stands up. "You know what? I'm going to have something stronger than wine. How about you?" she asks Edie. "Vodka? Do you drink vodka?"

"I'll stay with the wine."

Carla walks out to the kitchen.

"When did you move out of the apartment?" Edie asks Dean.

"Above the bakery? I stayed there until I was sure you weren't coming back. Don't laugh. I kept thinking, what if you came back and I wasn't there. You wouldn't know where to look for me."

"Oh, Dean."

"No. Really. I thought it could happen. When you were gone I changed. Oh, not all at once. But I could feel it happening. I'd tell myself, 'Well, you're not the same guy she left, so maybe . . .' Oh hell. Maybe I didn't change all that much. I just got older."

Edie nods. "Age changes us."

Roy and Carla return with the drinks, and he too has decided on something stronger.

"A toast!" Roy says, holding his whiskey aloft. But Roy has nothing more to say, and they all simply raise their glasses and drink.

Footsteps thud on the front porch. The doorknob rattles and turns, the door opens, and into the house pour Carla's sons, gangly towheaded teenagers who look more like twins than the twins already in the room.

Indeed, Roy hails them with, "It's the Trouble Twins!"

The boys drop heavy canvas duffel bags on the floor.

Carla stands up and asks, "Why are you coming in the front door?"

The boys' father follows them and answers Carla. "I parked on the street," he says. "Didn't want to block Roy's car."

"Why the hell not?" Roy says. "I live here, you know, Jay."

Jay smiles. Despite having forty pounds and almost as many years on his sons, his resemblance to them is startling—the round face, the ruddy cheeks, the broad piggish nose, the thin flaxen hair. And there's something of an adolescent's pleasure in his voice when he replies to Roy: "I keep forgetting."

"Take your dirty clothes right down to the laundry room," Carla says. "And be careful you don't let the cat out."

"We got a cat?" one of the boy says.

"No, we don't have a cat. It's hers. Now come in here so I can introduce you."

The boys step forward. They're all arms, legs, knees, and elbows, and they seem to be jockeying for space even when they're standing still.

"The taller one," says Carla, "is the baby. That's Troy. And his big brother is the little one, Brad. Don't ask me how that happened. Boys, say hello to—" She turns to Edie. "Why do I keep forgetting your last name?"

"*Dunn*," says Edie.

"Mrs. Dunn."

They both say hello, and then Troy steps forward to shake her hand.

"Mrs. Dunn used to live in Gladstone," Carla says. "We were in high school together. And Mrs. Dunn's daughter, Jennifer, is downstairs. They're going to sleep in the bedroom down there. And she's our guest, so don't you two start hassling her."

The boys look conspiratorially at each other. Then they pick up their duffel bags, but before they can leave the room, Carla asks them, "Do you have baseball tomorrow?"

"Jesus, Mom," Brad says. "Have another drink, why don't you. You don't even know what day it is."

"Hey!" Jay gives his son a shove in the shoulder. "You don't talk to your mother like that."

"Can I get you a drink?" Roy asks Jay.

"I'll have a beer," Jay replies, then he heads for the couch and a seat beside Edie. "Where'd you come here from, Mrs. Dunn?"

JENNIFER SITS CROSS-LEGGED on the laundry room's cement floor. Mickey is curled on her lap, purring as evenly as a tuned engine.

Then at the sound of footsteps pounding down the stairs and coming closer, Mickey comes fully awake and sits up at attention.

The boys burst through the door, heedless of their mother's caution about the cat. But Mickey bolts the other way, going deeper into the laundry room and hiding behind the steel shelves that hold laundry and cleaning products.

Brad laughs at the sight of the cat running for cover, but his brother shuts the laundry room door behind them.

Jennifer pushes herself awkwardly to her feet. She can't seem to decide if she should follow Mickey and find cover.

"Is that your mom upstairs?" Troy asks.

"Hey, stupid," Brad says to his brother. "Who else would it be?" He heaves his duffel bag in the direction of the washing machine, and the heavy bag clangs against the appliance.

"She's kind of a babe," Troy says. "Anybody ever tell you that?"

"Only every boy who ever came over to our house."

"Just like this friend of ours keeps saying Carla—that's what he calls her, which is so fucking weird—is the hottest mom."

"Except she's our fucking mother," Troy says. He sets his bag down gently. He unzips it and takes out two sweating bottles of Budweiser.

"I didn't even see you take those!" his brother says.

Troy smiles. "You got to be quick." He holds one out to Jennifer. "You want one?"

"How old are you anyway?" she asks.

Brad points at his brother and pretends to pull the trigger of a pistol. "He's thirteen. I'll be fifteen in three weeks."

Jennifer leans against the dryer. "So you're fourteen."

"How old are you?" Troy asks.

"I'll be a senior in the fall."

Brad says to Jennifer, "You want the beer or don't you?"

"No thanks."

"We ain't going to get caught. They're getting blitzed upstairs, so they won't be able to smell it on our breath."

"And they sure as hell won't miss a couple beers," Troy adds.

Jennifer shakes her head.

"You probably don't even drink," says Brad.

Troy meanwhile has begun to unload his duffel bag, tossing out one wadded, wrinkled ball after another of T-shirts, socks, briefs, shorts, and jeans.

"Hey," Brad says, "she don't want to see your dirty underwear."

"We were at a ranch," Troy says. "But we were mostly swimming and fishing."

"And waterskiing," adds Brad.

"We should ask her," Troy says to his brother. "You know, what Clint said."

"Ask me what?" Jennifer says.

"Never mind," Brad replies.

Troy has pulled a Swiss Army Knife from his pocket, and he levers the cap from one of the bottles of beer. Brad grabs the other bottle from him and says, "It's a twist-off, you dumb shit."

Both brothers drink, and Brad belches.

Troy moves toward the shelving unit that Mickey is hunched behind. "Here kitty-kitty." He asks Jennifer, "What's your cat's name?"

"Mickey."

"Like Mickey Mouse?"

"Sure. Like Mickey Mouse."

"Only Mickey *Cat*, right?"

"Right."

Troy squats on the cement floor. "Here Mickey-Mickey. Nice kitty."

Brad hoists himself up on the washing machine. He asks Jennifer, "How long are you staying anyway?"

She shrugs. "I'm not sure."

"Like a day?" Brad asks. "Or a month?"

"I think it depends on how Dean's doing."

"How come?" Troy asks.

"That's who we came to see."

Brad says, "I thought my mom said she went to school with your mom."

"My mom was married to him."

Brad jumps off the washing machine. "To Dean? No shit?"

Troy says, "So Dean's your stepdad?"

"Jesus Christ," Brad says to his brother. "Don't you know *any*thing?

Since her mom and Dean got divorced, he and Jennifer aren't con-
nected." He turns to Jennifer. "Where's your real dad?"

"He couldn't come with us," she says. "He had to work."

"Maybe you'll stay until Dean kicks then?" Brad asks. "My mom
says that won't be long."

"But," Troy says, "we're not supposed to say so in front of Roy."

"He better not die here," Brad says. "That'd be too weird."

"YOU'RE THINKING OF moving back here?" Jay asks Edie. "I'd give
you a deal on rent. A brand-new three-bedroom, two-bath unit. A
luxury unit. And don't listen to Carla. She'll want you to buy, but
renting's the smart way to go in this market. This place I'm talking
about, all the space and convenience of a house but none of the head-
aches. You know, the mowing, the shoveling."

Edie leans back and holds up her hands in surrender. She laughs
nervously. "I'm not in the market."

"If you change your mind, let me know."

"Listen to Mr. Welcome Wagon," Carla says.

BRAD AND JENNIFER are now seated on the couch in the rec room,
while Troy sits on the floor in front of the television, clicking through
the channels with metronomic regularity.

"Christ," Brad says to his brother, "you're making me sick. Pick a
station."

"I'm looking for MTV."

"It's channel forty-five. God, how many times do I have to tell you?"

Jennifer surveys the room just as her mother did earlier. "Are
your mom and stepdad rich?" she asks Brad.

Troy turns away from the television screen just long enough to
interject, "Mom makes more than Roy."

"You have nicer furniture in your basement," says Jennifer, "than
we have in our living room."

THE TELEPHONE RINGS and Carla gets up to answer it. A moment later she returns and says to Roy, "It's your mother."

With a sigh Roy stands and heads into the kitchen. Before he picks up the receiver he lights a cigarette and inhales deeply. "Hey, Mom. What's on your mind?"

"Is he asleep?"

"Mom. It's not even ten o'clock."

"He's usually asleep by this time."

"Well, this is a special occasion. I guess he feels like staying up."

"It's no good if he gets overtired."

"The bed's all ready for him. If he's tired, he can turn in anytime."

"Is she spending the night there?"

"You mean Edie? I told you. She and her daughter are staying here. Carla's idea."

"Huh. If you say so. Have you checked his temperature?"

"His temperature is fine, Mom."

"You might have to help him to the bathroom during the night. Even if he goes before bed. And he should probably stop drinking anything after—"

"Mom, Mom. I'll take care of him. You relax tonight. Get yourself a good night's sleep."

"And you'll call if—"

"If anything comes up. Yes. I'll call you."

"And if you have to take him back to the hospital, you'll come get me?"

"Yeah, Ma. I'll come get you."

GARY DUNN LOOKS at his watch, at the house, and then back at his watch. The street lights have come on, and in their cones of pale blue light insects circle and drift.

"Well, hell," Gary says, then gets out of his car and steps into the street, jingling his keys and whistling an unrecognizable tune.

He steps onto the porch and rings the doorbell.

The inner door swings open, and Gary takes it upon himself to open the screen door so there's nothing between him and the tall blond woman who says, "Yes?" It's only a single syllable, but it's probably enough to make most men take a step back.

"I'm here to see Mrs. Edie Dunn," he says.

Carla turns to look into the living room and ask Edie if she wishes to receive visitors. But it's enough to allow Gary Dunn to walk into the house.

"Hey!" Carla says.

Gary is already past her, scanning the room for his wife. "Edie?" he calls out. "Are you in here?"

Edie gets up from the couch. "Gary? Oh my God. *Gary?*" She moves away from the man walking toward her and stands, of all places, between Roy's chair and Dean's.

"What the hell!" Roy says. "Is this—?"

And Dean finishes the question: "Your *husband*?"

In his profession as insurance salesman, Gary is accustomed to entering rooms where he's not known, and he smiles now and steps forward and begins to introduce himself. He shakes Carla's hand and Jay's and Roy's.

"Hello, I'm Gary Dunn." When he comes to Dean he says, "You must be Dean. I've heard a lot of good things about you. Gary Dunn. I'm pleased to meet you."

They shake hands.

Gary turns and extends his hand to Edie as well. "How do you do? I'm Gary Dunn."

Dean reaches up between Gary Dunn and his wife. "Careful," Dean says. "She's got a bad wrist."

Gary leans forward as though he needs to see Edie's right wrist clearly. "Oh jeez, Edie. Did I do that? I'm *so* sorry."

"You want him out of here?" Dean asks Edie. "Just say the word."

Gary looks down at Dean. "Careful," he says. "This is me and my wife here."

Roy stands and hitches his trousers. "How'd you find her?" he asks.

Gary jabs his finger in Roy's direction. "I found *you*," he says cheerfully.

"You shouldn't be here," says Edie.

"I might say the same about you."

Carla raises her arms and says, "Hey, can we get organized here?"

"Where's Jen?" Gary asks as he looks around the room. "I know she's with you."

"Why are you here?" Edie asks.

Gary lifts his palms, smiles, and shrugs. "I came here to be with you, honey. You and Jen."

Dean struggles to his feet. "She doesn't want to be with you."

Gary's smile does not waver. "That's not really for you to say, is it?"

"You weren't invited here," Roy says to Gary.

Gary ignores the brothers and says quietly to Edie, "Why don't you get Jennifer and we'll hit the road?"

Roy steps forward. "She's not going with you."

Carla's sons and Jennifer have come upstairs, and from the kitchen they peer cautiously into the living room. Then Jennifer sees her father and runs toward him. "Dad!"

Gary opens his arms wide. "There she is! How are you doing, pumpkin?"

"How'd you know where to find us?" Jennifer asks. "Did Mom finally call you?"

"Oh, I had a pretty good idea where your mother was headed." Gary has his arms around his daughter, but he keeps his gaze fixed on his wife. "So why don't you two get your things together and we'll head back."

Seconds pass but no one moves. Gary gives his daughter a playful push. "Go on," he says.

Jennifer takes a few stumbling steps away from him and stares expectantly at her mother.

"I'm not ready to go back," Edie says.

"Well, do you what you have to do and get yourself ready." He nods toward Dean. "Kiss him good-bye or whatever the hell you came here to do."

Edie shakes her head slowly.

"Come on, Edie." Gary says. "This isn't where you belong. We can still put a few miles behind us but we have to get a move on."

Jay says, "Hey, Carla, have you got any plans for supper? Your sons haven't eaten a thing since lunch." He looks around the room. "Has *anyone* eaten?"

"I guess I'm not much of a hostess," Carla says.

Jay beckons his sons and then reaches into his wallet. He takes out three twenty-dollar bills and hands them to Brad. "You guys go to KFC." To Jennifer he says, "Do you have a driver's license?"

She nods.

"Brad here has got his permit," says Jay, taking his car keys from his pocket and tossing them to his son. "He can drive as long as a licensed driver is in the car with him. That's you, sugar. So the three of you go get us a couple buckets of chicken and the fixings."

Jennifer looks to her mother once again and Edie nods. Then the three young people head eagerly out the door.

"Well, well," Carla says to Jay. "Mr. Take Charge."

"Someone has to," Jay says. He takes a long swallow of his beer. "Now maybe you ought to put the breakables up high."

"I didn't come here for trouble," says Gary. "I just came to take my wife and daughter back home."

"The home she left," Roy says.

"And you with it," adds Dean.

"She left you too," Gary says. "She told me the whole story. You think you can do a better job now of giving her what she needs?"

"Don't, Gary," says Edie.

"Maybe we should hear it from you," Gary says to Edie. "Come on. Tell everybody what your marriage to this guy was like."

Roy steps toward Gary. "You weren't invited here."

"I'm just supposed to sit back and not do a thing when someone tries to hide my wife and daughter away from me? Do you people know a goddamn thing about what a marriage is?"

His question brings a laugh from Carla. "Mister, everyone in this room is an expert on what a marriage *isn't*!"

Gary reaches for Edie's hand again. "Let's go," he says.

Roy steps between Edie and Gary and pushes Gary in the shoulder. "I told you!" Roy says.

Gary pushes back, and this shove has the force of a blow.

Edie rushes into the space between them. She puts her arms around Gary, but this is not an embrace. She's pulling him toward the door, and though he could stop their movement at any time he allows himself to be led away.

"Please, Gary," Edie says. "Let's just go. Please, I'll go with you."

Roy has regained his balance, and he's moving swiftly to intercept Gary and Edie before they reach the door.

Edie keeps one arm around Gary and holds the other out to halt Roy. "No, no," she says. Caught between these men and their belligerent claims on her, Edie feels her allegiance lies with the Lindermans. But she will do what she can to remove the threat of violence from this home and its occupants.

"He's my husband," she whispers, and she feels Gary relax under her touch.

When they're almost at the door Gary says, "What about Jennifer?"

"We have a motel room," Edie says. "Tonight it will be ours. Just ours. But let's go. Let's *go*."

Edie grabs her purse from a table, and then she and her husband are on their way out while Roy, Dean, Carla, and Jay watch them leave.

"Tell Jennifer we're at the motel!" Edie calls back to them. "We'll pick her up in the morning!"

To anyone looking out a window from another house in the neighborhood, Gary and Edie Dunn are just another middle-aged couple walking toward their car, heading home after a sociable evening with friends. You'd have to be very close to them to see how tight his grip is on her shoulder.

Inside the house Roy and Carla peer out through the parted curtains. Dean has remained in his chair, but he says loudly, "She didn't want to go with him. I know she didn't."

"Well," Jay says, "she married him. And she went."

BRAD TIGHTLY GRIPS the steering wheel at ten and two o'clock, and he checks the side and rearview mirrors frequently. Jennifer sits in the passenger seat and gazes out the window as Gladstone reveals itself, street by leafy street, avenue by neon avenue. From the back Troy leans into the space between the bucket seats.

As they near Gladstone's commercial district, they stop at a red light. At one corner of the intersection is a small white house with a hand-painted sign in the lawn that says Little Tot's Day Care. Troy points to the house. "That's where Brad's girlfriend lives," he says.

"She isn't my girlfriend," Brad says.

"You said—"

"She's not. Okay? She's *not*. So shut the hell up."

The light changes to green, and Brad speeds away from the intersection.

"What's her name?" Jennifer asks. "The girl who isn't your girl-friend."

"Michelle."

"And why's Michelle your girlfriend but not really?"

Troy thrusts his head forward to say, "He took her to the movies last week."

"I didn't *take* her. I met her there."

"But she's not your girlfriend," says Jennifer.

"She's more or less everybody's girlfriend," Brad says. "She's pretty much a slut."

Jennifer shakes her head. "Wow. Nice talk."

"You don't know her."

She looks away from Brad and directs her next statement to the glittering windows of Eagle Auto Parts. "You don't either," she says.

Troy leans farther into the space between the seats and looks to his brother. "Hey," he says, "should I ask her? You know. What Clint said?"

"I don't give a shit."

"But *should* I?"

"You said that before," says Jennifer. "Ask me what?"

Troy wriggles himself even farther between the seats. "This guy Clint, at the ranch where we were—"

"Older guy," Brad says.

"Yeah. Older. Like nineteen. Anyway. He told us . . ." Troy pauses and looks to his brother again.

Brad turns his father's Thunderbird down a street lined with fast food eateries—Wendy's, Burger King, and, in the middle of the block, Kentucky Fried Chicken, its giant white bucket revolving over the roof.

"Okay. Well, Clint says girls want it just as bad as guys."

"*It?*" Jennifer says.

"You know," Troy answers.

"Yeah," Brad says as he parks close to the entry to Kentucky Fried Chicken. "You know."

"Why don't you ask Michelle?" Jennifer says to Brad. "Now, are we going to get some fucking chicken or what?"

IN ROOM 106 Gary threads the chain through the lock and stands with his back against the door. "Now," he says, "let me see that wrist."

They can barely see each other's faces in the dark room, but Edie steps forward and extends her bruised right arm. Gary takes her hand tenderly, but rather than inspect the injury he pulls her close to him.

"I told you I'm sorry." He kisses her lightly on the forehead.

"I know you are."

His hands are now up inside the back of her T-shirt.

Edie wriggles away from him. "I think we should talk, Gary."

"We can talk when we're back home. Right now I need to know you're still mine."

"Yours . . . What the hell does that mean?"

"You know goddamn good and well what it means."

The room is small, and when Edie takes a backward step she bumps into the bed. The contact startles her and she moves quickly in the other direction. Gary takes a sidewise step to remain in front of her.

"What have you been doing here?" Gary asks her. "Why'd you come?"

"You know why I came. You met Dean. You could see—"

"Did you fuck him? Just once more? For old times' sake?"

"Oh my God. Do you *hear* yourself?"

"That's not an answer. You said you wanted to talk. So *talk*."

"Do you know the first thing about me? Do you? All the years we've been together and you can ask me something like that!"

"You still haven't answered the question."

The compressor in the window air conditioner kicks in with a clunk and then begins to hum at a higher pitch. In that instant, as if her mood is tuned to that machine, Edie's expression changes from angry defiance to resignation. She folds her arms and shakes her head sadly. "Please, let's not do this. Tomorrow we'll go home and we can put things back the way they were. I shouldn't have come here. It was a mistake. I'm sorry. I was angry."

Her apology seems to alter Gary's temper as well and he says, "You know what my dad said when I told him I was going to marry you? 'Don't do it,' he said. 'A divorced woman—she's got that past she'll always compare you to.' 'Not Edie,' I told him. 'She wants to get as far away from that time as she can.' And since you didn't talk much about it, I let it go. I didn't want to hear about your life with another man. But maybe I should have asked. Maybe I should have tried to find out if I was doing just what the other guy did that made you leave him."

"No. You're not like him. You're nothing like him."

He spreads his arms wide. "Come here," he says.

Edie walks slowly, dutifully into her husband's embrace.

"This is what I wanted," he says. "This is all I ever wanted."

Seconds later his hands are under her shirt and sliding up her back again.

I THINK THIS beer's getting to me," Dean says. "I'm going to have to go to bed."

Carla says, "The kids will be here with the food soon."

Dean shakes his head. "I'm not all that hungry."

She stands up. "I'll show you the room we fixed up for you."

Roy waves her off. "I'll take him up." He extends his hand to his brother and gently pulls him to his feet. He asks Dean, "You going to make it okay?"

Dean pulls away from his brother's grasp and holds both arms out to his sides as if the carpet has begun to ripple underfoot. "Just give me a second to get my balance." He takes a deep breath, then exhales. "Okay," he says and moves slowly toward the stairs. He ascends them one at a time.

"We're not in any hurry," Roy says, following close behind.

Once they reach the top, Dean stops and leans on the banister. "Christ," he says. "Okay. Ready. Show me the way."

Roy takes his brother's arm and leads him toward a bedroom at the end of the hall, then hurries ahead and turns back the bedspread and top sheet. "Here you go."

Dean climbs between the sheets so slowly it calls to mind a man about to lie down on a bed of iron.

He groans and his brother covers him. "Are you warm enough?" Roy asks. "Can I get you anything?"

"I can't believe she went with him," Dean says.

"It was just to get him out of here. She'll be back."

Dean closes his eyes. His breathing slows and goes deeper. But just as Roy moves toward the door, Dean says, "Promise?"

Roy returns to the bedside. He bends over and kisses Dean on the forehead. "I promise," he says.

GARY IS TRYING to pull Edie's T-shirt up and over her head, and she's not fighting him, not exactly, but the shirt is snug.

"Just wait," she says, and she steps away from him and pulls off the T-shirt herself.

He hurries to close the distance between them, and once he does he pushes the straps of her brassiere off her shoulders.

"Don't you want to get into bed?" she asks.

When she turns toward the bed, he keeps his hold on her, lifting her hair and kissing her neck. She tucks her head into her shoulder to discourage him and again she says, "Just *wait*."

Gary persists and Edie takes a step toward the bed. She reaches behind her, finds his hand, and pulls him with her. She bumps against the mattress and manages to turn him around, and she pushes him onto the bed. He falls backward with a laugh.

Edie gets onto the bed and straddles Gary's legs. She unbuckles his belt and unzips his trousers. Gary reaches for her, but Edie pushes him back down. "Huh-uh," she says.

He laughs again, and again he allows himself to be controlled. He throws his arms out to his sides.

She pulls his shirttails out of the way, then reaches inside his boxers, and when she has a hold of his cock she pulls it out. Studiously, determinedly Edie begins to slide her hand up and down. It might seem her arm is moving though a darker shadow in the darkened room, but that's only the bruise on her wrist that makes it seem so.

Gary gives a little groan and after a moment he says, "My balls."

Obediently Edie fondles his testicles.

When he reaches for her again, she leans back out of his grasp.

"At least take off your bra," he says. "Let me see you. Come on. Let me see those tits."

"Have I ever told you, Gary, how much I hate that word?" But she says this softly, almost lovingly. And she doesn't alter the rhythm of her strokes.

"You should have thought of that before you had such great ones. Tits. Tits, tits, tits." He laughs but now begins to squirm under her touch. "Would you put your mouth there? Would you use your mouth? Would you?"

"Shh." She squeezes harder with both hands and pumps faster.

"Come up here," Gary says. "I want inside you."

But he has barely uttered his request when he gasps and ejaculates.

Before his spasms have subsided, Edie clambers off the bed. "I'll get a towel," she says.

She returns and tosses the towel at his crotch. "Did you bring other clothes?" she asks. "Because you got some on your pants."

"I've got a suitcase in the car. I'll get it in a minute."

"I'm going to take a shower."

"Take your time. I'll probably be ready to go again when you come out."

"Since when?"

"Since I been doing nothing but think about you for a couple days. Wondering if we'd ever do this again."

"Well, you found me."

Gary props himself up on his elbows. "You knew I would, didn't you?"

Minutes later the sound of the shower fills the room like wind-blown rain. Gary has wrapped the towel around his cock like a turban, and he's lying back with his fingers interlaced behind his head.

AS HE PULLS up in front of the house, Brad miscalculates and scrapes one of the Thunderbird's tires against the curb. He hits the brakes too hard, and Jennifer and Troy both lurch in their seats. One of the buckets of chicken slides onto the floor of the back seat.

"*Shit*," Troy says. "Shit, shit."

"Just pick it up," his brother says. "And don't say nothing about it."

"Brad! There's all sand and shit on the floor!"

"So don't eat out of that bucket. And put it where we don't either."

All three of them get out, and Brad calls out to Jennifer, "Hey, you want to go somewhere? I bet my dad will let me take the car."

She's carrying a bucket of chicken, and she doesn't even break stride. "I'm not interested in going anywhere with you," she says. Just before she steps onto the porch she stops, turns, and says, "And the next time you see your girlfriend? You better fucking apologize."

"TOOK YOU LONG enough," Gary says to Edie. "Did you leave any hot water?"

"Did you want to take a shower?" Edie asks.

"Later," he says, propping himself up on his elbows. He no

longer has the towel draped around his genitals, but his trousers are still unbuckled and unzipped. He asks, "Why'd you get dressed again?"

"I don't have anything else to put on."

"Why do you have to wear anything? You used to sleep naked."

"Not all that often."

"I sure as hell remember when you did."

"That's why you remember it. It didn't happen very often."

"You want one of my T-shirts? I got a couple clean ones in my suitcase."

"No thanks."

Gary peels back the bedspread and top sheet. "Well, climb in here now. Maybe you'll feel different once you're under the covers."

Edie stares down at her husband and the bed with an expression so dispassionate she might be contemplating the purchase of a mattress or bedding.

He slides across the bed to make room for her. "Come on. He pats the empty space next to him. Right here."

Edie lies down so slowly she seems to be trying not to wrinkle the sheets.

"There you go," says Gary. He raises his arm and she accepts the invitation—or is it a command?—and rolls closer to him, resting her head on his chest.

He sighs with satisfaction and says, "I found you."

"Was I lost?"

"You know what I mean. You didn't tell me where you were going. You didn't even leave a note."

"But you figured it out."

"Come on, Edie. Give me some credit. It's not like I just walked across the street and knocked on the door and there you were."

"And was I lost the first time you found me?"

"You tell me," Gary says, smiling up at the ceiling as if a mural has been painted there, displaying his memory. "What if I wouldn't have gotten hungry for a doughnut? What if I would have walked into a different bakery? Hell yes, I found you. I saw you behind the counter and I thought, There she is. That's the girl for me."

For a few minutes they lie quietly, their eyes open to the motel room's darkness. Then Gary says, "That's your ex-husband, huh? I guess it's the cancer that's got him whittled down to a twig."

"Dean's always been thin," says Edie. "He was a track star in high school. He ran the mile."

"You know what we used to say to those track guys? They'd run past the baseball diamond and someone would always yell out, 'What the hell are you running from?'" Gary chuckles softly at this memory, and then he gently nudges Edie. "But you're the one who ran off. Funny. Anyway, he don't really seem like your type."

It takes a long time for Edie to answer. "I guess he wasn't," she says. "Or you wouldn't have found me in the bakery."

"Or here?"

This time it takes so long for her to reply that Gary might think she's fallen asleep.

"Or here."

CARLA SEARCHES THE shelves of her pantry. "Shit, I know I've got some paper plates in here," she says.

"You told us to tell you when you say a swear word," Troy says. "Well, you just said one."

"Roy's not joining us?" Jay asks.

"He's outside smoking," Carla says as she searches another cupboard. "A pack a day habit keeps you outside a lot."

"It won't kill us to eat off the real thing," says Jay.

"The dishwasher is full," Carla says, "and I'll be damned if I'm going to wash dishes tonight."

"Mom! You said another one!"

"Just stack them," Jay offers.

"And I'll be goddamned if I'll get up tomorrow to a sink full of dirty dishes."

"Never used to bother you."

"Oh, fuck you, Jay. Just fuck you!"

"*Mom!*"

The paper plates are not lying flat on a shelf but instead are wedged in vertically. When Carla finds them she jerks them out—napkins and plastic forks and spoons tumbling out too—and they sail across the kitchen.

Two of the plates hit Brad on the shin and he says, "Nice shot, Mom."

"There!" Carla shouts. "Now you can eat your goddamn chicken. Now you've been fed."

"Hey, guys," Jay says to his sons. "Why don't you grab one of those buckets, and we can take it over to my place? You can sleep there tonight. Your mom's kind of stressed out right now."

Brad and Troy both look to their mother. Even when drunk and angry, she is still the highest authority in their lives.

"Go ahead," she tells them. "Let your father spoil you for another night."

Brad is careful about which container of chicken he grabs. Troy however turns in the other direction. "I'll get your stuff too," he says to his brother.

"Huh-uh," their father says. "Let's go. I've got anything you'll need."

"My retainer," Troy says.

"You'll be okay without it for a night," his mother says. "Go with your father." Then she says to Jennifer, "How about you? Have I put the fear of God into you? You can go with them if you like."

Jennifer shakes her head no.

Only Troy says anything in parting. To Jennifer he says, "It was nice meeting you."

"Yeah, sure," she says.

Once they've walked out the door, she turns to Carla. "Where are my mom and dad?"

"They went to the motel. They'll pick you up in the morning."

"Maybe I should go there."

Carla's smile is sympathetic and knowing. "No, honey. Trust me. You shouldn't."

EDIE HAS BEEN lying awake for at least an hour, listening, and now she begins to move away from her husband with excruciating slowness. If another hour is required to get out of bed without disturbing him, she'll take an hour.

She has slid close enough to the edge to extend one foot to the floor, and the rhythm of Gary's snoring has not varied. She risks the other foot, and now she's sitting up. She waits. If Gary were to wake at this moment, she could tell him she's going to the bathroom. But if he sees her move toward the door, she'll have no answer.

Now she's standing. She gazes down at him. His mouth hangs open, yet his forehead is wrinkled like a frown.

Edie takes her first steps toward the door, cautiously lifting her purse from the top of the dresser. But just when she reaches for the doorknob, Gary snorts and rolls onto his side. He's turned toward the empty space where Edie lay. But he's sunk so deeply into a confident slumber that Edie can open the door without disturbing him. Perhaps he's dreaming a dream that keeps her close beside him.

And then she's out. If the door were made of glass, she could not close it more gently.

The night is so calm and quiet she can hear a dog bark blocks away, and the occasional rush of cars and trucks on the highway even farther in the distance. Crickets are scraping their all-night songs, and in the air is the odor of late summer rot, grass clippings and fallen blossoms melting into the earth. And another smell, a familiar one—baking bread, a Gladstone bakery, Flieder's perhaps, preparing the next day's bread and rolls for the citizenry.

She opens the door of the Volkswagen and sits behind the wheel, leaving the door open. She's still waiting, watching.

But when the door of Unit 106 remains closed, she turns the key in the ignition. The car starts, and she shifts into reverse, allowing the Rabbit to roll slowly across the gravel of the parking lot. Not until she comes to the street does she slam her door shut, turn on her lights, and speed away.

EDIE TURNS OFF her headlights again before she turns into the driveway and parks behind Roy's red Celica.

There's not a light on in a single window. She gets out of the car and walks across the porch. She twists the doorknob without knowing what the result will be. The door opens.

She makes her way carefully through the house, sometimes navigating by touch, sometimes by the faint light above the kitchen stove.

Jennifer is sound asleep when Edie enters the downstairs bedroom, but the light is still on beside the bed and the girl is lying on top of the covers. Mickey however is awake, and he watches Edie warily. She returns the cat's stare and puts a finger to her lips.

The suitcases are on the floor at the foot of the bed, and just as Edie lifts the largest and begins to back out of the room, Mickey wriggles free from under Jennifer's arm, leaps from the bed, and meows urgently at Edie.

Jennifer comes awake but barely. She props herself up on an elbow and looks around the room as if she's not certain where she is. "What?" she says sleepily. "What is it?"

"Shh," Edie says and hurries over to her daughter's side. Crouching by the bed Edie gently strokes her daughter's hair. "Go back to sleep, honey. Everything's okay."

"Are you coming to bed?"

And then Jennifer sees the suitcase by the door.

"In the morning," Edie says softly, "your father will come for you. You'll ride back with him. I'm going on ahead alone. Everything is okay with your father and me."

The cat jumps back on the bed and inserts himself between Edie and her daughter.

"And Mickey," Edie says, stroking the cat, "will ride with you."

Jennifer's expression says she doesn't really understand what's happening, but sleep is too alluring for her to comprehend what her mother has said.

Edie stands up and switches off the lamp by the bed. "Sleep well, sweetheart."

"'Night," Jennifer says. She puts her arm around the cat again, and immediately he curls into her embrace and begins to purr.

The girl's eyes are already closed before her mother reaches the door. Only Mickey is awake to watch Edie leave, and human tears hold no meaning for him.

RATHER THAN LUG her suitcase through the house, Edie leaves by way of the back door. Just as she comes around the corner of the garage, a voice says, "Sneaking off without saying good-bye?"

Edie gasps and drops her suitcase.

"I almost said 'again,'" Roy says as he steps off the porch.

"Oh Jesus!" Even in her fright however, Edie has kept her voice down. "What the hell are you doing out here?"

"Came out for a smoke," he says and holds up his cigarette as proof. "But I believe the question is, what the hell are *you* doing?"

Edie sets her suitcase upright. "Can you do me a favor?" she asks. "Would you tell my husband—and Jennifer too—that I drove on ahead, and that I'll meet them back in Granite Valley? Tell them I wanted some time alone, some time to think. Tell them—oh, I don't know . . . Tell them I'll have supper waiting for them."

"You know I'd do anything for you. But come on. We have too much history between us. What's going on?"

She carries her suitcase back to the Volkswagen. "You really want to help me out? You'll tell them exactly what I just told you."

When she opens the car's back hatch, Roy puts the suitcase in for her. "Sure, sure, of course," he says. "You decided to drive back home alone, and you had to leave in the middle of the night. Whatever you say."

She looks up into his face, and she must see something in his expression, something that causes her to sigh and say, "I'm not going home."

"Where are you going?" Roy says softly.

"I don't know. I'm just going. And if you give them the message I asked you to give, I should have enough of a head start to get far away before he has a chance to come after me. This time he won't know where I'm going since I don't know myself. But by the time they get to Granite Valley there'll be a message on the answering machine telling them I'm not coming back. I'll get in touch with them. Eventually."

Roy inhales sharply. "My God, Edie."

"This time Gary might cut me loose for good. His pride probably won't let him come after me again."

"And your daughter?"

Edie looks away. "Jen is busy with her own life. She'll be fine."

Roy drops his cigarette in the driveway and crushes it with his shoe. "Listen, I've got an idea. Let me go with you. I don't care where. You don't want your husband coming after you? We'll change our names. We'll—"

Edie begins to laugh.

"I'm serious!" he says.

"Oh, I know you are. I know. But be someone new? I'd like to take another shot at being *me*. Look, I don't have much time to explain this . . . When Jennifer was born Gary bought a movie camera. For the first few years he filmed just about everything—Jennifer's first steps, her first ice-cream cone, her first Christmas. Not long ago he pulled out the projector. 'It's movie night,' he said. He was probably feeling guilty about spending so much time at work. But all right. We set up the screen, and the three of us sat there watching the herky-jerky images. Even though Jennifer was in every frame, she was bored sitting there watching it and didn't mind saying so, but Gary kept the projector running and pretending we were all having a great time. At some point he asked me if I'd get him a beer. So I stood up and walked in front of the projector, and when I did Gary said,

'Stop!' I was right in front of the screen, and I was wearing a white T-shirt, and the movie was playing on me. I looked down and saw myself—holding Jennifer's hand on a playground. 'There you are!' Gary shouted. 'It's you!' I knew what he meant. But I suddenly had this sick feeling. It was me all right. I was the screen. And it was what people—men especially—had been doing all my life. They'd seen what they projected on me. And now when I look at myself I wonder if that's what I'm doing too—just seeing someone else's movie. So no, Roy. I don't want a new identity. I want to figure out the old one."

"Maybe I'll follow you," he says. "You can't stop me."

"That's right. I can't. But you won't. You'll stay with Dean. And Carla. And your mother."

Roy takes out his billfold. "You'll need some cash," he says.

She puts her hand over his. "I'm fine," she says. "But thank you."

He looks up at the house's second-story windows. "Dean might be awake," Roy says, "if you want to—"

"I can't. I'm sorry. Tell him . . . tell him I was just too much of a coward to say good-bye."

"Then don't say it to me either," Roy says, and he opens the car door for her.

Edie says nothing. But before she climbs in behind the wheel, she stands on tiptoe and kisses Roy Linderman lightly on the lips.

Roy continues to hold the door open. "You need anything," he says, "anything at all, call—you hear?"

She nods as she turns the key in the ignition.

"And if you want to know when Dean . . ."

She shakes her head no.

"All right then." He closes her door.

Edie puts the car in reverse. She has backed out of the driveway and driven halfway down the block before she turns the Volkswagen's lights on.

ROY CLIMBS THE stairs slowly. He passes by the room where his wife sleeps and enters instead the room where his brother lies.

Dean's enlarged liver makes most positions uncomfortable, so he sleeps on his back. Roy approaches the bed and leans over his brother. He lowers his palm close to Dean's forehead, but then stops his hand a few inches away.

He crosses around to the other side of the bed, slips off his shoes, and lies down. His sigh is enormous.

"Well, she's gone," Roy says.

And when Roy's eyes close, Dean's open, as if the brothers had agreed to sleep in shifts. Not that there's anything to see. Though morning is approaching, the windows remain as dark as midnight. But this is the hour when birds detect some lightening in the morning sky, and the dawn chorus has begun, the trilling echoing through the neighborhood, all variations on the same song: "I'm here, I'm here—I made it through another night."

Someday a morning will come when Dean won't be able to rise from his bed unaided, but this is not that day. He swings his legs off the bed and slowly and stiffly sits up. Then he stands and with his feet wide apart in the stance he has adopted to keep himself steady, he shuffles over to the window.

He presses his forehead to the glass. He stares for a long time, and though the dawn always arrives in imperceptible increments, arrive it does. And Dean is confirmed in what he sees.

"Roy?" He raises his voice. "*Roy?*"

Dean's brother stirs and grunts a reply.

"Why," Dean says, "is Edie sitting in her car in the driveway?"

THREE

Edie Pritchard

2007

Even if she were not alone in the apartment, no one would be able to hear Edie Pritchard scolding herself, so softly does she whisper her own name.

"Edie, Edie."

In the living room she looks on the coffee and end tables, on top of the television, and on each of the shelves of the small bookcase. She walks to the kitchen and looks on the table, and on each of its four chairs. She looks under the table and on the counters and behind the sugar, flour, and coffee canisters. She looks in a drawer filled with a tangle of pencils, pens, rubber bands, playing cards, keys, postage stamps, and laundromat tokens. She runs her hand across the top of the refrigerator and comes away with nothing but dust. Just as she pulls out a sofa cushion, someone knocks on the apartment door.

Edie sighs and walks to the door, and just before she opens it she glances at the coat hooks on the wall. There, balanced across the hooks, empty in this season, is the envelope, white, letter-sized, but bulging with its contents. She grabs it and slaps herself lightly on the head with it before opening the door.

For a moment Rita and Edie face each other across the threshold as if for no other purpose than to demonstrate how they differ. They're close in age—in their sixties—but it doesn't seem as though the years have exacted a harsh penance from either one. Handsome women, many would certainly say, and both dressed in faded denim—jeans on Edie, a skirt on Rita Real Bird. Edie wears a red-and-blue plaid Western shirt with pearl snaps; Rita's T-shirt says Gladstone Arts and Crafts Festival. Both women wear their hair long and loose, though Edie's has all gone gray and Rita's is still improbably black. Rita is six feet tall, wide faced, wide shouldered, and wide hipped. She's deeply tanned and ruddy cheeked, while Edie has become more delicate with age.

Rita is carrying a plate covered with a gingham cloth napkin. "Muffins," she says and walks past Edie.

She doesn't stop until she gets to the kitchen. She puts the plate on the round wooden table and puts her hands on her hips.

"Well," she says to Edie, "he won't put on his goddamn leg. Again."

"I'm sorry," Edie says.

"Maybe you can talk to him."

"I'm not sure what I'd say."

"I don't think it much matters. As long as it's you saying it." Rita points to the envelope, which Edie has been holding with both hands as if she's worried it could be snatched away. "What have you got there?"

"This? Oh, I went through some photo albums and pulled out pictures for my granddaughter. I thought it'd be fun for her to look at these."

"When's she coming again?"

"She said they'd be here this afternoon."

"They?"

"A boyfriend, I'm told. He's driving."

"Uh-oh."

"Why do you say that?"

"You know. Boyfriends. This is the girl who lives in Spokane?"

Edie lays the envelope carefully on the table. "With her mother. Her father is way up in the woods somewhere in Idaho, and they were going to stop and see him on the way here. The family tour, or something like that."

"Good luck with that. Those dads generally don't like to be found. How long since you've seen your granddaughter?"

"When she was just eight? Seven? I'm not really sure." Edie laughs nervously. "Those Rocky Mountains . . . I guess both Jen and I have had trouble crossing over them."

"So she and the boyfriend are coming to see Grandma . . . How old is she now?"

"Eighteen. She just graduated this spring."

"Coming all that distance . . . That means spending some nights along the way."

"It's 2007, Rita. Their world isn't our world."

Rita's laughter booms through the apartment. "Shit, don't tell me you never climbed into a car with someone you shouldn't have!"

Edie says nothing but lifts the napkin and uncovers four muffins, plump, sugared, perfectly browned, and still warm.

"Look at those!" Edie says. "Blueberry?"

"You probably already had your breakfast," Rita says. "Maybe you want to save them and impress your granddaughter. And the boyfriend."

"I might do that."

"Where you going to have them bunk down, if you don't mind my asking?"

"Lauren can have the guest room. And he can sleep on the sofa."

Rita smiles slyly. "So you're keeping the young lovers apart, huh? How about when you go to work?"

"What do you mean?"

"You keep them in separate beds all night, and then you leave in the morning and they can fuck all day."

Edie shrugs.

Rita shakes her head. "I worry about you. What you don't know about human nature . . . Well, I've got the extra bedroom. Someone's welcome to it."

"Don't you want to check with George?"

"He won't mind. That son of mine hardly ever leaves his room anyway."

"That's good of you to offer. I think we can work it out. But thank you."

"And don't worry about coming over to talk to him."

"Are you sure?" Edie asks.

"He just sits in front of that damn computer all day anyway." Rita squares those wide shoulders of hers. "Okay," she says. "I'll get out of your way. You probably want to get on with cleaning something that didn't need cleaning in the first place."

But after Rita leaves, Edie doesn't clean anything. She opens the sliding glass door and steps out on the balcony, a space just large enough for two white plastic lawn chairs. She doesn't sit down but leans on the rail and gazes out across the parking lot and beyond, to the street that winds down from this height to the community of Gladstone, Montana.

Custer Ridge Apartments, a matched pair of two-story buildings that look as though they're balanced on the slope of a butte east of the town, are less than twenty years old, and though the buildings are what Gladstone residents would call out of town, the road up the hill is paved, which it wasn't back when Edie Pritchard was growing up here. When she was in high school, a gravel road led up to this height, winding around the rocks and the few pines and junipers clinging to the slope, and here, with the lights of the town twinkling below, lovers parked, their cars sometimes so close that the wheedling, the begging, the struggling, the heavy breathing, the moaning from one car might be heard in another. All the radios were tuned to the same station, and a song that played in one car—"Poor Little Fool" perhaps—played in others as well. From one dark interior came the glow of a cigarette, in another the glint of a beer can or liquor bottle, in another the flash of a pale garment and paler flesh. Eventually engines coughed, whined, and growled to life, and their headlights swept down and across the hillside.

EAST OF BILLINGS, Montana, on a summer afternoon, a dusty black 1995 Chevy Blazer speeds along Interstate 94, the speedometer steady at eighty miles per hour. Inside, the stereo's bass is booming so loudly it seems part of the car's system of propulsion.

Billy Norris wears a T-shirt with a red-and-orange Back Avenue Brewery logo on the chest. The sleeves of the shirt have been cut off, revealing his narrow shoulders. His hair hangs almost to his shoulders, and he curls loose strands back behind his ears. When he nods in time to the beat, he bites down on his lower lip and reveals a gap between his front teeth.

On the seat next to him, Lauren Keller has her bare feet up on the dashboard, and the hem of her sundress has ridden up her thighs. She wears her hair in dreadlocks that look like tightly twisted coils of hay. A tiny sparkling stone pierces the wing of one nostril. She fans her face, though the air conditioner is on its coolest setting.

Jesse Norris in the back seat is playing a game on his phone. He's a bigger, more muscular version of the driver, but the family resemblance is there—the long neck, the heavy brow, the hooded eyes, the shoulder-length hair.

"For Christ's sake," he says to Billy, "can you turn that shit off?"

"This is Jay-Z, man. *Kingdom Come.*"

"And what the fuck has either got to do with you?"

Billy raises his middle finger and turns the ear-thudding volume even higher. "Just because you don't like any music that's not about a hundred years old."

Lauren sits up quickly and pulls the hem of her dress down as if she could be assaulted by sound. "Jesus! Billy! What the fuck!"

Billy smiles and shouts, "Hear it okay back there?"

Jesse reaches forward and slaps him lightly on the head. "I hope you go deaf. Asshole."

Lauren turns the volume down to a barely audible level. "How much further?" she asks. "I have to pee."

"To Gladstone? Too far for you to hold it, that's for sure."

"Then you need to stop."

"How about if I just pull over?"

"Just pull off at the next town. Or rest area."

"This part of the world," Jesse says, "that might be a hundred miles or more."

Billy twists around. "And when we stop," he says, "we'll maybe get out and I'll fuck you up good."

Jesse laughs. "You going to go all Jay-Z on me? Come on back here, little brother. I would love that. I would fucking love that."

Lauren claps her hands over her ears. "Oh my God! What's *with* you two? You're driving me crazy!"

For miles then they travel without speaking. The snow-streaked mountains are far behind them, and they're making good time across the sunbaked prairie, mile after mile of tawny rangeland and rolling grassy hills that barely blush green. The occasional clumps of stunted trees and random eruptions of rock look like mistakes in this landscape. The flat-topped distant buttes rise only so high and then stop abruptly.

Billy points to a roadside sign. "Look! Pompeys Pillar. Remember, Jess? Dad was always promising we'd stop there."

"Threatening, more like," Jesse says.

"But we never did. That's where Lewiston Clark wrote his name on a rock. Or carved his initials or something."

"Lewis *and* Clark," says Jesse. "Not Lewiston. Jesus."

"Whatever. What do you think? We should stop, right? Like Dad never did."

"Keep going," Jesse says. "It's nothing special. Just a man's name on a rock."

EDIE IS OUT on the balcony when a Chevy Blazer pulls into the lot, its muffler rattling.

The girl is the first one out of the car, followed by two young men. She grabs the top of the open door and stretches like a cat. She pulls at the ropes of hair that fall from her scalp in every direction. She adjusts the straps of her sundress higher on her shoulders and smooths the fabric. Lauren Keller. Who else could it be?

Edie doesn't call out to them, though her voice would surely carry that distance. She doesn't wave either, though the taller of the two young men, the one who climbed out of the back seat, is looking in her direction. She goes back into her apartment and waits for the young woman who bears little resemblance to any of the photographs in the envelope.

"I WASN'T SURE when you'd get here," Edie says, "so I fixed a salad, and I thought I'd heat up a couple frozen pizzas. Does that sound okay?"

Lauren asks apologetically, "Does the pizza have meat, Grandma? I'm trying not to eat meat."

"One's cheese and one's sausage. How will that be?"

"Great!" Billy says. "Sausage for me."

"I'll eat either," says Jesse.

"How about something to drink? I have iced tea, Sprite, Diet Coke, and Miller Lite."

In one voice they all ask for beer.

"Are you sure?" Edie asks her granddaughter. "Beer?"

"I'm sure, Grandma."

Edie brings the beers and sets them on the coffee table, then stands back and looks at the trio as if she's trying to solve a puzzle.

All three are sitting on the sofa, with Lauren in the middle. She and Billy are the couple, aren't they? They seem closest in age. Both of them call her Laure and glance furtively in her direction when one of the straps slips from her shoulder. How do they know to look just then? It's not as though that narrow strip of cloth sliding across flesh makes a sound. And it's not as though its fall reveals anything.

Some puzzles resist solving however, and Edie excuses herself. "I'll put those pizzas in."

In the kitchen she calls Rita.

"That bedroom you offered?" Edie says. "I might take you up on that. I've got an extra one here. The boyfriend has a brother."

"Ho-ho! The brother—we know how that goes! History repeats itself, down through the generations!" Then Rita quickly adds,

"Okay. Uncalled for. Sorry. Sorry. Well, I'll warn George and get the bedroom ready."

"I haven't even offered yet. They might not—"

"I'll put the just-in-case sheets on then. Just in case."

JESSE LOOKS AROUND the room the way a prospective tenant might, appraising the navy blue armchair, the glass-topped coffee table with its copy of *People* magazine and the wet rings from the beer cans, the wooden end tables and the matching brass lamps. Except for the rocking chair with the sagging cane seat, this could be the waiting room in a doctor or lawyer's office.

Billy stands and moves toward the television set. "Do you think your granny'd mind if I turned on the TV?"

Lauren wrinkles her nose. "Don't call her a granny."

"Why not?"

"I don't know. Just don't."

"Because she looks like a old stripper and not like a granny?"

"Hey, you can't—"

Before she can finish, Jesse interrupts with a question to his brother. "Did you hear Derek's old man caught him looking at porn? And get this. He was looking at one of those MILF sites."

"What'd his dad say?"

"It was what Derek said to his old man. He told him there was a site like that for grandmothers too. 'Is that your thing, Dad,' he said. 'Because I'll show you how to find 'em.'"

Billy shakes his head. "He's going to kick Derek's ass out on the street again."

"Your granny I bet could be on one of those sites," Jesse says to Lauren. "You think she'd fuck somebody in front of a camera? She could make a shitload of money."

Lauren puts her hands over her ears just as she did in the car. "My God," she says and jumps to her feet. "I can't believe it! You two are sick, you know that? Sick!" She hurries out of the room to the sound of the brothers' laughter.

"DO YOU NEED any help, Grandma?" Lauren asks. She stands in the doorway with her head turned to the side as if she's trying to determine whether her grandmother could have heard what Billy and Jesse said.

"Frozen pizza, honey. Not much to do. Maybe get the salad out of the fridge?"

"Billy won't want any. He's not much for vegetables."

"While you're here," Edie says to her granddaughter, "would you like to go with me to see . . . Well, I'm not sure what she'd be to you. She was my mother-in-law. Mrs. Linderman. From my first marriage. I try to look in on her every few days."

Lauren doesn't say no but her features pucker.

Edie quickly says, "If you'd rather not . . ."

"She's old?" Lauren says.

"Well, yes. She's in her nineties. And her health is not good. She's in a nursing home."

"I don't do too good with old people," Lauren says. "Especially if they're sick."

"I understand," Edie says and smiles. "Your mother said something like that when we made a trip here. She was about your age."

"Do you think we're a lot alike, my mom and me?"

What can Edie say? "I hope not"? Or "It's too soon to say"? She steps over to the stove and opens the oven door. "Could you take a look at these for me? I can never tell when they're done."

Lauren walks across the room and bends over to look inside the oven.

"Careful she don't push you in," a voice says, and both women turn quickly to see Jesse standing in the doorway.

Lauren closes the oven door and says, "They're not ready. I'd give them a couple more minutes."

"You need any help?" Jesse asks.

"Like I told Lauren," says Edie, "not much to do with frozen pizza."

Jesse sits down at the table. "Billy's a goner," he says, nodding in the direction of his brother in the living room. "He found that Callahan program. Man, he can't get enough of that damn family."

"I don't believe I'm familiar with the program," Edie says. "But I get so many channels I don't know most of what's on."

"It's like a reality show," Lauren says. *Calling the Callahans*. About this family that lived in California, but then the mom got divorced and they had to move to Chicago, where her relatives are. And she's got twin daughters—"

"Hot daughters," Jesse interjects.

Lauren gives him a dirty look and goes on. "And the family just gets settled when the dad comes back, and he wants to get back together with the mom. And she's not sure . . . Anyway. Billy loves that program."

"He wishes they'd adopt him," Jesse says. "Especially with those twins—"

"It's the *mom*," Lauren says, shaking her head. "What's her name? He's got the hots for the mom."

"Maggie," says Jesse. "She used to be a movie star or something."

"Yeah. Maggie. It's fucking pathetic. Sorry, Grandma."

"Nothing I haven't heard before, honey."

"I'm pretty sure it's the family thing," Jesse says. Then to Edie he explains, "We had a pretty crazy family life. Really unstable. So Billy likes to watch other families. See if he can figure out what makes them happy."

"I'm sorry to hear that," Edie says. "About your family, I mean."

"Hey, it was what it was. One year we moved around so much Billy missed a whole year of school. From Pocatello to Great Falls and then back again. Mom's folks to Dad's. Then to Mom's sister's in Miles City. Then back to Pocatello. All the way out to Oregon once. Then back to Montana. That's how come I know the road well as I do."

"All that moving," Edie says. "Weren't *you* affected?"

Jesse smiles as if she came close to a truth but missed it. "I was older, so I didn't have the needs Billy had. Now I get all fidgety if I stay in one place too long."

"Bismarck," Lauren says, "is where we're headed next. They've got cousins there."

"It'll be old home week," says Jesse.

Edie turns to Lauren. "You didn't say how your visit with your father went."

"Speaking of fucked-up families, you mean?"

Edie flinches in surprise at how quick and sharp this teenager's tongue can be. "That's not what I meant, honey. I'm sorry if it came out that way."

Lauren is looking in the oven again. "These are done," she says. "What should I put them on?"

Edie takes two dinner plates down from the cupboard and holds each in turn while Lauren uses a fork to slide out first one pizza and then the other. The smells of tomato sauce, sausage, and burnt crust rush into the room.

"We couldn't find him," she says to Edie. "My dad."

"Which was weird," Jesse adds, "because I'm usually pretty damn good at finding people. But if a man doesn't want to be found, those Idaho mountains are a good place to stay lost."

Lauren says, "Daddy always had this dream of heading for the wilderness so he could live off the land. He wanted to build his own cabin. Hunt and fish for his food. No electricity. No telephone. Just getting by on his survival skills, he said."

"His skills," Jesse says, "and what he could make from cooking and selling meth."

Although she's on the other side of the kitchen, Lauren aims a listless kick in Jesse's direction. "Don't *say* that. You don't know that. Not for sure."

Jesse turns up his palms. "Lots of ways to survive, Laure." To Edie he says, "Some folks on the mountain told us somebody was running a meth lab. She just doesn't want to think that could be dear old dad."

"It could have been anybody," Lauren says.

Billy appears in the kitchen doorway. He points to the plates of pizza. "I thought I smelled food."

"How's the Callahan family?" his brother asks him. "Chrissy and Carly and the whole crew?"

"Chris is maybe getting engaged."

Lauren has drawn a bread knife from the wooden block on the counter. "I'll just cut these in fourths, okay?"

No one objects, and no sooner has she sliced the pizzas into eight equal portions than Billy takes a piece and begins to eat.

"Hey," Jesse says to his brother, "manners. Sit down."

"Pizza ain't a sit-down supper."

"It is when this lady goes to all the trouble to fix it for you and set out a nice table."

Once Billy sits down, Jesse says, "Let's bow our heads, and I'll say a couple words before we dig in. I'm sure the Lord can get past that big bite Billy already took out of his pizza." He reaches out, and the others understand what he is asking for and they join hands.

All heads are lowered, and all eyes are closed as Jesse begins a prayer. "Thank you, Lord Jesus, for this good food set before us and for the good company we find ourselves among . . ."

Edie and her granddaughter both lift their heads and open their eyes.

" . . . and for this kind lady opening the door to us, strangers who have traveled these many miles."

They look in each other's direction, and in an instant an understanding seems to declare itself in their interlocked gaze.

EDIE AND HER granddaughter rise in unison to begin clearing the table.

Jesse stands and pushes his chair back under the table. "That sure hit the spot, Mrs. Dunn. Thank you. Now if you ladies will excuse me, I'm going to unload the car."

Jesse taps Billy on the arm. "On your feet, soldier. I'm not lugging everything up here by myself."

Billy scrambles to his feet and heads for the door.

"Forgetting something?" Jesse asks his brother.

"What? Oh. Thanks for the supper, ma'am. What kind of pizza was that anyway?"

"You mean the brand?" Edie asks. "I'm not sure. Giovanni's, I think."

"Well, ma'am," Billy says with his gap-toothed smile, "that's going to be the pizza for me from here on out."

Once the brothers are out the door, Edie says, "'Ma'am.' I'm still not used to being a ma'am."

"Their dad really tried hard to bring them up with like good manners. But he wasn't around all that much, so . . ."

"Oh, I'm not complaining about their manners. I just meant . . . Never mind. But the first time a young man calls you ma'am, you'll know."

Lauren begins to search the cupboards. "Grandma, what else do you have to eat? When Jesse and Billy come back in they'll probably be hungrier than when they went out."

Edie looks at her quizzically and then says, "I have some chocolate chip cookies. Store-bought. And there are homemade blueberry muffins I thought we'd have for breakfast. But are you sure? They ate almost a whole pizza each."

Lauren finds the package of cookies and puts it on the counter. "You can say good-bye to these," she says. "They'll be smoking for sure out there."

"Smoking?"

Lauren pinches her thumb and index finger together and raises them to her lips. She inhales as if she's sipping through a straw. "You know," she says. "*Smoking*? Like weed? Marijuana? Makes you hungry?"

Comprehension crosses Edie's face like sunlight. "Oh. Oh! You must think your grandmother is completely out of it."

"No, ma'am," Lauren says, and the two of them burst into laughter.

RED-EYED AND SMELLING faintly like skunk, Jesse and Billy set down their bags right inside the door, an assortment of nylon duffels and packs in various sizes and colors. A new-looking royal blue rolling bag is the only piece that could rightly be called luggage.

"Where should we put these, ma'am?" asks Billy.

Jesse has brought in a black guitar case as well.

Edie turns to her granddaughter and says, "You and Billy can take my room. Jesse, you can have the guest room down the hall."

"No, Grandma," Lauren says. "We can't put you out of your room. We can sleep on the floor. It won't bother us."

Edie reaches over and rests her hand on her granddaughter's arm. "This will work just fine. I'll sleep right here on the couch. I've fallen asleep here on lots of nights when I've been too tired to get up and go to bed. It's perfectly comfortable. Besides, I believe I'm the only one who'll fit."

Lauren gets up to help the brothers. She grabs the handle of the rolling bag. "What do you think of this, Grandma? Mom gave it to me for graduation. Think she was trying to tell me something?"

LAUREN HAS CHANGED into a sleeveless white nightgown that is so free of adornment it looks like little more than a square of gauzy fabric with a hole cut for her head. It comes to midthigh and is so sheer it does little to conceal the young woman's slender, narrow-hipped, small-breasted body.

"Are you sure you don't want to borrow a robe? I know it can be chilly in here."

"I'm fine, Grandma."

After a shower Billy has put back on the T-shirt and the baggy cargo shorts he wore earlier. Jesse is also wearing shorts, but he is shirtless, his torso rib-skinny but tight with ropy muscle. Both are barefoot.

For a long time Jesse has been tuning his guitar, bending his ear close to the strings until he gets the notes exactly right.

Finally he asks, and he asks it only of Edie, "What's your favorite song?"

"My favorite? I'm not sure." She laughs. "Something old. Of course."

"A Beatles song maybe?"

"Maybe."

"Which one?" Jesse smiles his wide wolfish smile. "Because Beatles songs are practically my specialty."

"Oh, now I can't think of any titles."

"'Yesterday'?"

Edie shrugs.

"'Michelle'?"

Edie shakes her head no.

Jesse picks out the opening to "Norwegian Wood," though there's no indication that anyone in the room recognizes the song.

Edie asks, "Where did you learn to play?"

"High school. Me and a few guys started a band. Had a set list and everything. Classic rock. That was going to be our thing because we could play that anywhere. Bars. Schools. County fairs. Then just before our first gig, Mom and Dad packed us up and we moved again."

"Was that in Miles City?" Billy asks.

"Great Falls."

"Then it was just Dad."

"If you say so."

"What was the name of your band?" Lauren asks.

After a long moment Jesse says, "Javelin."

"How about this one?" Jesse asks and once again his question is directed to Edie alone.

Then he begins to play in earnest, and the opening chords of "Layla" ring out and fill the room. Yet when Jesse starts to sing he lowers the volume again, and his voice is little more than a whisper. "'What'll you do when you get lonely.'"

He's not looking at Edie now but is bent over the guitar again.

Edie nods. "That was a good song."

BILLY IS ALREADY in bed and under the sheet. Lauren is looking through her grandmother's closet, and when she finds an empty hanger she hangs up the dress she's worn that day on the back of the bedroom door.

She walks to the edge of the bed but she doesn't get in, not yet. "What the fuck was that all about?" she asks. "Jesse singing to my grandmother."

"Jealous?"

"Don't. It was weird. Didn't you think it was weird?"

"Hey, I told you. Fucking Jesse, man. You thought that was strange? Stay tuned."

Lauren turns out the lamp and climbs into bed, her back to Billy.

"Do you smell cinnamon?" Billy asks. "I smell cinnamon."

"That's like potpourri or something. On top of the dresser."

"Can you put it somewhere? It's kind of making me sick. Or hungry."

Lauren sighs and gets out of bed. While she crosses the room Billy scrambles and arches his body under the covers. She puts the small crystal dish in the dresser's top drawer.

Bars of light from the parking lot seep through the blinds, enough light for Lauren's body to be outlined under her nightgown as she walks back toward the bed.

As soon as she gets back into bed, Billy presses his body to hers.

"Ew. Put your underwear back on."

"Come on," he says, putting his hands under her nightgown. While one hand gropes for the waistband of her underpants, the other hand slides up toward her breast.

"Don't," Lauren says.

She tries to wriggle away from him, but she's right at the edge of the bed. When she squirms away from one of his hands, that allows his other hand to go where it will. "Billy!" she says. "My grandma is right in the other room!"

"We can be quiet."

"No."

"The hell. It wasn't that long ago we did it on the toilet seat in your mom's house, and she was just down the hall in the goddamn kitchen. And how about when Jesse was right over there in the other bed?"

His hand has reached her breast and he squeezes hard.

"Ouch! God *damn* it, Billy!"

"Okay, okay." He rolls away from her, throws back the sheet, and gets out of bed.

He stalks around to Lauren's side of the bed and positions himself right by her head. He takes hold of his semi-erect penis and waggles it up and down near her face.

"You want to be quiet?" he says. "Here. Put this in your mouth. That'll be nice and quiet."

He places his other hand on her head, wrapping coils of her hair in his fist like lengths of rope. He moves closer, his legs spread and pressing against the mattress.

"If you don't get that out of my face," Lauren says, "I'll fucking bite it off."

He relaxes his hold on her hair.

"I mean it, Billy."

She leans out from the bed, bares her teeth, and snaps twice in the direction of his penis. Her teeth make a clacking sound in the air.

He laughs. But he steps away from the bed.

EDIE IS SITTING on the couch in her nightgown and robe looking at the photographs.

One in particular holds her attention.

It's a photograph of three generations of females, taken on the occasion of Lauren's christening, almost eighteen years ago to the day. Lauren, an unusually chubby baby, sits on a green brocade couch in a flowing baptismal gown, and she's propped between Jennifer and Edie, who once looked more like sisters than mother and daughter. But the years have done something to Jennifer that passed her mother by. Perhaps it was all that time Jennifer spent under the sun's rays; perhaps it was some long-suppressed bitterness that finally revealed itself in her features. Whatever the cause, her looks have grown coarser over time. Jennifer has a hand in front of her daughter to keep her from toppling over, yet she still manages to look at the camera. Edie however is looking away, as though someone outside the frame has just called her name.

And that is exactly what happens. While Edie is staring at the photograph her granddaughter enters the room.

"Hey, Grandma," Lauren says softly.

To hear herself called that while that picture is in her hand surprises Edie, but she recovers quickly. "Hi, honey. Is everything okay?"

"I can't sleep," Lauren says. "It happens to me a lot."

Edie puts the photograph back and tucks the envelope between the sofa cushions.

"Billy never has any trouble falling asleep. Anyplace, anytime, he closes his eyes and he's out."

"Lucky man."

"For sure. I saw the light on. But if you're getting ready for bed—"

"No, no. Come. Sit." Edie pats the cushion next to her. "You must have inherited your condition from me. I've always had trouble sleeping too."

"It's the worst when I know I have to like get up early the next day."

"Well, you can sleep as late as you like tomorrow. I'll try to be quiet when I get up. I'm sorry I can't take the day off, but another woman in the office is on vacation this week."

"Don't worry about it, Grandma. We'll be fine. I think we saw a mall when we were driving into town."

Edie nods. "Prairie View Shopping Center. It doesn't have as many stores as they hoped for. Plenty of folks still drive to Billings to do their shopping."

"We'll probably hang out there."

"Our downtown isn't completely dead. There are a few little shops you might like. And we have the Pioneer Museum. It's small but some of the displays are interesting."

Lauren laughs. "You don't have to keep apologizing for Gladstone, Grandma."

"I don't want to mislead you, honey. We don't have a lot here."

"But enough for you, huh?"

"It's my hometown. I was born here. And I've lived here longer than anywhere. Which is only two places. Gladstone and Granite Valley."

"Mom said you hid out here after you and Grandpa split up."

"Hiding? Is that what I was doing?" Edie thrusts her arms in the air. "Here I am! You found me, didn't you? But Granite Valley was your grandfather's place. I couldn't stay there."

Lauren nods knowingly, a motion that sets her dreadlocks bobbing. "Mom said if Dad hadn't left, she would have."

"And then she left anyway."

"Because of Kyle."

"And what's the status there?"

After a long pause Lauren says, "They're back together."

"You're not happy about it?"

"I can't stand him. He's like this superconfident macho prick. But hey. If that's Mom's type . . . She's the one who has to live with him."

"Relationships don't always make sense to those of us who are looking at them from the outside."

"He's younger than Mom, you know. Kyle. Like ten years."

"I didn't know that."

"I think it's kind of a big deal to Mom," Lauren says, falling back against the sofa cushions. "Whatever. I'm not going back to Spokane."

In this new position Lauren's long legs are exposed, and Edie can't take her eyes off the tattoos high on her granddaughter's left leg. Three small dark blue hearts trail down her inner thigh as if they were dripping from her vagina. Lauren must sense where her grandmother's gaze is focused, and she tugs at the hem of her nightgown, but that doesn't do much. Lauren closes her legs and crosses them.

Oh, the irony! The woman Lauren can't live with was once the girl that Edie couldn't abandon. And Edie is back in the town she left so many years ago.

"Does your mother know?" Edie asks. "That you're not returning?"

"I mean, I didn't come right out and tell her. But she can figure it out. She knows I want to be with Billy. And I pretty much packed up everything before we left. It's either in the car or in a box in Gina's basement. She's like my best friend. My best friend besides Billy, I mean. We worked at Subway for a while. Me and Gina. Before I got a job at Express."

"Is Express a food place too?"

"Grandma!" Lauren laughs. "Don't you have an Express here? It's a clothing store."

"But not a job you'd go back to."

She shrugs. "I could pretty much get a job at any Express. And Billy could walk into any Hardee's, and they'd for sure hire him because he worked at one before. I mean, he doesn't want go back. But if he absolutely, *absolutely* had to, he could."

"How did you and Billy meet, if you don't mind my asking? Were you in school together?"

Lauren shakes her head no. "He went to Southwest. Plus he's a few years older than me. No, Billy kind of like saved me one night at a party. We were at this girl's house and her parents were out of town, and she was going to have a little party. A *little* party. But people started showing up from all over. And a bunch of Southwest guys were there. Really drunk. And trying to start fights. Brittany—that's whose house we were at—tried to get them to leave, but they wouldn't go. They were trashing the house and driving all over the lawn and tearing up the grass and the shrubs and shit. Finally they said they'd leave if we'd go with them."

"*We?*"

"Gina and me and this other friend of Brittany's. So we said yes and were about to leave with them, and Billy came running over and said, 'Don't do it.' At first he scared me because he grabbed my arm and he was all serious like. But he just kept saying, 'Don't do it. Don't get in the car with them.' And I don't know why, but I believed him. And then the rest of the night I kind of hung out with him, and all we did was talk. He didn't try anything or try to get me to drink or anything. We've kind of been together ever since."

"What about your friend? Gina?"

Lauren exhaled. "Yeah. Sure enough. Something bad happened. I'm not going to tell you what, Grandma. But it was not good. Not good."

"So Billy saved you from Gina's fate. And what do you and Billy have planned now?"

"Billy and Jesse think maybe we should stay in North Dakota. Either Bismarck because, like I say, they have family there. And somebody, maybe a cousin or an uncle, I forget which, has a big house. We can stay as long we like, he said."

"The cousin?"

Lauren nods eagerly. "Or the uncle. Or maybe we'll go up to Williston. Billy and Jesse could both get jobs in the oil fields no problem. Oil workers make so much it's *crazy*. Billy thinks maybe we could work half the year and then take off and travel the other half. Just drive around the country and, when we come to some place we like, check into a hotel or motel and stay as long as we like. A place with an indoor pool in the winter and an outdoor one in the summer. Then if the money gets low, back to Williston. Why do you look like that, Grandma? Did I get the town wrong? Isn't it Williston?"

Edie looks down at her hands, folded in her lap. "It's Williston."

"I mean, we're young, right? Well, I am anyway. Billy and Jesse, kind of. What did you do when you got out of high school?"

"I had a job in a bank," Edie says. "And I was about to get married."

"Oh wow! You and Grandpa got married way back then?"

"Not your grandfather. My first husband."

Lauren strikes herself lightly on the forehead with the heel of her hand. "Duh! My bad. I keep forgetting. He's the one who died, right?"

"The one who died. Yes. That's right."

"So you were like a widow when you were pretty young?"

Edie shakes her head no. "Dean died years later. When your grandfather and I were still married. And your mother was about your age."

Lauren waves her hands and slumps in confusion. "God, I can never keep all this family shit straight. And I just gave up with Billy's relatives. I don't know who's who."

"Except Jesse."

"Except Jesse. Yeah. Jesse I know."

Edie smiles kindly at her granddaughter. "I understand," she says. "Families can get pretty tangled."

Lauren sits up again. "So you got married when you were my age? What did your folks say about that?"

"Not folks. Just my mother. My father had died a few years earlier. My mother said she knew Dean and I would get married eventually, so why not get to it. And people married younger then."

"Yeah," Lauren says thoughtfully. "I don't think Mom much gives a shit either."

"Hey, Laure." A voice startles both of them, and they look up to see Billy standing in the entrance to the living room. In a voice husky with sleep he asks, "Are you coming back to bed or what?"

His eyes are bleary and his hair is matted on one side. His boxers barely cling to his narrow hips. In addition to the tattoo on his upper arm, Edie sees another on his shirtless torso. On the surprisingly deep concavity of his sternum is a yellow lightning bolt outlined in blue, an electric shock right over his heart.

Lauren jumps up from the sofa. "Yep, I'm coming."

She turns to Edie and says, "Good night, Grandma." Then she adds in a voice pitched only to Edie's ears, "It scares him sometimes when he wakes up and I'm not there."

EDIE HAS TUCKED a fitted sheet around the sofa cushions and on top she's spread another sheet and a blanket. She's brought her own pillow from the bedroom. She has also brought the clock radio and placed it on the end table where its red numbers now burn through the darkness. The alarm is set for the usual hour. She takes off her robe and lays it on the coffee table. She lies awake for a long time, and like every woman who lives alone, she watches the entrance to the room where someone could step in from the darkness. Even as she slides into sleep she is turned in that direction, and in that position she remains throughout the night.

EVERY MORNING AT work Edie's first task is to print out a copy of the day's appointments. She carries this sheet into the dentist's office. Dr. Hackett is thick and solidly built, her hair cropped close, which emphasizes her big head and outsize features. Both her manner and physical bearing convey that she has the physical and emotional strength to carry out any painful procedure that her profession might require.

"Shit," the doctor says when she looks over the patient list. "Joan Busch. I was afraid she'd be back. Was it just last week?"

"I can call back and cancel. Tell her you had an emergency."

Dr. Hackett shakes her head. "She's one of those women who has nothing better to do than sit around all the goddamn day and wonder if her teeth feel okay." The doctor sets down the appointment sheet. "What the hell. We'll get it over with."

Edie is on her way out of the office when Dr. Hackett says, "I see Kenneth Aldinger is coming in too."

"For a cleaning. Yes."

"For a cleaning he doesn't need."

"Is that what Bonnie said?"

"That's what I said," Dr. Hackett replies. "You know what I'm talking about. Kenneth Aldinger is in hot pursuit."

"He doesn't quite know what he wants."

A laugh as booming and bawdy as Dr. Hackett's would turn heads in a crowded bar. In a dental office it's close to violence. Dr. Hackett says, "Hell, if ever there was a man who knows what he wanted it's Ken Aldinger. And that's you, my dear. Just last week Denny and I were at the country club, and Ken Aldinger came up to me and asked me if I'd give you some time off so you could go to Denver with him."

"What did you tell him?"

"That you're a grown-up. You can go wherever you damn well please. But if you're asking me what I advise, I'd say go."

"I'm too old."

"For what?"

"Going to Denver."

Dr. Hackett waves her hand dismissively. "Bullshit. And let's stop with the going-to-Denver euphemism. I'll tell you what you ought to do. When Ken Aldinger comes in today, you take him back in the X-ray room and fuck his socks off. And then let him give you the life he wants to give you. Wouldn't you like to live in that big house of his? Drive around town in something other than your little shit-box Honda? Sleep in for a change instead of coming to work and listening to people complain about their goddamn teeth? Aren't you sick and goddamn tired of going home to an empty apartment?"

"You know I've been married twice before, don't you?"

"And you think Ken Aldinger is keeping count? He doesn't give a shit."

"I've learned how to live alone," Edie says. "I have my routines. And I like my apartment."

Dr. Hackett turns her attention back to the list of the day's patients. "Fuck your routines," she says. "You can learn some new ones."

Edie turns to leave the office but stops in the doorway. "His *socks*?"

"I have confidence in you."

FROM THE RECEPTIONIST'S desk Edie can look out onto Gladstone's downtown business district when she's stared too long at the computer screen. People walk in and out of Payless Shoes, J. C. Penney, and Anytime Fitness, but no one enters or exits the heavy glass doors of Stockman's First National Bank, where Edie worked in her first full-time job out of high school. Back then a steady stream of customers drifted into the bank to deposit their paychecks, to pay their mortgages or their car loans, to cash a check, or to flirt with the tellers, all of them women. Someone unfamiliar with Gladstone and its stores and businesses might believe that the bank is closed, like the Pioneer Cinema down the block, with its empty marquee, or Beierly's Boots and Saddles, with its sheets of plywood where the plate-glass windows once were.

As Edie looks out at the main street, she sees Ken Aldinger walk by. Twice. He's a tall, slim man who carries himself stiffly straight like the military officer he once was. It's a hot day and he doesn't have an office to go to, yet he's the only man on the street who's wearing a suit and tie.

BOTH MEN ARE smoking, which prompts Jesse to say, "Not too many places left where we can do this."

Jesse is shirtless and wearing the baggy cargo shorts from the night before. The man on the adjoining balcony looks to be about the same age as Jesse. But he has a weightlifter's muscled upper body; his gray T-shirt is strained tight on his biceps, shoulders, and pectorals. His bulked-up torso, held up by only one leg, makes him look unbalanced, as though he could topple over if he moved too quickly. His amputated leg ends just above the knee, and the skin there appears as if it's been folded, tucked, and stitched inside the stump.

"I meant smoke," Jesse says.

"I know what you meant."

"We're here with Mrs. Dunn's granddaughter."

"So I heard."

"Kind of traveling around the country visiting family."

"Good for you."

Jesse moves closer to the other balcony. He points to the man's stump. "Where'd you get that?" he asks.

"Get? *Get?*" The man says, turning toward Jesse. His brow is so heavy and low he'd look as though he were glowering even if he were smiling. And he's not smiling. He says to Jesse, "I didn't *get* it. I lost it."

"Iraq?"

The man turns back toward the parking lot. At the edge of the asphalt, near the rusting dumpster with its shape reminiscent of a beached ship's hull, two crows search for garbage.

"Afghanistan," the man finally says.

Now Jesse extends his hand. "Jesse Norris. I'm sorry, man."

The man looks at Jesse's outstretched hand. "Why? Was it your fault?"

"Fuck. You know what I mean."

The man inhales deeply on his cigarette, exhales, and then flips the butt out over the balcony. "George Real Bird," he says, though he doesn't move to shake Jesse's hand.

"Pleased to meet you," says Jesse. "Did they give you a leg for your trouble?"

"What the *fuck* kind of question is that?"

"I mean, you fought their fucking war for them. You ought to get something in return. Like a—what do you call it—a fake leg."

"Prosthetic."

"Yeah. Prosthetic. At least. And a big fucking pension."

By a combination of hopping and balancing hand-over-hand along the railing, George Real Bird moves around the balcony to move closer to Jesse. "You know what it's like wearing one of those goddamn legs? Try jamming your foot into a fucking steel shoe about four sizes too small, strap the shoe on with buckles that bite into your leg, and then walk around on that all fucking day. And the money? Sure. It's enough so you can just sit instead of walking around on your fake fucking leg." George Real Bird leans back from the balcony and stares at Jesse. "So what do you think? You ready to enlist?"

Jesse holds his hands up in surrender. "Not me, man. I can't take orders worth a shit."

"Maybe you want to give me one of those inspirational talks? All about how I need to suck up my warrior spirit and keep fighting, how I can't let something like a missing limb hold me back?"

Jesse leans close to George Real Bird. "What you need," Jesse says, "is what I've got. Some weed so kick-ass you won't care about your legs or your feet or your fingers or your toes."

George Real Bird shakes his head. "No thanks. I don't go for anything stronger than Pepsi and Marlboros. And I sure as fuck don't need anything that'll kick my ass. That's been taken care of."

DR. HACKETT, BONNIE the hygienist, and Edie sit at a table by the window in Applebee's. "What time's the next appointment?" Dr. Hackett asks Edie.

"Not until one thirty."

Dr. Hackett twists around in her chair to look toward the kitchen just as the waitress comes their way balancing a tray of salads. She sets the bowls down in front of the women.

"About time," Dr. Hackett says and eagerly picks up her fork. She eats her salad faster than the other women, and when she finishes she sets her bowl to the side. "You see who's coming in this afternoon?" she says to Bonnie. "Ken Aldinger."

"I saw," Bonnie says and glances at Edie.

"What do you think?" Dr. Hackett asks Bonnie. "Is the man trying for the cleanest fucking teeth in town?"

Bonnie Yoder is a shy young woman, a practical dresser with a trim figure, straight brown hair, and pleasant features.

"I guess," Bonnie says.

Dr. Hackett leans across the table and says, "He. Wants. Edie. You haven't got that? He doesn't give a damn about clean teeth and healthy gums. The man might look like he's ready for the home. But he's just an old horny toad. I told Edie—"

Edie puts her fork down on the tabletop with such force it makes a noise like a mousetrap snapping shut.

"Do you think," Edie says, "it would be too much to ask if we could have a conversation that isn't about Mr. Aldinger or any other man?"

Dr. Hackett rises slowly. She drops her napkin on the table and picks up her purse. She takes out a ten and a five and slides the bills under her unused knife. "That should take care of my share," she says. "You two take your time. I'll watch the front desk until you're back."

She starts to walk away and then stops. "Which one of you is going to take care of the dogs next week when Denny and I leave? Or is that subject off limits too because they're male?"

"I'll do it," Bonnie says. "I said I would."

After the doctor has left the restaurant, Edie says, "I'm sorry. I shouldn't have said anything."

"I'm surprised you took it as long as you did."

"I've heard her say things to you too."

"My husband says she talks like that because she's not getting any at home."

"Well, if she's not getting it at home, she's not getting it."

Bonnie pushes her bowl aside. "Maybe you could sue her. The things she says—that's sexual harassment, I bet."

Edie smiles at the suggestion. "I don't think courts look kindly on sixty-four-year-old women claiming they're being sexually harassed, especially not in an office with nothing but women. Besides, at my age we're supposed to be flattered. Not filing law suits."

"You're sixty-four?"

"Just like the Beatles' song."

"How about this," Bonnie says. "When is Mr. Aldinger coming in? I'll come up to the front and check him in, and you can just wait in the back until he's in the chair."

Edie waves away the offer. "I can handle Ken Aldinger. That's not the point. And aren't we doing it now? Talking about men?"

"I thought we were talking about work," Bonnie says. "But maybe there isn't any difference."

"The thing is, I like Ken Aldinger. He seems like a serious, sensitive man, and I think you'd agree there isn't an abundance of that type in our part of the world."

Bonnie nods eagerly. "He's such a gentleman."

"I used to have an aunt," Edie says, "who was obsessed with people's illnesses. And the more serious the problem was, the more fascinated Aunt Ethel was. I still remember how she'd sort of say under her breath, 'She has to see a specialist in Billings.' Or 'They opened him up and the cancer was everywhere. Nothing they could do but sew him back up again.' And sometimes it was just a word. 'Complications,' she'd say. She loved that word. 'It turned out he had *complications*.'"

Edie looks at Bonnie so intensely that the young woman involuntarily leans back from the table. "What I don't want in my life are complications. However many years I have left I would like them to be free of complications. And Ken Aldinger, no matter how much of a gentleman he is, no matter how kind or how sensitive, would come with complications."

THE PRAIRIE VIEW Mall is nearly deserted, and Lauren Keller has the floor and the merchandise of rue21 to herself. She moves through the store with astonishing alacrity, lifting a scarf or a T-shirt and holding it up and then dropping it again, pulling a dress from its hanger and bringing it to her body only to put it back, trailing down a line of jeans with her finger as if touching the denim for an instant were enough to tell her all she needs to know.

On a bench outside the store Jesse and Billy sit and eat their pretzels.

"I don't get it," Billy says to his brother. "Don't they got all kinds of organizations to do shit for them? The VFW or American Legion or what not?"

"That's not what I'm talking about, man. I'm talking about what the government *won't* do for them. And the shit they don't want to ask their wives or their folks or anyone else to do. You know, like get dope for them. Or women. Or porn videos."

"Get women?" Billy says. "Fuck, man. That's nothing but a goddamn pimp. And who watches porn videos anymore? You got a computer, you got porn."

Jesse takes another bite of his pretzel and then tosses it into a nearby garbage receptacle. He leans closer to his brother. "We'd be like personal assistants. These veterans have needs and we serve their needs. Especially the ones who are crippled up or disabled. I mean, think of a blind guy. He can't do shit for himself. Or somebody who got his hands blown off. And they all got money. Pensions and disability and all. And guns. We'd have a fucking arsenal in no time."

"Why'd you throw that away?" Billy says, pointing to the garbage can. "I'd have eaten it. And how we going to talk women into this deal?"

"First off, these are fucking heroes. Men and maybe even women who lost an arm or a leg or an eye or got their heads messed up defending our country. I mean, who doesn't want to help them? Hell, dope dealers might be willing to give a discount."

Billy shakes his head. "No fucking way. And what about Cousin Mike? You said we could get on with his construction crew. Or head up to Williston. Them guys make so fucking much money they can't spend it fast enough."

"You want to break your back doing construction? Or work even harder on an oil rig and maybe lose a finger or two in the bargain? What I'm talking about is hardly even working. Doing errands is more like it. Besides, Mike isn't really a cousin. Dad just said that to impress us or something. Like there was somebody in the family who wasn't a fuckup."

Now Billy wads up the waxed paper that held his pretzel and tosses the ball toward the garbage can. He misses. "And how do we find the vets who're going to pay us for doing this shit? Nail up a sign? Hey, Need Dope? We'll Score for You! Or put an ad in the paper? Looking for a Woman to Blow You? And I'm supposed to be the stupid one."

"Help out a couple of these guys," Jesse says, "and word will get around. They'll find us."

"Even if they do," Billy says, shaking his head, "then we got to set something up with dealers. And with women? Shit, man. It's just more trouble than it's worth if you ask me."

"Leave it to me," says Jesse. "I can get us started with connections. And as for women, they'll be lining up to volunteer once they find out what we're trying to do for our wounded warriors. Some of those dudes got their dicks blown off. And others got PTSDs or something so they can't get it up. A woman might not have to do anything more than sit on someone's lap. If that's not easy money, I don't know what."

Billy shakes his head even harder. "That's still pimp work. Is that who you want to be? Hello. My name is Jesse Norris and I'm a goddamn pimp and a dope dealer. Jesus, man. Have some pride."

"You know what your problem is?" Jesse asks. "You've got no fucking imagination."

As if this remark has the force of a physical blow, Billy lurches on the bench. "Okay," he says. "Here? Are we supposed to start up this business here?"

"Probably not enough of those guys here. Though maybe I'll see what we could do for the neighbor before we leave. I bet the government pays him a fucking bundle every month for hopping around on one leg."

Their conversation stops when Lauren comes to the doorway of the store and signals for them to come inside. She says, "They've got men's stuff in here too."

Two boys, no older than fourteen or fifteen, walk by, their attire so similar they could be wearing the cowboy uniform—boots with riding heels, Wranglers that bunch around their boots, hand-tooled belts with big silver buckles, snap-front shirts, wide-brimmed straw hats pulled low. They're walking as though they have a destination in mind, but then they see Lauren Keller standing in the doorway of rue21—and to them she must look like a clothing-store mannequin come to life. Her long legs and cutoffs hanging loose and low on her hips, and her hair, her hair in that style they've seen only on television . . . The cowboys stop in their tracks, and for a moment they stand between Lauren and the Norris brothers.

Lauren gives the cowboys a little finger wave, but before they can respond to that gesture—oh, perhaps there's time for their hearts to speed up a little—she reverses the wave and shoos them on their way.

As they walk off, one of the boys punches the other in the shoulder as if he's to blame for their embarrassment.

Billy points to where the cowboys just stood. "I think they left a little cow shit on the floor there."

"That could be their shit," Jesse says.

Lauren is still standing in the store's doorway.

"Go ahead," Jesse says to his brother. "Let her dress you up like her own little Ken doll."

Billy gives his brother the finger. Then he stands up and follows Lauren into the store.

EDIE ENTERS HER apartment and calls out hello, but no answer comes back to her. Beside the door is the table with the small bowl waiting for her keys, but she keeps them in her hand as she moves from room to room.

In the sink are three bowls and three spoons. Juice glasses with dried pulp clinging to their sides are on the counter.

The doors to the bathroom and to Edie's bedroom are open, and she glances briefly into both. Towels are draped unevenly over the shower bar. Edie's bed is made but clumsily so. Lauren's new royal blue suitcase is open on the floor, and nylon duffel bags lie close by.

The door to the guest room is closed, and Edie knocks. There's no response and she knocks again. She opens the door slowly, peers into the room, and then walks in. Jesse's bed is also made, more neatly so than Lauren and Billy's. His guitar case is open, and Edie bends down and plucks the B string. She can see into an open duffel bag, and there, among the balled-up socks and the carelessly folded jeans and T-shirts, is the barrel of a gun. The sight is enough to make her react as if it were a rattlesnake. She gasps and takes a step back.

Perhaps she's mistaken. The shape after all is wrong—rectangular, not round. But there's no mistaking the color—blue-black steel. With her foot she prods the shape through the nylon. The feel of it gives back just enough information. Yes, it's a gun. Here. In her home.

She bends over slowly and reaches hesitantly toward the bag, its unzipped top gaping open like a smiling mouth.

"Looking for something?" a voice behind her says.

Edie lurches backward as Jesse Norris steps from the doorway into the room.

"Your . . . your guitar," she says.

"What about it?" He looks at his duffel bag, and he knows what she has seen.

"I hope it's all right," Edie says. "I strummed it. To hear the sound. That was all."

"Yeah? Would you like a lesson?" But he flips the guitar case closed.

They're facing each other now, Jesse in the middle of the room, close to the foot of the bed, and Edie almost against the wall.

"I wasn't sure if you were still here," she says. "I didn't see your car in the lot."

"Yeah, I'm still here. As you can see." He steps toward the door and she follows. "Billy and your granddaughter dropped me off. They're headed someplace down by the river. We talked to a fellow in a sporting goods store who told Billy where the fishing's supposed to be good. So they went to scout out the location. He's thinking maybe he'll go fishing tomorrow."

"Tomorrow."

Jesse laughs. "You probably thought you were getting rid of us!"

"You're welcome to stay as long as you like," Edie says.

Staying close to the wall, Edie leaves the bedroom. She walks to the kitchen. She can feel Jesse following, his bare feet so close behind hers he's almost stepping on her heels.

Edie is still holding her keys, and at some point she has shifted them in her hand so that she carries them as women are advised to do when they are crossing a dark parking lot. Now she tosses them on the counter. She opens the refrigerator and takes out a bottle of chardonnay. "It's become my habit," she says in a voice that's strangely formal, "to have a glass of wine at the end of a workday. Can I pour you a glass?"

"Sure," Jesse says, slouching in the same chair he sat in the night before. "Unless you have something stronger."

Edie doesn't say anything. She sets the wine bottle down and opens the cupboard below the sink. She reaches back behind the garbage can and takes out a bottle of Wild Turkey 101. She sets it on the table.

Jesse raises the bottle. "Strong enough," he says.

Edie picks up one of the dirty juice glasses from the counter. "I don't suppose you remember which one is yours?"

"Doesn't matter," Jesse says cheerfully. "We pretty much share everything."

But Edie takes a clean glass from the cupboard and hands it to Jesse. "Do you want ice?" she asks. "Water?"

"I'll take it neat," he replies. "Isn't that what they say? *Neat?*"

"I believe you know the answer to that, Mr. Norris. I believe you know many more answers than you let on."

"Well, it's true I've had more schooling than Billy." He uncaps the whiskey bottle and pours himself a generous portion. Across the room Edie pours her chardonnay into a wineglass.

"I had almost a year at a community college," he says. "Before I got interrupted."

"*Interrupted?*" Edie leans back against the counter.

"You know how it is."

"I'm afraid I don't. And school wasn't exactly the kind of knowledge I was referring to."

Jesse looks out toward the living room. "I like your balcony. I was sitting out there having a smoke. Bet you see some sunsets from there. You want to go out?"

Edie shakes her head no.

"I met your neighbor out there this morning. George?"

"George."

"Jesus, what a hand he got dealt, eh?"

Edie sets her wineglass down on the counter. "We can discuss George Real Bird's hard luck some other time." She crosses her arms and, in a voice as precise and official as she would use speaking to a dental patient, she says, "Mr. Norris, you have a gun in your luggage."

Jesse points toward the living room and beyond. "You sure you don't want to go out on the balcony? Looks like a thunderstorm might be coming our way. Some big-ass thunderheads blooming in the west. Should be impressive."

"You brought a *gun* into my home."

Jesse shakes his hand as though he might have just pinched his fingers in a door. "Woo-hoo! We got a little lightning flashing in here, don't we?"

Edie's steady gaze at Jesse doesn't waver.

"You don't have a gun somewhere around here?" he asks.

"I do not."

"Woman living alone out here on the prairie, I'd think she might want to have some protection on hand."

"This is Gladstone, Mr. Norris. Not Tombstone or Dodge City. And it's 2007. Not the Wild West."

"You sure about that?" Jesse says with a sly smile. "And what's with the 'mister' business? We know each other better than that, don't we . . . Edie?"

She stares at him for a long moment. He doesn't flinch under her gaze however, and she is the one to look away. She picks up her wineglass and heads out of the kitchen. "Go ahead and watch your sunset," she says. "I'm going to change my shoes and go for a walk."

As Edie walks past him, Jesse leans lazily out from his chair and says, "It's not even loaded."

Edie takes a quick sideways step and then stops, out of Jesse's reach. "I've been around long enough to have heard plenty of stories of some person who was shot with a gun that someone swore wasn't loaded."

"If you really need to know," he says, "I brought it along because of Lauren's dad. Up in those mountains there's all kinds of folks who don't want strangers coming around trying to find somebody. Meth dealers, like I said before. Survivalists. Religious nuts. Plain old outlaws."

"Keep it in your bag," Edie says. "And keep the bag zipped. As far as I can tell you're the closest thing to an outlaw around here."

EDIE HAS BARELY walked half a mile when she has to turn around and head for home. The thunderheads have risen now to blot out the sun, and the sky has darkened to the same dark blue as that gun's barrel. Thunder booms and cracks overhead. Jagged lightning streaks crack and thud into the earth not far down the hill, and Edie picks up her pace. Soon she's jogging, slowly and stiffly, but jogging—though when she comes to the steepest part of the hill that climbs toward the apartment complex, she has to slow again to a walk. But she's close enough. A few fat drops splat on the asphalt and on the surrounding prairie, releasing a mingled odor of salt and sage, but Edie steps through the apartment building door scant seconds before the great rush of wind and the near-horizontal torrent of rain arrive. For a moment she stands with her back to the door as if she has to brace it against an onslaught that wants to force its way inside. Wind and rain pound the building, and Edie looks out the window next to the door. It's difficult to see much of the parking lot through the pulsing cascade, but it doesn't look as though the Blazer has returned. She climbs the three flights of stairs and walks down the hall to her apartment.

Jesse has turned on the lamp next to the sofa, where he sits. His glass of whiskey is on the coffee table, and in his hands are a few photographs from the envelope.

He looks up at her and smiles. "Get wet?" he asks.

Some people get bleary-eyed from drink, but Jesse's eyes glint sharply and seem to have lost none of their ability to focus. He holds up the pictures, fanned out in his fingers like a hand of cards. "Hey, what did Laure think of these?" he says. "You've got her whole damn childhood right here!"

Edie wants to grab the photos from him, but she stops and sits down in the rocking chair.

"I was watching you from the balcony," says Jesse. "You move right along, don't you? I checked all the windows, by the way. All shut down." He holds a photograph overhead. "I believe this is my favorite. God *damn*."

He has it turned so Edie can't see the image. She doesn't ask him what's pictured there, and he quickly lowers it and mixes it back into the batch. He pulls out another, and this time he allows her to see it. "Who'd have thought Laure would ever have been fat?" he says. "But she was a chunky little thing, wasn't she?"

Edie says, "Those aren't yours."

"What? Yeah. No shit." He flips through a few more photographs. "I kind of get now what Laure's mother's problem with you is. No daughter wants a mother who's better looking than she is. And then Mrs. Keller loses out on the other side too when she has Laure. I mean, Lauren's mom isn't a bad-looking woman, but you get what I'm saying."

Minutes pass. Jesse continues riffling through the photographs but so rapidly he can't really be seeing what's there. The wind gusts even harder, and rain strikes the balcony's door with a sound like a hundred brooms slapping back and forth across the glass. Edie leans forward in the rocking chair, the palms of her hands pressed together.

Finally she says, "What do you want from me?"

Jesse picks up his whiskey, takes a small sip, and then carefully sets the glass down on a coaster. He straightens the pile of photographs, making certain that all the edges align. He puts them back in the envelope and folds the flap over. Only then does he look at Edie.

"Want something? From you? Why would you think something like that?"

"Intuition," Edie says. "Experience."

He shakes his head slowly. "You've fed us. Given us beds and clean towels." Jesse picks up his glass again and holds it toward her as if he's about to propose a toast. "Shared your liquor. What more could we ask for? No, I should be the one asking." He pauses and smiles the smile that no doubt has charmed women of all ages. "What do *you* want from *me*?"

Edie says, "I want you to leave."

Jesse laughs. "I'd like to oblige you. I surely would. But I've got no car. Not to mention it's raining like a son of a bitch. I believe you're stuck with me. So we'll just have to find a way to spend our time together that brings us both a little pleasure."

Swiftly and wordlessly Edie rises from the rocking chair and leaves the room. She walks down the hall to her bedroom. She doesn't slam the door behind her, but she pulls it shut with enough emphasis that Jesse can surely hear it close, and perhaps even the lock being turned.

The wind has died, but the rain continues to tap insistently on the sliding door to the balcony and every one of the apartment's west-facing windows.

Jesse watches the hallway as if he expects Edie to return at any moment. When it's clear that she's not coming back, he sighs and rises from the couch. He picks up his glass and drinks off what remains. He puts the glass down and heads down the hallway.

At the door he knocks. "Hey. Hey, Mrs. Dunn. Don't go away mad."

He puts his ear close to the door and says, "You know, if it was up to me, we'd be on our way tomorrow. Hell, tonight. We'd head out tonight. Storm or no storm. But Laure—Laure wants to kind of get back with family."

He steps back from the door as though he expects it to open. When it doesn't, when no sound comes from the other side, he knocks again and waits. Still nothing.

"But if we're still here Sunday," says Jesse, "I'll need you to give me a recommendation on a church. That's maybe something you didn't get about me. I might not look like it, but I'm pretty regular about church attendance. Denomination doesn't matter so much to me. Methodist, Baptist. Whatever. I figure Jesus doesn't care."

He puts his ear to the door again. "Hey. Hey! Everything okay in there?" He pauses. "I hope you're not in there snooping through someone else's things. Not nice, Mrs. Dunn. Not nice at all."

Very slowly he backs away from the door. "But I forgive you," he whispers.

WHEN BILLY AND Lauren walk in Jesse doesn't even look up from his beeping, pinging Game Boy. "Still raining?" he asks them.

"Not like before," Billy says. "We was down by the river, and I thought we'd get washed away in a fucking flood."

Billy's carrying a twelve-pack of Busch beer, but the carton has been opened and three cans are missing. He sets it down on the coffee table. He takes out a beer and holds it toward his brother. "You ready for one?" he asks Jesse.

Lauren bends over and shakes her head. Droplets spray from her dreadlocks as if those tubes of hair had been filled with water. When she stands up straight she sees her grandmother walking toward her from the bedroom.

"I thought I'd order Chinese food," Edie says brightly. "How does that sound?"

"Sure," Billy says.

"That'd be great," Lauren says. "I can get something vegetarian."

"And they'll deliver," Edie says over her shoulder as she walks to the kitchen. She takes a China Palace menu from a drawer and takes it to the living room. Tossing it on the coffee table she says, "Let me know what you want."

Billy is still holding the can of beer out to his brother. "You want a beer or not?"

Jesse reaches out for the beer but says nothing.

Billy notices Jesse's empty glass. "What the hell have you been into?" he asks.

Jesse turns off the Game Boy and puts it on the coffee table. He pops open the can of beer. "You order for me," he says to Edie. "You know what I like."

MILDRED LINDERMAN, ONCE as tall and big shouldered as most men, is now little more than a skeleton in a flannel nightgown. An aluminum walker waits by her bed, but she doesn't look as though she has the strength to sit up, much less support her weight on that metal frame. She lies flat on her back, unmoving but for her eyes. And those eyes are sunk deep but open wide and gleaming like dark stones on a streambed.

Mildred's eyes follow Edie until she is standing alongside the bed, and only then does she stop watching her. Edie parts the curtains and peers out across the parking lot of the Cottonwood Elderly Care Center. Her Honda Civic is parked in the shade of the trees, and Lauren is waiting in the car. Edie looks at her watch and then sits down in the bedside chair.

"I have company this week," Edie says, speaking slowly and enunciating clearly, though she seems to know that her words don't register. "My granddaughter. Lauren. She's waiting out in the car, so I'm afraid I'll have to cut my visit short today. You might remember my daughter, Jennifer, Lauren's mother—she came with me when I made that trip to see Dean. She came reluctantly, I might add. And Jennifer and Lauren visited me here on at least one other occasion, when Lauren was just a toddler. Not in school yet, and that's why they were able to come in September. Oh, I agree. I agree. September always shows Gladstone off to its best advantage. As I recall they came during the county fair. Lauren just couldn't get enough of the animals. Rabbits, especially. Wasn't it the Collins girl who raised those big Belgians? My God, those rabbits were almost as big as Lauren. I remember how she petted one of the rabbits so carefully it seemed like she thought its fur could peel right off."

Edie leans forward as if she's listening to Mildred, although the old woman hasn't spoken. She seems to be drowsing, though her eyes are still open.

"Was that the trip when Jennifer and I had the falling-out? It might have been. You might be right about mothers and daughters. Nothing like that went on between you and your boys. Who knows what it was that time. Nothing. Everything. It never took much with Jennifer and me. But there was one argument I remember well. Jennifer hadn't been married for even a year, and she was going to run off with someone. This was a young man who sold insurance with Gary. My husband then. He came to Gladstone when Dean was sick. Yes, the same trip. But Gary came to fetch me. Actually he was ready to drag me back by the hair if need be. And I was just as determined not to go. You never knew that, did you, Mildred? You were so sure I walked out on Dean. But you only knew his side of things. His and Roy's. And I bet Dean was more understanding than Roy, wasn't he? As if it was Roy I divorced. But that's 'neither here nor there,' which is something my mother used to say. And now how did I get to talking about her? Mothers and daughters, I guess. But back to Jennifer. She was bound and determined to go off with that salesman. I tried everything. I tried forbidding her. Not that that *ever* worked with Jennifer. I tried arguing. Finally I asked *why*. 'I want to be loved,' she said. '*I want to be loved.*' 'My God, Jen,' I said to her. 'Listen to yourself. You have a husband who loves you. Your father loves you. *I* love you.' And she looked at me, and she said, 'Not enough, Mother. Not enough.' And I couldn't help it, Mildred. I thought she meant *me*. She was doing that because *I* didn't love her enough."

Edie sits up straighter in her chair. She tilts her head to stop the sudden tears from spilling down her cheeks. Then she resumes talking. "But I don't know, maybe she was right. Maybe it was my fault. Maybe her shortcomings were from no one loving her enough. From *me* not loving her enough. But what *is* enough?"

Edie rubs Mildred's arm.

"And now Jennifer's daughter has shown up here in the company of two young men I don't trust any farther than I can throw them. And I have that same helpless feeling I had with her mother. I know there's nothing I can say or do to pull her away from them."

Edie pauses.

Then she goes on. "Funny that now, after all these years—yes, after almost half a century—*now* I'm asking you for advice. Now, when I never asked before. Now, when it's too late. Telling you these things, you who never had a problem with your boys. You were devoted to them, and they were devoted to you. You can rest easy on that account."

Edie looks at her watch and then stands up. "And now I have to run. I'm sure my granddaughter is growing impatient. Yes, maybe next time she'll come in. Maybe when we have more time."

Edie has almost reached the front door when a young nurse who works in Mildred's wing waddles toward her. "Is she vocalizing today?" she asks Edie. "I was walking by, and I thought I heard you two talking."

"Sorry," says Edie. "That was all me."

The nurse slumps a little with disappointment. "When I heard your voice I was hoping . . ."

"Has she been talking? At all?"

"The last time her son was here. He walked in, and she sort of brightened up and said, 'Dean?' But that was it. And since then, nothing."

Edie shakes her head sadly. "Roy. That was Roy who was here. His twin brother was Dean. He died almost twenty years ago."

The nurse winces. "Roy. Of course. Roy. What's the matter with me?"

"How long ago did she say Dean's name?"

"Well, it was a Sunday of course. You're Saturday and he's Sunday. This was at least a month ago."

"If I hear so much as a word from her," Edie says, "I'll be sure to let you know."

"You never know. She's a tough old gal. She's got about five things wrong with her, and any one of them would kill most folks."

"She once told me," Edie says, "that she'd dance on my grave."

EDIE CLIMBS INTO the car and says with the kind of mock enthusiasm that seldom fools anyone, "And we're off! What sights would you like to see?"

"I don't know," Lauren says. "Maybe like where you used to live? Or where you went to school?"

Edie turns the key in the ignition. "Let the grand tour begin!"

EDIE DRIVES DOWN one of the blocks that make up Gladstone's business district. It's a Saturday morning, but the street is as deserted as on a Sunday and Edie has no trouble finding a place to park.

She points across the street, to the building with the letters Bronze Glow Tanning Salon stenciled on the large front window.

"I used to live there," she says to Lauren. "In an apartment upstairs. My first home. Well, mine and my husband's. And down below was a bakery, so we smelled pies and cakes and cookies all the time. Which was wonderful at first but then became too much." Edie closes her eyes. "It's funny. Most of my life I've lived in other places, but in my dreams I'm so often in those rooms"—Edie opens her eyes and points to the windows over the tanning salon—"and I'm never in the rooms I'm currently living in. I suppose a psychologist could tell me what that's all about."

Lauren points to the narrow storefront next to the tanning salon. The sign in its window says Baubles, Bangles, and Beads. "Is that an Indian store?" Lauren asks. "You know, like Indian beads?"

Edie shakes her head no. "It's just a craft store."

"I know there's a bunch of Indians living around here. Jesse said your neighbor is."

"That's right."

"That must be weird."

Edie comes out of her reverie now and turns to her granddaughter. "No," she says. "It's not weird. Not at all. Why would you say that?"

"I don't know. Just, you know. Indians."

"Rita was my friend in grade school and in junior high. And then she moved away. But she came back to Gladstone before I did, and when I came back Rita helped me find a job and a place to live. I feel very, very lucky to have her for a friend and neighbor."

Lauren shrinks back in her seat. "Okay, Grandma. Okay. Did you know Mom goes to a tanning place? She thinks she looks better with a tan. I've tried to tell her it just makes her look old. You know, because it dries out her skin and all. And then she's like cooked her hair with all the dye jobs. I wish she'd let me fix her hair and dress her." Lauren shrugs and sighs. "But she thinks it's all working for her."

"Your mother," Edie says, "has always been pretty."

"I tried to tell her she can get cancer from those tanning beds." Lauren waves her hands as if she wishes to erase what she's just said. "I know, Grandma, I know. I'm pretty tan. But I kind of have to be. I'm thinking I'll try to be a model, and I'm pretty sure models need to have good tans."

"A model?"

"It wasn't my idea! But we were watching *America's Next Top Model*. Billy and Jesse and me. And Billy and Jesse said I was prettier than any of those women. And it's kind of true, plus I've got the long neck and the long legs you need. And boobs, okay, yeah, but not like too big."

"I think it's a hard life, honey."

"Plus I know like how to wear makeup and how to dress. Girls have always asked me for advice. I could maybe do something in fashion too."

"I'm sure you could. Well, what would you like to see next?"

"Can I ask you something, Grandma? When you broke up with your first husband and Grandpa Gary too, what did you say? I mean, did you just like come right out and say, 'Hey, I don't love you anymore'?"

"Oh, I don't remember. It was so long ago. With Dean, I'd left Gladstone and after I'd been gone for a while I called him. Yes, I suppose that's what I said. Something like that. It sounds so cruel now. But I don't think I had to say anything to your grandfather. He knew. We both knew. Over and done. Why do you ask?"

"And then did they like argue? Did they try to talk you out of it?"

"Talking was pretty much over by that time. And when people don't love each other anymore, you can't really argue them into it. But you still haven't answered me."

Lauren points to the windows over the tanning salon. "So if you still lived up there, you could look out and see yourself now." Then she laughs. "I don't know what made me think that. I just get these like really crazy ideas sometimes."

Edie looks up at the windows too. "I'm not sure we'd recognize each other." Then she shifts her gaze to her granddaughter and touches her lightly on the shoulder. "Are you thinking of breaking up with Billy?"

"I sort of tried to last spring. But he talked me out of it. Mostly he cried. That's what did it, the crying. That and Jesse told me how bad it would bust Billy up if I dropped him."

Edie keeps looking at her.

"Really," Lauren finally says. "It's all good."

"Whatever you say." Edie puts the car in gear but doesn't drive away from the curb. "Anything else you'd like to see?"

"Do you have a Starbucks here, Grandma?"

"Billings I believe is the closest Starbucks. But they've got good coffee at Jitters. It's right over on Fourth Street. Close enough to walk."

"No, that's okay," Lauren says. "How about where you went to high school?"

"It's just a school," Edie says. "Like every other high school in America." Then she must hear herself because she adds, "Okay. Home of the fighting Wildcats here we come."

They drive through Gladstone on rain-washed streets, under canopies of cottonwood, box elder, and ash, but Lauren never looks up from her phone. Edie pulls in behind Gladstone High School, a two-story brick building with wide expanses of blacktop on three of the school's four sides.

"When I was a student here," Edie says, "about a hundred years ago, there was only a small parking lot back here. Then they tore down houses and apartments to make room for more cars."

She points to the far northeast corner of the block. "Over there was the apartment building where my friend Nancy's grandmother lived. I think we ate lunch there almost every day when I was a freshman and a sophomore."

She points toward a section of the school built of a paler brick than the rest of the building. "And that's the new gym," she says. And then she laughs. "The new gym must be fifty years old now!"

"My school was pretty new," Lauren says. "But they put like way too much glass in it, and on sunny days it was so hot you could hardly stand it."

"I remember a hot day in the fall," Edie says, "and my boyfriend was supposed to pick me up after school. He was older and he'd already graduated. Well, when I came out, he wasn't there. I waited and I waited. I sat right over *there* on the steps. And while I was waiting Dean Linderman came along and he sat with me until my boyfriend showed up. And when he finally drove up he told me he couldn't come earlier because he was watching the World Series. That was the end of the two of us. And the start of Dean and me."

Lauren says, "And then he died, right?"

"Well, no, not . . . yes, yes, I suppose. Then he died."

"That was his mom you were visiting?"

"His and Roy's, Dean's twin brother. Yes."

Edie takes another long look at the steps where she waited on a sunlit afternoon. "Why is it," she says, "I keep remembering what I'd just as soon forget."

"WHEN WE LIVED there," Edie says as she stares at the little brick bungalow she has parked in front of, "there were elm trees up and down this block. Trees so big and leafy cloudy days and sunny days didn't seem much different. And we had lilac bushes on either side of the front door. Three blocks that way"—she points south—"lived the Spillers. A young couple who had two little girls. And both the mother and father worked some nights, and when they did, I baby-sat their girls. The mom usually came home first, and when she did she paid me—paid me very well, I might add—and sent me on my way. One night the father came home first. Don Spiller. He paid me, and I started to leave, but he said no, no, he'd walk me home. When we got right *there*"—Edie points to the sidewalk leading to the front door—"I thanked him but he kept walking with me. Then when we got right up there by the lilacs—it was May and they were in full bloom—he grabbed me and kissed me. I'd been kissed before but never like that. This was a *man* and the way he held me was different and the way he kissed was different. Even while it was happening, even while I was afraid he was going to do more than just kiss me— that he was going to rape me right there in the bushes—I thought about his girls and how they were home alone. I felt responsible, like if Mrs. Spiller came home while her husband was here trying to stick his tongue down my throat she'd be mad at *me*. And Mr. Spiller must have assumed I was going to welcome his . . . his . . . what he was doing. That I was a girl getting this kind of attention from a grown man—why wouldn't I think this was wonderful? Why wouldn't I swoon in his arms? Why wouldn't I let him do whatever he wanted? But when I kept trying to pull away, he finally let me go and I went inside and locked the door behind me."

Edie turns back to her granddaughter and says, "And that was the end of my babysitting for the Spillers. My mother was angry that I kept saying no to Mrs. Spiller. 'You need to earn your own money,' she told me."

"What's 'swoon,' Grandma? You said swoon."

"It's . . . it's sort of giving in, collapsing."

"Like turned on?"

"Something closer to fainting."

"Oh. Why didn't you tell your mom what happened?"

Edie stifles a laugh, and the sound that comes out is half a sigh and half a cough. "She wouldn't have believed me. She would have asked me what I did to encourage him."

Lauren nods in eager understanding. "Mom thought I was flirting with Kyle."

"That's the boyfriend who's younger?"

"I could have told her to look at how he looks at me."

"But you didn't."

Lauren shakes her head no.

"I'm sorry, honey."

"That's why I'm not in like a real big hurry to go back. One of the reasons."

"And that's why I can't stand the smell of lilacs. Come on. Let's go to Jitters."

BECAUSE JITTERS JAVA occupies the space that was once Shaw's Rexall, Edie and her granddaughter wait for their coffee at the counter where Edie once drank lime phosphates. Ahead of them in line is a woman who, when she receives her coffee, turns and says, "Edie! I've been meaning to call you."

"Well, here I am. What did you need, Joan?"

This woman looks to be Edie's age, but the sun has toughened her face and arms like animal hide. Her hair with its loose curls is raven black. Her eyes are heavily outlined, and she has given her lips a shape not quite theirs with bright red lipstick.

"I know it's a ways off," Joan says, "but we're putting together a committee for the next class reunion, and someone said you might be willing to serve on it."

Edie shakes her head. "No. Sorry."

"Are you sure? There wouldn't be all that much work. Think about it. Tomorrow we're having an organizational meeting at Keith and Mary's. Down by the river? Right next to Frontier Park?"

"I know where they live."

"If you come, bring a suit. We might go *swim-ming*." She sings the syllables of that word and smiles coyly at Edie.

Edie puts her arm around Lauren. "Sorry," Edie says. "I have company. My granddaughter."

Edie and Lauren carry their coffee and cappuccino to a small table.

Lauren says, "What was her deal, Grandma? What's all that about swimming?"

Edie sighs and seems to be considering whether she should provide an answer. Finally she says, "It's silly. I can't believe any of this matters."

But she moves her chair closer to Lauren.

"On our graduation night there was a big party down by the river. That's where the park is she was talking about. Bonfires. Beer. And some of us went swimming. I say swimming but not really. Splashing in the water, not much more than that. On a dare, because the water was so cold. My God, it was cold. But we undressed before we went in. I mean, nobody had a bathing suit. So we stripped down to our underwear. Bras and panties for some girls. Just panties for a few others. And nothing at all for one or two girls. Joan remembers that I was one of the girls who took everything off. But I wasn't. Yes, I stripped down to my bra and panties before I jumped in. And does it matter to me? Not really. Except it just seems like every time I run into someone who knew me then, I feel like a part of me vanishes. I mean, Joan might as well carry an eraser with her. Every time we bump into each other, she rubs out another part of me."

"Have you told her?" Lauren asks. "Have you said, 'Look, bitch, that's not what I did'?"

Edie shakes her head no. "I don't give a damn if she thinks I was naked or wearing my prom dress. I wasn't the best-behaved girl back then, and I sure as hell wasn't modest. Maybe I would have taken everything off. That's not the point. It's that when she's remembering me she doesn't remember *me*. I mean, all of us are someone else in the eyes of others. And for all I know, maybe that other is as true, as real, as the person we believe we are. But the thing is, when you're back home, you never have a chance to be someone other than who you were then. Even if you never were that person."

Edie pauses and looks away from her granddaughter. "And Dean's mother—if she remembers me at all anymore, it's just as the woman who ran out on her boy and broke his heart. But what makes me think we have any right to control the memories of others?"

When Edie turns back to her granddaughter, she sees in her eyes a look both bewildered and alarmed.

"Oh God, what am I *doing*?" Edie says. "Here I am, yakking away and with one sleazy story after another. Nude swimming. Bad boyfriends. Attacked by a father. I'm sorry, honey. You should have just told me to shut up."

"That's okay, Grandma. I don't mind. You probably needed someone to talk to."

"And you wanted to see Gladstone and now I've made it seem awful. It's not. Really. It's a nice town. No better and no worse than most towns."

"You know what we did on my graduation night?" Lauren asks brightly. "We got high and went bowling. Me and Billy and Jesse."

"Is Jesse always with you and Billy?"

"Not *always* always but pretty much all the rest of the time. It's weird because Billy says Jesse needs us and Jesse says Billy needs him. Jesse said we're like the three Mouseketeers."

"Don't you ever need to be alone?"

"Not really."

"But how about you and Billy?" Edie asks. "Sometimes it needs to be just the two of you."

Lauren slaps the tabletop as if her grandmother has just said something hilarious. "Oh, Grandma! He's not with us *then*!"

"I meant, finally it has to be the two of you."

Smiling widely, Lauren holds up both hands with three fingers showing. "The three Mouseketeers!"

"THEY'RE OUT ON the town tonight," Rita says. "Is that right?"

Edie and Rita stand on Rita's balcony, drinking white wine and looking westward, where the thin clouds that drifted in late in the day have taken on a yellow-orange tint, though the sun has not yet dropped below the horizon.

"It was my idea," Edie says. "I gave Lauren some money and suggested they go out to eat and take in a movie. 'Come with us,' she said. But I told her I was tired. Which was not a lie."

"How much did you give her?"

"Fifty dollars."

Rita doesn't say anything but sucks air through her teeth.

"Cheaper than trying to come up with another meal idea," Edie says.

"How about you? Did you eat?"

"I fried an egg. Which was just right."

"Well, here's my prediction—they'll take that money and eat cheap at Hardee's and then go to a bar and drink what's left over."

"Lauren's only eighteen."

Rita scoffs. "Shouldn't take them more than a couple tries to find a bar that'll serve her. By the way, what's with that girl's hair? I know it's supposed to be some kind of style, but it just looks like she never washes or combs it. Lord."

"She wants to give me a complete makeover. I told her it was too late for me."

Rita leans back to examine Edie. "At least you wash your damn hair." Then Rita holds her glass up to let the dying light shine through the wine. "Guess who called me today? Cousin Dennis."

"This is the cousin who isn't really a cousin?"

"One and the same. By the way, I finally figured out how that got started. We were together so much when we were kids and we got along so well it put a fright into my mother. So she told me Dennis was my cousin. And she got *his* mother to tell him the same damn thing. By the time we figured out what was what, we were both with someone else."

"And what was your mother's objection to him?"

"She thought he wasn't good enough for me. She finally let it slip. 'You can do better than some Indian,' she said. So when I brought

Norman home to meet her, she all but fell to her knees and bowed down to that white boy."

"How was it," Edie says, "that neither of us had a mother who was on our side?"

"It was pretty simple with my mother. She didn't like herself, so she didn't like Indians."

"And now Dennis is back . . . How do we like his chances this time around?"

Rita nods thoughtfully. "I believe he'll fare very well. Very well. How about you? Would you like me to see if he has a friend?"

"I'll pass," Edie says.

"Wouldn't you just like some male company from time to time? Someone to go to a movie with?"

"You know what? I order these movies from Netflix, and most of the time I return them unwatched."

Rita leans closer to Edie. "Okay. I can see I'm being too subtle. *Go to a movie* is a euphemism. I mean sex. Wouldn't you like someone to have sex with? Don't you miss sex?"

Edie wrinkles her nose. "Kissing? Would kissing have to be involved?"

"I think you'd get to call the shots on that one. But physical contact, for sure. No sex without physical contact."

Edie laughs. "What I think I miss is having someone in my life I'd *want* to have sex with. I'm not sure about the act itself."

"You want someone to love."

"Do I?"

"But maybe you should start with sex. And don't give me that shit we're too old. When I'm too old for that you can just kick some dirt on me."

Edie says, "When I was young I wanted love but sex is what I got. Later, when I wanted sex, I got love. It kept going back and forth like that . . . I kept believing one had to lead to the other, that they were two streams that had to merge into one river. And maybe at times they did. Maybe I was wrong to want both, maybe I was wrong to think of them as separate. Men didn't seem to much care about the difference."

"I'll go you one better," Rita says. "Norman could tell me he loved me when he had his hands around my throat and his cock inside me. I swear to God, he was never more tender than when he was kissing a bruise he'd given me just an hour before."

"You win," says Edie. "But I didn't think we were competing."

"We're not." Rita lifts her glass to her lips and drinks. "So that's what you used to want. What about now?"

"I'm not sure," Edie says. "Maybe not to want at all."

"How's that working for you?"

"You know, at lunch this week I had a little outburst. I told Dr. Hackett I was sick of how men kept turning out to be the subject of every conversation the three of us—she and Bonnie and I—had. And now here *we* are. Talking about men."

Rita reaches across the space separating them and takes Edie's hand. "Honey, we're not talking about men. We're talking about *us*."

They both turn back toward the west. The sun has set and the horizon is smudged with violet. The trail of a jet, a gold streak against the depthless blue, dissipates like a watercolor brushstroke.

"And how," Rita says, "did the sightseeing tour go?"

"Well, I don't know how it was for Lauren, but it surprised the hell out of me. We were in Gladstone *today* but I kept seeing Gladstone *then*."

"It's your hometown. It's your history. What did you expect to see?"

"I guess I thought the past was dead and gone."

"You better ask me to come along next time you contemplate an excursion like that. I can give you a few lessons in then and now."

The door behind them slides open, and George Real Bird steps onto the balcony. He's dressed in his usual attire—snug gray T-shirt, khaki cargo shorts—but tonight he's wearing his artificial leg. And that smooth, pink attachment with its chrome steel joints practically glows in the waning light of evening. With stiff steps he walks over to lean on the balcony rail closest to Edie. He reaches into the pocket of his shorts and pulls out a crumpled pack of Marlboros and a Zippo lighter. He raises a cigarette to his lips and lights it. Then he flicks his wrist, and the Zippo closes with a clank.

"Just waiting for it to get dark, huh?" he says.

"Like a couple of vampires," his mother replies.

"How's your leg doing, George?" Edie asks him.

"Feels like shit," he says. "But I thought maybe if I try it just an hour or two a day, I'll eventually get used to it."

"That sounds like a wonderful plan."

"Just like it did," Rita says, "when I suggested it months ago."

George ignores his mother's remark and says to Edie, "You promised me you'd go dancing with me if I got this leg working."

Edie laughs. "I believe I said I'd come to *watch* you."

George smiles and wags his finger in her direction. "Well, just be ready."

"I'd be proud to watch you dance," says Edie. "Your mother and I both would be. By the way, did Lauren and the boys stop by earlier? I told her you might be interested in going out with them."

"I passed," George says. He inhales deeply and then blows a lungful of smoke into the night air. "That Jesse is the kind of trouble I don't need."

"Trouble of what sort?" Rita asks.

"Oh, you know. He's always got the cure for what ails you."

Rita says, "And what pray tell would that be?"

George shrugs. "This and that."

"My God," Rita says. "Can you give me a straight answer?"

"You remember Darryl Whitman? Same deal."

"That boy." Rita shakes her head. "Lord. Ended up in Red Lodge and broke his mother's heart."

George seems to notice that Edie is trying not to hear this exchange. "So what did I walk in on? What are the two of you plotting out here?"

Rita swirls her wine. "I was telling Edie that I've renewed my acquaintance with Dennis Old Coyote. You might recall—"

George interrupts her with his laughter. "Now that Grandma Lou is dead!"

"He's *not* my cousin, you know."

"Yeah, Ma. I know. What's Cousin Dennis doing with his life now? Is he still on the rez?"

"He's retired, more or less. And no. He's living on his sister's ranch. Helping out since her husband had a stroke. And he's not—"

George holds up his hand. "'Retired, more or less'—what's that mean anyway? *I'm* retired more or less."

"I told you. He's working on the ranch. He worked for Montana-Dakota Utilities for many years, you know."

"Okay. He's a pillar of the community. You have my blessing." He pushes himself away from the balcony rail and heads toward the door. "I'll let you two vampires get back to it," he says.

"DON'T, BILLY," LAUREN whispers. "*Don't.*"

Edie lies still on the sofa, feigning sleep, though she can see through the slits of her eyes a dim, shadowy version of what's going on—the three of them have just returned from their night out.

Lauren twists away from Billy, who's trying to put a hand down the back of her jeans.

"Just *wait*," Lauren says. But then she laughs. And Billy laughs too.

Jesse, following behind them, puts a finger to his lips. "Shh."

And then Lauren and Billy are gone, down the hallway to the room where Edie has always slept alone. Jesse remains behind. He stares at Edie as though he's trying to determine if her breathing is a sleeper's or a pretender's.

"Are you awake?" he whispers.

Edie neither stirs nor replies.

Then he's gone too, off to his own bedroom.

The children are home. Edie feels under her pillow to that space between the arm of the sofa and the cushion for the hammer that she's been keeping there. With her hand around its handle, she finally drifts toward sleep, but she can't quite reach its shore. Yes, the children are finally home.

EDIE WAKES UP to the smell of burnt toast and coffee. The sun has not yet risen, but enough light has entered the apartment for objects to acquire their outlines of form and solidity. And birds have already started up. When she sits up on the sofa, she sees Jesse in the kitchen sitting in a chair that allows him to watch her. She reaches immediately for the robe lying on the coffee table and manages to put it on without standing up.

Jesse gives her a little wave. Then he gets up from the chair and, coffee cup in hand, comes into the living room.

"Have a bad dream?" he asks her. He's shirtless and barefoot and dressed in the same baggy shorts he's been wearing since he arrived. "You were sort of twitching all over," he says. "Like a dog chasing rabbits in his sleep."

"How long have you been up?" Edie asks.

"Never really went to bed. Did you hear my guitar? I was trying to keep it down. Playing helps me sleep sometimes. But not last night. About an hour ago I said hell with it. Made that coffee quiet as I could. Then I got hungry. That's a for-shit toaster you got, by the way."

"You didn't bother me," Edie says.

"Didn't seem like I did." He sits down in the rocking chair and nods in the direction of Edie's bedroom. "I'd like to get those two up so we can hit the road early but they'll be so pissy they'll be miserable company. So let 'em sleep, I decided."

"Any place you need to be by any particular time?"

"Nope. Free as birds, we are."

"Must be nice," Edie says and stands up and begins to fold the bedding.

"Were your ears burning last night?" Jesse asks. "Because we were talking about you. Lauren says you've had some rough luck in your life. A husband who died on you. Another one who walked out. But I guess a true Montanan like yourself is tough enough to stand up to the hard times."

Edie stops folding and sits down on the sofa. She shakes her head slowly. "That girl," she says. "I don't know how she can get so many things so wrong. For the record, Dean Linderman died of cancer some twenty years after we were divorced. As for Lauren's grandfather walking out, it was plain either he'd have to get out or I would. As it turned out, we both did."

"And you came back here. Lauren says you're none too happy in Gladstone."

"She has that wrong too."

Jesse nods. "Sure," he says. "Sure. You got yourself a nice little life here. But you ain't got all you want."

"And what is it that I don't have?" Edie asks.

Jesse smiles slyly. "You tell me."

Edie smooths a few of the sheet's wrinkles as it lies across her lap. "As for being a 'true Montanan,'" she says, "I'm not even sure what that means."

"We love our freedom," Jesse says. "Simple as that."

"Is there a place where they don't?"

"And we like to do things our own way. Without someone in an office a hundred or a thousand miles away telling us different."

Edie doesn't say anything in reply. She stands now, she has to in order to finish with the sheet. And once it's in a folded package as tight and compact as a flag that might have covered a serviceman's coffin, she hugs it to her bosom. "But I've lived enough years in the West," she says, "to understand something about young men like you. I've seen them in bars and on street corners and in their cars and trucks. You love your freedom all right. Free to be some sort of outlaw. If I could pry my granddaughter loose from you and your brother, I would."

"Well, Granny, you can let go of that dream. She's ours."

THE BLAZER IS packed, the back section of the vehicle heaped with nylon packs and bags and Lauren's graduation suitcase. Jesse's black guitar case has been propped upright in the back seat like the family dog that has to see out all the windows. A few of the doughnuts left over from those Edie bought this morning at Albertsons are in a white bag on the center console. Billy is behind the wheel; Lauren is in the seat across from him; and Jesse is in the back seat, looking for all the world like their child, his fingers already busy with his chirping Game Boy.

The thank-yous and good-byes have been said, grandmother and granddaughter have embraced, and now Edie stands back from the car, her arms folded as if there were a chill in this summer morning. Lauren's window is down, and Edie says to her, "Will you call me when you get where you're going?"

Lauren laughs. "How can I when I don't know where that is?"

ON HER RECEPTIONIST'S desk, Edie has an index card with over a week's worth of dates written down. Next to each date are penciled check marks, no fewer than five marks for a date and as many as ten for the day before, a Monday.

When Kenneth Aldinger walks past Hackett Dental Care for the third time this morning—it's not yet ten o'clock—Edie marks his appearance with a check. But then she jumps up from her desk, goes outside, and runs down the sidewalk. She catches up to him in front of McFarland's Ace Hardware, and when she steps in front of him and spreads her arms wide, he has no choice but to stop.

"Mr. Aldinger," Edie says. "Stop. Just stop. What are you *doing*?"

He gestures vaguely in a direction past Edie. "I was just . . . I was going to—"

"No." Edie shakes her head. "No, you weren't going anywhere. You were walking past my door. You've been doing it over and over, day after day. Do you think I can't see you?"

He turns and points in the other direction. "My office," he says, "my office is right over—"

Edie says, "No. N-O. There's nothing you do in or out of your office that requires you to walk up and down this street. I know what you're doing, Mr. Aldinger. You're after me or something. I can see you, you know. Every time you walk by. Every day."

No doubt with the intention of getting past Edie, Kenneth Aldinger steps quickly to the side, toward the bags of grass seed and fertilizer stacked for display in wheelbarrows outside McFarland's. She's too quick for him however, and with both hands she grabs his arm.

He looks down at her hands encircling his upper arm. The dark wool of his suit wrinkles in her grasp, but he makes no attempt to pull away. Edie Pritchard is touching him, and though there is nothing approaching affection in her grasp, here they are. *Here they are.*

Edie detects a shift in this moment, some flex or twitch in the muscle of the arm she holds, some gleam in his eye, something that she recognizes as the first stirring men feel when a woman stands close to them. She lets go and steps away.

"Your teeth, Mr. Aldinger, are fine. You don't need to come into the office again. Not for a very long time. And you need to find yourself a different street to walk up and down."

Kenneth Aldinger takes a moment to compose himself, to become once again the successful businessman, the civic leader, the church deacon. Then he turns and walks away from Edie Pritchard, crossing the street with a stiff-backed bearing that doesn't allow him to look anywhere but straight ahead.

LAUREN AND BILLY are conducting their quarrel behind a two-story farmhouse badly in need of paint and repair, a shelter wanting shelter. Because the yard is more dirt than grass, and the uncut weedy grass is almost as tall as the surrounding fescue, the farmyard is barely distinguishable from the prairie. A small stand of scrub oak marks the end of the property line, but none of its shade reaches Lauren and Billy where they sit in the glare of the midday sun, she in a flimsy aluminum lawn chair and Billy cross-legged at her feet.

"Jesus, Laure. We're not talking about you fucking somebody else. This is just you and me. We're going to fuck anyway, right? The only thing that's different is somebody's going to pay to watch us. So instead of doing it for nothing, we'll be doing it for money. Get it? We'll be getting paid to fuck. If you can come up with a better goddamn deal than that, I'd like to know what it'd be."

"Whose idea was this? Jesse's, right?"

"Nah, nah. He said it's totally up to you."

"And I said no."

"But he did say we'll have to find some way to make money. He's thinking probably selling pills. Matt is bringing a shit-ton back from Canada. Jesse said we'd help him move it."

"*We?*"

"Well, him and me." Billy turns his palms up. "But you know what happens if he gets caught dealing. That's prison."

Lauren is wearing sunglasses, and she tilts the glasses up on top of her head so she can turn the full force of her glower at Billy. "Boo-fucking-hoo," she says.

"I got to do my part too," says Billy. "How would you feel about visiting both of us in the slammer?"

"'The slammer.' Ooh, listen to you."

"I'm just saying, you know. You got to go into it with your eyes open. Now, if we go the other route"—Billy begins to draw circles inside circles in the dust—"we let Garth watch us, we get maybe fifty bucks every time."

"Fifty dollars. A fuck of a lot of good that'll do us."

"I don't know what your problem is. You know you look good. You didn't have a problem letting me have those pictures. Or those you took yourself. I mean, come *on*. What are you getting all modest for now?"

Lauren springs forward in her chair. "Did you show those to any-one? *Did you?*"

"I told you I wouldn't."

"You swear?"

"Do I swear? Okay. What the hell. Yeah. I swear I didn't."

"Not even Jesse?"

Billy laughs. "*Especially* not Jesse."

She leans back in the chair and lowers her sunglasses. After a long moment she says, "So . . . Garth, huh?"

"What can I say? He's nothing but an old horndog."

"Does Marilyn know?"

"How should I know?" Now, instead of circles in the dust, Billy makes slashing diagonal lines. Lightning bolts.

"What did he say? When he asked—"

"He didn't ask *me*."

"Oh my God! No, don't tell me!" Lauren stands so swiftly that the chair tips over.

"Jesse got him to agree he wouldn't be in the room—"

"Jesse?"

"He'd be like outside the door. Or we could do a movie—"

"And who's going to hold the camera? Like I don't know the answer to that!"

"We could do it ourselves, I bet."

Lauren gives him the finger and walks away.

ONCE THE FULL moon gains some height, it's like a yellow spotlight trying to fix its beam on the farmyard, plenty of light for Jesse to cross the yard and find Lauren, sitting in the lawn chair. She's drinking a beer, and she's still wearing her sunglasses.

"There you are," Jesse says.

"Like it's a big secret."

"Mosquitoes will eat you alive out here."

Jesse walks around in front of Lauren. He grabs ahold of a low branch of one of the oaks and pulls on it as if he's trying to determine whether it will support his weight. "The moonlight too bright for you?"

"What?"

"The shades. Or maybe you're going for the movie star look."

Lauren doesn't say anything.

"Marilyn and the girls are going into town. I think I'll ride along. You want to come?"

"Not really."

"Suit yourself. You need anything?"

"Kind of late to go shopping, isn't it?"

"Hey, that's Marilyn. Takes her a long time to get organized."

Jesse is still hanging on to that branch, and now he lifts his feet off the ground and gently swings back and forth. "You're okay staying here with the menfolk?"

"Why wouldn't I be?"

"A joke, kid. I was making a joke." He lets go of the branch and drops to the ground. "Billy said he talked to you about Garth."

"Yeah."

"And he said you weren't too keen on the idea."

"That's a fucking understatement."

"Hey, you don't want to, nobody's going to force you. I get it. I really do. Only . . ."

"Only what?"

"Nothing, nothing. It's your decision. Totally. It doesn't matter. Forget it."

"*What?*" Lauren asks. "What doesn't matter?"

"There's a little more to it. I mean, more than Billy knows."

"You mean like you're going to prison if I say no?" Her voice drips with scorn.

Jesse laughs. "What the hell did he say to you anyway? Jesus. No."

"Then *what?*"

"Well, I know Garth wants to come off as this jolly old hippie who doesn't give a shit about anything but smoking weed and blasting his music so fucking loud it makes your ears bleed, but I'm pretty sure he's having a problem getting it up. So that means he's worried about Marilyn too because they've always acted like they're both free to, you know. Get it wherever they can find it."

"He told you all this?"

"Sort of. But I kind of got the rest from Marilyn."

"And watching somebody fuck is going to help him get it up? Why doesn't he watch porn like everybody else on the fucking planet? Or take a pill like any other old man with a limp dick."

"Jesus, Laure. That's icy. Besides . . ."

"What? *What?*"

"I don't think it's watching just anybody fuck. It's you. Hey, you know you have this . . . effect. You can't blame the guy."

"Yeah. Yeah, I can."

"Okay," Jesse says and holds up his hands. "Not another word about it. You said no. That's the end of it."

"Except now I don't want to be like even in the same room with him."

"Well, don't say anything to him. Or to Marilyn. They're letting us crash here." Jesse slaps at his arm. "Fucking mosquitoes. Okay. I'm going. And you don't want anything from town?"

"No."

Jesse starts toward the house. He has almost outpaced the reach of the moonlight when Lauren calls after him.

"Hey, you know what you sounded like before? Trying to talk all sweet and reasonable? Like a fucking pimp."

Jesse laughs.

LAUREN ENTERS THE house through the back door and blinks in the kitchen's bright overhead light. She walks to the refrigerator, opens it, and takes out another beer.

Standing over the kitchen table, measuring ingredients into a stainless steel mixing bowl is Garth. He's the size of an NFL lineman. His long salt-and-pepper hair is tied back in a ponytail. His beard is long enough to cover his throat.

Without looking up at Lauren he asks, "Find what you're looking for?"

"Yeah." She deftly twists the cap off the bottle. "You want one, Garth?"

"Not while I'm working." He picks up a half-teaspoon measure and dips it delicately into the baking soda, which he drops into the bowl. "By the way," he says, "both your boys went with Marilyn."

"Billy went?"

"Uh-huh."

She looks from one corner of the room to another. "Randy?"

"He's in the living room. Watching *Finding Nemo* for about the eleven thousandth time."

She walks over to the doorway where she can see for herself.

Garth wipes his hands on his jeans and says to Lauren, "How many beers are left in there?"

"Three, I think. Yeah. Three."

"Let's check, shall we?" He walks to the refrigerator, opens the door, and peers inside. "One, two, three. Right you are, Miss Keller." He closes the refrigerator and with a smile asks, "And how many people are living in this house?"

"Counting Jesse and Billy and me?"

He spreads his arms expansively. "Why not?"

Lauren's forehead puckers with concentration. "Eight?"

"Eight. That's very good. And when Matt returns, which could be at any time, nine. Now then. Marilyn's girls don't drink. Randy—obviously not. Marilyn likes her wine, so she rarely drinks beer. Still, hot weather—she'll crack a beer. So that's five of us. And three beers left? Who's going without?"

There's nothing threatening about Garth, nothing except his size, but perhaps that's enough. Lauren starts to back away from him. But then stops and stands firm.

"Well, Miss Keller? Who?"

Lauren shrugs. "I don't know."

"And who put those beers in the refrigerator?"

"I don't know. Marilyn?"

"Marilyn. That's right. Marilyn. And when she comes back tonight, she'll put some more in there. And who gave Marilyn the money to buy the beer? Or the food you see in there? You're catching my drift here, aren't you? And those muffins I'm making for everyone's breakfast—who bought the ingredients? Who's doing the baking? Now, I don't want to go all Little Red Hen on you, but if you want to drink the fucking beer and eat the fucking muffins maybe you should give some thought to how you can make a contribution around here."

Lauren walks back to the refrigerator, opens its door, and puts her opened bottle of beer back inside. Then she slams the door so hard that its contents clink and rattle.

"Your muffins suck," she says and steps out the back door.

Lauren walks around to the front of the house and then continues down the dirt driveway until she arrives at the blacktop county road that runs past the farm. She looks up and down the highway, but there's nothing but darkness in either direction. She steps out into the road and stands right in the middle. The only terrestrial light comes from a farmhouse in a far-off fold of hills. How far away? A mile? Two? Three? Distances are as difficult to gauge out here as the light from stars.

She reaches into her back pocket and takes out her phone, the light from its screen so bright out here in the darkness it seems as though the phone is looking back at her. Then she punches in a number.

WHEN THE WIND blows hard from a certain direction—west by northwest—the window in Edie's bedroom hums and whistles in its frame. And though this usually occurs in the fall or winter, Edie wakes up and looks toward that window. Then the phone buzzes and vibrates again on her bedside table, and she comes fully alert. She opens its shell.

"Grandma?"

"Lauren? What is it, honey? Where are you?"

"Do you think I could come and stay with you, Grandma?"

"Is something wrong, Lauren?"

Her granddaughter doesn't answer.

"Where are you? Can you tell me that?"

"I just thought . . . I don't know. I thought it would be different."

"Of course you can come here. Of course you can. You can come here."

"The thing is, I don't have any way to get there."

"What's going on there, honey? You can't get a ride here?"

"No, no . . ."

"Could you take the bus? Would that be possible?"

"I don't really have any money. Or a way to . . ."

"Lauren. Are you all right? Listen to me. Are you *okay*?"

"Oh sure. It's just that—"

"And you're not in trouble?"

"Oh no. Nothing like that. Nothing like you mean. But could you maybe come get me?"

"Of course I can. You just tell me where you are."

"I'm not sure."

"You're not *sure*?"

"Well, I mean, Bismarck. We're in Bismarck. Kind of. We're on a farm. Kind of a farm. I mean, nobody's like farming. It used to be a farm."

"Okay, okay. That's fine. But you'll have to tell me how to get there."

A sound comes through the phone that could be the halting breaths of a girl who believed she had reached an age when her tears would finally be under her control. Or it could be nothing but electromagnetic dust, all the particles, beams, waves, and weakening signals that come between what one person's tongue sends and another person's ear receives.

"Lauren? Did you hear me?"

"I'm not sure. I'll try."

"Or could you meet me somewhere?"

"I don't think so. Maybe . . ."

"Just tell me where you are, Lauren. I'll come for you."

There's another silence, long enough for Edie to check whether the connection has been lost.

"I'll call you, Grandma. Or I'll text you. Can you get texts?"

"I'll be waiting, honey. But is there anything—"

"I have to go," she whispers.

And this time there can be no doubt. The call is over.

"HOW MANY TIMES have I told you kids not to play in the road?" Garth shouts.

Lauren puts her phone back in her pocket.

"You can't be out there playing in the traffic!" he says, laughing.

Lauren takes a last look down the highway. Then she walks back up the driveway. When she's almost to the porch, Garth holds an opened bottle of beer out to her. "You might as well drink this," he says. "You can't just leave an open beer in the fridge. It'll go flat."

She takes the beer, but she doesn't step onto the porch.

"You want one of those sucky muffins?" he asks. "First batch is about to come out of the oven."

"What kind?"

"Oat bran. With walnuts and raisins. Guaranteed to lower your cholesterol. Not that you need to worry your pretty little head about that."

"Thanks but no thanks," she says.

"Suit yourself. There'll be plenty if you change your mind. No one else likes them either."

She looks back at the road. "Did they say when they'd be back?"

"Nope. Once you let Marilyn loose in Walmart, she's liable to wander around in there for hours."

"Jesse hates Walmart."

"Does he now? Well, I'm with him on that. But if you want to understand America, you got to put in your time at Walmart."

He turns to go inside but then stops, holding the screen door open for her. "You coming?" he asks.

"Not yet."

"Okay," Garth says. "Come in if the mosquitoes get bad."

As soon as he goes in Lauren steps onto the wide wooden porch. She paces from one creaking end to the other, drinking her beer and staring up and down the highway.

AN OVERHEAD FLUORESCENT light in Walmart flickers, dims, brightens, then dims again. Marilyn is pushing a cart loaded with toilet paper, Tide laundry detergent, paper towels, and Diet Coke. She says, "They better fix that before someone has a seizure right here."

Marilyn is a big woman, tall, heavy breasted, and wide hipped, and she leans on the handle of the cart for support. But even as she lumbers through the aisles, that large body sways in a way that causes both men and women to slow down and watch her approach.

Jesse walks alongside the cart like a child who has been admonished to stay close to a parent. Marilyn turns to him and says, "So whatever you and Matt have planned, it can't be anything that people can get strung out on or OD on. So no meth. No speed. No heroin for sure. No crack or coke. If it just makes you feel good, probably yes. If it kills the pain, maybe yes, maybe no."

"Doesn't leave much."

"What can I tell you? Garth's real old school."

"How about oxy?" Jesse asks.

"Borderline. Judgment call."

"X?"

"Probably okay. But in my limited experience, North Dakotans don't go for it in a super big way. I have no idea why. But no matter what, you have to know if you're looking to deal something in volume, there just isn't that big a market here. I mean, the whole goddamn state has fewer people than Minneapolis. And it's not just a problem of fewer buyers. It's the wrong ones. Sooner or later you'll sell to someone you shouldn't."

"So weed, I guess."

"Oh, and Garth won't stand for selling *anything* on a reservation."

"Jesus."

"His house," Marilyn says. "His rules."

"The thing is," Jesse says, "Matt didn't go up to Canada to shop around. He's for sure coming back with something. I just don't know what. Maybe he talked it over with Garth before he left."

She shakes her head no. "If he did, honey, I'd know about it."

Up ahead Billy is approaching. He waves as though either he or his brother has been lost for days. Behind him are Marilyn's daughters, Tiffany and Sarah, gangly girls smiling in the heaven of a discount store. They wave too.

Jesse pulls Billy away from the others. Once they are halfway down the pet care aisle, Jesse says, "The camcorder's got to have a zoom, okay?"

Billy nods enthusiastically. "A JVC looks like it's the easiest," he says. "Except the guy says it can be a problem in low light. But then he told me a bunch of shit you can do to make it work okay."

"But a zoom, right? It's got to have a zoom."

"Yeah, yeah. But it ain't cheap."

"It'll pay for itself," Jesse says. He takes out his billfold and hands it to his brother. "Go to a different checkout than the one she goes to."

When Jesse walks back to meet Marilyn again, she stops the cart, looks at him, and smiles. "I've been thinking on your problem," she says. "You could always move out. Then you can sell anything you fucking well please."

THE CAR TURNS off the highway and up the driveway, its headlights sweeping across the porch and illuminating the girl sitting on the step. She stands up and all but runs down the gravel drive.

The car has barely come to a stop before Billy gets out and hurries to meet her. "What's the matter?" he asks her. "Garth?"

She shakes her head no.

As they walk toward the farmhouse, Garth turns on the porch light and steps outside. "Need a hand?" he asks.

"Not while I have my two strapping young centurions here," Marilyn says. She pops open the trunk and says to Billy and Jesse, "Just take all that shit to the kitchen."

Marilyn and her daughters head toward the porch while Billy, Jesse, and Lauren take the bags and boxes from Walmart and the Bottle Stop Liquor Store around the back of the house.

As they walk through the dark, Billy asks Lauren, "Why'd you want to stay here with him? I thought—"

"*What?* No. I thought you were still here."

"He didn't say anything? Or . . ."

"Not exactly."

"What the fuck does that mean?"

"Hey," Lauren says. "why are you getting mad at *me*?"

Jesse has overheard them, and he laughs and says, "Kids, come on now. No fighting. Don't make me give you a time-out!"

The two girls go into the living room and sit on the floor with Randy for yet another viewing of *Finding Nemo*. The adults gather in the kitchen, amid the smell of fresh-baked muffins and under the bright overhead bulb where a few insects now circle and flutter.

THE RED NUMERALS on the clock on Edie's nightstand say it's 11:28. She climbs out of bed and goes out on her balcony. The night is warm and a faintly yeasty aroma travels on the air, the smell perhaps of the bread that bakes while others sleep.

A voice says, "I don't want to scare you." But of course it's too late.

Edie startles and turns toward the sound. George Real Bird is sitting on the adjacent balcony in one of the plastic patio chairs. "Sorry," he says.

"My God," she says. "George. What are you doing out here?"

He holds up his cigarette. "Getting my nicotine ration. You start as late in the day as I do, you got to put in some long hours to get it all in. But I'm out here most nights. What's your excuse?"

Edie fans her face with her hand. "I still don't do well with air-conditioning. It's too chilly when it's running, and when it cycles off it's too stuffy."

"You could just open your windows. It's not going to rain."

Edie smiles. "Our own private weatherman."

George holds up a finger and corrects her. "Weather *advisor*. Without the expert training provided by the United States military, the Iraqi weather officers wouldn't have been able to use the Tactical Meteorological Observation System, which enabled them to predict that it was going to be hot and dry. Followed by more hot and dry."

"I'm sorry, George. Does everything remind you of over there?"

George Real Bird exhales a cloud of smoke. "Only the stars. Or the sun. Or wind. Or clouds." He looks up at the night sky. "Speaking of which, if these clouds would move out we'd have a great view of the full moon." He points up and off to his left. "Right. Up. *There*."

"I see you're not wearing your leg tonight."

"Don't need it to smoke. But I was wearing it all evening."

"I appreciate that you're giving it another try. And I know your mom does too."

"Yes'm, Miz Edie, I'm-a-tryin'."

"I mean it."

"So do I. I plan to take you up on that promise to go dancing. I think the damn thing needs an alteration though. Maybe shorten the inseam."

Edie laughs politely. "When I first came out here, something reminded me of a summer night long, long ago. Dean and I—Dean was my first husband—"

"I can keep track. Dean. Yeah."

"And we were living in an apartment downtown right above the bakery. Summer nights—my God, it was stifling. Anyway. We woke up one night to the sound of a car horn honking. Both of us got up to look, and down in the street was Dean's brother, Roy. He was sitting in a little red convertible. An MG, maybe? Something new, for sure. Back then it seemed like Roy had a different car every month.

"When he saw us he waved for us to come down. We didn't sleep in much, but I put on a robe and I think Dean pulled on a pair of gym shorts.

"'Let's go for a ride,' Roy said. Dean didn't want to go. He had to get up and go to work in a few hours. We all had to go to work. But Roy and I talked Dean into going. The car was a little two-seater, and the twins sat in front. I sat in the back, sort of. Up on the trunk. Like in a parade. But there wasn't a soul on the street to see us. I'd been so hot in bed, and riding around, with the wind blowing my hair back and cooling me off . . . it just felt wonderful.

"After we drove around the streets for a while, Roy headed out of town. West. No one was on the highway either. At least that's the way I remember it. Nobody but us. I don't know how far we went. Quite a ways. Because when we turned around and headed back toward Gladstone, the sun was coming up.

"'Let's not go back,' I said. 'Let's just keep going.' Totally impractical. Totally impossible. But Roy looked over at Dean. Dean just shook his head. I knew we'd never do anything like that again."

George clears his throat and asks, "And what was it you *were* doing?"

"I'm not sure. Riding around in a convertible on a summer night? There must have been more to it. Leaving? I still don't know. But we came back. And here I am."

They fall silent for a long moment. Then Edie says, "When you said something the other night about Jesse being trouble, what did you mean? Specifically."

"Well, he's doing a little dealing."

"Drugs, you mean?"

"A little weed. Some pills. But I believe he has bigger plans. Men like him, they always have plans."

Then George must see something in Edie's expression that tells him he mustn't frighten her further. "But your granddaughter? She'll be okay," George says. "Both those boys are crazy about her. They'll look out for her."

Edie takes her cell phone out of the pocket of her robe and looks at its silent, closed shell. "I hope you're right."

TWO DAYS LATER the message arrives.

Edie's been keeping the phone right beside the computer at her desk, and when she hears the ping she picks up the phone and flips it open and reads the message.

Name on mailbox is Solon north of Bismark

Edie's about to respond when a door opens in the back of the office. She pauses, her finger hovering over the phone's keyboard.

A minute passes, then another, but neither the dentist, the hygienist, nor a patient appears.

Finally Edie types a reply.

I'm coming. Leaving tomorrow. Give me more info if you can.

FROM HER BALCONY Edie watches the parking lot. When she sees
Rita's Ford F-150 truck pull into the lot, Edie goes back inside. After
ten minutes have passed—enough time for Rita to kick off her shoes
and perhaps pour herself a glass of wine—Edie calls.

"Hey, are you up for a road trip?" she asks. The cheeriness in her
voice must sound forced to any ear.

Rita laughs. "Where to?"

"Lauren sent me a text. Apparently things aren't working out,
and she'd like to come back to Gladstone. I'm heading to Bismarck
tomorrow to pick her up."

"Not working out how?"

"She didn't provide any specifics. But in the company of those
two? I can only imagine."

"Is she in trouble, did she say?"

"She didn't. I'm thinking she's probably just tired of babysitting
them."

"I wish I could," Rita says, "but I've finally got an appointment for
George at the VA hospital. We're leaving real early for Fort Harrison."

"Is there something—"

"No, no. But they've agreed to look at that leg and see if he needs
to be refit. It's funny. As long as they know he got the original leg at
another facility, they're willing to say maybe there's a problem."

"Well, for sure," says Edie. "You've got to go. I understand."

"The thing is," Rita says, "it was so hard to get this appointment I
don't dare reschedule. You know, he's finally trying with the leg, and
if it turns out it just needs an adjustment—"

"Please. Now you're making me feel bad for asking. I bet we'll
back before you. You're not going to try to do it all in one day, are
you?"

"We'll play it by ear. My cousin's daughter lives in Helena. We
could probably stay with her. Maybe," Rita says, her voice brighten-
ing, "you should ask Mr. Aldinger if he'd like to ride along with you."

"I'm sure he'd pay for gas!"

"And the motel," Rita says with a laugh.

Edie doesn't laugh along with her.

"Are you worried about making this trip, hon?" Rita asks.

"I just thought it would be fun. A couple of chicks on the open road. Sort of a senior version of Thelma and Louise."

"Maybe I can check the bus schedule. George is a big boy. He doesn't need to have his mommy drive him."

"Oh, stop, *stop*. You take George. That's where you need to be. Somebody has to make those army doctors do right by him. I'll be fine."

A small *clink* comes across the line, the sound perhaps of Rita's wineglass hitting the telephone's mouthpiece. "Is there something you're not telling me?"

"Well, I'm a little uneasy about having a teenager live with me. You know me. I've got my routines. And it's not a life that'll be very appealing to a young woman."

"Maybe once Lauren comes back here the boredom will get to her, and she'll want to hit the road again. Back to her mother maybe."

"I believe," Edie says, "that door is closed. And locked."

"Well, ours is open. Why don't you come on over? We're going to order a pizza and I'll pour you a glass of wine."

"Thanks for the offer. But I believe I'll fry an egg and get to bed early. I'd like to get an early start in the morning."

"You and your fried egg. Okay, hon. Have a safe trip. George will have his cell phone, so you know how to get in touch with us."

EDIE GOES TO the bedroom where Jesse slept, the room that now will be Lauren's. She has not put any bedding back on the bed, and the bare mattress gives the room an institutional look. From the closet shelf Edie takes laundered sheets and a pillowcase, a thin cotton blanket, a bedspread, and a pillow. But after she makes the bed, the room still looks underfurnished. A motel room perhaps.

She goes to the kitchen, and from the drawer under the toaster she takes the envelope of photographs. She takes out three: one of Jennifer holding an infant Lauren and smiling in fear and amazement at the baby cradled in her arms; another a school portrait of

Lauren in perhaps second grade, front teeth missing and hair tamed in pigtails; and finally another mother-and-daughter picture, both of them wearing matching red turtlenecks and kneeling in front of a spindly Christmas tree. Jennifer still looks amazed but no longer afraid, and though Lauren is only eleven or twelve, she already possesses the wide-eyed, dimpled prettiness she'll carry into adolescence. Edie takes these photographs into the bedroom and inserts them into the frame of the mirror attached to the dresser. There. A teenager's bedroom.

EDIE BOUGHT HER rolling suitcase before a trip to Minneapolis for a dental convention. It was only her second trip on an airplane, and she'd heard how important it was to carry on luggage rather than check it, and she'd gone to J. C. Penney and picked up this maroon-and-green plaid number. As she rolls it across the parking lot now, the collapsible handle twists in her hand, and the wheels don't track straight.

Standing in the lot near Edie's car is a tall man dressed in a short-sleeved white shirt and khaki trousers. He's smoking, and his back is turned to Edie. At the sound of those clattering wheels, he turns around.

"Roy?"

"Might as well take my car," he says, and he pats the top of his black Toyota Highlander as though it's a pet.

Once again Edie asks the question that is his name. "Roy?"

"Were you expecting someone else?"

"I wasn't expecting anyone."

Roy opens the passenger door of his car. "I just don't think my legs could handle a trip in that little Honda of yours."

"A trip?"

"I thought we'd take a drive to Bismarck together. If that suits you."

"Did you come to rescue me, Roy? Is that it?"

"I don't have a bad leg anymore," he says. "Because now the other one is in such sad shape they're a matched pair."

"Answer me. Because I don't need you here."

Roy Linderman smiles the smile that has closed hundreds, perhaps thousands, of deals over the years. "You? Rescue *you*? Shit, the Edie I knew people needed rescuing *from*, not the other way around."

"Don't bother, Roy. What are you doing here?"

"Your friend Rita called me."

"What did she tell you? How did she know how to find you?"

"Whoa, whoa." Roy backs up awkwardly. "My name and number are in the Billings phone book. And she said you're taking a little trip and you might like some company."

"'Like some company'? Or *need* some company?"

"Hey, hey, Edie. Take it easy. Your friend is concerned about you. You don't need me here, I get that. And I don't need to be here. Let's say we're doing it for Rita. Come on. Hop in the car. We can hash it out while we drive."

Roy takes a set of keys from his pocket and presses a button on the fob. "Here," he says. The liftgate opens like a yawn, and Edie steps back as though something in the vehicle's dark interior has frightened her. Then Roy walks over to her, picks up her suitcase, and slides it into the back right next to his own black rolling bag.

"You won't smoke in the car," Edie says.

"Is that a question or a command?"

"I'm not getting in if you plan to smoke."

"I promise," he says and raises his right hand as if making a pledge.

Once they are both settled in the soft leather seats and their seat belts are securely fastened, Roy Linderman looks over at her. There's something he wants to say, it's apparent in his eyes. Yet when he finally speaks—"This is the hybrid," he says, "it'll get better mileage than your Civic."—it's equally plain that those are not the words he might have rehearsed over the years for the occasion when Edie Pritchard once again climbed into a car with him.

"TELL ME ABOUT this granddaughter," Roy says. They're on the highway, and he has the Highlander doing eighty, as easy behind the wheel as he's ever been. "She anything like her grandmother? And

I have to say—I'm having a hell of a time with that. You a grand-mother, Edie? God *damn*!"

"*You* have a hard time! Try living it. She's . . . oh, I don't know. She's eighteen and thinks she's more grown-up and sophisticated than she is, which might be why she's unhappy in whatever this lat-est chapter is."

"But she's . . I mean, wherever she is, it's of her own free will, right?"

"I believe so. But she's with these two brothers—"

"And we know what kind of trouble that can mean," Roy says.

Edie stares out at the low hills in the distance. "I'm aware of the irony here."

"Rita made it sound like they're just a couple of fuckups."

Edie turns to Roy. "One of them has a gun. A pistol. I saw it in his luggage."

"Shit, this is Montana. Who *doesn't* have a gun? Hell, look in the glove box. No, no, I'm kidding. You remember that trip we made up to Bentrock? Those brothers? What the hell was their name?"

"Bauer."

"Bauer. You got a pretty good memory. That's right. The goddamn Bauer brothers. And then Dean went out and got himself a pistol. What the hell was he thinking anyway?"

"Dean had a *gun*? My God."

"Nothing came of it."

She raises her eyebrows as if she can't quite believe he'd say some-thing like that. "Roy. Please."

"Yeah," Roy says. "Okay. Sorry."

"Dean seemed to believe," Edie says, "that the more of himself he kept from me, the more I'd love him. I tried very hard to cure of him of that. Obviously I couldn't."

"That whole episode with the Bauers seems like it happened on another planet."

"Another century," Edie says. "Another life."

The terrain they drive through has begun to change. The ocean of grass that previously surrounded them is broken now by an occasional outcropping of pale sandstone that looks like a whitecap on that sea. Then, mile by mile, the grass becomes sparser until the jagged rocks burst through, larger and larger, like bones. They've entered the Badlands. A country of compound fractures.

After a few minutes of silence Roy returns to the subject. "You were saying. The brothers?"

"Oh, I don't know. Maybe Rita is right. I hope so."

"As I recall," says Roy, "not everyone was happy with you and Dean as a couple."

"That would be your mother."

"Dad sure liked you."

"Or were you talking about yourself?"

He doesn't reply.

"But to answer the question you're not asking," Edie says, "no, my granddaughter and I are not close. But she called me."

"And you answered."

"What can I say? I'm a good dog. I come when I'm called."

The landscape smooths out, and once again they're traveling through rolling grassland.

"Go over this again for me," Roy says. "You know she's in Bismarck but not *where* in Bismarck?"

"Not *in* Bismarck. Someplace outside the city. A farm she said."

"Christ, Edie."

"I'm working with what I've got. And if it doesn't suit you, turn around right now and I'll do this on my own."

"I'm just asking if you've got a plan. That's all."

"You know as much as I know."

"Oh, I doubt that," Roy says. "I doubt that very much."

THEY'VE BEEN ON the road for less than an hour when Roy has to stop for a cigarette. He pulls off the highway near Beach, just inside the North Dakota border. The rest area is built on a small rise, and the elevation is enough to allow Roy and Edie a view of the highway they've just traveled, gray strips cutting through green-and-yellow undulating countryside. The trees are so distant and few they look like black bristles caught in the creases of hills.

Roy and Edie sit at a picnic table full of messages, initials, and symbols that have been gouged into the wood over the years: LW + SG. I ♥ Jamie. Go Fuck Yourself. Eat me. Hawks Rule. Lilya 4ever. Edie mindlessly runs the tip of her index finger over and over in the grooves of that 4.

Roy lights a second cigarette from the butt of his first. He inhales deeply and then tilts his head back and blows the smoke up into that huge, vacant blue sky.

"Don't answer this if you don't want to," Edie says. "But what was it like at the end? With Dean."

"Mom never said anything on one of your visits?"

"I wasn't about to bring it up."

"Yeah. I get that. Well. It wasn't as bad as it could have been. I mean, not *good*. For sure. But all things considered . . . Yeah. It could have been worse."

"You don't want to talk about it," says Edie. "I understand."

"This is something you really want to hear? Okay. This was a couple months after you went back to . . . where?"

"Granite Valley."

"And he was at our place when you left, right?"

"Just for a night, I thought."

"It turned into a few. But that was okay. It was long enough for us to get a hospital bed moved into Mom's place. A tight fit, let me tell you. But it gave him a little more comfort. You know, with its adjustments and all. Hospice provided it. Hospice—they were champs. Anything we needed. The bed. Drugs for the pain. Which Dean tried to avoid. I finally said, 'This isn't like running a damn race. It's not like you're a winner if you can push through the pain. You don't want to suffer. Mom doesn't want to see you suffer. *I* don't want to see you suffer. Take the fucking drugs.' So he did. And they helped. You could see that. Before, he had this strained look all the time, and then he relaxed and looked more like himself. Anyway, one night he and I were watching a ball game. Then he said he was tired and was going to call it a night. This was during the playoffs, mind you. But I helped him get settled. Then I went out in the other room with Mom. She was watching *Dallas*. She couldn't get enough of that show, and I couldn't fucking stand it. I had enough soap opera in my life at the time. So I closed my eyes, and I dozed off for a few minutes. I woke up when the news came on. Mom was just tiptoeing back into the room after checking on him. 'How's he doing?' I asked. She smiled and said, 'Sleeping like a baby.' And I knew. I just fucking *knew*. I was in there like a shot. But he was gone. *Call it a night?* Shit, he sent me away so I wasn't there to see the end. So, yeah. It could have been worse. It could have been a hell of a lot worse."

Edie reaches across the picnic table and covers Roy's hand with hers. "I'm sorry," she says. "I'm so sorry."

"Yep," Roy says. "I know."

He drops his cigarette and grinds it out in the gravel. He stands up. "Okay," he says. "Let's see if I can make it to Bismarck now without having another nicotine fit."

As they walk to the car they both wipe away tears with an identical motion, a quick swipe with the heel of the hand.

"Hey, you asked," Roy says, and they both laugh. Through their tears they laugh.

EDIE SAYS, "WHAT'S that cologne you're wearing, Roy?"

"Dolce & Gabbana, I think."

"Well, you're wearing too much of it. I could smell you even when we were outside."

"You need me to open a window?"

"I'm just saying. For future reference."

"Shit." Roy raises his hand and with his index finger makes a check mark in the air. "Another one on the debit side," he says and turns the fan up on the air conditioner.

"God, Roy. *Still*?" Edie shakes her head sadly.

"Sorry, kid. Can't turn it off."

"Does Carla know what you're doing today?" Edie asks.

Roy whoops a laugh. "Carla! We haven't exchanged so much as a how-d'ya-do for maybe ten years. Believe me when I say Carla doesn't give a shit what I'm doing. Not today or any other day."

"What happened?"

He runs his fingers loosely around the steering wheel. "About a year after Dean died Carla and I moved to Billings. A Realtor there wanted her to come work for him, and he made her an offer so damn good she couldn't say no. So off we went. The move was okay with me, even though I couldn't land anything with a dealership in Billings. But I got something with a used car dealer. And, as it turned out, Mr. Jeff Joseph, of Joseph Realty and Associates, wanted Carla to come work for him not just because she was so damn good at selling houses. He was trying to save some money and cut down on his time on the road. If she was right there in Billings he wouldn't have to keep driving up to Gladstone and checking into a motel for a night or two for their dates." Roy laughs again. "*Dates.* That's the word Carla used when she finally broke the news to me. 'I've been dating another man,' she said. *Dates.* Jesus Christ. I still can't get over it."

"I'm sorry, Roy. It doesn't sound like Carla."

"I think what you mean is that it sounds *exactly* like Carla. She saw an opportunity to improve her circumstances and she took it. But we'd all have put money on it being my shenanigans that would break us up. The hell of it is, once Carla and I moved in together, I more or less changed my ways."

"So when you and I saw each other at the nursing home, you and Carla were—?"

"That's right. Which was what you no doubt saw as the hopeful look in my eye."

"Why didn't you say something then?"

"Would it have made a difference?"

"We're friends, Roy. And family."

Roy groans. "Oh Christ, Edie. Don't do me like that." He reaches across the space between them and jostles her shoulder. "The next thing you'll be telling me you think of me as your goddamn brother.

Besides, you never told me that you and—what's his name?—had split."

"Gary. But you knew I was back in Gladstone."

A few miles pass before Edie says, "At least you were spared the indignity of marriage counseling. My God, what a shit show that was. I don't know how many times Gary would look up and say, 'Excuse me?' What? I was never sure if he really wasn't listening or if that was just the impression he wanted to give. One time I looked over at him, and he had his little pocketknife out and he was cleaning his fingernails. But our therapist, Dr. Snell, bless his heart, kept plugging away. Gary's indifference. My . . . I don't know what it was. Stubbornness? Like giving up on our marriage was some kind of failure on my part. I'd already failed with Dean. No, no, don't say it. I know, it takes two—but that was how I felt. I just wanted to keep this second goddamn relationship alive. If it died it wasn't going to be because I quit. And then one day our therapist was working *so* hard and finally he leaned forward and said in his high squeaky voice, 'But you two love each other—I know you do.' And I said, 'No. We don't.' And that was that. I guess all we needed was for one of us to say it and make it official. Gary was gone in no time."

"What a fool."

"Come on. You have no idea what living with me would be like. No idea."

"I'm guessing you wouldn't let me smoke."

"That'd be the least of it."

"And what was his problem anyway? Your husband. Indifferent, you said? I have a hard time believing that."

"Just resign yourself to the fact that some things will always be a mystery to you."

They drive into the Dakota Badlands, and though the violent eruptions of rock are similar to those on the Montana side, every formation here is tinged with orange as if the fires that created this country have only recently been extinguished.

"Scoria," Roy says. "A hell of a lot of petrified wood out there too."

"We had a big chunk of it in the garage when I was a little girl.

Something my dad picked up and brought home for God knows what reason."

"Frowned on now. Supposed to leave it out there."

"One more way the world's changed. Now we're not supposed to take away anything that belongs there and make sure we don't leave behind something that doesn't. Erasing our tracks. I think I've been pretty good at that."

Roy pats his pocket as if to reassure himself that, though he can't smoke, his cigarettes are still there and waiting for him. "Can I tell you about something, Edie? Something that happened long ago? Hell, you probably won't even remember it, but it's been bugging me all this time."

Edie says, "Are you sure it's not something we're supposed to leave out there?" Then she sighs and asks, "How long ago?"

"Well, we were out of high school, but you and Dean weren't married yet. Maybe the summer after we graduated?"

"Jesus, Roy."

"Yeah, well. Like I say. It's something that's been bugging me. But if you don't remember—"

"I didn't say that. You haven't told me yet."

Roy shifts in his seat. "Okay. We were at a party. Out at Dennis Rooney's ranch—"

"Which wasn't a real ranch. Stables, as I recall."

"Well, everyone called it the Rooney ranch. Anyway. Dennis's folks were out of town, and we were down in their basement rec room."

"I remember that basement. All the trophies on the walls. Everywhere you looked, some dead animal was staring at you. Deer. Elk. A moose, I think. Maybe even a bear?"

"Yeah, the Rooneys were big-time hunters. But let me tell this now, damn it."

"I'm not stopping you."

"You were wearing a dress, a summer dress. Does that help?"

"Yes. Yes! Doreen Mueller's wedding. She married that soldier from Laramie. What was his name? Older guy? Everyone knew

Doreen was pregnant. The wedding was on a Saturday afternoon, and after the reception at the church we drove out to Rooneys'. And you're right. It was the summer after we graduated. Doreen was a year older."

"This isn't about Doreen. I don't give a damn about Doreen. This is about Dennis Rooney. Dennis Rooney and you."

Edie shrinks back in surprise. "Dennis?"

"We were sitting around in the basement. Sort of in a circle. You and Dennis were sitting across from each other. A cooler was on the floor right by you, so Dennis asked you to get him a beer. And another. And another. And he asked you to get one for whoever was sitting next to him. Might have been me since I was sitting across from you too. And he kept asking because you had to bend down to open the cooler and reach around inside, and when you did Dennis got a look down your dress. A damn good look, if you know what I mean."

A Chevy Tahoe pulls alongside them, and for as long as it takes that vehicle to pass, Roy falls silent. Once the Chevy is well ahead of them he continues, "He'd ask for a beer, you'd bend down and get one, and every time he'd laugh his ass off. And here's what really got me. Dean saw what was going on, and he didn't say a goddamn thing."

"Was that," Edie says, "why you and Dennis got into that little scuffle outside the bowling alley?"

"You remember that? It didn't amount to much. Some shoving back and forth. But yeah. It was. Not that I said so to Dennis. I was just needling him, trying to get him to maybe throw a punch so I could kick his ass. But that should have been Dean's job."

"His *job*?"

"You know what I mean."

"Dean was supposed to pick a fight at the bowling alley?"

"Come on, Edie. Dean should have put a stop to it."

"Can I tell you something about your brother? Dean once said to me he thought he wasn't *supposed* to be jealous. So he tried not to show it. Gary on the other hand once told me that if he was jealous it was because I was doing something wrong. But why wasn't it *my* job, Roy? It was my dress he was looking down."

"You didn't know—"

"Are you sure? Maybe I liked it. The attention. I looked pretty good back then. Maybe I was testing my powers."

"Oh Jesus, Edie, you looked—"

"And you must have gotten a pretty good peek yourself, right? Since you knew what Dennis was doing."

"But it was a *trick*. He tricked you. It was a fucking stunt. He was taking advantage—"

"Roy, Roy. Will you *listen* to yourself? You're talking about something that happened almost fifty years ago that didn't mean much to me then and means nothing to me now."

"'*Nothing*—'"

"Nothing! Except that you've had it tucked away all this time. It makes me worry about you, it really does. A boy looked down my dress. My God, Roy. *Let it go.*"

"Hey, you think I haven't tried? You don't think my life wouldn't run a hell of a lot smoother if I didn't keep replaying scenes like this? I could make a movie out of these memories."

"I think," she says gently, "you'd be the only one who'd want to watch that movie."

A mile passes, perhaps two, before Roy answers. "Dean," he says. "Maybe Dean would have watched."

They leave the Badlands behind and are back among the low treeless hills and tawny prairie grass. Edie looks out at the distant fields where oil wells dip their beaks over and over into the earth. "I remember that dress," she says. "Pale blue with little white flowers. I loved that dress."

THEY'RE STOPPED ON the interstate. The two lanes heading west are shut down, waiting to be resurfaced, and now the eastbound lanes are stopped as well and a line of cars waits for a massive road grader to cross in front of them.

"You ever been to Bismarck?" Roy asks Edie.

"I don't believe so."

"You'll like it. Nice city. Clean, bright. I used to go there fairly often. Did a lot of business with a fellow who had a used car lot on the south side of the city. I think we both thought we were screwing each other, so it was a pretty good working arrangement."

Edie checks her phone again.

"Dean and I once went to Bismarck together," Roy says, "so he could run their marathon. Did you know he started running again? Before the cancer of course. The Bismarck race was in September, and the day of the race was ungodly hot. The route took them along the Missouri River, so it was humid too. And the only day in North Dakota history when the wind wasn't blowing. Runners were dropping right and left. Dean finished though, by God. Later when he was sick he said dying wasn't as hard as running the Bismarck Marathon. 'You don't look as bad either,' I told him."

For a few minutes they sit silently. Edie stares at her phone as though attentiveness alone will be enough to bring forth a communication. Roy watches a trio of highway workers, two men and one woman, sitting on the back gate of a pickup truck and drinking water from a plastic gallon jug.

"Can I ask you something?" Roy says.

"Uh-huh."

"I mean *really* ask you something. Can you put the phone down?"

She slips the phone into her purse, but she doesn't look at Roy. Instead she looks out the window. A few antelope are out there, perhaps a hundred yards away, and one of them lifts its head to look in their direction. It cocks its head as if trying to puzzle out what these machines and creatures are, so slow-moving in a landscape that seems to offer no impediment to motion.

"All right," she says. "Ask."

"Now I know I put this to you on another occasion, but I think you'll agree things are a little different now. What do you say we just take off? Leave it all behind us. You and I will go make a new life together. We have clothes in our suitcases. I've got money in my pocket and more in the bank. Just you and me. We can keep heading east—Minneapolis, maybe Chicago. Or we can turn around and go west. Seattle, Spokane. San Francisco. Or maybe some little town where no one knows us and we don't know anybody." Roy holds up a hand as though he's the one assigned with stopping traffic—"Wait. Just let me get this out. I'm not asking you to do anything more than what you're doing right now. Just be by my side. The two of us."

He stops abruptly as if the words of his speech have suddenly congealed and stopped in his throat. He's the one who looks away now, over to that torn-up stretch of highway, its concrete pulverized to rock, gravel, dirt, and sand.

"Go ahead," Edie says.

He laughs a little and turns his face back to hers. "All I'm saying is I wouldn't put any conditions or make any demands on you. Hell, I can't even count on getting it up every time. I just want to be with you, Edie. I don't know how many days I got left, none of us do, so . . . Shit. You know what I'm saying. I just want to make sure you understand what I'm proposing."

"Don't be dramatic. If you take after your mother, you've got a lot of years left. And what about your mother?"

"She doesn't know I'm alive. She sure as hell wouldn't know I'm gone. Don't bring her in on this."

"Let me see if I have this right. A man is asking me to run off with him and he says sex won't be part of the bargain. Whoa! Whatever I might have had once I guess it's gone now!"

"That's not what I said. I just meant—"

"That I shouldn't get my hopes up? Where's the Roy I used to know? The man who'd promise anything if it'd help him close the deal. Do you ever watch that TV show? What is it, *The Apprentice*? I don't believe you'd last more than a single episode."

He reaches over and takes a gentle hold of her wrist. "Please, can you be serious about this? I just want an answer. And if it's no, I'll never ask again."

She stares at his hand on her wrist, her gaze so unwavering it has the power to make him release her. When he does, she says, "I'm going after my granddaughter. That's all I have in mind right now. I appreciate your willingness to accompany me, but if you can't concentrate on the task at hand . . ."

Roy shakes his head slowly. "You don't even know—"

"We're moving!" Edie says, pointing to the car ahead of them. "At last."

Within minutes they're back up to highway speed. Roy's vision is locked on the road ahead, his jaw clenched, his hands gripping the steering wheel tightly at ten o'clock and two.

THEY SIT IN a booth in Perkins. The lunchtime crowd has come and gone, diners drifting back to their offices and their retail jobs in the stores in the neighboring Gateway Mall.

"What do you suppose this is the gateway to?" Roy asks.

"The West?" Edie suggests.

"What about us? We're heading in the other direction."

"The East then."

"Maybe that's why people live *here*. So they don't have to decide."

"Maybe." Edie flips open her phone again.

"Anything?"

She shakes her head no and closes the phone.

"What's the plan then?" He sips his coffee. "You're in charge here. I await your orders."

"Well, a farm north of the city. The Solon farm? That's the name she said was on the mailbox."

"A *farm*? We're in North Dakota, for Christ's sake."

"I don't know what to tell you. I keep waiting for something more."

Roy finishes his coffee and swipes the bill off the table. "What the hell. Maybe we'll get lucky and find her standing on the side of the road somewhere."

THEY DRIVE NORTH on winding River Road. Off to their left the wide Missouri River blinks in and out of view whenever there's a gap in the towering cottonwoods. A high grassy bluff hems them in on the right.

"Whatever became of Carla's boys?" Edie asks.

Roy opens the shade on the sunroof. "Troy's down in New Mexico. Teaching high school. Married to a pretty Mexican woman. They've got two girls, and Carla's down there every chance she gets. They call her—shit, I can't remember now. Something Spanish for grandmother. Brad's still in Billings. He had an accident waterskiing a few years back. So now he's got a brain injury, though you'd never know it to meet him. But that's what the doctors say, so who am I to argue. And that's supposedly the reason he can't hold a job. I think it's mostly bullshit if you ask me but then nobody did, so I keep my mouth shut. Carla pays all his bills. Out of some crazy sense of guilt, I guess. She's got a few things to feel guilty about, but not where those boys are concerned. Maybe if I had kids myself I'd get it, but I don't."

"For some kids it's never enough," Edie says. "I don't believe Jennifer ever forgave me for wanting to be anything besides her mother."

"That'd be Brad, all right."

"They were good-looking boys, as I recall."

"And those good looks got Brad in a shitload of trouble. He had something going with a married woman—this was before the water-skiing accident—and her husband, a husband with a gun, was looking for Brad. I knew the husband a little, and I was able to talk him down. Carla never knew about it, which was just as well. I told the fellow that Brad was nothing but a weaselly little prick who wasn't worth going to prison for."

"You'll forgive me," Edie says, "if I smile."

"Yeah, well. Those years are behind me. And would it make any difference if I said I was never involved with a woman who was happily married?"

She reaches over and touches him on the forearm. "Roy. If they were happily married they wouldn't have been interested in you in the first place. That's what it means to be happily married."

"Now there I'll have to disagree with you. There's plenty of women perfectly content in their marriages who still have a little curiosity they'd like to satisfy. People like to think that's only men, but in my experience the sexes aren't so different as they're made out to be. I'll give you a for instance. Years ago I had a little something going with a married woman—a happily married woman. We never ended up in the sack together, but we were close. Not an affair exactly but some kind of thing. She once told me she wished she'd be cast in a movie she'd have to do a love scene in. That's what she called it. But a sex scene was what she was talking about. And she and the actor would be in bed together. Going at it in front of the camera. Because that was her role, her job. She'd have to do it."

"And she told you she was happily married?"

"That's what she told me. But everyone could see she and her husband were happy together."

"She wasn't."

BECAUSE GARTH HAS been baking again, his phone is dusted with flour and baking powder. He blows on the keypad, raising a tiny white cloud, and shuts the phone. Then he tosses the phone down on the counter disgustedly and walks out the front door.

He finds Jesse on the front porch, playing his guitar. Tiffany sits nearby, endlessly impressed with his version of "Layla," perhaps the only rendition she's ever heard at twelve years old. Garth orders Jesse into the kitchen, and he tells Tiffany to go upstairs with her sister and Randy. Lauren and Billy are in the backyard, laughing in the dark as they try to set up the croquet set they found in the barn. When Garth says he wants to talk to them inside, they shrug and follow him in.

Marilyn is in the bathroom, having just taken a shower. When Garth knocks on the door and then enters, she's wearing nothing but a towel. She smiles expectantly at Garth, but if there's an invitation there, he ignores it. "Get dressed," he says curtly. "Then come down to the kitchen."

And now they're gathered there. Jesse, Billy, and Lauren are seated around the table. Marilyn stands apart, leaning against the cupboard.

Garth walks over to Jesse and stands so close that Jesse has no choice but to look up like a child about to be scolded.

"All right," Garth says sternly, "let's hear it. What the hell kind of big scheme did you and Matt have cooked up?"

Before Jesse can answer, Garth continues. "Because it's sure as fuck over now." He turns to Marilyn as though she's the only person who's capable of understanding what he's about to say. "Matt got himself arrested. Some sheriff out in Bumblefuck Falls, Montana, pulled him over for a busted headlight. Searched the car and found over a hundred pounds of Ecstasy. And he had a young Canadian couple with him. I might not have all the details right, but it sounds like Matt crossed the border on a motorcycle and then this young couple picked him up on the US side. All part of the plan apparently."

Garth stops and glares at Jesse. "Any of this sound familiar to you?"

Jesse doesn't say anything.

"Wait," Marilyn says, shaking her head. "*Wait*. How do you . . . Did you talk to Matt?"

Garth ignores her and continues to stare down at Jesse. "What about it? Do you have any part in this?"

Jesse shakes his head no.

Garth kicks the leg of the chair Jesse is sitting on.

"I said no," says Jesse.

"Because this is a fucking federal offense," Garth says. "So if there's anything that's going to bring the law to that door"—he points toward the living room—"you better fucking say so."

Jesse shakes his head again.

Garth turns to Marilyn. "I talked to his lawyer. Matt gave him my number. Hoping I'd go his bail. Or pay the lawyer. Or both."

Billy and Lauren stare down at the table.

Garth asks Jesse, "Where in hell did Matt get the money to make a buy like that?"

Jesse says nothing.

"Him and his sister had some money from when their dad died," Billy says.

"Insurance," Jesse adds. "Plus they sold his house."

Marilyn says, "On the street—"

Garth answers before she completes her question. "Three, maybe four million? Sound about right?" he asks Jesse.

"I didn't know he was bringing in that kind of weight."

"Did you have a connection lined up around here?"

"No," Jesse says.

"Nobody'll come knocking on the door asking about a delivery?"

Billy says, "We thought, you know, like a few pills. Sell a handful in a bar maybe. At a concert. Like that."

Garth walks to a cupboard and grabs a bottle of ibuprofen tablets. He brings it to the table and shakes it in front of Billy. Garth then hands the bottle to Billy.

"Look at the label," Garth commands. "Two hundred and twenty pills in there. And how much does this weigh? A pound? Not even. And Matt had over a hundred goddamn pounds. You thought you'd maybe sell a *handful*? Shit. You could fill the fucking bathtub with what he was carrying."

Garth walks over to where Lauren is sitting, and rather than loom over her as he did with Jesse, he gets down on one knee in front of her. He reaches forward and with both hands grabs onto of the back of her chair. Lauren shrinks back but, of course, she cannot escape the cage that his arms have formed.

"Do you see, darlin'?" he says. "Do you see what you're mixed up with here? These two will land you in trouble you don't need a bit of. You deserve better."

Marilyn says matter-of-factly, "She's just a kid, Garth. And that's her boyfriend you're talking about."

Garth pushes himself stiffly back to a standing position, but while he is still bent over Lauren he says softly to her, "Save yourself."

He looks at everyone in turn again. "Is Matt anything to any of you?"

His gaze lingers on Marilyn. "Don't look at me," she says. "He's your cousin's kid."

Garth continues to stare at her. It's the kind of unwavering, baleful look that's usually supposed to elicit a confession. Marilyn stares right back at him and says nothing.

Garth turns to Jesse. "You?"

Jesse says, "We both had temp jobs with a book distributor last winter. Like I told you before. In Redmond. Just outside Seattle. Then Matt quit early because he heard there were opportunities out this way. 'Come out and we'll join up,' he said. So here we are. But I know what you're saying. Federal prison? Huh-uh. Not for us. So long, Matt."

Billy adds eagerly, "We'll probably try to find something in town." He looks at Lauren. "Right, babe? Like we was talking about before. I mean the pills was actually just kind of an add-on. They was never supposed to be the whole deal."

Garth continues to stare at Jesse, and now Jesse stares back, only Jesse's look is as dead-eyed as roadkill.

For a long moment no one moves or speaks.

Finally Marilyn says, "Well, fuck this," and she walks over to the stove where a full muffin tin is resting. She takes out a single muffin and holds it up as if she were displaying a work of art for bidders. "And what kind are these?"

Her question momentarily unsettles Garth, but then he says, "Cranberry walnut."

"Do I know the muffin man? I believe I do." She smiles and sings, "Who lives on Drury Lane . . ."

LAUREN, BILLY, AND Jesse have been given the attic for their bedroom. It's a long narrow room, its beams and studs covered over with sheetrock and with rectangles and squares of carpet remnants on the floor. The roof's pitch is so steep that only in the middle of the room is it possible to stand up straight. There are two mattresses on the floor, the length of the room apart, a single mattress for Jesse and a double for Lauren and Billy. The attic smells of mildew and wood rot with an undertone of the funk given off by the mattresses. Through one of the windows comes the constant hum and rattle of the air conditioner in Garth and Marilyn's bedroom a floor below.

Lauren's eyes are open, but since she's lying at the edge of the mattress and turned toward the tight dark space where floor, wall, and roof meet, she can't see much more than she would if her eyes were closed. Tonight the air is unmoving and the dark and the heat seem inseparable.

She hears a soft *Shh*, yet she hasn't made a sound. Billy is lying beside her, and he has one hand on top of her head, loosely gripping a handful of her dreadlocks. He's worked his other hand inside her tank top, and his fingers are busily tickling and pinching her breasts. Does she doze off for a moment or two? It's difficult to tell, just as it's difficult to tell where one's body leaves off and the attic heat begins.

There is the hand teasing first one breast and then the other. And the hand that twists its fingers in the cylinders of her hair. And the hand that caresses a path up her thigh, higher and higher, until it insinuates its way inside the elastic of her underpants.

And at that touch—in that instant—she comes fully awake.

She jerks herself away so abruptly she rolls off the mattress. When she tries to sit up she bumps her head against the wall. She crawls and scuttles around the mattress until she can stand up.

"What the fuck! What *the fuck*!"

She's looking down at the mattress now, at the mattress and at Billy and Jesse, lying where they could both reach her, their bodies pale shadows in the dark room.

"I had a bad dream," Jesse says. "I crawled over and—"

"Garth! You said it was *Garth*! But it was you who had those . . . those *ideas*! It was you, it was you all the time. You fucker! You *fucker*!"

"Laure," Billy says, "Laure, Laure—"

"Get away get away get away get *away*!"

But it's neither Billy nor Jesse who moves—it's Lauren. Bent low to keep from hitting her head on the ceiling, she moves quickly around the mattress. Once she's clear of that makeshift bed and the brothers she grabs her clothes and hurries down the stairs.

"Laure!" Billy calls after her. "*Wait*, Laure!"

"Let her go," Jesse says.

In the living room Lauren pauses for a moment as if, like a sleeper who has been roused from a dream, she can't be sure of her location. But then she runs out the front door, the screen door banging behind her.

She leaps from the porch, and though she's barefoot she keeps running, down the driveway, where the gravel and the stones can bruise and cut her feet. But she doesn't stop until she's out in the road again, the blacktop still warm with the heat of the day, exactly where she stood before, helpless, hopeless, and looking off in every direction but the one she came from.

She pulls on her cutoffs and reaches for her phone. Surrounded by so much darkness, the bright screen seems as though it could be a beacon visible for miles.

IN HER ROOM at the Holiday Inn Express, Edie pulls back the covers and breathes in the odor of freshly bleached bed linens. As she climbs into the bed, she gives a little sigh of satisfaction. She has just closed her eyes when her phone dings. Edie brings the screen up close to her face to read the text.

10 or 11 miles north of bismark on dreary lane farmhouse

Edie sits up and types a reply.

Be there tomorrow. Soon enough? OK?

The answer arrives almost instantly.

ok

With the phone still in her hand, Edie grabs her key card and leaves the room. She walks across the hall and knocks softly on the door. Then she knocks again, harder, loud enough to wake anyone who might be sleeping inside.

But Roy has not been asleep. He answers the door barefoot but still dressed, though his shirt is unbuttoned and his belt is unbuckled.

The sight of Edie in his doorway—Edie in her nightgown—does something to him. He's surprised, of course, but confused too, and in his confusion it almost seems as though he wants to close the door on her.

Edie steps inside and holds her phone up to his face. "She called! Texted, I mean. But she said where she is!"

Roy however is not looking at the phone.

"Dreary Lane!" Edie says. "How hard can that be to find?"

Then she must realize where Roy's gaze and mind are directed. She wraps her arms tightly around herself. "Oh, Roy. Jesus. Don't tell me."

He shrugs helplessly.

"God damn it, Roy! I'm not the girl whose dress you looked down in Dennis Rooney's basement! These are sixty-four-year-old boobs!"

He turns his back on her and walks across the room, back to the desk where his glass and his bottle of Jack Daniels wait. As he walks he buckles his belt and shakes his head. "Doesn't matter, Edie. Doesn't matter. It's you. Don't you get that? You. You*you*you. However the hell it works between men and women, love, or imprinting or some other bullshit. For me it's you. No one else. Never has been. Never will be."

"It's *not* me. It's some idea of me. Some . . . an obsession or something."

He turns around to face her. "How can it *not* be you? I've known you longer than almost anybody."

She's shaking her head. "But most of that time we've been apart. People don't stay the same. They change."

"Yet here we are," he says. "There has to be a reason for that."

Edie holds her phone up again. "Here's the reason. *Dreary Lane!*"

He sits down heavily in the desk chair and swivels around until he's no longer facing her. He lifts his glass of whiskey and drinks. Then he says, "Can I tell you about a fantasy I've had, Edie?"

With that single question, he drains away all the excitement she felt over Lauren's text. She slumps and closes her eyes and feels behind her to find the bed. She sits down. If she didn't know before what matters most to him on this trip, she knows now. And it's not the address on her phone.

"Go ahead," she says. "I'm listening." Her attention is how she must repay him for accompanying her. Tonight she'll listen; tomorrow they'll find Dreary Lane.

"I used to think, what if Dean and I were identical twins? The kind where people can't tell which one is which. No, hell—where *you* couldn't tell us apart. So you'd be waiting for Dean to come pick you up and take you to a movie or something. Only I'd show up. Or at a school dance. I'd walk across the gym and ask you to dance, and of course you'd say yes. And then later when you were married and living above the bakery, and I knew Dean wouldn't be going home from work right away, I imagined I'd walk in and . . . and you'd welcome me. You'd never know the difference. And as long as I'm probably creeping you out—after Dean was dead, I imagined showing up. Crawling into your bed. 'Hey, Edie. It's me again. It's Dean.' And you wouldn't be able to resist. You'd know it was Dean's ghost."

He's drunk. But that doesn't make his confession any less chilling. She's always known how Roy feels about her, but she didn't think he'd be willing to sacrifice his identity to have her. She realizes all over again how tightly, intricately entwined the lives of these brothers have been, knots that not even a death can loosen.

"After I moved back to Gladstone," Edie says, "you could have called me. You could have asked if I wanted to meet for coffee. The way two people would who share as much history as we do."

"I was ashamed of my own thoughts. Hell, I've been ashamed of them most of my life. And this is coming from a man who's got plenty of *deeds* to be ashamed of. Besides, I thought if I stayed away, I could cure myself."

"What a waste, Roy. What a waste. And you make me feel guilty. Like I've been a part of your wasted life."

"Hey, don't feel sorry for me, Edie. I knew what I signed on for."

"You make it sound like you took a vow."

She rises from the bed and walks over to the desk. Though this brings her close enough to Roy that he could easily reach out and touch her, he doesn't move. He doesn't even look at Edie as she picks up the whiskey bottle.

"I don't believe in ghosts," she says.

He still doesn't look at her.

"Have you got another glass?" she asks.

"Bathroom," he says.

She returns with a plastic glass half filled with water. She uncaps the bourbon and pours a generous amount into the glass. "I hope," she says, "this doesn't taste like your toothpaste."

After taking a long swallow, she goes back to sit on the bed. "Do we have to watch sports?" she asks. Roy has a baseball game on.

He picks up the remote control and tosses it onto the bed.

Edie puts her whiskey glass on the nightstand. She stacks up the pillows on the bed so she can sit up. She begins to scroll through the channels. She pauses just long enough on The Weather Channel to see that the forecast for the next few days is constant: sunny and hot. Then she switches to another channel and another until finally she lands at Turner Classic Movies, with *Robin and Marian* just starting.

"Do you mind?" she asks Roy. "I can watch this every time it's on."

"Knock yourself out," he says.

"But fair warning—I'll probably bawl like a baby at the end. I always do."

In the darkened motel room with the only light coming from the flickering television screen and from the amber light of the parking lot, the man and the woman wordlessly watch the movie and drink their bourbon.

Halfway through the film, when Robin Hood and his men have returned to Sherwood Forest, Roy asks Edie, still without turning to look at her, "What year is your Civic?"

"A ninety-seven."

"How many miles?"

"Closing in on a hundred thousand, I think. I put so few miles on it, but I bought it used—"

"You'll want to put in a new timing belt pretty soon. When you do, might as well replace the water pump too. You do that, you'll be set for another hundred thousand."

To this advice, Edie merely says, "Thanks."

She swirls her whiskey in its glass. She continues to stare at the television, but it takes only a slight shift of her gaze to keep watching Roy as well. She watches, and she waits.

WHEN EDIE WAKES up it's not light from the parking lot leaking into the room but sunlight. She's on the bed, and still on top of the covers, though at some time during the night she must have pulled the hem of the bedspread over herself. Or someone did it for her. And at some time Roy moved from the desk chair to the chair beside the bed. He's sleeping there now. The television is off, and Edie was spared her tears since she fell asleep before Marian told Robin that she loved him more than God.

Edie picks up her phone from the nightstand, opens it, and then closes it again.

She slides quietly off the bed. The carpet muffles her footsteps. At the door she turns and looks back at Roy. His mouth is open. He slept with his false teeth in. She turns the doorknob slowly and slips out.

WHEN SHE WALKS into the motel's breakfast room an hour later, he's already there, sitting at a table facing a television tuned to CNN. No other guests are there. Edie waves to him and then steps over to the counter with its cereal dispensers, juice pitchers, plates of doughnuts and pastries, and coffee urns. She's ready for the day dressed in a yellow sundress.

As she approaches with coffee and a doughnut, Roy raises his Styrofoam cup. "I finally got my wish. Edie Pritchard spent the night in my bed."

The line is surely meant to be humorous, but he delivers it with a straight face.

Edie however smiles at him. "And was it good for you?"

"Nope," Roy says and stands up. "Just can't do it. I thought I could, but I can't. I'll wait for you in the car. Take your time."

Edie takes a bite of the doughnut but then puts it back down on the paper plate. She grimaces when she sips her coffee. She looks up at the television. Another politician has made another speech in another town in Iowa. On her way out of the room she drops her uneaten doughnut and most of her coffee into a garbage bin.

ONCE AGAIN THE sound of the rattling wheels on Edie's suitcase cause Roy to turn around.

"You want to open the back?" she says, pushing down the handle of her suitcase.

"You checked out?" He drops his cigarette and grinds it on the asphalt. "You must be pretty damn sure."

"Why, did you keep your room?" Edie asks.

"Dreary Lane? Not a hell of a lot to go on. I guess I don't share your confidence."

Edie turns toward the east and squints right at the sun. "We're getting a good start."

Roy pops open the liftgate. He lifts her suitcase and slides it inside. "What the hell," he says. "Let's go find your granddaughter."

"HEY, SUNSHINE. UP and at 'em."

Lauren blinks her way to wakefulness and sees Marilyn standing over her by the couch. On the living room floor a few feet away, Randy is watching *Finding Nemo* again. He's eating Honey Nut Cheerios out of the box.

"Trouble in paradise?" Marilyn asks.

"What? Oh. It was so hot up there."

"Get yourself up and ready. I'm going to town, and I need you to come along."

Lauren sits up. She glances over at Randy and straightens her tank top, making sure everything is tucked in. "To town?"

"That's right. Chop-chop. Get a move on. I need to shop for Tiff's birthday, and since she thinks you're pretty much the second coming of cool, you, my dear, will be my shopping advisor. We're going to the mall."

THEY HAVE BEEN traveling for two miles without speaking when Marilyn says, "How did you hook up with those two anyway?"

Lauren stares out her window at the sunlit prairie rolling past. Just when it seems her silence is permanent, she says, "Billy's my boyfriend. Jesse's his brother."

"Yeah, I got that," says Marilyn. "That's not what I'm asking."

Lauren says nothing.

After another mile of silence Marilyn asks, "Was that the plan all along? Come out here and make a big dope score and get rich?"

"Not hardly."

"So now what?"

"Billy said maybe we'll get like jobs or something."

"Here? In Bismarck?"

"I guess."

"And is that what he said? We? *We'll* get jobs? Because I'm about to tell you something, and you're not going to like hearing it."

"I bet."

Marilyn takes a hand off the wheel, rests her elbow on the window ledge, and leans on that hand. "I used to live with a guy like your Jesse."

"He's not *my* Jesse. *Fuck.* How many times do I have to tell you. *Billy.* Billy's my boyfriend."

Marilyn ignores this and continues. "We'd been together for over a year, and things were going pretty good for us. He dealt weed. A little coke too, but weed was the main thing. Like I say, we were doing okay. Until we weren't. He lost his connection and the money ran out fast. So I got a job waitressing, something I'd been doing off and on since high school. If you can waitress, you can always find work."

"Is that the lesson for today?"

"You'll know when I come to the lesson, honey. You won't be able to fucking miss it. Now let me finish. I was waitressing at a diner that only did breakfast and lunch, which are lousy meals for tips, which meant I wasn't bringing in enough money—not enough for him anyway. But he had a plan. Men always have a fucking plan. And his was to pimp me out. Now, it wasn't like we were strung out or anything. Like some crackhead and his ghetto whore who'll do anything for a fix. We were a regular couple. That's what I thought anyway. Except it was okay with *my* guy if I spread my legs or sucked cocks for anyone who'd pay. Yeah. A real fucking sweetheart. 'Huh-uh,' I told him. 'I'm not doing it.' Now, he had a motorcycle, and one day we were riding out in the country, and we were heading back to the city. I'm on the back and he's driving fast. Fast and then *faster*. I mean, every fucking curve in the road I think, Oh shit, we're not going to make it. And finally he stops. Out in the middle of nowhere. And he tells me, '*I thought about killing us both. What do you think about that?*' I mean, what the fuck could I say? 'Please don't,' I said. Like a little kid. 'Please don't.' 'Then don't give me any more shit.' I knew what that meant. I didn't want to get back on that motorcycle. More than anything I didn't want to get on. What else could I do though? But that night when he was asleep, I took off. Got out to the highway and started hitchhiking. Now this is the hilarious part. A guy picked me up and took me where I wanted to go. A city where I knew a couple who'd let me crash at their place. But he didn't drop me off there. He took me to a corner of a parking lot where he proceeded to beat the hell out of me and rape me. And he wasn't about to pay me for the privilege."

"When's the lesson?" Lauren says.

Marilyn shakes her head sadly. "Not for a few years. I still had a lot of nasty shit I had to get through. And plenty of it I instigated. Including running off with the husband of that couple who let me stay with them for a few months. But I can tell you're getting impatient, so I won't bore you with any more lurid details. I'll just give you a visual aid and then move on."

Marilyn is wearing a chambray work shirt over her sundress. With her left hand she pulls her shirtsleeve up to her elbow on her right arm. Steering now with her left hand, she extends her right arm toward Lauren. The pale line on her inner arm is no thicker than a pencil would make, but it's a serious scar, a determined scar, running from her wrist almost to her elbow.

But she doesn't give Lauren much study time. She pulls the arm back and rolls her sleeve down. She laughs a mirthless little laugh. "And now," she says, "I'm just showing off. No, the lesson is when I met Garth. Because then I learned there was such a thing as a man who'd never ask me to do something I didn't want to do. Someone who's been a better father to my girls than the man who was their actual father. And in case you were wondering, Randy's his."

They are traveling south now on the four lanes of Highway 83, and they've entered the corridor leading into Bismarck, the gaudy miles of fast food franchises, big box stores, strip malls, discount centers, and auto dealerships. Then they're in the city, and they drive past the state capitol, a nineteen-story limestone tower that looks like a brick balanced on end. They keep driving, through residential streets, and into the business district.

Marilyn doesn't speak again until they've stopped for a freight train at a crossing that divides the city like a suture. "You might look at Garth," says Marilyn, "and think he's just making it up as he goes along, but he's got a code. Take that business with Matt. Garth made it clear to Matt before he left that he was welcome to come back anytime, but he couldn't be peddling his wares out of the house. He had to be doing that on his own time on his own turf. You understood that, right? Garth won't have anyone coming to the door looking to score. And no drugs on the premises either. I mean, no weight. I tried to explain all this to your . . . to Jesse and your boyfriend—"

"Billy."

"Right. Billy. Garth'll let almost anyone crash at our place rent free, but you have to make a contribution. Like in a commune, which Garth says he once lived in, though when he describes it, it sounds suspiciously like rehab. But anyway. He won't assign duties or anything. You're just supposed to find a way to kick in. Garth thought maybe you could watch the kids, but Randy's scared of you and I'm not sure I want you any-fucking-where near the girls. So when we're at the mall, I suggest you look around for stores that might be hiring."

Lauren has been intently watching the rumbling procession of train cars, but now she looks at Marilyn. "So like the whole shopping-for-your-daughter thing was just bullshit?"

"Not at all. I really don't know what Tiff wants. Except to be you. And while we're at it, let's see if we can find a way to nip that in the bud, shall we?"

FOR HOURS ROY and Edie have been traveling up and down the streets, avenues, county roads, and main highways north of Bismarck. They've driven through housing developments so new their streets have only recently been graded, and they've followed dirt and gravel roads that have ended at farm ponds, hay fields, and cow pastures. No matter how unpromising a lane, road, or path might seem, they've turned onto it.

Roy asks, "Are you religious, Edie?"

"Why? Have we tried everything now but prayer? But no, that gene skipped our family."

"Ours too. No, I was wondering because Carla got religion. One of those no-name-make-your-own-personal-Jesus-brain-dead denominations. How she could believe that happy horseshit was beyond me."

"I used to think maybe there's a God who dreams up a special punishment for each one of us. And mine was to have twin brothers both want me."

"Well, shit, Edie. Nothing deep there. We were men. No reason we should be exempt."

They take another turn only to end up in someone's long driveway. Roy simply follows it until they come to a massive brick mansion where a man in shorts, flip-flops, and a pink polo shirt is hosing off a riding lawn mower in front of a triple garage. He's drinking a Coors Light.

Roy rolls down the window. The man aims the hose in the other direction and comes just close enough to hear what Roy has to say.

"Excuse me!" Roy calls out. "We took a wrong turn somewhere. We're looking for Dreary Lane."

The man shakes his head no. "Not around here."

"You're sure?"

"Yeah, I'm sure."

"The Solon farm?"

The man laughs. "Does this look like anyone's farm?"

Roy takes a deep breath. "The name doesn't mean anything?"

"You're lost, man. And you're in my driveway."

"Okay. Thanks anyway." Then Roy rolls up the window, puts the Highlander into reverse, and begins to back down the driveway. Edie raises her middle finger to the man with the hose. He probably sees her gesture, though he can't hear her say, "Prick."

Roy turns onto the main road and speeds off with a spray of dirt and gravel. "I believe," he says, "your frustrations are beginning to show."

A few minutes later he stops the car at an intersection of two county roads, one paved and one dirt. The stop sign is riddled with bullet holes. Roy turns onto the road that's paved.

"By the way, Miss Edie, when did you turn into such a badass? Flipping off strangers. Drinking whiskey. Spending the night in a man's motel room."

"Is the Holiday Inn a motel?"

"Holiday Inn Express then."

"I don't think anyone has ever called me a badass."

"How's the fit?"

She taps her chin. "Edie Pritchard. Badass. Yeah, maybe."

A tractor is poking along ahead of them, and Roy accelerates and passes it and the sunbaked farmer driving it. "Edie Pritchard," Roy says.

"Yes, Roy Linderman?"

"No, I just mean . . . It's interesting. Not Dunn. Back to Pritchard."

"Well, I never had quite enough time with it, so yes. Back to Pritchard."

"Sure, sure. I get it. It's just that . . . When we were checking in yesterday, it occurred to me there was a time when we both could have checked in as Lindermans."

"A very short time. Dean and I weren't together very long. Not when you look at all the years since."

"The long view. I've never been very good at it."

"You haven't, have you? But time forces it on all of us."

They're back inside Bismarck's city limits now, and Roy turns into the Prairie Falcon Fuel and Truck Stop. "Let's see if someone here knows where we can find Dreary Lane."

Roy parks the Highlander near a line of semis. He leaves the windows open, and the fumes of diesel fuel, of trains, buses, and trucks, drift into the vehicle and fill Edie's nostrils. It's an odor that all but issues a command: "Better get moving."

A few minutes later Roy comes out of the gas station. He climbs into the car and says, "Nobody's ever heard of a Dreary Lane. And there's a young guy in there who says he'd know. He plows roads and driveways out this way."

"How about the Solon farm?"

"That name," Roy says, "means nothing to nobody."

He bends forward, crosses his arms on the steering wheel, and rests his head on his arms.

"Are you that tired?" Edie asks.

"My back. Sciatica."

"Maybe if you wouldn't sleep sitting up in a chair."

He turns his head and looks at her but says nothing. Then he sits up straight and starts the engine.

"There's a café here," she says. "Shall we go in? You didn't have much breakfast."

"I'm fine."

"Do you want me to drive?" Edie asks.

"Nope."

"And you don't want to take a break?"

"Nope."

"Is there something you usually take for your back troubles?"

"Ibuprofen," he says. "It's hard on the stomach though. Especially for someone who likes his whiskey. So I try not to take too much."

"You could try to go easy on the whiskey."

"I could." Roy has turned the vehicle around, and he's about to exit the gas station's lot. "Which way?" he asks.

"Back up north, I guess. Maybe there's a road we missed."

"Not fucking likely," he says. But he turns into the line of cars flowing north.

Only when they are traveling again through the open country north of the city, through the sunlit rolling hills where the road curves for reasons that don't reveal themselves to the eye, does Edie begin to speak.

"Maybe you don't want to talk about any of this," she says, "but I'm still trying to figure out what happened last night."

"It's complicated," Roy says with a shrug.

"It's *not* complicated," Edie says. "I got into your bed and you decided to sit up in your chair."

"I had the feeling I was where you wanted me to be."

"Did it ever occur to you to ask me what *I* wanted?"

"Did it ever occur to you to tell me?"

"My God," she says. "You sound like a teenage girl who wants everything to be just perfect her first time."

"Nothing wrong with that," Roy says. "What the hell. I had a little too much to drink. I think you did too."

"Jesus. You know what they used to say? That Roy Linderman—he can talk any woman into the sack. But me? You talk *out*."

He says nothing to this, and they travel in silence for a few miles. Then Edie turns and looks at Roy. "I have a theory about you," she says. "You probably don't want to hear it."

"I probably don't," he replies. "But I will anyway, won't I?"

"All these years you've wanted me only because you couldn't have me. And because you couldn't, you turned me into this, this ideal. So if you saw my stretch marks or how one boob is bigger than the other, you might have had to let go of your obsession. And what if, God forbid, it turned out I was lousy in bed? What then? Would your life suddenly lose its meaning?"

"Did it ever occur to you what I wanted was for you to love me back?"

"And did it ever occur to you that maybe I did? But just not the way you wanted? Maybe you need to take what you can get."

On the road up ahead a cyclist is pedaling hard, his spandex-clad ass up in the air and his helmeted head down low. Because there's no paved shoulder, Roy has to pull out to pass and, as they go by, the rider gives them the thumbs-up sign.

"That must mean," Roy says, "we're heading in the right direction."

"I can't think of any other possibility," Edie replies.

LESS THAN AN hour later, Roy and Edie pass the cyclist again. This time they're traveling in opposite directions, his out of an out-and-back completed. They regard him with envy since they have no way of knowing where they are on their journey. Halfway or just starting? As far from their finish as they'll ever be?

But then Edie turns to look back at a farm they've just passed.

"Wait." She says the word so softly it's as though she's afraid of breaking a spell. "I think that's it."

Roy pulls over with care as if it's not gravel but glass crunching beneath the Highlander's tires.

"We just passed it," Edie says. "That's their SUV out front."

"You're sure?"

"Yes, yes! I'm sure!"

Roy makes a U-turn and speeds the quarter mile down the road to the farmhouse. He pulls into the driveway behind a black Chevy Blazer. Its license plate is from the state of Washington.

The Highlander has barely come to a stop before Edie is out the door. Roy watches her stride up the driveway, away from him and toward a girl who has Edie's blood, however diluted, running through her veins.

Roy gets out of the car and walks back down to the road, and there he stops at the mailbox. There's nothing to indicate the farm's address, but sure enough, the letters S O L O N are stuck to the black metal. He walks by the weeds growing around the post, and then he sees it—the G that lost its adhesive and dropped to the ground. He picks it up and tries to stick it back in place, but it won't stay put. He bends down and picks it up again. This time he opens the mailbox and places the glow-in-the-dark letter inside. "It's been good to know you," he says.

He takes another step toward the road, where he can see the remains of an animal crushed by a passing vehicle. The animal—a raccoon? a possum?—is no longer identifiable, its carcass mashed so flat it has almost been absorbed by the road itself. Not even the outline of its body is discernible. Whatever the creature was it had fur, and a few tufts of hair still rise above the surface as if they've sprouted from the asphalt. Roy steps forward tentatively.

"Roy! She's here! Lauren's here!" Edie calls to him from the porch.

Roy plods up the driveway.

Tiffany has answered the door, but she doesn't invite Edie inside. She calls out, "Hey, Lauren! Someone's here for you!"

It's not Edie's granddaughter who appears however but Marilyn in an old pair of Converse high-tops, shorts, and a once-white T-shirt so stretched out it could have been Garth's. All are spotted and streaked with paint. Her hair is tied back, and she's pulling off a pair of canvas work gloves. She and Edie look at each other through the screen door.

"Hello," Marilyn says. "What can I do for you?"

"I'm Lauren's grandmother."

"Uh-huh. You've traveled a ways."

"Well, yes. From . . . Is Lauren here now?"

"Down in the cellar. She's been helping me put up some shelves."

"Could I see her?" Edie asks. "Could I talk to her?"

"I don't see why not." Marilyn starts to open the door and then sees Roy limping toward the house. "Hello," she says. "Who's this? Grandpa?"

He steps onto the porch. "Just the chauffeur," he says.

Marilyn opens the door wide and, with a sweeping gesture, ushers Edie and Roy inside. "Your own personal driver?" she says to Edie. "Must be nice." To Tiffany she says, "Go tell Lauren to get her butt up here."

Marilyn takes a step back and looks Edie up and down. "So, Lauren's grandmother, I'm Marilyn Hoffman. That was my daughter Tiffany who answered the door. Sarah, my other daughter, is around here someplace. My husband is off fishing with our boy, Randy, and Lauren's boyfriend."

She leads them to the kitchen and asks, "Can I get you something to drink? Coffee? A cold beer?"

"I'm fine," Edie says. "Thank you anyway."

"No thanks," says Roy.

"You've traveled some miles," Marilyn says. "From Washington, I understand."

"You're thinking of Lauren's mother," Edie says. "We came from Montana."

"Well, you could certainly pass for the mom," Marilyn says. "But here you are—the grandmother, and of a teenager at that." She gives Roy the kind of look that coconspirators might share. "Can you believe it?"

Roy says simply, "I've known her a long time."

Marilyn cocks her head as though she's waiting for further explanation, but none is forthcoming. "How did you find us?" she asks Edie.

"Lauren called me. And sent me a text."

"And that was good enough to find your way *here*? I wouldn't have thought that girl could give directions out to the barn."

Tiffany and Lauren emerge from the basement, and at the sight of each other Lauren and Edie rush into an embrace.

Marilyn says to her daughter, "Go find your sister. You two make sure your room's clean."

"Lauren," Edie says, "this is Mr. Linderman. Roy, this is my granddaughter."

"Mr. *Linderman*?" Lauren says to her grandmother.

Edie nods.

Jesse suddenly appears, torso and feet bare as usual and eyes blinking as though he's trying to clear away the world of sleep to bring the real one into focus.

"If it isn't Sleeping Beauty," says Marilyn. "Come see who's here for a visit."

Jesse smiles at Edie. "Hello, Grandma. Who's this? You bring your boyfriend?"

"So you know each other?" Marilyn says.

"We've met," Edie says. "But a 'visit'? No, Lauren's going to leave with us. We can't stay."

"Whose idea is this?"

"Both of ours," Edie answers. Her arm is still around Lauren.

Marilyn gives them both a long, hard look before she says to Lauren, "Then you better go pack up your shit."

"Can I give you a hand?" Edie asks her granddaughter.

Lauren nods and they leave the kitchen together.

As they walk past him, Jesse says with a laugh, "Bye-bye, Miss American Pie!"

"Well, that's that," Marilyn says. She pulls her work gloves back on. "Now if you'll excuse me. I'm in the middle of a project. You can let yourselves out."

Jesse and Roy watch Marilyn head back to the basement. "That Marilyn," Jesse says, "she sure as shit doesn't care about winning Miss Congeniality."

He opens the refrigerator and takes out a beer. "What about you?"

Roy nods, pulls out a chair, and sits down at the table.

Jesse brings over two cans of Bud Light, and then he sits down too. "So," he says, "I guess Lauren can't put up with us any longer." He sips the beer and with a dainty gesture wipes foam from his upper lip. "Can't say I blame her."

"Probably just missing home. That's my impression anyway," Roy says.

"Must be nice to have a home to miss. Billy and I, we're still trying to nail that down."

"Billy?"

"My brother. Lauren's boyfriend. If she's gone before he comes back . . ." Jesse holds up his beer can. "Don't know if there are enough of these in the world to help him get over her. He'll be howling at the fucking moon."

"Why don't you take him out and get him laid? In my experience that mends broken hearts a hell of a lot quicker than beer."

"Has that been your modus operandi?" Jesse asks.

"It's worked a time or two."

Jesse wags his finger back and forth between Roy and the other side of the room as though someone else is there with them. "You and Mrs. Dunn?" he asks.

"What's your question?"

Jesse smiles. "Any old answer will do."

"Old friends."

"Ah," says Jesse. He raises the beer can to his lips and in a few long swallows finishes it. "Old friends who travel the country together."

"Is that another question?"

"Nah." He belches and then goes to the refrigerator. "You want another? You got time. Lauren's got her shit scattered all over upstairs. And you should see the bathroom. Fuck, man, she could start her own drugstore."

"I'm fine," Roy says. "So how long you been here? In North Dakota, I mean."

Jesse shrugs. "Kind of lost track of time."

"And how have you been filling your days?"

"You know. A little of this, a little of that."

"I do know," Roy says, and for the first time all day, he smiles the Roy Linderman smile. "That just happens to be my line of work. A little of this. A little of that."

"Very unpredictable line."

"A man's just got to keep his eyes open for where the deals are. Take you, for instance." Roy leans closer to the younger man. "I hear you've got something I've been looking for. Mrs. Dunn said you've got yourself a handgun. Did she say right?"

Jesse laughs but he seems unsettled. "Caught her snooping around in my gear. But yeah. Yeah, she said right."

Roy smiles again. "She's not too knowledgeable when it comes to weaponry. I've been trying to get my hands on an automatic."

Jesse nods. "Glock. Nine millimeter."

"That'd be what I'm looking for, all right. I'll tell you what." He pauses and reaches into the front pocket of his khakis and pulls out a money clip, but he keeps it out of Jesse's sight. From the clip he extracts a number of bills that he carefully folds over. When he holds up the bills a hundred is the only one visible. He says, "If what you've got is in decent condition, I'll give you a good price for it."

"What would that price be?"

"Let's see the gun. What'd you pay? You're entitled to make a profit."

"I got to know if it's worth the trouble of climbing the fucking stairs."

Roy pinches the bills between his thumb and forefinger and reveals a second hundred. "First, let's see what you've got. Then we can find a number that's fair."

Without another word Jesse leaves the kitchen.

Alone in the room, Roy places the folded bills on the table and sets his beer can on the bills.

Jesse returns. He's carrying a blue-nylon duffel bag. "You might get out of here before dark after all," he says. "They're already in the bathroom."

Roy simply holds out his hand.

Jesse unzips the duffel and extracts the handgun, which he hands to Roy. The pistol's sleek blue-black polymer surface is so unadorned it could pass for a child's toy.

Roy ejects the magazine immediately and inspects it. It's empty. Then he works the pistol's slide to verify that a bullet is not in the chamber either. He turns the automatic over in his hand. "Second-generation 17?" he asks Jesse. "This has got some years on it."

"It'll do what you ask it to."

"Is it registered?"

Jesse pulls a face. "Shit, man. Come on."

Roy hefts the gun in his hand. "I'll give you three hundred."

"Hell, I paid three fifty."

"Did you now. An unregistered Glock. At least ten years old. Three fifty."

"I was trying to help a buddy out," Jesse says.

Roy puts the gun on the table near the beer can and the money. He points to the duffel bag. "You have ammunition in there?"

"A box. Almost full."

Roy picks up the gun again. He asks Jesse, "You ever fire this?"

"I've not had the occasion."

Roy smiles at this. "Okay. Four fifty. You throw in the ammo. And at that price I'm helping somebody out too."

Jesse extends a hand, and the two men shake. Then Roy lifts his beer can, exposing the folded bills. Jesse slides the bills away quickly and counts them. "I guess," he says, "you had a number in mind all along."

"I knew how high I'd go if that's what you mean. Now. The ammunition."

Jesse feels around in his duffel again, takes out a box of cartridges, and hands it to Roy.

Roy opens the box and runs his finger down the rows of gleaming brass and lead. "Federal," he says. "You get these at Walmart?"

"The guy just threw them in with the gun. Does it matter?"

"Not to me," Roy says, and once again he releases the magazine. He sets the pistol down and proceeds to take a cartridge from the box and push it into the magazine. Then another—*snick*. And another—*snick*. Each time the spring resists slightly, then gives way to the human hand and the will it enacts.

With each cartridge snapping into place, Jesse winces a little as though something sharp were scraping its way through his gut. He says, "The guy I bought it from was an addict. He was so fucking hard up I probably could have got it for ten bucks. Crack cocaine. How fucking stupid can you get."

"So you're telling me," Roy says without looking up from his task, "you paid three hundred and fifty dollars for something you could have gotten for ten?"

"Like I say. I was helping out a buddy."

"So he could buy crack."

"Hey, he could have put a bullet in me and taken everything I had."

"Interesting relationship. You and your buddy."

"Like I say. A crackhead. A different fucking creature altogether." Jesse reaches into his duffel bag again. "As long we're buying and selling here, I might have something else in here that would interest you. How about something to help you stay awake on those long road trips?"

Roy says nothing. He picks up the pistol now and rams the magazine into place. He stands up and pulls back on the slide to chamber a round.

Jesse jerks back in his chair. "What the fuck, man?"

Roy puts the box of cartridges into the pocket of his trousers. He lifts his shirt and tucks the pistol into the waistband of his trousers and pulls his shirt down over the gun.

"You sure you want that in there?" Jesse asks. "Pretty dangerous if you ask me. Aimed right at your manhood and all."

"My *manhood*?" Roy says and laughs. "If you knew a fucking thing about the gun you used to own you'd know what it takes to fire it."

"Hey, you bought it. Stick it wherever you like."

"Fucking A I bought it. Now you listen. When we leave here today? I don't want to see you in my rearview mirror. You know what I'm saying?"

For a long moment Jesse simply stares up at Roy Linderman. Then he must see something in the older man's eyes that compels him to answer. "Yeah," he says. "I hear you."

As he's leaving the room, Roy says, "Tell them I'm waiting outside."

When Roy reaches the car he opens the front passenger door and puts the Glock and the box of ammunition inside the glove compartment. He takes a cigarette from the pack and lights it.

Moments later Lauren and Edie exit the house, Lauren carrying her graduation suitcase and Edie carrying a green-plastic garbage bag.

Roy drops his cigarette in the dirt and grinds it out with his heel. He opens the Toyota's liftgate and says, "Just toss it all in there. Let's get a move on."

Climbing into the car, stifling in the heat of the midday sun, Edie turns to her granddaughter. "Don't you want to say good-bye to anyone?" she asks.

"Fuck no," Lauren says, climbing into the seat behind her.

WHEN ROY DRIVES into the parking lot of the Holiday Inn Express, he asks Edie, "What do you think? You want to head back or stay another night?"

"How's your back?"

"It's holding up."

"Then I'd just as soon get going."

He looks at Lauren in the rearview mirror. "How about you?" he asks. "You want to vote?"

"Do they have a pool here?"

"Nope."

"Go then, I guess."

"I'll check us out," he says. "You two can wait here."

Roy gets out of the vehicle, leaving its engine running. Edie and Lauren watch him walk across the lot.

"What's the matter with his leg?" Lauren asks.

"He was in a car accident," Edie says. "Years ago."

"Like when he was a kid?"

"Not much more than that." Edie twists around in the seat to look at her granddaughter. "You want to tell me what happened back there?"

"So does he have like one leg shorter than the other one? Because he walks kind of like this kid I went to school with. He was in a bad accident when he was in like fourth grade, and after that his leg was all shriveled."

"When you called me," Edie says, "you sounded like—"

"And this is the really *awful* awful part. His dad was driving. Can you imagine? To be all crippled like that. And your own dad did that to you. And now this guy's like a serious addict. Oxycodone and shit like that. Does Mr. Linderman take a lot of pain pills?"

"No, he's fine," Edie says impatiently. "He lives with it. That's all. He just lives with it."

Lauren is tapping away on her phone. "Do you know how to get on the Holiday Inn Wi-Fi? It says we're close enough. So if you know what the password is—"

"No, no, I don't. Lauren. What happened?"

Lauren answers with a deep sigh. She drops her phone into her purse. "Jesse. He . . . he touched me."

"He touched you how? Did he hurt you?"

She snorts a laugh. "Not hardly!"

"Then—"

"You know. Like putting his hand where he shouldn't."

"Did Billy know?"

"It was probably his fucking idea. Those brothers. I mean, come *on*."

"But you're okay?" asks Edie.

"Plus the whole vibe there. Garth and Marilyn were just this weird couple. He was always like cooking muffins and talking about how we all have to work together. But I never saw him do anything but those muffins. And Marilyn, she wanted me to help with her kids. But I just don't get kids. At *all*."

"But you're all right? That's the important thing."

Lauren frowns at her grandmother. "Yeah. I told you."

Roy Linderman is walking across the parking lot, pulling his suitcase. After rearranging the suitcases, he climbs in behind the wheel and asks, "Ready to hit the road?"

Lauren leans forward from the back seat. "Could we maybe have lunch first?"

Edie and Roy exchange the look common among tired, indulgent grandparents. Then Roy says, "Is Perkins all right?"

EDIE, ROY, AND Lauren are seated in the same booth where Edie and Roy sat upon arriving in Bismarck. This time however Roy and Edie sit side by side. The only other customer in the restaurant at this hour is an obese young man in overalls sitting at the counter and eating a slice of French silk pie.

Lauren orders a vegetable omelet, French fries, and a Diet Coke, Edie a Cobb salad and iced tea, and Roy asks for coffee and a slice of apple pie. Once the food arrives, Lauren is the only one who displays any enthusiasm for the meal.

She has almost finished her food when she says, "They'll come after me, you know. Billy will. So Jesse will too."

"You're sure about that, are you?" asks Roy.

"Oh yeah. I'm sure."

"Most men," he says, pausing to sip his coffee, "you walk out on them, that's the end of it."

"That's not Billy," Lauren says.

"Okay," says Roy. "Let him come." He turns around, looking for the waitress and the bill.

"I have to go potty," Lauren says and slides out of the booth.

Once she's gone, Roy says, "Potty. Jesus. She swears like a fucking sailor but now she has to go potty."

Edie puts her hand on Roy's arm. "I tried to ask Lauren what happened back there, and I wasn't sure how much she'd say in front of you. As it turned out, she didn't say much to me either. Just that Jesse touched her."

Roy doesn't move his arm. "Touched her how?"

"She was pretty vague on that subject. But you met Jesse. What do you think?"

Roy looks off in the direction of the restrooms. "Whatever happened she seems to have recovered."

"Do you remember Donnie Vaughn? That's who he reminds me of."

"Donnie?" Roy laughs. "Yeah, that works. The famous Don Vaughn. I hope he never trapped you in that big old DeSoto of his."

"I got out in time," Edie says.

"Jesus, Edie. Do you have any idea what you're in for? Taking her into your home?"

"That's exactly what Rita said," Edie says. "It'll work or it won't."

Roy raises his eyebrows. "But a teenager? You're not out of practice?"

Edie laughs. "It's like riding a bicycle, Roy. Once you've fucked up as a parent you never forget how to fuck up again."

"Come on. Go easy on yourself."

"I'll see to it she gets a job. Maybe sign her up for classes at the college."

"She'll be the fucking terror of Gladstone."

The waitress sets the bill down on the table, and Roy picks it up and gets out of the booth. "I'll meet you outside," he says. "But first"—he leans down and whispers—"I'm going potty."

When Lauren returns she asks, "Where's Roy?"

"Mr. Linderman went out to have a cigarette."

Lauren makes a face. "His car smells like an ashtray."

"Well, it's his car. Listen, have you called your mother?"

Lauren shakes her head no.

"Don't you think you should?"

"And tell her what? That I'm not where she never knew I was in the first place? Because she didn't give a shit anyway?"

"Do you want me to call her?"

"Hey, it's a free country. But believe me. She does. Not. Give a shit."

"Okay," Edie says. "We'll wait until we get to Gladstone."

"How far is it anyway? Is it like a couple days from here?"

"It's only a few hours, honey. We'll be there before dark."

"Oh, okay." Lauren sighs with relief. "I wasn't sure. We didn't come like directly here. First we drove up to Minot. Or some small-ass town around there. That was where like all their *family*—" Lauren makes air quotes around this word—"was supposed to be. Then they treated us like we had AIDS or something. So right in the middle of the night Jesse said, 'Fuck it. Let's go.' Then we tracked down this friend of Jesse's. Matt. He was like so weird. Taking too many of his own drugs or something. And then a few days later we went to Garth's."

"And that's where it happened?"

"Where what happened?"

"Jesse? You said he—"

"God, Grandma! Can't you give that a rest? I told you. It wasn't that big a deal."

"Okay, Lauren." Edie can't keep the exasperation out of her voice. "But let's not forget. You called me."

Edie slides across the booth, but before she can stand up, Lauren reaches out toward her grandmother. "I'm sorry, Grandma. It was just, I don't know. It just wasn't like it was supposed to be."

Suddenly Lauren blinks and her pretty features bunch up and then crumble. "I thought I'd be *important* to Billy or . . . or somebody. Not just a fucking toy."

Edie covers Lauren's hands with hers, and looks into her granddaughter's tearing eyes.

"I thought I'd *count*. For *something*."

Edie's own eyes begin to glisten. "You matter to me, honey."

But this must not be what Lauren wants to hear. She grabs a napkin and wipes her eyes and nose. "We better go," she says.

LAUREN LEANS INTO the space between the front seats. "Hey, are there any songs about that river? Jesse says there's more songs about rivers than any other water. More than like oceans or lakes or anything."

They are speeding along on Interstate 94, that section of highway that rises into the tawny hills west of Bismarck and Mandan, twin communities built on the eastern and western banks of the Missouri.

Edie begins to sing, "'My Bonnie lies over the ocean / my Bonnie lies over the sea . . .'"

When she stops, Roy begins to sing, in a deep, surprisingly tuneful voice, "'Away, I'm bound away / Across the wide Missouri . . .'"

Edie looks at him admiringly and says, "Mr. Linderman. My goodness. I had no idea."

"Two years of choir," Roy says. "Miss Egan brought out the best in me."

"I bet she did."

But Lauren has become bored with her own question. She tugs on the shoulder strap of her grandmother's sundress. "That dress is really cute, Grandma. Did they have it in other colors?"

"I think so. But I don't know if they'd have it in your size, honey."

"That's okay. I was just going to say it's like not a really great color for you. Blue? Did they have it in blue?"

"I'm not sure," Edie says, and she and Roy exchange a look.

"We'll check," Lauren says. "From now on I'm going to be your personal wardrobe consultant."

"I'm not that much of a shopper, honey."

"You will be!"

Edie turns to Roy. "How's the shopping in Billings?"

"Better than in Gladstone."

Lauren however is finished with this topic too. She lies down on the backseat. "Wake me when we get there," she says.

A few minutes later Edie turns around and looks at her granddaughter. "I wish I could sleep like that," she says to Roy.

"When I was her age," he says, "I could damn near fall asleep at will. Now I can't go more than a couple hours before I have to get up and move around."

"My mother used to say if your conscience is clear, you won't have any trouble sleeping. Of course she said that knowing I had insomnia."

"Your mother was something else. Scared the hell out of me. Did I ever tell you what she said to me at your wedding? She looked me up and down and then asked, 'Well, did she get the right one?' 'Hell yes,' I said."

"She might have loved Dean," Edie says, "as much as she was capable of loving anyone."

"Mothers and grandmothers loved him."

They have landed on a subject they are both wary of, and as a consequence they fall silent for a few miles. In the absence of conversation, Roy turns up the volume on the radio. It's tuned to a public radio station and its classical music, and as they travel through this bone-dry landscape, the sounds of Handel's Water Music fill the car.

Edie turns again in her seat to look at Lauren. Then she says quietly, "I had the radio on this morning, and there was an interview with a psychologist, a woman, who was talking about young girls. Apparently their self-esteem really seems to drop about the time they're in middle school. That really struck me. Because that's about the time boys are really discovering girls. I mean, really giving them a look, right? Wasn't that about the time some of us started dating? So why, if girls are getting all that attention from boys, why wouldn't it *raise* their self-esteem?"

Roy remains silent.

"Come on, Roy. You must have a theory."

He takes a deep breath. "It must be something about the way we look at you."

Edie nods and turns to look out the window. "At last," she says.

The hum and thump of tires on pavement. The occasional whoosh of a passing car. The regular chuffing breaths coming from a young woman fast asleep. After ten minutes of these disparate sounds of traveling, Roy asks Edie, "What kind of vehicle were those boys driving? A Blazer, wasn't it?"

"I'm not sure. It was black. Why?"

"Because a black Explorer has been dogging us for a while. And I don't think it has Montana or North Dakota plates."

Edie turns in her seat to look.

"It's a ways back," Roy says. "But sort of holding its distance. No matter what my speed."

"It was an SUV," Edie says. "I know that." She looks out the side-view mirror. "But aren't you the one who's supposed to know cars?"

"I do," Roy says. "It's my memory of cars that's the problem. Wake her up. Ask her."

"Oh, let's let her sleep."

"Fine," Roy says. But only a minute later he pulls onto the shoulder of the road. "Hell, I can't take the suspense."

And once the Highlander's highway hum changes pitch and rolls to a stop, Lauren opens her eyes. "Why are we stopping? Where are we?"

"Nowhere," says Roy.

Only a moment later the black Explorer passes, and once it does Lauren asks, "Did you think that was Billy and Jesse?"

"It crossed my mind," Roy replies.

"I told you."

"That you did." Then Roy puts the Highlander in gear and pulls back onto the highway.

WHERE ROY PARKS, in front of the cinder-block rest stop, his car is only one in a line of vehicles, their license plates mostly from North Dakota and Montana but also from Wyoming, Idaho, Arkansas, and South Dakota. Right next to them is a Subaru Forester packed tight and with suitcases lashed to the roof as well. Its license plate is from Alaska.

"Where are all these people going?" asks Edie.

"It's America," says Roy. "We're a country on the move. And we all have to take a leak. Anyone else?"

"I'm good for now," Edie says.

"I'll go," Lauren says. She unbuckles, and when she opens the door a gust of wind almost blows it shut again.

Before Roy exits the car, he says to Edie, "At least she didn't say *potty*."

Edie watches them walk toward the gray squat building, its shape and material suited to withstand the wind that howls and swirls around this hilltop.

Roy comes back out of the building before Lauren, and he lights a cigarette.

When Lauren comes out she sees Roy and walks over to join him. She spreads her arms wide as though she wants to make a sail of her body. "God," she says, almost shouting. "Is this like a fucking tornado or something?"

"You know," Roy says, "your grandmother won't say anything, but your language bothers her."

"You think? She said it doesn't."

"It does."

"Well, I guess you know her better than me."

"I guess."

Then Lauren asks Roy, "Hey, did you know my mom?"

"Not really. I met her. That was all. When she was about your age."

"Was she pretty? She's always telling me how great looking she used to be."

"I don't remember her all that well. But sure. I guess. Pretty girl."

"How about my grandpa?"

"Again," Roy says, "I met him once. Can't really say I knew him."

"But him and grandma were still married?"

"That they were."

Lauren smiles coyly at Roy. "That must have been tough for you, huh?"

"You know, you're about one half as smart as you think you are." Roy glances over at the car where Edie sits waiting. "Did your grandmother say anything to you on this subject?"

Lauren smiles and shrugs. "I can usually tell what's what."

"Must be a wonderful talent to have."

"Sometimes it's more like a burden."

"You're bearing up well." Roy inhales deeply, holds the smoke, and then exhales toward the sky. "You keep looking down the highway," he says. "You still think your boyfriend is coming after you?"

"I know he is."

"So was this some kind of damn test? You call your grandmother to come get you just to make your boyfriend chase after you? Because I'll tell you something, you put a man to the test often enough sooner or later he's going to flunk."

"Little lady."

"What?"

"*Young lady*. When somebody older says that they usually say, I'll tell you something, *little lady*. I'll tell you something, *young lady*. Like every fucking time. *Young lady*. I was just waiting for you to say it."

"Jesus." Roy drops his cigarette onto the concrete and steps on it. "You are something, you know that?"

The notes of Lauren's laughter are carried off on the wind.

AS THEY PULL back onto the highway, Roy nods in the direction of Lauren in the back seat and says, "She's pretty sure they'll be coming for her."

"Not 'pretty sure,'" Lauren says. "Like *really* sure."

"It wouldn't surprise me," Edie says. "Think about it. Men. If their dog runs off, they'll chase after it." She laughs a little. "They don't want to think about their runaway ending up in someone else's yard."

Lauren laughs too and joins in. "Or like somebody else is scratching the dog behind the ears."

"But it'd be all right," Edie adds, "if someone else fed the dog."

"Or scooped the dog's shit!"

"All right," Roy says and adjusts a vent on the dashboard that doesn't need adjusting. "I believe I'll stay on the outside of this conversation. I'm just the driver here."

"Gary came after me," Edie says. "As you recall."

"Hardly a lost dog situation," Roy says.

"I didn't say *lost*," Edie replies. "I said a *runaway*."

"Was that what you were? A runaway?"

"I suppose," Edie says and shifts her gaze to the fields of sunflowers growing close to the highway, all those flowers turning their faces toward the late afternoon sun.

"We don't have to talk about it," Roy says and nods in the direction of the back seat.

"Oh, I don't mind," Edie replies, "and I don't mind who hears about it. At first I wasn't running away *from* Gary; I was traveling *to* Dean. You should know. You set things in motion with that phone call."

"I remember."

"But then by the time I got to Gladstone, I was definitely running away."

"And you were going to keep running."

"Which was obviously impossible. I had a child. I was a mother." Edie turns up her palms in a gesture of surrender. "Now here I am. Right back where I started."

"In the car with me, you mean?" Roy asks. "With someone after us?"

"Gladstone," Edie says. "I meant Gladstone. I'm back in Gladstone."

Lauren, who is perhaps uncomfortable with the subject of a woman in motion, reaches forward to flick a few strands of her grandmother's hair. "Hey, Grandma. Have you always had long hair?"

"I had a couple flirtations with short hair. But yes. Mostly."

"Because I'm thinking when I get my hair cut we'll cut yours too. Like, *really* short. And we'll change the color too. And we'll switch your lipstick too. Like really red. Oh, you'll look wicked, Grandma. Won't she, Roy?"

"Yep," he says with a smile. "*Wicked.*"

"And when we hit the bars," Lauren says, "the cowboys will all be like, 'Whoa, who is *that*?'"

"Let's not get ahead of ourselves, honey."

THEY'VE RISEN FROM the alkali valleys and passed the hayfields waiting for the second cutting. The strange rivers have been crossed. They're in Montana now, less than half an hour from Gladstone. They've fallen silent as travelers so often do as they approach their destination. They can see the familiar water tower and count the church spires.

As the road begins to curve down a rimrock bluff, Roy says, "You'll have to give me directions to your place, Edie. I'm not sure I know the way coming in from this direction."

"Just before you reach the bottom of the hill you'll take a hard right," she says. "And then climb back up again."

"So you live where we used to—"

"Exactly."

"Huh. I must have gotten turned around in that new development. If there's any place I should recognize, it's that hill."

Edie smiles. "A lot has changed."

"Truer words . . ." Roy leans forward to get a better look at something that's no longer there. "Now am I remembering right? There used to be a little graveyard up here. Or not a graveyard, more like a couple headstones with an iron fence around them. It was all grown over. Jesus. Did I dream that?"

"You're remembering right," Edie says. "It was supposed to be the family plot of early settlers. The Campbells."

"My God," Roy says reverently. "It's all coming back." He turns around to address Lauren. "We used to drink and party up there on that hill. And more. It was our—what?—lovers' lane? But that wasn't what we called it."

"Thrill Hill," Edie says.

He shakes his head and laughs. "One night a bunch of us were up there drinking and scaring the shit out of each other with ghost stories. Some of the stories had to do with those graves. I can't remember how it started, but the big dare was, would anyone go climb over that fence and kiss those gravestones? Only one person would take that dare and that was your grandmother."

"I once kissed Wayne Hedrick," says Edie. "Or should I say let him kiss me. If I was brave enough for that . . ."

Lauren asks, "Like how did you prove you did it?"

"I believe," says Edie, "I had to leave lipstick on the stone."

Lauren shudders. "Yech."

"So that was your grandmother," Roy says.

"Was it?" Lauren asks her grandmother. "Was that you?"

"If that's how he remembers me," Edie says with a shrug. Then she says, "The graves were moved when they put in the new road and built the apartments."

They have almost arrived at the parking lot for the Custer Ridge apartment complex. Although the lot faces west, the sun has almost set, and the evening's lengthening shadows will soon vanish in the dark.

"Who's hungry?" Edie asks. She looks from Roy to Lauren and back to Roy. "We should go out for supper. My treat. What do you say? Lauren? We could go to Applebee's. They have salads."

"I'm not all that hungry, Grandma. That was like such a big lunch."

"Roy? How about you? All you had was a piece of pie. And you didn't have much breakfast."

He shakes his head no. "I've still got over two hundred miles to travel."

Roy parks next to Edie's Honda Civic and says aloud what they all know. "Here we are."

Edie reaches over and lightly lays her hand on Roy's wrist. "Why don't you stay the night? I don't feel right about you spending hours more on the road. You've had a long day already. Stay. Give your back a rest. I've got room."

After a long hesitation he says, "I better not."

"Sure?" Edie says.

After another hesitation he says, "I'm sure." He pushes a button that pops open the liftgate. "I'll give you a hand with your things."

The evening is warm, and though the wind here is almost calm, something still brings the sharp odor of sagebrush from the surrounding hillside.

Lauren has already begun taking her bags from the car. When Roy approaches she thrusts out her hand and says solemnly, "Thanks for everything, Mr. Linderman."

He shakes her hand. "Don't be giving your grandmother a hard time now. Young lady."

Lauren laughs. "You have to come back," she says, "after I get through with her makeover. You won't even recognize her!"

"I don't believe that's possible," he says.

WHILE EDIE HUNTS through her purse for her keys, Roy and Lauren wait patiently by the apartment door with their load of suitcases and bags. "I'm sorry, I'm sorry," Edie says. "I know I have them . . ."

"Take your time," says Roy. He looks up and down the hall. "Are these all two-bedroom units?"

"What? Oh. No. Some of them are one-bedrooms. That's what I wanted, but there weren't any available when I was ready to sign a lease. So he let me have a two-bedroom for the same price."

"You always were a skillful negotiator."

"And," she says, "I didn't even have to flash an ankle."

Roy turns to Lauren and says, "Your grandmother has always had very persuasive ankles."

Lauren rolls her eyes.

"Here they are," Edie says. She brings forth her keys and unlocks the apartment door.

The apartment isn't completely dark, but the interior dimness is like the murky view from under water. Edie reaches for a light switch, but before her finger touches it a light flashes on in the kitchen.

Startled, she lurches back. And from out of the kitchen steps Jesse with Billy close behind.

"Hey, slowpokes!" Jesse says. "What the hell kept you?"

Lauren edges behind Roy and Edie.

Edie asks, "How did you get in here?"

Jesse holds up a key. "Did you really think," he says, "you could send us out on the town with a key and I wouldn't make a copy?" He shakes his head in mock sorrow. "You're losing it, Grandma."

"Did you look for us?" Billy asks Lauren.

She nods.

"We parked over behind the dumpsters."

Roy's anger has finally overridden his confusion and surprise. "What the hell are you doing here?"

"We didn't even have to drive that fast to beat you," Billy says.

"I'd like to say we came for a visit," says Jesse. "You know, sit down, share a pizza and a beer. Shoot the shit. Take some time and get to know each other a little better. But that wouldn't be the truth. We came to get Miss Lauren here and be on our way." He points at Lauren with a wiggling index finger. "This'll be easy won't it, honey? You're all ready to go. You won't even have to pack up your things."

Lauren has dropped her bags just inside the door, and at Jesse's remark she starts to reach down.

"She's not going with you," Edie says.

"Oh no?"

"And you're leaving right now," says Edie, stepping in front of Lauren and her suitcase.

"If you say so." Jesse's smile grows wider and he turns his palms up. "But she's going with us."

The evening grows darker, the last light dying in the western sky too. Only the light from the kitchen doorway, like a cave's open mouth, illuminates the apartment. These people however make no move to step out of the shadows.

"You can't be here," Edie says. "This is trespassing. And I'm calling the police."

Jesse throws his arms in the air dramatically. "Oh no, Grandma. No, no! You can't be doing that." He takes a step back. He lifts his shirt, revealing not only his rib-skinny torso but also a pistol sticking out from the drooping waistband of his shorts. He pulls his shirt back down immediately.

"Wait!" Lauren says. "*Wait*! Fuck. *Fuck!*"

Roy has seen the gun as well. "Son of a bitch," he whispers.

Jesse lets his arms dangle at his sides in imitation of a gunfighter's stance. "What do you think?" he says to Roy. "Shall we see who's quicker on the draw? Shoot it out over the women here? Go ahead. Go for it."

"Billy," Lauren says. "*Billy. Do* something!"

But Billy says nothing. He has become as much a spectator to his brother's act as anyone.

Roy lifts his shirt. "I'm not carrying."

Edie looks up at Roy. "What's he talking about?"

"He didn't tell you?" Jesse says. "The two of us played a little version of *Let's Make a Deal* back at the farm."

Edie continues to look beseechingly at Roy.

Jesse's hoot violates the apartment's quiet. "Ho-ho! Keeping secrets, are you, Roy?" Jesse flips up his shirt again and just as quickly pulls it back down. "That gun you were so upset about, Grandma? Your boyfriend here offered me so fucking much for it I couldn't say no. But he put enough money in my pocket I could have bought a goddamn arsenal."

"Not quite," Roy says.

"No? Well, old Garth was willing to sell me his pistol for about a tenth of what you paid me." Jesse pats his waistband. "Of course it's not the fancy fucking firearm you bought. But this'll do. This sure as fuck will do."

Lauren says, "Garth had a gun?"

"When Marilyn found out?" Billy says. "*Whoo!* She about shit. If it was up to her, he'd have given it away."

"This is all true?" Edie asks Roy.

He nods.

"And where is it now?"

"In the car. In the glove box."

Edie takes a deep breath and lets it out slowly. "Is the car locked now?"

Roy nods again.

"Give me the keys."

Roy shakes his head no.

"I mean it," Edie says. "Give me the keys."

Roy reaches into his pocket, takes out the keys, and holds them just out of her reach. "What the hell are you doing, Edie?"

"Why, I'm going out there for your gun. He's got one"—she points to Jesse—"so we should have one too."

"I don't think so," Jesse says to Edie, and he reaches to his waistband and pulls out the gun.

"What's that?" Roy asks. "A Hi-Standard? Twenty-two long rifle?"

"Fuck if I know," says Jesse. "But I believe my barrel's longer than yours." Jesse giggles at his own remark, but no one else acknowledges its humor.

"Sears used to sell that model. Good target pistol."

Five people are clustered around the door as if they don't quite know how to say good-bye. Edie keeps holding her hand out for Roy's keys. Billy is trying to find a way to step in front of his brother and get close to Lauren. She in turn edges farther behind Roy Linderman.

"You keep trying to make conversation," Jesse says to Roy, "and I haven't got a fucking thing I want to say to you. And you got nothing to say I want to hear. Now, move away from that door, Grandma."

While Roy is focused on Jesse, Edie grabs the keys from his hand. She turns and opens the apartment door.

Jesse waves his gun in her direction. "Hey, hey, hey, Grandma. Where do you think you're going?"

"I told you. To get a gun."

"Jesus-fucking-Christ! Do you not understand what the situation is here? I don't want to have to shoot you!"

"You do what you have to," she says. "But you better do it quick. Because if you don't shoot me first I'm going out to the car to get that gun."

Edie hesitates and then steps outside. She closes the door quietly behind her. Her footsteps make hollow thumps as she walks down the hallway.

"Fuck! Fuck!" To Roy he says, "What's with her? Huh? Does she not care if she lives or dies? Is she fucking crazy?"

"Easy," Roy says and makes a calming motion with his hands. "Easy. You don't want to shoot anybody. Come on. Put it away."

Jesse lunges toward Roy, raising the gun and jabbing it toward Roy's head as if the weapon's real threat were to poke out an eye. "See," Jesse says, "that's where you're wrong. I want to shoot *you*. I want to shoot you so fucking bad I'm getting a hard-on just thinking about it!"

Roy raises his hand. "Okay, okay. But wait. Just wait. Hear me out. I've got another deal for you."

"I bet you do. I just bet you do."

"Laure," Billy says, "Hey, Laure. Come on . . ."

She steps back and presses against the wall next to the door.

"You want to hear the deal," Roy says to Jesse, "or not?"

"Make it fast. Because if she comes back here with a fucking gun in her hand, all hell is going to break loose."

"You saw what I'm driving? The Highlander? That's a 2007. Got a little over ten thousand miles. And I'm willing to swap it straight up for your—what are you driving? An Explorer?"

"Blazer."

"A Blazer. All right. I'll take your piece of shit Blazer off your hands. And you drive away in a damn near brand-new vehicle. But you *drive away*. Now. This offer expires the second that doorknob turns."

Billy reaches out and lightly slaps his brother's arm. "Hey, Jesse. What do you think? A new car'd be cool."

"We can do the paperwork right here," says Roy. "Registration is out in the car."

Jesse cups his hand to his ear. "Do I hear her coming?"

"She's not even your girl," Roy says.

"He's kind of right about that," says Billy. "I should be the one—"

"Shut up."

"We'll just trade pink slips," Roy says, putting a protective arm around Lauren, "and you can be on your way."

"You shut up too!" Jesse points his finger at Roy as though for the moment he's confused the finger with the gun barrel. "Go look out the balcony," Jesse tells Billy. "See what the fuck she's doing out there."

"Going for the gun might have been bullshit," says Roy. "She probably took the keys and drove off. I would."

"So we ain't getting his car," Billy says.

"Grandma wouldn't," Lauren says.

"Go!" Jesse shouts at his brother.

Billy pushes aside the wide slats of the vertical blinds and slides open the balcony door. The parking lot lights have come on, and their pale light flashes weakly into the apartment. The wind rattles the blinds and makes a noise like cards being shuffled.

"Maybe you don't have the title for your vehicle," Roy says. "Fine. Not a problem. I'll just sign the title over to you and hand over the keys, and you can drive off."

"Do you ever fucking stop talking?" Jesse says to Roy. Then he calls out to Billy, "Well?"

"I can't see her. Maybe she went out and called the cops. Huh, Jesse?"

"She didn't take her purse."

"Wait! She's coming back!"

"And? Is she carrying the gun?"

"I can't tell! Maybe . . ."

"Please, Jesse," Lauren says. Her words are muffled as she speaks into Roy's shoulder. "Please. Don't, don't. I'll go with you. I'll . . . Whatever you want."

Roy pulls her closer.

"Get out of the way," Jesse says as he steps toward the apartment door.

Roy is blocking Jesse's path, but it's Billy Roy speaks to. "Listen to me, Billy. You don't want her this way. Not by force. I know what I'm talking about here. You don't want a woman who doesn't want you."

The doorknob turns, and Roy presses back against the door with all his weight.

"Fuck, man," Jesse says. "Get out of the way."

But Edie has a strength or force that no one on the inside could anticipate or understand, and before Jesse can reach the door or Roy can let go of Lauren and brace himself even harder, Edie somehow manages to push her way inside.

And yes, yes, she has the gun, yes. She's staring at it in her hand, an alien object, carried into her world from another, its dark shape looking as if it were formed from darkness itself.

She asks, "Is it loaded?"

The question could only be directed to Roy. "Yes," he says. "Loaded and racked."

"I don't know what that means." She turns the gun over in her hand, scrutinizing its surface. "Does it have a safety?"

It's Jesse who answers her: "It's ready. Just pull the trigger."

He's holding his own gun at his side. All of them—Jesse, Billy, Lauren, and Roy—stand perfectly still, a tableau, watching Edie as if her performance were about to begin.

And it does.

She raises the pistol with both hands and with her arms extended points the barrel at Jesse.

He flinches and holds a hand up in front of his face, but he comes back to himself quickly and he laughs. "You going to shoot me, Grandma?" He still has not raised his own pistol.

"I think so," Edie says.

"I think so too." He points to the gun aimed at his head and to the hands holding it. "Look here," he says. "You can't have your hand up top like that. The slide's going to come back and take a big fucking bite out of your hand." Jesse looks to Roy. "I'm right, right? Tell her."

"That's right," Roy says and reaches for her hand on the gun. "Here, let me—"

She jerks the gun away like a child unwilling to share a toy. And then she raises the pistol again, this time with one hand. Her aim at Jesse's head is still steady.

"They'll put you in jail, Grandma."

"And they'll bury you."

Jesse is the one who can see Edie's eyes. All he has to do—all he can't help but do—is look beyond the gun barrel. Long ago her eyes lost the green shine of her youth. Now they're the dusty green of late summer. But something has perhaps come back in the last few moments, and now they gleam darkly.

Is that what Jesse sees? Are Edie's eyes more convincing, more persuasive, than the black round vacancy of the muzzle?

"Jesus-fucking-*Christ*, woman!" Jesse says. He lifts his T-shirt and returns the pistol to the waistband of his shorts. He sniffs and draws his shoulders back. "She ain't worth it, you know. You'll find that out, sure as hell."

Then Jesse signals to his brother. "Saddle up, pardner," he says, the joke dying in the darkening air. "We're heading out of here."

"In his car?"

"His car? Fuck no. *His* car. We don't need his charity. We're walking out of here of our own free will. Not because someone paid our way out the goddamn door."

As the brothers move toward the door, Edie keeps the gun aimed at Jesse's head and her finger on the trigger. Billy looks beseechingly at Lauren. He wants to say something. But words are lost to him, and he follows his brother out the door.

The second the door closes behind the Norris brothers, Edie drops the gun. It hits the floor with a thud, a sound that seems to reverberate through all the rooms of the apartment. Edie sinks to her hands and knees.

Lauren kneels beside her grandmother. "Grandma, Grandma. It's okay. They're gone. It's *okay*."

Roy picks up the pistol, holding it by its barrel as if it were a tool for hammering nails. He carries it to the coffee table and sets it down gently. Then he walks out to the balcony.

"Grandma?"

Edie gets off her knees and sits back against the door. "Honey," she says to her granddaughter, "it might be a lot of things but okay isn't one of them."

Lauren nods. She sits down next to her grandmother and puts an arm around her shoulders. Edie grabs and squeezes her granddaughter's hand.

Roy comes back in from the balcony. He slides the screen and then the heavy glass door shut, and when it closes it seems as though the room's breath has stopped. He walks over to Edie and Lauren, who are still sitting on the floor.

"They drove off," he says. "For now."

"For good," Lauren says. "Billy'd come back if he could but Jesse won't stand for it. He's got all this weird family pride."

"Still," says Roy, "I'll stay here." He points to the sofa. "Right there. I'll be right there."

Edie holds her hands out to Roy. "Help me up," she says.

He pulls her to her feet.

"But you can't stay," she says.

"Just for the time being," he says. "Until we can be sure—"

"No," she says, looking up at him. "Don't you understand? If you don't leave, I might get used to having you here—*needing* you here— to feel safe. No, I have to get through the night without you here. If

I don't, I'll feel like I can't make it without you here. You or another man. You have to go, Roy. If it doesn't work . . . Well, then I'll know."

"Edie . . . just tonight."

She shakes her head no and pushes him away.

"I'll leave the gun."

Edie hurries over to the coffee table, picks up the gun—by the barrel, just as Roy carried it last—and carries it to him. She presses it toward him so insistently he can't help but take it from her hand.

"You take it," she says. "*Take it*. I don't want it here. I don't want to see it or touch it ever again. I don't want to be who I was when I held it in my hand."

Roy shakes his head and starts to speak, but Edie puts her hand over his mouth. "Go, Roy. You have to go. Thank you. Thank you so much for everything. For being my brother . . . I know it's not what you wanted. But thank you."

"But, Edie—"

She steps back and grabs the front of his shirt. "Go," she says. "*Now. Go!*" She pulls so hard that Roy can't help but move toward the door.

Lauren understands something that he doesn't. She's on her feet now, and she opens the door for him. She hugs him and says, "Thank you, Uncle Roy."

In his confusion he steps out the door, and as soon as he does Edie closes the door.

The sound of the deadbolt locking into place is not so different from the sound of a semiautomatic pistol's slide being pulled back.

THE NEXT MORNING is a Saturday, and the alarm on Edie's clock radio is turned off. Nevertheless Edie is awake and out of bed at seven. On her way out to the kitchen to make coffee, she sees the corner of a small piece of paper under the apartment door.

She picks it up. It's a business card for a Billings real estate firm, Joseph and Associates, and Carla Linderman is the name of the specific associate on the card. On its back is a handwritten message.

Edie,
If you ever need <u>anything</u>, call me. Roy
406-223-3964

Edie sighs and shakes her head. She carries the card to the kitchen and puts it in the drawer where she's placed so many other items she wants to save but has no real place for.

EDIE DRIVES RIGHT up to the entrance of the Prairie View Mall, though at this hour—minutes before five o'clock—the parking lot is largely deserted.

Before Lauren gets out of the car, Edie tells her, "I'll be right here at nine o'clock."

"I have to close tonight," Lauren says, "so I won't be done till like nine thirty."

"I don't mind waiting."

Lauren opens the door and swings those long legs out. Then, just as quickly, she climbs back into the car and slams the door shut. "I can't, Grandma. I just can't go in there."

"What's the matter? Don't you feel well?"

Lauren shakes her head no.

Edie reaches out and presses the back of her hand to her grand-daughter's forehead. "You don't feel warm."

"I don't feel like *sick* sick. I just hate going in there. I hate-hate-*hate* it."

"Has somebody said something?" Edie's expression darkens. "Has somebody done something? Have they—"

Lauren shakes her head furiously. The dreadlocks lash back and forth across her face. "No. No-no-no. You always think something like that. No. It's just . . . it's like so *boring*, Grandma. And people come in and they stare at me like I'm an alien or something."

Edie glances at the clock on the Honda's dashboard. And then she steals an even quicker glance at her granddaughter. At that long sleek body and those ropelike coils of hair. Alien indeed. Edie says, "It's only for a few hours, Lauren. You can last a few hours, can't you?"

"But it's every *day*, Grandma. Every fucking day!"

"I don't know what to say, honey. It's only a part-time job. What is it—twenty hours a week? And you've been there less than two months."

Lauren wipes the tears from her cheeks. "Fuck. My mascara."

"I'll tell you what," says Edie. "You go in there and see if you can't get through your shift. If you can't, call me and I'll come get you. And tomorrow we can start looking around for something else. Maybe at the bank? In the meantime—"

"Yeah. Right." Lauren climbs out of the car and slams the door so hard the car rocks on its springs.

Edie leans forward and bumps her head over and over against the steering wheel.

EDIE SIPS HER wine, a rose the color of those wispy clouds in the west that she and Rita look out on from Rita's balcony.

"She says she feels like an alien," Edie says.

Rita shakes her head. "If she'd cut off those damn curls or whatever she calls them, she'd look like any other white girl wandering around the mall."

Edie shrugs helplessly. "I thought she'd have made some friends by now."

"Give her time. And a haircut."

"I thought . . . Oh fuck it. It doesn't matter what I thought." With a few long swallows Edie finishes her wine.

The screen door makes a metallic scraping sound as it slides open. George Real Bird comes out onto the balcony.

"Here to watch the sunset?" his mother asks.

"There'll be one again tonight? Hot damn."

"Smart-ass," Rita says, but as her son hops up next to her she rests her hand affectionately on his shoulder.

He's carrying a liter of Diet Pepsi, and he rests that on the balcony rail as he pulls his squashed pack of Marlboros from the pocket of his shorts.

Edie asks, "That new leg wasn't the answer?"

He smiles at her. "You were really counting on going dancing, weren't you?"

"You promised."

George pinches a cigarette out of the pack. "I realized," he says, his tone more serious than the usual banter that goes on between Edie and him, "I didn't know what kind of dancing you hand in mind. You know, Indian or white. And then I realized it didn't make a goddamn bit of difference. I don't know how to do either one. I can't dance. That's just the truth. So what the fuck do I need another leg for?"

Love and anguish illuminate the look that Edie and Rita exchange. It's a look only parents can share, and like all parents they know to keep the look from their children's sight.

THE HEAT HAS come on during the night, and the early morning air in the apartment is redolent of hot dust. Edie shivers as she walks down the hall to the bathroom.

After she steps from the shower and dries off, she removes the flannel robe from the back of the bathroom door, wraps it around herself, and knots it tightly. She walks to the kitchen with a turbaned towel on her head.

There on the table is a note, and she steps back in recognition and retreat. Is this who she has become, a woman people would prefer to communicate with in writing rather than addressing their words to her face?

Hi gramma
Sorry I had to <u>borrow</u> your car. Please don't
call the police or anybody because you can get
it back in a few days. I'll text you where I leave
it. I bet uncle Roy will give you a ride there.
    Billy and I have been texting and we talked
a couple times. He really wants to get back
together & its going to be different. He and
Jesse have gone there separate ways.

> *I know you don't think so but Billy & I are*
> *meant to be together so thats what I'm going*
> *to do.*
> *Thank you so so <u>much</u> for everything.*
> *Love you,*
> *L*

Carrying the note Edie walks to her granddaughter's bedroom. The girl's gone, and the bed is left unmade. The photographs that were stuck in the mirror's frame are gone too, though the musky odor of Lauren's perfume lingers in the room.

Edie walks out onto the balcony. None of the cars in the parking lot look the way they looked the night before. Their windshields and back windows are white with frost, but where her Honda had been parked there is now an empty rectangle of black asphalt. Edie's sigh is a small, brief cloud in the morning air.

Back inside, the note still held tightly in her hand, Edie walks into the kitchen. She opens the drawer that's filled with everything else in her life she can't quite get rid of. The card with Roy's telephone number is easy to find, and she carries it and today's message to the telephone.

The phone is in her hand. The phone is in her hand . . .

"Uncle Roy," she says and laughs a little.

And then Edie puts the phone back on the hook. She opens the cupboard under the sink and drops both handwritten messages into the garbage can.

THE WIND BLOWS hard this morning from the northwest, and as it sweeps swiftly across the plains it carries with it cold from the Rockies' far-off icy heights. It's that wind that finds Edie as she walks down the hill on her way to work, that wind and nothing else that causes tears to spring to her eyes as she leans hard into every gust.

ACKNOWLEDGMENTS

Many, many thanks to my agent, PJ Mark, and to my editor, Kathy Pories. Their advice, insight, and commitment to this novel have been invaluable.

Thanks also to Brunson Hoole, Michael McKenzie, Stephanie Mendoza, Lauren Moseley, and everyone at Algonquin Books. A writer could not be in better hands.

I'm grateful to copyeditor Robin Cruise for her sharp eye and enthusiasm.

I'm very fortunate to work with such wise, dedicated professionals.

Finally, a special thank you to my wife, Susan, to whom this novel is dedicated. She was my inspiration and my test case for all things Edie. I couldn't have written this book or any other without her support. And I doubt I would have wanted to try.

THE LIVES OF EDIE PRITCHARD

Do You Know This Woman?
An Essay by Larry Watson

Questions for Discussion

DO YOU KNOW THIS WOMAN?

An Essay by Larry Watson

M y family is rife with twins.

My great-grandfather was a twin, my mother was a twin, aunts, uncles, cousins, a nephew and a niece are all twins. And as I learned in 2013, this preponderance of twins is an occurrence not limited to my closest relatives.

That was the year I attended a Fisketjon family reunion in Bismarck, North Dakota, my hometown. Over a hundred descendants came to the event, among them contingents from Norway, Guam, and throughout the United States. I received an invitation because my grandmother (who gave birth to two sets of twins) was a Fisketjon. She immigrated to the United States from Norway, as did a good many other Fisketjons.

At a banquet on the final night, my cousin (whose father was a twin) stood up and asked the assemblage how many of them were twins or had twins in their immediate families. So many raised their hands—many more than the statistical average birth rate for twins. A rush of twin stories followed, most of them humorous and one or two heartbreaking. As you would expect, many of the anecdotes

368 AN ESSAY BY LARRY WATSON

featured mistaken identities, even though, as genetics decrees, most of the sets of twins were fraternal.

But of course, twins needn't be identical to cause confusion. I remember as a child listening to my mother and her twin sister visiting in another room. I couldn't tell who was talking, and when the conversation became a heated argument, I couldn't tell whose position was whose.

Was it at the Fisketjon reunion when I decided I would do something more with twinship in my fiction? It might have been. In previous novels and stories, I'd often included twins, but mostly those characters had simply been a way to pay homage to my clan. Twins as primary characters, I thought, would allow me to explore a theme that had always interested me: uncertainty about identity. I began to work on a novel whose working title was *Edie and the Linderman Twins*, and as originally conceived, the story featured twin brothers who were in love with the same woman.

But something happened in the writing that I hadn't expected. It was not the twins, but Edie, the woman they loved, who came to dominate the story, largely because she was the one who embodied the theme of confused identity. The confusion, however, was not in how Edie saw herself—or how she saw the Linderman twins—but in how others saw her. Pragmatic and unpretentious, she was a woman with a realistic sense of self. But she was also beautiful, and beauty often blinds people to qualities of heart and mind that can be every bit as rare as beauty.

Edie possessed, for example, both physical and emotional strength when she was the only person who could rescue her brother-in-law after a horrific highway accident. When Edie saw her young husband obsessively pursue a doomed attempt to salvage his pride—and impress her in the process—her patience and understanding were strained to their limits. She struggled to keep her frustration from turning into anger when her husband's sexual desire diminished— and his brother's longing for her became almost uncontrollable. When a man she once loved was dying of cancer, she was willing to disrupt and dislocate her settled middle-class existence just to pay him a final visit. A very different test of her loyalty came when she had to choose between returning to an abusive, possessive husband or abandoning her teenage daughter. And many years later, Edie placed her own life in jeopardy in order to save her granddaughter from a pair of dangerous, predatory young men.

Many of the tests—and revelations—of Edie's strength, courage, loyalty, and intelligence occurred during a series of road trips. Those urgent, often harrowing journeys, undertaken at twenty-year intervals and each with unnerving parallels to the others, became the basis for the novel's structure, a novel that had come to focus on the stages of Edie's life, from the time she was a young wife to being a grandmother. Hence the novel's final title, *The Lives of Edie Pritchard*: the story of a woman who often found that others, men usually but not exclusively, had projected on her an identity that suited their needs rather than hers.

For most of her years, Edie lived in Gladstone, Montana, the small town where she was born and grew up. People there knew her, or believed they did. *Edie Pritchard . . . Was it her dad who died when she was just a girl? About as pretty and popular as any gal at Gladstone High . . . but what was it she did on graduation night? She worked at the bank, didn't she? And wasn't she married to one of the Linderman twins? But was it Dean or Roy? I could never keep those two straight . . .*

Perhaps it was this that drew me to Edie's character most of all: through her many lives, despite others' attempts to define her, she was sure of who she was. I hope you recognize her.

QUESTIONS FOR DISCUSSION

1. In *The Art of Fiction*, John Gardner wrote, "In nearly all . . . fiction, the basic—all but inescapable—plot form is: A central character wants something, goes after it despite opposition (perhaps including his [sic] own doubts), and so arrives at a win, lose, or draw." What does Edie want, and what stands in the way of her getting what she wants? Does she win, lose, or come to a draw?

2. There are actual twins in *The Lives of Edie Pritchard*, but throughout the narrative there are elements—characters, episodes, incidents—that parallel others. What are some of those examples of "twinning" in the novel? What are the effects of those similarities?

3. Important conversations and significant moments in the novel often occur in automobiles. What do you make of that?

4. How does Edie change over the years? How does she remain unchanged?

5. Roy Linderman figures importantly in all three parts of the novel. How does he change over the years? How does he remain unchanged?

6. Mother and daughter relationships loom large in the novel. How do they add to our understanding of Edie and her world?

7. Gladstone, Montana, is the setting for important action in all three sections. It's Edie's hometown, and though she doesn't seem nostalgic or overly fond of it, she keeps going back. Why? What keeps bringing her back and what finally keeps her there?

8. So much of the novel is dialogue and action. What are some effects of the story being told through those narrative modes?

9. Have you ever been treated like Edie? Have you seen others treated like her?

10. After Edie leaves Gladstone in 1968, Roy Linderman is largely absent from her life. Yet he's present at crucial moments in later years. How would you characterize the relationship between them? Does it change over time?

11. On more than one occasion Roy Linderman asks Edie to go away with him. Why is "going away" so important to his proposal?

12. How do Edie's relationships with women differ from her relationships with men?

13. There are many minor characters in the novel—Mildred Linderman, Gary Dunn, Rita Real Bird, George Real Bird, Lauren Keller, to name just a few. What importance do these characters have to the overall narrative?

14. Did you return to your hometown and if not, why not?

15. Did you hope that Edie and Roy would eventually end up together? Why didn't it happen?

Raised in Bismarck, North Dakota, **Larry Watson** is the author of ten critically acclaimed books, including the bestselling *Montana 1948*. His fiction has been published internationally and has received numerous prizes and awards. His essays and book reviews have appeared in the *Los Angeles Times*, the *Washington Post*, the *Chicago Sun-Times*, the *Milwaukee Journal Sentinel*, and other periodicals. He and his wife live in Kenosha, Wisconsin. A film adaptation of Watson's novel *Let Him Go* starring Kevin Costner and Diane Lane was released in 2020.